# Quest for Osiris

Book 3 of

The EGYPTIANS! Trilogy

**Jay Palmer**

ISBN: 1-7324989-2-X
ISBN-13: 978-1-7324989-2-1

## Books by Jay Palmer

The VIKINGS! Trilogy:
- DeathQuest
- The Mourning Trail
- Quest for Valhalla

The EGYPTIANS! Trilogy:
- SoulQuest
- Song of the Sphinx
- Quest for Osiris

Jeremy Wrecker, Pirate of Land and Sea

The Magic of Play

The Seneschal

Viking Son

Viking Daughter

Dracula – Deathless Desire

The Grotesquerie Games

**Cover Artist:** Jay Palmer

**Website:** JayPalmerBooks.com

# ACKNOWLEDGMENTS

Thanks to those researchers and authors who provide the rich source material to indulge enquiring minds!

**Bibliography** (and recommended reading!):


- "The Ancient Egyptian Books of the Afterlife", by Erik Hornung, translated by David Lorton
- "Dictionary of Ancient Egypt", by Ian Shaw and Paul Nicholson
- "Book of the Dead", by E.A. Wallis Budge
- "Egyptian Magic", by E.A. Wallis Budge
- "Bulfinch's Mythology", by Thomas Bulfinch
- "Dictionary of Occultism", by Lewis Spence
- Marvel Comics, by Stan Lee


Special thanks to Edith Hamilton, author of "Mythology", for introducing me to the intricacies of my favorite subject!

To a learned educator, an inspired poet,
and a trusted friend, Elizabeth Hayden.

## Chapter 1

## The City of Thoth

# KARL

*They'd escaped the Field of Wheat!*

Karl stared at his companions, long and angrily, and then turned away. In despair, he dropped to his knees on the gray, gritty sand. This land was as bad as Yggdrasil, deadly and maddening. They'd survived their first threat … by luck alone; *the Field of Wheat had defeated them all.* None had guessed its true nature, and without the warnings of the Mad Hermit, they'd all have fallen into the Duat … and become half-animal demons. Only the Mad Hermit's warnings, his parental desire to protect Alarika, had saved them …

*She'd been planning to betray them all along!*

Nate called his name, but Karl just shook his head. When he finally rose, Karl surveyed their two surviving wagonloads of supplies, waterbags, and few remaining animals. They'd been smart enough to provision themselves, yet they were worse off than they'd been on the roots of Yggdrasil. While they now had better provisions, no ghostly footprints marked their path. They had no idea where they were going, and no amount of supplies was likely to last if they were forced to wander blindly through an unknown realm.

Torn between fury and relief, Karl wondered if they were still dreaming, or how much of their dreams had been real. He truly felt that he'd visited Castle Bristlen, reported everything to Rafe and Seren, and held little Eric, Athelwynne, and Roselyn again. Karl would've preferred to stay there, but if part of their souls had remained behind, then they were better off returning.

*Yet … how could they keep going … knowing that one of them was a traitor?*

"Alarika," Karl said, deepening his voice. "You've proven yourself disloyal …"

*"I'm no subject of yours!"* Alarika snapped.

"Without cooperation, lands like these devour mortals," Karl said. "Join us … or depart. Take whatever provisions your camel can carry. Seek your gods alone."

Alarika glared, but Karl never flinched.

*"If not for my father …!"* she hissed.

"He didn't care about us anymore than you did," Karl said. "Swear fealty to me, now, or go!"

Immobile as a mountain, Alarika stood stiffly. Tense moments passed, and then she sneered.

"What value do you place upon my oath?" Alarika asked.

"Little," Karl said.

"It shows you're amenable," Eloise interjected.

"I don't need you," Alarika said. "Countless dead have made this journey … alone!"

"Remind your father of that when your hands and feet turn into snakes," Karl said.

The desert woman stared, glancing at them all.

"I have a price," Alarika said.

Karl resolutely returned her glare, his jaw clenched.

"Help save my father," Alarika said.

"The Seer can save him, if anyone can," Eloise said.

*"Swear it!"* Alarika snapped.

"We help all sworn companions," Karl said.

Alarika gritted her teeth, glaring daggers.

*"You command … I obey,"* she hissed through taut lips.

"I'll hold you to that … until we're really home," Karl said.

Wary glances swapped all around.

"The light's that way," Nate broke the silence. "If the Lady spoke true … then that glow is coming from the Seer."

Karl glanced; along the horizon, only one distant spot glowed brighter than the few stars. They had no proof that the distant glow was their destination, but it was as good a direction as any.

"I'll lead," Karl said, and he walked back toward his horse.

Hours later, they seemed no closer.

*"Weary warriors unequal opposition,"* Roselyn said suddenly.

Karl looked around at the nodding heads.

"Camp," Karl declared.

"If we stop, will the ground open up?" Sister Aspertine asked.

"Our gods want their people to reach them," Alarika said. "They wouldn't make it impossible."

"We face challenges, not barriers," Elaina said. "I suspect that we can pause to rest … as long as we don't give up."

Camp was quickly set, as they needed no tents, and hadn't thought to wish for firewood. Food and drink was shared in plenty, and blankets spread out upon the sand. Yet conversation was unpopular; everyone seemed preoccupied with their memories of the Field of Wheat.

*"Pleasant … dreams …,"* Nate said snarkily, and not even a groan replied.

The next morning, Karl watched them shake and roll their blankets in silence. Sister Aspertine and Nate kept sneaking glances at each other … and when their eyes met, looking away. Eloise and Roselyn both seemed furious, on the verge of open war. Henry remained oddly distant, and he walked with his shoulders slumped and head bowed, as if hopeless. Alarika snarled whenever anyone came by her. Phil looked sad, and kept staring blindly at the one glow on the horizon as if lost in thought.

*"Trouble,"* Elaina's voice whispered in Karl's ear.

Karl startled to find that Elaina had silently crept up behind him.

*"If we're not together, we won't get far,"* Karl agreed.

*"Keep them moving … and hoping,"* Elaina said.

*"Pass around some Water of Life,"* Karl whispered. *"Make everyone drink."*

*"You're our leader …,"* Elaina suggested.

*"You're the only one nobody wants to kill,"* Karl replied.

A wan smile brightened her face, and then Elaina gave Karl a wink and walked away. Soon she was approaching everyone with a flask of their precious Water of Life. Karl hoped that its effects would enhearten everyone … without energizing their feuds.

When Elaina finished, Karl ordered everyone to mount up. Nate and Phil each drove a camel-drawn wagon, their horses tied to its rear. As one, they resumed their trek toward the distant light.

The endless night's sky irritated Karl, but when crossing a desert, better eternal starshine than a single day of burning sun. Yet they had to find something soon … before their rivalries exploded.

Elaina shared bread and cheese as they rode, climbing among the laden wagons, and then riding to each companion in turn. Karl asked Henry to sing a sea chanty, but his half-hearted effort was swallowed by the scratches of hooves and wheels plowing through the crunching sand. Hour after hour they rode, until Karl felt that another sleep-time was approaching.

Suddenly Phil stood up on his driving board and looked out.

"I see something!" Phil shouted. "It's … buildings!"

"Make camp!" Karl ordered.

"Why …?" Eloise asked. "There're buildings …!"

"If those buildings are places to rest, then we'll sleep in them tomorrow," Karl said. "If not, we'd best face them fresh."

Reluctantly, they dismounted and began unrolling their blankets. Phil suggested cutting up boards from Nate's wagon to make a hot supper, but Karl didn't want to create fire or smoke … in case someone in those buildings was watching. Roselyn said that she'd stay up late to guard them, and warned Nate that she'd wake him up when she needed to sleep.

The next morning, Karl awoke Nate with a kick, and his glare exhibited his displeasure. Ashamed, Nate slunk off, but nothing had bothered them during the night. Henry helped Elaina pass around bread, salted pork, and some Water of Life, and then they mounted and rode toward the city.

The city was magnificent; huge, gleaming structures of giant stone blocks, like the pyramids, but looking freshly chiseled and stacked, as if newly-made. Towering obelisks loomed over the high wall surrounding the city, their four-sides sharply peaked at the top, pointing at the stars. Other structures surrounded them, but few seemed roofed; Karl saw only one tall building such as those he'd seen in the palace of Ptah Shabaka.

The twin gates of solid gold, covered with majestic decorations, dwarfed the puny entrance to Castle Bristlen. As they rode closer, they spied recognizable symbols in raised gold: measuring scales, human hearts, one huge feather, and the giant shape of a man with the head of a long-billed bird.

"The City of Thoth," Alarika announced as they rode closer.

All heads snapped to face her.

*"You know what city this is …?"* Roselyn snarled.

"That's Thoth, with the head of an ibis … a sacred Egyptian bird," Alarika said, pointing at the figures on the doors. "He's the Scribe of Osiris, the God of Wisdom, and the Weigher of Hearts."

"You mentioned him before … in the desert," Elaina said.

"Al-Hassim and Ptah Shabaka also mentioned Thoth," Eloise said. "Their servants called Thoth 'Divine Intelligence', and said that Thoth was born of Ra and Maat."

"May Ptah Shabaka spit out his tongue before Anubis!" Alarika said. "He blasphemes … and not from ignorance. Our people have dwelt in Egypt for 5,000 years. Over the centuries, many pharaohs have ruled, wisely or foolishly, and gods have fallen in and out of favor."

"Your gods cycle …?" Elaina asked.

"Not our gods, our pharaohs," Alarika said. "Pharaoh Akhenaten was a worshipper of Ra, the sun god, whom he renamed Aten. His priests declared that Akhenaten and his wife, Nefertiti, were Aten's sole representatives on Earth. Akhenaten abolished the worship of Atum and his children, dismissing their priests and demolishing their temples."

"Your kings, I mean, pharaohs, rule your faith?" Sister Aspertine asked.

"They try … not always successfully," Alarika said. "After Akhenaten's death, many angry priests justly cursed his Ba and his Ka. His Sheut is now trapped; Akhenaten wanders hopelessly forever. Even today, in the desert, many Egyptians have spied Akhenaten's shade."

"Then … who were Thoth's parents?" Eloise asked.

"Thoth was Self-Begotten, the Moral Law, born with Maat, for neither can survive without the other," Alarika said. "All heavenly bodies move by his command. Thoth invented writing, and alphabets, and brought light to the darkness of ignorance. Thoth is the Scribe of the Underworld … and the author of the Pyramid Texts."

"Pyramid Texts …?" Eloise asked. "A written diary of a god …?"

"The Pyramid Texts are the oldest form of Kitab-al-Mayyit, the Book of the Dead Man, and Kitab-al-Mayyitun, the Book of All Dead." Alarika said.

"Those books exist …?" Eloise asked excitedly. "Can copies of them be acquired?"

"They're expensive … and no translations exist to the tongue of England," Alarika said.

"Seek treasures later," Karl said. "Tell us more."

"Thoth is the ibis-headed god," Alarika gestured to a tall statue with the face of a long-beaked bird, easily seen over the wall as they rode closer. "The lunar crescent rests on Thoth's head, for Thoth created the radiant Sun-disk and dimmed the moon's light. Thoth rides upon the side of Ra's boat, and arbitrates all godly disputes, for he is the Master of Magics, the Spring of Wisdom, and the Judge of the Dead. His power is unlimited; Thoth alone rivals Osiris, but he bows to him, for his wisdom commands that Osiris must rule.

"Thoth is the winner of all games. When Re cursed Nut, that she couldn't bear a child upon any day or night, Nut begged for help from Thoth. Once spoken, the curse of Re could never be recalled, but in his wisdom, Thoth approached Khonsu, the Moon-god, and challenged him to a contest of draughts. Game after game they played, and Thoth always won. Their stakes grew high, and finally Khonsu, the Moon, wagered half of his moonlight … and lost.

"Thoth gathered up a year's worth of the dim, wagered moonlight of Khonsu, and combined it into five extra days of sunlight, which he set between the end of the old year and the beginning of the new. On these five days alone Nut could birth a child. Thus did Thoth lengthen the year … and the moon was forever diminished, so that unto this day its glow ebbs and grows.

"When mortals die, if they reach the City of the Gods, then they must present themselves to Thoth for judgement."

"The weighing of the heart," Karl said.

"When we reach our destination, Thoth will judge us," Alarika smiled.

Most of the companions paled and exchanged worried glances, and looked up apprehensively at the approaching city. As they drew near to its closed golden gates, no movement showed.

"Wait," Alarika said, and she raised both hands and began to pray in Egyptian. When she finished, the twin doors opened a crack, but not wide enough to squeeze through. Alarika glanced back at her companions, then repeated her chant in English.

*"Oh Thoth, who makest*
*Osiris triumphant*
*over his adversaries,*
*let we be made triumphant*
*over our adversaries.*
*Before the Circle of Gods*
*about Ra and about Osiris*
*and the Great Circle*
*of Gods in Heliopolis,*
*on that Night of the Eve's Provender*
*and the Night of Battle*
*when befell the Defeat of the Sebau,*
*and the Day of Extinction*
*of the adversaries of the Inviolate God."*

As she finished her prayer, the gleaming, golden gates of Thoth slowly opened wide. Karl spurred forward, yet Roselyn stretched out her arm and stopped him.

"Recall what I said about traps," Roselyn warned.

"Advise," Karl said.

"Wait … and watch," Roselyn said, and she drew the sword of Hel, spurred, and alone rode toward the city.

"Elaina … Eloise," Karl said. "Take the buckboards. Give Nate and Phil your horses."

Quickly they swapped while Roselyn proceeded, and by the time that she'd cantered through the wide gates, both squires rode up beside him, and Henry and Alarika joined them.

*"Don't wait if anything attacks Roselyn!"* Karl whispered.

Suddenly laughter filled the air, shrill and sarcastic. Roselyn jerked her head in each direction, but nothing could be seen.

*"Harpy …!"* Elaina screamed.

Seeing nothing, Karl glanced back to see Elaina, eyes bulging, pointing upwards.

Above them flew a monstrous horror, a vulture with the head and torso of a woman, a twisted fusion of human and animal, resembling an avian Mad Hermit. This woman had dark brown skin which matched her long feathers. She bore black eyes, a beautiful face, and round, exposed breasts, but below her waist, feathers sprouted into a vulture body and talonned vulture-feet. A long, feathery tail trailed her, and where arms should be, powerful wings stretched wide, catching the winds. The harpy shouted at them in the language of Egypt.

"Mortal food," Alarika translated.

*"Watch her!"* Roselyn shouted, and seconds later, she suddenly twisted in her saddle and swung her sword at a second harpy, diving low at her back.

The second harpy arced sharply, darted around Roselyn, and then pumped her wings to gain elevation, rising out of sword range. Both harpies flew to land side-by-side atop the summit of the golden arch atop the open gates, looking down at Roselyn.

"A woman warrior …!" the first harpy laughed.

"She spotted me … while looking at you!" the second harpy complained.

*"Never trust the foe that presents itself,"* Roselyn scowled.

"We're outmatched!" the second harpy laughed.

"Whatever shall we do?" laughed the first harpy. "Surrender … to a mortal?"

"Better than dying!" Roselyn warned.

Both harpies laughed.

*"Behind you!"* Sister Aspertine screamed.

Roselyn spun just in time to see a third harpy dive upon her, talons bared. With movements worthy of a Valkyrie, Roselyn fell from her saddle, using her horse as a shield. Rather than strike Roselyn, both sets of vulture-talons stabbed deep into the neck of her stallion. It screamed and reared, clenched by its mane, and Roselyn leaped up and plunged the sword of Hel deep into the stomach of the winged harpy.

Impaled, the harpy screamed, a woman's wail, and tried to fly off, but Roselyn seized a feathered vulture-leg, flung it to the sands just outside the gates, and sliced deep into one of its wings.

From above, the other harpies screamed in outrage, and flapped their wings threateningly.

"Don't kill it!" Karl shouted, and he spurred forward. Roselyn's glare matched any berserker's, but she stopped her next strike mid-swing … a second before decapitating it, just as Nate and Phil rode up, trailing Karl.

*"Never pity an enemy!"* Roselyn argued

"They can talk …!" Karl interrupted her. "Perhaps we can …!"

"Negotiate …?" one of the harpies laughed down at them. "Trade …?"

Both harpies convulsed with laughter.

Karl rode inside the City of Thoth, glanced at the countless sparkling sculptures and monuments, and then turned to look up at the bird-women.

"You speak English," Karl said.

"You speak stupid," one harpy retorted.

Both harpies spread their wings and dove inside the city, making Karl slash the air with his sword, but instantly they banked, flitted just under the archway between the open gates, swooped over Nate, Phil, Henry, and Alarika, and winged toward Eloise, Elaina, and Sister Aspertine. Sister Aspertine screamed, jumped from her horse, and dove under the wagons, but Elaina jumped to stand, drawing their attention, and then leapt with her dancer's agility onto Eloise's wagon, standing protectively over her daughter.

*"LADY!!!"* Eloise screamed, and she arose, fury in her blue eyes. Flames burst from her cupped hands, and the startled harpies swooped away from her and Elaina.

Sister Aspertine, who'd jumped under Elaina's wagon, scampered across the sand on her hands and knees to hide under Eloise's wagon. By the time that she'd made it, Henry and Alarika rode up, Nate and Phil trailing behind them. Alarika repeatedly slashed her khopesh through the air, holding the harpies at bay, while Henry watched her back. Nate joined them, while Phil fetched Sister Aspertine's mount, which had started to bolt, and brought it back. Karl frowned; three more harpies had appeared flying above the gate, a total of six, all laughing.

Roselyn was kneeling on both of the wounded harpy's wide wings, the sharp point of Hel's blade lightly stabbing between its bare breasts.

"Enough!" Karl shouted to the flying women. "Draw back, or we kill your sister!"

All six of the harpies laughed, including the one that Roselyn held hostage.

"Release her, and we'll kill her!" one of the harpies shrieked.

"You wish a deal?" another harpy taunted. "Give us one of your own … freely … and we'll spare the rest of you!"

The other harpies laughed at this, wheeled around and flew down low, then beat their strong wings, blowing up a thin cloud of sand that engulfed the companions, and then they rose back up to hover over them, watching the companions try not to shield their eyes.

"Bring the wagons inside!" Roselyn shouted.

Karl rode back, into the sandy cloud, gave his reins to Phil, and then jumped onto Elaina's wagon. Holding his sword ready, he grabbed and shook its camels' reins. Elaina took Eloise's reins, as Eloise's hands still cupped flames. With an *'eek!'*, Sister Aspertine waited until their cart rode out from overtop her, and then she jumped onto its back. Karl glanced over at Eloise, still holding a ball of fire in each hand.

"I didn't know that you could do that," Karl said.

*"My flames are harmless,"* Eloise whispered.

*"Good bluff,"* Karl whispered back.

They drove both sets of camels forward, past Roselyn, still holding her sword upon the wounded harpy, her badly-wounded horse fallen beside her. One at a time, they drove the wagons between the gold gates, into the city, as the five remaining harpies flew over them.

Reins in one hand, sword in the other, Karl glanced back, outside the gate, to see that Alarika had dismounted, and was holding her khopesh against Roselyn's prisoner. Almost pressed against her back, Henry stood wielding his khopesh and watching the flying harpies.

Roselyn grabbed a bow stashed upon one wagon. With amazing speed, as Karl jumped down, ran back, and touched his blade against the wounded harpy's neck,

Roselyn raised her bow with an arrow nocked. Before any reaction was possible, an arrow streaked upwards and stabbed deep into a flying harpy's upper chest. The harpy screamed as the arrow stabbed between her left breast and shoulder, and then she fell hard onto the sands near Nate.

All four of the unharmed harpies laughed.

Nate jumped off his horse and stepped toward her, sword raised, but the harpy unexpectedly kicked at him, and one sharp talon tore a deep, bloody gash out of the front of his shin. As Nate cried out and fell, she jumped atop him, biting and battering him with her wings. Then she screamed: Nate had grasped the arrow-shaft sticking out of her and repeatedly yanked it. As Phil jumped off his horse and ran to help, Nate threw her down, onto her back, his one hand on the bloody arrow. He stabbed his sword hard through her right wing, and then gripped her throat.

"Wait!" Karl shouted, running out onto the sands as the other harpies flew upwards, one barely dodging another of Roselyn's arrows. "Please, let's talk!"

He waved at Roselyn, who held her next shot, but he also glanced at her, seeing the slight shake of her head, which told him the last four harpies were too high to insure a strike.

*"Enemies should be slain,"* Roselyn said as Phil reached the pinned harpy that Nate held down and held his sword against her cheek.

"We don't kill unless …," Karl began.

*"Valkyrie slay the wounded!"* Roselyn shouted.

"This isn't Valhalla," Karl said.

"I agree with Roselyn," Alarika said.

Karl shook his head, and Roselyn scowled, and then she briefly examined her horse, laying at her feet, slowly twitching and bleeding to death.

"Eloise, can you heal my horse?" Roselyn asked.

Hearing Roselyn address Eloise, everyone startled. Eloise paused before replying.

"Nate needs healing first," Eloise said.

"Nate will live …," Roselyn said.

"Wife, Roselyn's horse could die …," Karl said, and Eloise reluctantly nodded.

*"Why hold my throat?"* Karl heard the harpy whisper to Nate. *"Why not hold … what you really want …?"*

*"No!"* Phil shouted, pressing the tip of his sword hard against her skin.

"Nate, mind on your duty!" Karl ordered. "Henry, Sister Aspertine, Elaina: watch the other harpies, and warn us if they swoop."

Karl walked over to Nate and Phil, and placed his sword upon the harpy's other cheek.

"Why attack us?" Karl demanded.

"Fresh meat," the harpy grinned. "Also … it's fun."

"Phil, go help Alarika and Roselyn bring the other one over here, away from the gate," Karl said, and after Phil departed, he looked closely at the harpy. She had dark Egyptian skin, wild, thick black hair, and teeth like a wildcat. Her naked breasts were impressive, her face young and beautiful, but like the Mad Hermit, she was only half-human.

"How did you learn English?" Karl asked.

"Harpies are the lovers of Thoth, He Who Knows All," the harpy grinned wickedly. "You know all about lovers, don't you … *lover?*"

"We need to find the City of the Gods …," Karl said.

"You really are stupid, aren't you …?" she laughed.

"Silence!" Nate ordered, and he jerked on the arrow stuck in her shoulder, which was badly bleeding, and made her scream.

"Enough, Nate," Karl said. "We have a healer …"

"Does she taste good?" the harpy asked, grinning. "Have her heal me, if my pleasures you seek …!"

"We only seek passage …," Karl said.

The harpy licked her lips provocatively.

"If you knew the pleasures of harpies …!" she began.

"I know that harpies feel pain … and can die," Karl warned.

"Harpies can give you …," she began.

"Nate, yank it again," Karl said.

She screeched as Nate obeyed, and Karl knelt beside her.

"This is your last chance," Karl said. "Healing … for cooperation."

"Kiss me … and I'll answer," she grinned evilly.

Nate looked up at Karl questioningly.

"Don't even think it," Karl ordered Nate.

The harpy blew Nate a kiss.

Roselyn, Alarika, and Henry struggled the other harpy over to them, and they hurled her onto the sand beside her sister. She flopped free and thrashed, but her wing was partially severed from the top, where her elbow should've been. She bit back screams and thrashed in pain.

"Easy!" Karl knelt beside her, one hand on her shoulder, and easing her back, he straightened her bent wing. "We can heal you … if you'll help us."

The harpy hissed, thrashed high, and suddenly bit hard onto Karl's arm, but her fangs only crunched upon the rings of his armor.

"Mail," Karl explained as he pulled away from her snapping teeth and held up his armored sleeve. "Rome conquered your lands before the North wore it. Now who's stupid …?"

Karl walked over to the other harpy, and with a sudden swing, he turned his naked swordpoint down … and stabbed her through her non-wounded shoulder. She screamed in pain.

"Leave them here," Karl said. "Without wings, they're not flying anywhere."

The two harpies shrieked and cursed at them, but the companions walked away. The wounded harpies flopped around and screamed from their own exertions. Phil half-carried Nate, who was badly limping.

"Take Nate to Eloise," Karl said to Phil.

"It doesn't hurt …," Nate hissed through gritted teeth.

Karl kept an eye behind him, at the two harpies on the sand, watching them writhe, assuring himself that they were helpless.

"Where are the rest?" Karl asked, and Henry, Elaina, and Sister Aspertine pointed to four dark specs flying amid the dim stars.

The companions gathered beside Roselyn's wounded horse. Blood pooled thickly beneath it, streaming through the narrow gaps between the slate flagstones that floored the city inside the golden gates.

"Alarika, where do we go?" Karl asked.

Alarika looked up at the high stone walls and tall monuments.

"One gate in, one gate out," Alarika said.

"Can't we go around the city?" Karl asked.

"The path to my gods lies through the cities," Alarika said. "They wouldn't allow mortals to cheat …"

"There must be a way through," Elaina said. "Their gods want the faithful to reach them."

"Our gods require you to prove your worth," Alarika said.

"I need quiet," Eloise interrupted them.

As Eloise began her healing chant, she held up her finger, then slid it into the deep wounds on the horse's neck. It neighed and writhed, and Henry, Alarika, Roselyn, and Phil held the horse and tried to soothe it, while Sister Aspertine and Elaina kept close watch upon the four remaining harpies, who were circling amid the stars. Nate was clinging to a wagon wheel, favoring one leg.

*"Karl!"* Elaina and Sister Aspertine shouted at the same time.

Karl looked up: the four harpies had divided into groups of two, each pair flying off in a different direction. Then they dove, straight down, and Karl shouted.

"Weapons out! Roselyn, bow!"

All but Henry abandoned Eloise, who cried out, poking the back of her own neck with her bloody finger.

Weapons rose against the distant, diving harpies, but their flights on both sides dipped below the tops of the walls, swooping outside, hidden from sight.

*"The wounded . . . !"* Karl shouted, but too late.

From each side, two harpies came flying over the sands, winging faster than Karl had thought possible. The wounded harpies upon the sand cried out as, two-by-two, the flying harpies slashed over and past them, long talons extended. Ripping sounds, followed by tall splashes of blood and feathers, came from each of the wounded harpies. The flying shapes never slowed . . . and dexterously dodged Roselyn's arrow.

Seconds later, all four remaining harpies flew high, and Karl could hear them laughing.

"Keep watching them," Karl snarled. "Phil … with me."

Karl and Phil walked back outside the gates onto the sands, but they didn't need to approach closer. The two harpies on the sand lay ripped apart, unmoving, slain by their own sisters. Karl and Phil glanced at each other, then walked back inside.

"No wonder they wouldn't deal," Phil said softly.

Karl frowned.

"It's too easy," Karl said, looking at the monuments filling the walled City of Thoth.

"A trap …?" Phil asked.

"Exactly, but we can't go back," Karl said. "The Duat will eat us."

"Nate and I follow you," Phil said. "Even if I have to beat him …"

"When I want you two fighting, I'll tell you," Karl said.

Looking at the others, Karl shook his head. Rafe and Seren's squabble over Radsvid had nearly killed the whole company in Yggdrasil. Their immediate threats were flying high above them … and laughing at them, yet Karl wasn't sure if he could count on half of the companions … if they were presented with an opportunity for revenge.

# Chapter 2

## Truth Revealed

## NATE

Nate hated himself.

Even as Eloise, lost in her healing chant, knelt and stuck her finger in his wound, withdrew it, and then lifted her skirt almost to her knee, and touched the same spot on her shin where Nate had been raked, Nate scowled. Eloise screamed, and Nate felt a strange, warm tingling, a brief connection to Eloise, and then the pain in his leg lessened, although it didn't fade entirely. Elaina caught Eloise as she collapsed, and Nate tried to help, but he staggered, too weak to support her. He glanced down; the worst of his wound had suddenly stopped bleeding, and when he wiped away the blood with his hand, the skin under it looked unbroken, pink and swollen, but partially healed.

Rapidly, deeply, Eloise puffed gasps, and slowly she allowed her mother to right her back onto one knee. The identical spot on Eloise's leg swelled, and grew red and puffy.

"I'm sorry," Nate said to her.

Eloise had to refocus her eyes before she grasped his meaning.

"It's the price of healing," Eloise said, straining to regain control. "The Seer could redirect the pain, but … I'm not him. Here, let me see your other …"

"No, it's just a scratch …," Nate refused, looking at the smaller rent that the harpy's back talon had made in his calf.

"Then … let's look at the bite," Eloise said.

Nate ran his fingers across his cheek, just above his jaw.

"Does it show?" he asked.

"The punctures are small, but they could get infected … or be poisoned," Elaina said.

Nate shook his head.

"I can't inflict unneeded pain upon my baroness," Nate said.

"All magic hurts," Eloise said. "Losing you would hurt worse, as would waiting until you're really sick … and explaining to Sara Tiller why I didn't heal her son."

"Just heal me … enough to get us to the Seer," Nate said.

Eloise smiled wanly, and then took a deep breath, which seemed difficult in her weakened state. She muttered a prayer whose words Nate couldn't translate, and she placed a finger over each of the teeth punctures on his lower cheek. The warm tingling returned, and with it arose a connection, an unexpected familiarity, with Eloise, and Nate cringed and shuddered. He didn't want a connection with his knight's lady, especially not an intimate bond. As she withdrew her fingers and placed them on the same place on her smooth cheek, the tingling that he felt grew briefly hot, and their connection strengthened. Yet Nate blushed scarlet, and tried to force the connection away with his own will, even at the cost of his own healing.

Eloise startled, suddenly looking confused.

"What …?" Elaina asked her.

"I … don't know," Eloise said. "It was working … and then it … stopped."

"Maybe the Lady doesn't like me," Nate said, ignoring their curious gazes. Nate stood and tested his leg. It stung badly, but putting his weight upon it didn't make it any worse, so he turned away.

"If you feel indebted, protect Eloise," Elaina said. "She needs rest."

Ignoring the agony of his leg, Nate bent and picked up Eloise in his arms, shrugging off Elaina's attempt to help.

*He didn't deserve help. He didn't deserve anything …!*

*"Mind on your duty!" Karl had ordered him …*

Everyone hated him. He hated himself.

*Why'd he done it?*

*He'd known that she was a nun …!*

*He'd been only having fun, competing with his brother, and then …*

*… and then …!*

Nate couldn't look Sister Aspertine in the face. He tried not to meet anyone's eyes. He'd sunk so low in everyone's opinion that Karl had warned him not to play with a wounded harpy's breasts.

*Was he really considered so base, dominated by lusts …?*

Karl had two beautiful women fighting over him, and most of the women in Demril and Castle Bristlen sighed whenever he walked by. Nate couldn't refuse a woman's advances, not even if his life depended on it.

*He was weak …*

*He was pathetic …*

Eloise's blonde, natural beauty had never failed to escape his notice, but she was his baroness, and Nate had known her since he was little, barely able to lift a sword. Elaina's strong, attractive features, so like her daughter, had delighted him the instant that he'd seen her. Roselyn's immortal beauty overwhelmed him, but he didn't dare let her suspect; *she'd probably make good on her threat to tear out his teeth.* Alarika was beautiful like Roselyn, and had the exotic swarthy, enticing darkness of Egypt. Sister Aspertine …

*Sister Aspertine …!*

Nate flinched so hard he almost forgot that Eloise was still in his arms. Standing frozen, holding his baroness against his chest, Nate glanced to find both Eloise and Elaina staring at him. Limping slightly, he circled to the front of the wagon and loaded her aboard.

"Nate, is something wrong …?" Eloise asked.

Nate shook his head and started to walk away.

"Someone needs to protect Eloise," Elaina reminded.

With a deep sigh, Nate climbed onto the wagon, behind the driver's board, and sat on a barrel of water amid their stacked weapons, bags of supplies, and chests of treasures from the Field of Wheat. He drew his sword and looked up at the sky. The four harpies were still circling like the vultures they half-resembled. Nate frowned, remembering their voluptuous endowments; *these harpies were proof of his weakness!*

"Are we well enough to travel?" Karl asked Eloise.

"Roselyn's horse was hurt badly," Eloise sighed. "It shouldn't be ridden. I can travel … but not drive."

"Nate can drive," Karl said, nodding to Nate. "Roselyn, choose a different horse. Tie the extra horses to the back of the wagon."

Karl sent Sister Aspertine to ride with Nate and Eloise. At Eloise's request, Sister Aspertine agreed to keep watch on the harpies, but she glanced daggers at Nate as he picked up their reins; he couldn't blame her.

Phil drove the other cart, with orders to protect Elaina, who sat beside him, watching the harpies. Karl and Alarika rode on one side of the carts, Henry, with his curved Egyptian khopesh, and Roselyn, with her bow, rode on the other side.

Inside, the City of Thoth boasted dozens of huge metal statues, stone monuments, many square pillars, tall but supporting nothing, and wide gateways with no doors, existing only to display painted engravings and countless colorful pictures of Egyptians and their gods, often paired with hearts, scales, and feathers. They rode past splashing fountains, their deep pools bright with waters streaming into the starlit air.

Massive busts and giant statues of Thoth dominated the other monuments, showing his long, thin beak protruding from his small bird-head, with an ornate hood hanging from his brow down to his shoulders. Atop Thoth's head, many drawings and statues showed a wide crescent, often with a sun-disk between the quarter-moon's upturned points. Thoth wore no shirt, only a linen shift, like a skirt, which was upheld by a belt of gold, a large dagger on his belt, and leather sandals. Often he held a scroll in one hand.

Everything in this city honored the Egyptian God of Wisdom. Picture-writing covered every surface; Alarika read and translated a few passages, mostly prayers to Thoth, like the one that had opened the gates. The rest of them glanced with wonder at the magnificent artistry of the decorations, but mostly they watched the harpies wheel far above them.

A giant ruby, shaped like a human heart, gleamed from the center of a magnificent monument. They all gaped at it, radiantly reflecting the starlight; a priceless treasure. Alarika rode toward it, but Karl called her back, and Alarika reluctantly obeyed. They rode slowly past the ruby heart, and Karl had to remind them to keep their eyes off the jewel and upon the threats flying above them.

A huge, roofed temple rose in the center of the city, greater than any of the monuments, and twice as ornate. Gold and silver inlay filled many lines of its columns and decorations, and twin statues of Thoth flanked its tall silver doors. Both doors lay open, and they could easily see inside.

Countless scrolls filled the Temple of Thoth. Rows of tall, gem-studded, bronze shelves stood, shining in the light of countless oil lamps, stretching from floor to ceiling. A carpet of woven red rushes led across its center, the only open area in the shelf-crowded, scroll-filled hall. Between the shelves, statues of the gods and goddesses of Egypt lined each side of the red carpet, reaching three times Nate's height, all gleaming of gold. On the very end, Thoth sat enshrined in silver, upon a silver throne, larger than the rest, reaching to the ornate ceiling. The wall behind Thoth's sitting statue dazzled every eye with brilliant colors, between lines of strange writing shined depictions of colorful scenes where the gods and goddesses came to Thoth for counsel.

"Imagine if you could read those scrolls!" Eloise exclaimed.

"The secrets of centuries … of eons!" Elaina agreed.

"The wisdom … of the God of Wisdom," Alarika said.

"The Seer would kill to stand here," Eloise said. "He'd learn their language just to read these … even if it took centuries!"

"Odin must hear of this," Roselyn said. "He tore his own eye out for wisdom; nothing would keep him from here."

"If you want your eyes torn out, we'll do it!" shrieked a harpy's voice.

The four harpies sat, perched upon a wide monument not far away. Roselyn lifted her bow, but Karl gestured for her to wait.

"Can you read these scrolls?" Karl asked the harpies.

"We can read anything," one of the harpies laughed. "We're not stupid like you!"

The other harpies cackled wildly.

"What secrets lie in them?" Karl asked.

"None!" shouted another harpy. "Thoth is too wise for lies!"

They burst out laughing, and Nate wondered why Karl was bothering with them.

"We have knowledge that Thoth may want," Karl said. "We hold the secrets of other realms …"

"Yggdrasil …?" one harpy asked.

"The Elysian Fields …?" another harpy asked.

"Shambhala …?" a third asked.

"Asphodel Meadows …?"

"Mount Olympus …?"

"Takama-ga-hara …?"

"Axis Mundi …?"

"Themiscyra …?"

"Baltia …?"

"The Garden of Eden …?"

"Irkalla …?"

"Mictlan …?"

"Avalon …?"

The companions stood speechless while the harpies laughed uproariously, their white teeth sparking in the sun amid the duskiness of their skin and feathers.

"What wisdom have mortals that Thoth doesn't know?" one of the harpies challenged them. "You know the young realms … Thoth witnessed their births!"

*"Shoot …?"* Roselyn whispered.

"Not yet," Karl said. "When we strike, we kill them all."

Nate shook his head, despite the pain in his shin. The harpies' mouths seemed to be their nastiest weapon. Alone, one person might be goaded into stupidity. Together, they wouldn't make stupid mistakes …

*… like sleeping with a nun …!*

"Alarika, is there anything in those scrolls that'll help us?" Karl asked.

"Undoubtedly, but it might take years to find," Alarika said.

"Just another trap … to delay us, to trick us into abandoning our quest," Henry said.

"Let's keep going," Karl said.

As they rode around the huge library, they spied one monument excelling all others. Arising above every building, more than ten times the height of a man, stood a great golden scale, its thick balance-beam fifty-feet wide, with an empty golden pan hanging from each side. It rose on a single massive pillar, upon which the entire scale balanced. The golden scale shined in the starlight, impressive beyond imagining, but it also gleamed red, reflecting a glow from below.

The companions reined in short before the low wall surrounding the giant golden scale, looked down, and saw the source of the glow: molten lava filled the pool, almost twenty feet below them. Immense heat rose from the bubbling lava in waves that blurred their vision. The lava fumed, occasionally spitting thin gusts of flames high into the air. The lava pool extended all the way to the tall city walls on both sides, divided only by the massive main pillar of the golden scale.

No route across the pool of lava existed.

On the far side, they spied the gates to exit the City of Thoth.

The companions sat on horse, camel, and wagon … and stared at the impossible barrier.

*"Spear!"* Roselyn shouted.

They all looked up, and suddenly Henry threw himself backwards, off his saddle, rolled head-over-heels off the rump of his horse, and landed hard onto his feet. A second after he departed his saddle, a mighty spear plummeted down from the sky and pierced his horse clean through. His horse neighed and thrashed for less than four seconds, and then it collapsed dead.

Henry stared disbelieving.

"Roselyn taught you well!" Phil said to Henry.

*"Harpies!"* Roselyn warned, and she raised her bow and shot.

The harpies flew over them, clutching many weapons in their clawed feet, which they dropped, then darted aside as Roselyn's arrow shot past them.

The heavy weapons fell. Everyone scattered, dodging, and more horses and camels screamed. Bare-bladed swords and spears rained upon them, but the harpies flew off as soon as they'd dropped their weapons, easily swooping around Roselyn's next arrow.

*"Go on!"* one harpy taunted them. *"Reach the gate … if you can!"*

*"Maybe you can swim!"* another harpy laughed.

Alarika's white camel shrieked, and then fell onto its side, bleeding from its neck and hump. Another horse was badly hurt by the rain of weapons, and two more reared, but none of the companions were harmed.

"Good jump, Henry," Roselyn said, drawing another arrow without taking her eyes from the sky.

"Th-thanks," Henry stuttered. "I can't believe I did that."

"It's the Water of Life," Phil said. "I feel stronger, too."

Henry risked a smile at Phil. "True, but without Roselyn's training … I'd never have moved that fast!"

"Or well," Roselyn added. "You landed on your feet."

"The harpies waited … until we were staring at the scale … and struck while we were distracted," Alarika said.

"Thank God we weren't killed," Sister Aspertine said, looking at the dead and wounded horses and camel.

"Thank Roselyn," Elaina said.

"On a battlefield, the more something attracts your eyes, the less likely it's a threat," Roselyn said.

"We may have only moments before those bird-women return," Karl said, looking across the wide pool of lava. "We need to get to that gate."

"How?" Elaina asked. "If we could jump to those giant trays, then our weight would unbalance the scale … and drop us into the lava."

"Eloise, could you hold it steady while we …?" Karl asked.

Eloise shook her head.

"There must be a way," Eloise said. "Otherwise, no one could reach the City of the Gods."

"Thoth is the God of Wisdom," Alarika said. "We have to think our way across."

"Look at this," Elaina said.

Before her, centered before the scale, stood a stone monument, covered with carved images, but no writing. Centermost, it held a carved inset relief in a shape that they'd seen before.

"The heart!" Nate said. "That's … the shape of … that ruby heart!"

"What does it mean?" Karl asked.

"It's a key," Elaina, Roselyn, and Eloise chorused together.

After a brief exchange of wary looks, Roselyn continued.

"That's the lock, and the heart is the key," Roselyn said. "We need to fetch it and put it here."

Karl frowned. "I don't like it."

"What's not to like?" Phil said. "We solved the puzzle!"

"Exactly," Karl said. "It's too simple … too simple to prove ourselves to the God of Wisdom."

Nate suspected that Karl was right, but he didn't want anything to delay their departure from the City of Thoth.

"Do we go back?" Eloise asked.

"We don't separate," Karl said.

"Perhaps we should," Roselyn said. "The wagons are slow, and we've lost several mounts already. If we don't hurry …"

"Fine," Karl scowled. "Nate, Phil; go with Roselyn. She'll fetch the heart; you watch the harpies … don't fail."

Roselyn surveyed both boys. "I ride fast."

Nate mounted and turned a horse around, and suddenly Roselyn spurred and rode away at a gallop. Phil rode after her, and Nate spurred to get his horse moving, shaking his reins and shouting at it to hurry.

They rode around the huge library of scrolls, past fountains and monuments, and then Phil shouted.

*"Harpies!"* he pointed.

Ahead of them, all four harpies waited, standing on the very monument holding the ruby heart. Roselyn lifted her bow, but they waved their wings.

"Wait! We need to talk!" one harpy shouted.

Roselyn didn't shoot, which surprised Nate. Yet she didn't lower her bow, either. They slowed their horses and stopped only fifteen feet from the harpies.

"Speak," Roselyn commanded.

"You can't all leave," a different harpy said. "We're forbidden to allow it. But … if you'll help us … then we'll fly you three to the gate … and you can escape."

"You won't divide us," Roselyn said.

"The blackest of choices," the harpy said. "You can't all survive. For each death, one may live."

"I'll carry your words to Karl," Roselyn said. "Will you seek to harm us again?"

"We're honor-bound to stop you …," a harpy said, and before she could utter another word, Roselyn fired her arrow, and it pierced her chest.

The three other harpies screeched in fury. As the harpy pierced by Roselyn's unexpected arrow fell dead onto the stone tiles before the ruby heart, the rest dove at them. Nate and Phil slashed with their swords, and the bird-women swooped and winged away. Roselyn noched another arrow, aimed and released, but its metal tip only 'pinged' off the edge of a nearby monument as the harpy that she'd shot at flapped behind it.

*"Watch them!"* Roselyn shouted, and she jumped off her horse and stepped toward the dead harpy, tread on her wings, and lifted the gleaming ruby heart from its stand.

*"Yadda suun ka!"*

The strange, high-pitched voice, like a bird's whistle, came from nowhere, and suddenly an image appeared over the stand from which the heart had been removed. The figure of Thoth appeared, hazy and translucent, and above him flew a harpy. Thoth raised one hand and pointed at the harpy.

*"Yadda suun ka!"* the image of Thoth said.

The image of the harpy fell, as if blasted out of the sky. Then another harpy appeared, and the scene repeated.

*"Yadda suun ka!"* Thoth said again.

Roselyn glanced around and spied a harpy flying over them, just out of bow-range. Without hesitating, she clutched the jewel-heart and her bow in one hand, pointed her empty hand at the harpy, and cried out:

*"Yadda suun ka!"*

The harpy screamed and toppled, flipping as it plummeted, and when it righted itself, it flew away, screeching complaints.

"It's a spell!" Roselyn said. "A spell to hold off the harpies!"

"They're flying back toward the others!" Phil said.

*"Ride!"* Roselyn shouted, and she leapt onto her horse.

They galloped back the same route that they'd come. As they approached their companions, they spied three harpies flying toward the wagons, their talons again heavily-laden with weapons.

*"Yadda suun ka!"* Roselyn pointed at the closest and shouted.

The harpy was blasted sideways, and dropped its load of weapons, which crashed harmlessly onto bare flagstones. Roselyn pointed her hand at a second harpy, and repeated her chant; this harpy managed to fling its weapons at those near the wagons, but then it was knocked flipping in midair by Roselyn's spell.

*"Yadda suun ka!"* Nate shouted, pointing at the last harpy.

A strange tingle washed through his palm and fingers, as if passing from his forearm, and he could almost see a distortion in the air shoot from his fingertips faster than any arrow. It struck the third harpy, and she collapsed and spun helpless, her load of weapons scattering to fall to the ground, before she righted herself and flapped away.

Karl, Alarika, and Henry were standing on the backs of the wagons, Eloise, Elaina, and Sister Aspertine hiding under them. They watched this magic amazed, but Roselyn quickly explained … and boasted that she'd slain another harpy.

The spell worked wonderfully. Whenever a harpy dared show itself, at least one of the companions would shout the spell, and the harpy would be driven back. Everyone cheered.

Roselyn gave Karl the priceless ruby heart, and he carefully placed it into the recess … where it fit perfectly.

A loud, sudden grinding filled their ears, and as they looked up, the giant golden scale started to rotate. Slowly, deafeningly, it spun on its central support, the end of one arm moving toward them, the other away, until one end towered almost directly over their heads, its huge gold pan within easy reach.

Then, slowly, with even louder scrapes and grindings, the entire scale began to lower. Its massive central column descended into the wide pool of lava that bubbled and seethed around its base.

The closest of the twin pans, which was wide enough to be a gold raft for all of them, hanging on gold chains, clashed against the edge near them, and then fell to strike the surface of the lava, twenty feet below, and rested on the molten stone. To no one's surprise, both hanging pans melted, pooling into bubbling, liquid gold atop the red-burning lava. All of their chains fell limp, and where they touched the lava, the chains also melted.

The top bar of the scales dropped, close enough to touch, and then, with a crash that shook the whole city, its descent ceased. The gold balance-beam of the giant scales stopped, the top of the golden beam even with the flagstones that they stood upon, forming a long, smooth, metal pathway, a bridge across the lava pool, leading all the way to the gate.

"Excellent!" Eloise said, but Karl waved her back.

"I don't think so," he said.

Karl walked to the edge, behind the monument into which they'd placed the ruby heart. At a gap in the short wall, he examined their 'bridge': it was solid gold, three feet wide, with a tiny rail, barely a handspan tall, on each side. The beam was smooth and flat. From the edge at Karl's feet, there was only a short gap, maybe two feet wide, overlooking the lava pool, and from there the solid edge of the beam led to its halfway point, where it poised on a giant single hinge, and then onward to the other side of the pool.

"Henry, Alarika, and Roselyn; take my arm, and hold tight," Karl said. "Nate, Phil; watch the harpies, not us."

The three came and held Karl, and he edged his weight over the gap, rested a boot upon the scale, and slowly transferred his weight. At first, the thick balance-beam supported him, but then it suddenly lowered; the others yanked Karl back onto the flagstones as their walkway steeply descended.

"I thought so," Karl said. "It's a trap. If we ran, we might make it halfway to the balance-point before it tilted enough to drop us into the lava, but no farther. Once we're at the balance-point, in the middle, how will we get to the far end?"

"I could make it," Phil said, only briefly taking his eyes from the sky. "At least, I'll get to the middle. Then I could balance it until you get on."

"Getting on it isn't the problem," Alarika said. "We can all get on … but we can't all get off."

"Every problem has a solution," Elaina said. "Could we circle it, maybe climb the walls and walk them …?"

"I doubt it," Alarika said. "Thoth placed this puzzle before us … to be solved."

"The wagons can't go … and I doubt if we could get the horses across … or the camels …," Henry said.

"Take what supplies we can carry," Karl said. "Afterwards, we walk … if we can get across it at all."

"Could we … wedge it?" Eloise asked, looking at the thick beam. "So it doesn't tilt?"

"Unlikely," Karl said, looking down at the lava. "We might be able to keep it from going down on this end, but not from going up, which means the other end, where we need to go, can still drop down."

"Maybe we can wedge it in the middle," Sister Aspertine suggested.

"We won't know if that's possible until we're trapped in the middle," Karl said. "Where's that rope? Maybe we could tie it around …?"

"I'll try," Roselyn said. "As a Valkyrie, I …"

"You're not going," Karl said to Roselyn. "Nate, take your boots off; bare feet will give you better traction."

"Yes, my knight," Nate said hesitantly.

Nate pulled off his boots and stockings, leaving them on the ground. *Why him?* Roselyn had offered to go. *Was Karl so disgusted with him that he felt his life worthless?*

"Elaina, Sister Aspertine, keep watch on the harpies," Karl said. "Eloise, stand ready to do any magic. Phil, get the rope from the wagon and tie it around Nate. Henry, Roselyn, and I will hold the rope. If anything happens, we drag Nate back."

Nate looked down at the boiling lava pool while Phil tied the rope around his waist. The rope looked dangerously thin. *Was he about to die?*

"Try to get to the middle … and stay there," Karl told him.

No one said another word, but doubt shaded every expression.

Nate hitched up his swordbelt and mail coat, took a deep breath, and fixated on his golden path, hoping that it wouldn't drop him into the fire. Suddenly he dashed forward.

Barefoot, he ran ten paces before he came to the brink, leaped off the last flagstone, and over the open gap. His bare feet hit the cool golden rampway, and he kept running. Instantly the intense heat struck him, acrid fumes burning his lungs … and then the beam began to tilt. He felt himself dropping, but bowed his head and focused on his momentum, running up an ever-steepening hill. His bare feet provided more traction than his boots would've; the ramp tilted halfway; the golden end that he'd started on tilted low, and almost touched the fiery pool, before he reached the middle. There he fell flat, clinging to the tiny rails on both sides as tightly as he could. The beam's rocking movement slowed, and then it righted itself, raising his feet until he was looking downhill, clinging to keep from sliding forward. Long he held on, and the great scale's arm slowly balanced.

He'd made it onto the balance-bar … *but how would he get off?*

*"Look at the pivot!"* Karl yelled from behind him. *"See if there's a way to lock it … or jam it."*

The rope around Nate's waist had fallen over the golden lip of the ramp, leading back to the other companions, but only slightly. Suddenly two thin gusts of flames spat high into the air, as if on purpose, one near Nate, and one near the companions. Both gusts struck the rope; the simultaneous flame-spurts burned through on both sides. The central length of rope fell, leaving only flaming braided ends, one dangling from Nate's waist, and the other hanging from Karl's hands. The bulk of the rope fell to the boiling lava pool and instantly crisped into flaming cinders.

Expressions of frustration exchanged, but no one seemed surprised.

"That was our best rope …!" Phil complained.

Ignoring his brother, Nate leaned over the edges on both sides and looked down. The middle point protruded from the base underneath him, with rounded rivet heads as large as shields. A single pin, a sort of pivot bolt as thick as his waist, supported the entire beam, but no decorations or ornate carvings marked the surface of the rivet heads.

*"Nothing!"* Nate shouted back. *"It's all smooth … simple design!"*

*"Stay there!"* Karl shouted back, and it looked like he and the others were arguing again.

The heat wafting up from the pool baked him, threatening to singe off his hair and choke his lungs.

*"Harpies!"* Elaina and Sister Aspertine screamed at the same time.

Three harpies dove out of the night's sky, suddenly, plummeting toward Nate. Trapped and exposed, Nate yelled incoherently, but simultaneous shouts of *'Yadda suun ka!'* from half of the others knocked the harpies backwards, sending them tumbling in midair. Two harpies managed to regain their balance, but the third toppled below the edge of the scale-top, and only barely caught the hot rising winds in time to avoid splashing into the lava. Several more spells were cast at her, but she swooped under the beam and came out on the other side, close to the far gate. She slipped up and disappeared over the far wall.

Suddenly, all three of the remaining harpies flew back over the gate, into view, and landed together onto the beam on the far end. Their combined weight dropped that end, nearest the gate, and lifted the other side, where the companions stood. Tilting forward, Nate clung desperately, holding on for life. Behind him, his companions screamed as the gate-end dropped suddenly, and Nate felt himself starting to slide forward, down the smooth gold surface toward the lava.

He seized the short rails and clung tightly. Then the harpies took wing, flying directly toward him, up the length of the beam, just before the far end splashed into the pool, which it struck hard, shaking the whole beam. Shielded from the view of the other companions, the harpies flew fast, fangs bared as they smiled, anticipating their victim's helplessness.

Despite his risk of sliding to death, Nate raised a hand toward them.

*"Yadda suun ka!"* Nate shouted. *"Yadda suun ka! Yadda suun ka!"*

Backwards the harpies were blasted, and Nate reclutched the thin rim to keep from slipping face-first down the golden slope, and then he felt the beam before him rising, leveling out again. The harpies flew off, but he heard their cackling laughter.

Nate began to realize how desperate his situation was. He was trapped, and unless they figured out a way for him to run faster than he could fall twenty feet, he'd never make it off this tilting beam … except to splash into lava.

The scale took a while to stop rocking, and suddenly, just as the gate-end was about to descend again, the bar shook hard. Phil came running onto the golden beam. The bar tilted his way, and Phil fell, halfway to Nate, and tried to cling on. Nate quickly crawled away from him, up onto the rising end. Both boy's weight slowly balanced, and the bar evened out.

"What're you doing?" Nate demanded.

"Karl says that there's no other way," Phil said. "We all need to cross … and bring what supplies we can."

"But how are we going to get off?" Nate demanded.

"There's no exit that way," Phil nodded back at the others. "We'll be no worse when most of us are on the other side."

"That's crazy!" Nate said. "Eventually we'll have to sleep … and the harpies …!"

"That's why we're doing it now," Phil said. "Before we're too tired to face them."

Phil explained Karl's plan while the bar balanced, and Nate listened with disbelief. However, both obediently stood, and stepping carefully, each walked backwards at the same time. They paced off fifteen paces toward opposite ends.

From his edge, Nate examined the destination that they wanted to get to: the empty gap between the balance beam and the safety of the flagstones looked exactly the same as on the other side. Just over the gap, a wide patio led to a white stairs, which rose between cascading fountains of water to tall gates of pure silver, where great golden feathers, three times any man's height, rose on each side.

Then, as planned, Nate and Phil slowly approached each other, keeping the beam balanced. They switched sides, and then separated again, walking slowly apart. Balanced by his brother, when he each reached the edge, Nate described the exit to the others.

The harpies came diving down upon Phil as he stood on the far end, but chants from the others blasted them, and they flew off again.

The companions' work began, and balance became difficult. Soon Elaina, and then Eloise, Sister Aspertine, and Henry joined them on the beam, and they spread out, evenly balanced. Phil jumped off, onto the safety of the far side, and the others began shifting waterbags and weapons to him, along with Nate and Phil's boots, food and blankets, spare ropes, and other gear, while Roselyn guarded against the harpies.

The brides of Thoth flew just outside of spell-range, circling them. On the beam, Elaina and Eloise took turns, watching the harpies and shifting goods, with Nate balancing them on his end. Every time that a harpy flew by, at least three cast the spell, driving it back.

All too soon, everything was transferred, leaving only the wagons, the remaining horses and camels, and all the barrels and treasures that they couldn't carry. Nate grinned when he noticed how many rings, necklaces, and armbands his companions were now wearing; *apparently they didn't want to leave all their treasure behind.* Karl threw the extra weapons down into the lava pool, and then Alarika and Roselyn joined them aboard the balance-beam.

"Pass Nate, and move along," Karl told them. "He'll balance you, and have Elaina and Sister Aspertine get off … one at a time … as we balance."

As the others dismounted the scale, swapping sides while staying balanced was tricky, but the number of companions on the tilting bar soon dwindled. Finally Karl struggled to set a heavy water barrel onto his end, waited until they shifted their positions to balance it, and then he jumped on. Nate was more than halfway from the middle, and when Roselyn jumped off, both men quick-stepped toward the exit-gate. They shifted carefully, waiting until the beam balanced again, and then they slowly stepped toward each other.

"Okay, time for you to …," Karl started.

"I can't leave you …!" Nate argued.

"You won't have to," Karl said. "See that water barrel? I left it on that end to balance the last person, so I can get off …"

"Let me do it," Nate said.

"A good knight doesn't ask his squires to take all the risks," Karl said. "You were the best choice to climb out here first, as you're the youngest and lightest … you've done your part."

Nate shook his head; *he'd misunderstood Karl's purpose.*

"Master, everyone hates me," Nate said. "I need to do this."

Karl stared at Nate. "It wasn't your fault. Trust me: I know better than you … if the glares of women could kill then no man would be left alive. But I'll give you this chance … if you really want it."

Nate nodded. With a sigh, Karl patted Nate's shoulder, and then he inched past him and headed toward the far end. Nate had to walk to the center, balancing Karl and the barrel. As Karl reached the end, Henry reached out and took his hand, and Karl stopped to look back.

Nate leaned forward, prepared to run, and nodded again at Karl. Karl nodded back … and stepped off. The end with the water barrel dipped, and Nate dashed forward, running uphill toward the others…

The beam started to balance …

Evil laughter struck as three harpies flew over the rail, landed on the far end, and added their weight to the water barrel. Instantly it plummeted.

*"Yadda suun ka!"* half of the companions shouted, but their spells struck the bottom of the wide golden beam, which shielded the harpies from their eyes … and their spells.

Beneath Nate's feet, the beam tilted wildly, jarringly fast, and even barefoot, Nate couldn't maintain balance while running so steeply up a shaking path threatening to hurl him off. Nate dropped onto the golden ramp, grabbed the tiny rail on each side, and held tightly, trying to look back. Too late came the idea that he could cast his own spell, yet it wouldn't have mattered; the harpies flew off the descending arm seconds before it crashed hard onto the surface of the boiling lava, almost loosening his balance and flinging Nate off. As the far end splashed into the thick lava, the water barrel toppled off the beam. Its wooden slats burst aflame, and its water splashed out, hissed, sizzled, and evaporated in a thick cloud of steam.

Nate had been only a few paces from the edge of the beam, but as the bar shook with the impact of the other end, he lost his grip and started to slide backwards. He grabbed and scrabbled at the smooth rail to slow his momentum … when suddenly he realized: with the water barrel gone, no weight counterbalanced him. The beam shook and trembled, and then dropped; Nate fell, his end tilting wildly.

The screams of the others mixed with his own as he tried to scamper backwards toward the middle, but too late. His end crashed down, and the force of the impact hurled him head-over-heels, rolling him forward, toward the lava. Nate half-fell off the beam, clinging to the rail, his naked feet only inches above the boiling, molten rock. Desperately he clambered backs onto the ramp's end, burned by the rising waves of heat, but holding on. Once atop the tilted beam, slowly he inched his way back up the steep slope, wedging his toes against the insides of the rails, and pushing himself upwards, away from the fumes baking and choking him.

*"Go slow!"* Karl shouted from above him.

*"Careful!"* Eloise shouted.

The others were shouting, even Phil, but Nate ignored them and focused on climbing. He tried not to look back, to see the lava so close … *the lava he'd almost fallen into!* Nate clutched the rails and pulled himself higher, and slowly climbed upwards.

Minutes later, he reached the middle, and the beam began to level out. Breathing easier, and wiping away the sweat dripping into his fumes-stinging eyes, Nate inched for balance, and felt the scale's thick arm grow steady. Nothing had changed; a good runner could make it dip one direction, and then run the other, but he'd have to run uphill, and he'd only make it halfway before the beam started to descend. He'd never make it to the ledge before it dropped him to a scalding, fiery death.

*"Wait there!"* Karl cried. *"We'll figure something out!"*

*"No!"* Nate shouted back at him. *"Leave it to me! Don't interfere!"*

The companions fell silent. With their voices hushed, Nate could hear the hissing and bubbling of the molten rock beneath him, and the distant laughter of the three harpies circling them. He drew and lifted his sword.

*"Hey, ugly ones!"* Nate shouted. *"Bird-bitches! Feather-brains!"*

The laughter of the harpies changed, and their courses altered. They rose, and flew closer, but not close enough.

*"What are you doing ...?"* Phil shouted, but Nate waved him silent.

*"Leave them to me!"* Nate shouted. *"No spellcasting!"*

Nate tore his eyes from the approaching harpies long enough to spy the shock and doubt on his companion's faces ... all but Karl's.

*"You're in charge!"* Karl shouted. *"Call for help if you need it!"*

Nate nodded, not taking his eyes off the approaching harpies. The expressions on their beautiful faces looked murderous.

*"Use the spell ...!"* Eloise screamed, over-shouting the others' cries of dismay.

As they swooped down, the harpies glanced at the other companions, seeming surprised by their inaction. Yet Nate clenched his teeth and said nothing, watching as their sharp, cruel talons extended toward him.

Nate stood upon the beam, sweating in the heat. The harpies closed upon him, flying toward the center of the giant, golden scale. One harpy flew slightly above the others, and one glided off to the left, and the closest flew straight at him.

As they met, Nate threw himself down, onto his back, and swung at the same time. His sword arced at the first, and struck a leg, and a talonned foot severed, hit the gold beam, and bounced toward the molten rock. The bleeding, wounded vulture shrieked … and all passed without touching him. Nate stabbed at the second, and his point lightly penetrated a breast and gashed feathered ribs as she flew close. More blood sprayed Nate, but she flew away, cursing and dripping. The third, attacking from the side, dropped down upon him, battering him with her wide wings, and a sharp pain stabbed into his already-wounded leg.

Nate cried out and kicked hard into her stomach with his knee, but his already-wounded calf was caught in her talons; she was trying to drag him over the edge. She snarled and hissed, and Nate dropped his sword and grabbed her by a thick handful of feathers.

*"Yadda suun ka!"* Nate cried, pointing his empty hand right at her chest.

The blast struck her hard, and she fell back, almost pulling Nate with her. He seized his sword, and in the second it took her to recover, Nate swung a deathstroke. The harpy saw the blade coming too late; Nate split her skull, splashing himself in more harpy blood.

Screeches came from the two other harpies, and the first barreled down upon him again. Coated in red, Nate swung at her as she passed, but she rotated her body and he missed her entirely. The momentum of his swing almost tumbled him over the brink; he dropped to one knee and grabbed the tiny rail to stop his fall. Yet the top of the smooth golden balance-bar, including its rails, was now slick with blood, making his footing even worse. His wounded leg could barely support his weight; he gritted his teeth against the pain.

The second harpy, still trailing blood, hovered outside his range.

*"You'll never live, mortal!"* she called. *"Your friends left you to die!"*

"End my life, if you can," Nate challenged her, glimpsing behind him. "You won't distract me from your sister."

The harpy scowled and flapped away. Nate kept an eye on her, but turned to face her sister. The one-footed harpy was watching him intently, flying circles above him.

"Doomed human!" she scowled.

"We both know that I'm never leaving here," Nate said. "But I'll take you both out, if I can."

"Why?" she demanded. "Your friends have reached the gate …"

"Why not?" Nate chuckled. "What else do I have to live for?"

"Pain," the harpy answered. "We'll eat you alive …!"

"If I feared pain, then I'd jump off … into the lava," Nate said, glancing back to make sure that the other harpy wasn't flying at his back, then risking a glance at his bleeding leg; his pants leg was rent and soaked with his own blood … again.

"You've sacrificed yourself," she said. "You think you're noble, but you've no idea what doom you've earned …!"

"The Duat," Nate said. "Who knows? Maybe I'll become half-vulture …?"

Both harpies laughed.

*"A male harpy!"* the bird-maid behind him cackled.

"Maybe we'll fly to the Duat … to fetch you," snickered the closer harpy.

"We heard your leader," the harpy said. "You taunt us, but you desire us, too."

"He's wrong," Nate said flatly.

"Not attracted to us …?" the grinning harpy asked. "But you are, aren't you?"

Nate glanced behind him to see empty sky.

"Where'd she go?" he demanded. "Flying low, going to sneak up from below …?"

"Sister, don't attack!" the harpy shouted. "We may have … a new companion!"

Flaps of mighty wings arose, and Nate saw the other harpy rise up behind him, but she was keeping her distance, watching.

"Don't be ashamed," the harpy said. "All men love our shape …" She glanced at her breasts. "We're designed to be watched … and desired."

"You'll kill me …," Nate said.

"Yes, but we can make your death painful … or delightful … an indulgence beyond your dreams …," the harpy said.

"Paradise … or terrors beyond nightmares," the other harpy finished.

"Send your friends away," the closer harpy said. "We can delay your death … and make the interim wondrous."

Nate eyed them both, and the bleeding harpy flew around to join her sister, both facing him. Nate watched their round breasts bounce as they flexed their wings, flying in place.

*"Karl!"* Nate shouted. *"I'm doomed! Go find the Seer! I'll stay here … so you can escape!"*

*"Squire, you're not …!"* Karl began.

*"There's no way off!"* Nate shouted. *"That's the test: a sacrificial challenge! Go … while you can!"*

*"No!"* Karl shouted, and the others chorused his refusal.

*"Trust me!"* Nate shouted. *"Like you used to … in Castle Dunstay!"*

Karl paused, then nodded.

*"We'll never forget you,"* Karl said. *"Squire, I salute you!"*

The expressions on every face radiated confusion. Soft whispers passed between them, and then they turned away. Slowly, reluctantly, with many backward glances, they picked up their burdens, walked to the steps, and started to climb toward the silver gates.

Eloise burst into tears.

"We'll make you glad that you chose us," the harpy with two feet said, and she glided forward and descended onto the beam. As her weight settled, Nate slid backwards, stepping onto the dead harpy's feathers, to keep the beam balanced.

"You … are beautiful," Nate said.

Both harpies smiled, their white teeth bright, their eyes shining with malevolent anticipation.

"There must be … some way … a harpy can be pleased …," Nate said, shrugging.

Both harpies laughed.

"You'll fulfill us … and know fulfillment," the harpy said, and she took a talonned step forward.

Nate smiled. He set down his sword, displayed his empty hands, and scooted closer, sliding on the knee of his wounded leg. Slowly he reached out his hand to cup her chin.

"I give myself … to you, my beauty," Nate said.

Balancing on the bar, they slid closer, and his fingers reached out, touched her, and traced the curve of her jaw. She closed her wings around him, her young, lovely face nearing his, and they kissed.

Nate's hidden dagger flashed, stabbed, and imbedded deep into her heart. The harpy grunted, gasped, and blood spewed from her mouth. Wings fluttered weakly as blood dripped down her front. Then she collapsed in his arms.

The one-footed harpy screeched in anger, flew back, and then winged off to the side. Nate watched her fly to the far end behind him … and settle upon the beam. At once it began to tilt, slowly, and then faster; Nate dropped his knife, grabbed the thick feathers of both dead harpies, and pulled them toward him. Then, as the beam tilted fully, he threw himself upon them, as if protecting their corpses with his body, while clinging to the rail. He managed to grab his sword as it slid by, but his dagger scraped gold all the way down and plunked into the lava.

The wounded harpy took flight, before the far end struck the lava, and winged upwards. Nate clung tight, and held the corpses of both harpies beneath him.

Nate frowned, but the last harpy, already wounded, flapped its wings and rose warily, watching as the beam rocked back and slowly balanced.

"I know what you want, trickster," she finally said. "You won't get it."

"Let's talk about it," Nate said. "Come closer …"

"Two aren't enough!" the harpy said. "You need all three of us …!"

"Maybe," Nate said. "But I'm resting while you're flying … I'll bet I can last longer."

"You'll outlive me … but not by long," the harpy said. "Your death … is my duty."

The last harpy smiled at him; her face was truly beautiful. Then she spread her wings wide … and stopped flapping.

*"Noooo …!"* Nate cried.

Abruptly she fell, straight down, into the flaming pool beneath them. She smacked hard onto the lava's surface and, screaming in agony, burst into flames.

*"Damn!"* Nate cursed.

He heard the others shouting to him, but he ignored them. The last harpy had grasped his plan … and thwarted it.

Slowly an idea raised his eyebrows. It was risky, but it would be the only chance that he got. The others were still shouting at him, but he waved his hand for silence, and they stopped shouting.

Nate hesitated, then unbuckled his belt, shrugged off his heavy mail shirt, and laid it atop the dead harpies. Then he pushed the corpses of the two harpies, covered with his mail, backwards, as far as he could, until the beam began to tilt. Then he slid backwards, frustrated, across the center-pivot; *the harpy was right; two weren't enough.*

Slowly the beam balanced, and then returned to the center. Finally, with a heavy sigh, Nate stopped to take a breath.

*"Anything we can do?"* Karl shouted. *"We've still got some rope …"*

*"It won't work,"* Nate shouted. *"Hold on …!"*

Nate used his sleeves to wipe the blood from the bottoms of his bare feet, gritted his teeth, and braced himself to stand. Agony shot through his leg, but he'd get no second chance. Waiting would only make things worse.

Nate stepped to center, felt the beam below his feet tilt lower, and then the harpy corpses, covered in his heavy mail, started to slide. On the blood-slick gold between the rails, they slid the whole way, tilting the beam sharply, and finally the bloody, feathered bodies and his mail fell off the far end into the lava.

Before they fell off, Nate began running. Nate ran up the rising bar, ascending the slope. Bent over, his feet slapped gold. His twice-wounded leg flamed new torments, but he had no choice … *now he'd live or die.*

As Nate ran, the tilting beam slowed, but when the weight of the dead bird-women and his heavy mail fell off the far edge, the beam suddenly dropped. Nate's feet lost traction, but he kept running. His end of the bar was still above his head, but only for a few more seconds. Nate forgot his pains; he'd been drinking the Water of Life for days, and been trained by Reginleif the Valkyrie. He reached inside his gut to find the strength he needed.

Just as the beam approached level, Nate jumped the last few paces … but he didn't make it. He leap was too short; he stretched out his fingers … which might graze the white flagstones, but not even Roselyn could hope to catch it and hold on.

Hands shot out over the abyss, Phil's hands, and he seized his brother's arms. Held by Karl, Roselyn, Henry, and Alarika, and by a rope around Phil's waist held by Elaina, Eloise, and Sister Aspertine, Phil was leaning out over the ledge, and had barely avoided the falling beam.

He caught Nate as the beam fell. Then, with everyone helping, as the end of the beam splashed into the lava below, Phil pulled him up. Moments later, both Nate and Phil fell onto the safety of the hard, firm flagstones.

Cheers filled his ears, and hugs seized Nate from all sides.

His wounded leg collapsed, and he'd have fallen again without the hugs upholding him. He recognized every touch … only missing … the only hands that he cared about. Across the flagstones, peering between the happy faces, Sister Aspertine stood apart, still holding the rope, and looking at him glumly.

Finally the others realized that he was in pain and carried him to the steps. Eloise knelt and repeated her magic, and Nate had no strength to resist. To his surprise, the pain faded sooner than he'd thought. As Eloise cried out, Nate pulled back his leg, it still stung, too much to move quickly, but he couldn't let her suffer.

Alarika arose and approached the tall silver doors, flanked by giant gold feathers. She faced it and spoke another prayer to Thoth.

Silently the doors opened, and then countless voices cheered. A flock of a hundred harpies burst into the sky, flying all around them. The companions yanked their swords from their scabbards, and Roselyn drew an arrow and fitted it to her bowstring, but uselessly; *the harpies numbered too many to hope for victory.*

Yet the harpies didn't attack. The six familiar harpies, all of whom they'd thought dead, flew down from the cloud swarming overtop them and alighted onto the tops of the open silver gates, smiling down upon the companions.

"Well done!" one laughed, and the others chorused agreements. "We doubted that you'd make it, but you did!"

*"You … died …!"* Elaina gasped.

"No one dies here," a harpy explained. "Even the crocodiles of Osiris, which devour the hearts of the cruel and selfish, can't truly end a spirit's existence."

"Death sends all paradise … or to Aapep," another harpy said.

"So … the five parts of the soul survive," Alarika translated.

"Indeed, sister, but you needn't worry about that," the harpy said. "You've proven yourselves wise, and we've seen that your hearts are pure."

"You … gave us the power to stop you," Nate gasped, still flexing his sore leg, "… but the challenge was to have the spell … and find the wisdom to not use it!"

"Exactly," the harpy said.

"Maybe we should keep him," another harpy said, grinning wickedly. "He's smart … and a good kisser!"

The entire flock of harpies laughed.

"There're so many of you," Karl said. "Why …?"

"We exist to test, not overwhelm," a harpy said. "When a petitioner comes alone, only three of us engage, and we provide them the spell just inside the gate, or force them to solve a simpler challenge. Your victory is ours, for you bring hope to Thoth. Depart with his wisdom … and may your hearts balance."

"Can you tell us what's ahead?" Eloise asked.

"Challenges must be unheralded," the harpy said. "Go in peace, rest well, and recover before you brave the next city."

"We had to leave our animals …," Karl said.

"You won't need them," she said. "Seek the light, and you'll find … your next challenge … not far from here."

Amid cheers from the huge flock of harpies, the six took wing. The whole flock rose with them, and all flew back towards the center of the city. Soon the sounds of a distant, lively music wafted over the winds.

Elaina suggested that they make camp just outside the silver gates, and Karl agreed. Everyone but Nate and Eloise helped, as his wounds were only partly healed, and she suffered from the effects of healing him.

As the others worked or prepared food, Sister Aspertine approached Nate, who was sitting alone.

"I … I prayed … for you," Sister Aspertine confessed.

Nate swallowed hard.

"Sister, I …," Nate began, but she held up her hand.

"Best that we … don't discuss …," she whispered. "I … must bear … this shame …"

"My pain is worse than yours," Nate said. "I'm sorry, Sister Aspertine; I'd give you back … what I took, if I could. But … what you took from me, I gave freely, and I hope that you keep it."

"Keep …?" Sister Aspertine asked.

"My heart," Nate said.

Sister Aspertine looked horrified, and she hurried away, walking quickly across the sand. With his bad leg, Nate couldn't chase after her, and resigned that it was probably for the best. He frowned; he didn't regret telling her, but he doubted if she'd ever speak to him again.

## Chapter 3

## The City of Isis

# ELAINA

While the distant music of the harpies wafted across the starlit hills, the silence of the companions deeply troubled Elaina. Despite their victory, and the sounds of a riotous celebration in the city, everyone darted black glances … whenever they looked at anyone. Roselyn frequently sneered, and Alarika mumbled in Egyptian, words that anyone could interpret as curses. It didn't matter how hard or easy their road was; unless something lightened their internal animosities, the company wouldn't survive.

For dinner, Elaina feasted them on all the best foods that they'd dreamed up and carried across Thoth's golden scale. The roast fowls and vegetables were still tasty, and the eight of them emptied three bottles of Saxon wine.

*"We should go easy on our supplies …,"* Karl whispered to her.

*"If we don't placate them now, we won't last to drink the rest,"* Elaina whispered back.

They spread bedrolls upon the sand just outside of the city. Music at bedtime felt gladly familiar, but Elaina hated sleeping on sand … which got inside everything. Each movement of her companions grated on her sensitive hearing, and her own movements scraped and ground loudly, stealing her peaceful rest. When sleep came, it was troubled, broken by sudden awakenings. She'd bolt upright, fearing some attack, but one of the men, Karl, Henry, or Phil, was always awake, watching over them as they slept.

Nothing changed in the dim, starry sky, but Roselyn finally announced that they'd slept enough. No one agreed, but Elaina tried to set an example; she rolled from her blanket and jumped to her feet as the others groaned. Elaina felt filthy, gritty, and desperate to shake off the annoying sands. She wished that she could bathe, yet she had a duty to the company, so she smiled and tried to seem cheery … to contrast their sullen, bitter frowns.

Elaina shook out her blanket, rolled it tightly, and tucked it under her arm. At Karl's command, Nate cut and offered her a length of rope, but she didn't know what to do with it. Smiling, Nate unrolled her blanket, re-rolled it so that it was longer and thinner, and tied a loop of her rope around each end, so that it hung over her shoulder. Then Phil came and loaded her with a heavy bota bag and a small pouch of food; Elaina staggered, but she said nothing, noting that hers was the lightest load. In addition to a blanket and bota bag, each carried a larger portion of food than she, and most carried several bota bags. Except for her, Eloise, and Sister Aspertine, the others also carried heavy weapons, and Karl, Roselyn, Alarika, and Phil wore armor; Nate's mail had slid atop the harpies into the lava, but he carried their heavy ropes.

Elaina bit her lip and struggled; she may be the eldest, but she couldn't afford to appear burdened while carrying the least.

Henry offered to lead their way, and started their trek across the sand. The dim stars lit their route, and they walked far, rarely stopping, before they spied another city silhouetted in the light coming from the horizon. This city looked different from the first. Thick, black smoke rose from its center, but even the cloud of smoke was dwarfed by a sight so strange that Elaina couldn't recognize it; a great shadow hovered over the city, eclipsed by the light behind it.

"It's a giant tree!" Karl said. "Not as big as Yggdrasil, but huge."

As they approached, the outline of massive branches stood out, but its undersides flickered red, brighter than its starlit top. The wavering reflections of a huge fire glowed brightly underneath the massive tree, the source of the black smoke, illuminating its giant leaves.

"Rest … or enter …?" Sister Aspertine asked.

"Rest," Karl said. "If we'd entered the City of Thoth sleepy, we'd never have escaped."

Again, Elaina insisted that they eat well, but she was worried. They only had a few days' worth of food; they'd left the rest to be feasted upon by the harpies … assuming that they ate anything but human flesh.

"Eating too much will weaken us," Roselyn complained.

"We'll have less to carry …," Eloise snapped.

"Casting away food in a pack is easier than dropping rolls from around your middle," Roselyn retorted.

Elaina stepped between them, and both relented … with scowls of disgust.

After another filthy, restless night, or period of rest, if any could call it that, Elaina struggled to maintain her sunny disposition. She acquiesced when Karl insisted that they eat less, to save their provisions, and she shared a meager fare.

Unless absolutely necessary, no one spoke. Yet glares screamed, and Elaina struggled to be warm and friendly, even as looks of hate flashed between the others.

Slowly they approached the city topped with the giant tree. Like the City of Thoth, a great wall surrounded it, but this wall was bright white, made of flawless marble, with smooth sides and natural pink swirls within the stones, which stacked only fifteen feet high. This city had gates of polished shell, as if a giant scallop had been lifted from the sea and decorated with bronze fittings. It was split down its center and wide open.

Inside the open doors stood two golden statues of a sphinx, much smaller than their counterpart in Giza, facing all who entered. Around the sphinxes, and over the walls, they spied more obelisks, monuments, and the tops of many buildings.

Sweet scents filled the air. Along the tops of the walls, and seemingly all around its base, and even inside the city, shined blue and white flowers. Yet, as they walked closer, slogging across the wide sands, a faint whine floated on the winds. As they marched nearer the gate, they realized the sound was … a distant, unending, agonized scream.

The companions paused, and worried glances exchanged. Even Alarika seemed concerned.

"It's … part of a test," Elaina said, although she was never less certain.

They waited, but the agonized wail ended only momentarily, as if the screamer's suffering had briefly overwhelmed their power to vocalize, but then it began again.

"God help … that poor …!" Sister Aspertine began, but then she trailed into silence, unknowing who or what was crying out so pitifully, and she crossed herself.

"What … do we do …?" Eloise asked.

"Never fear," Roselyn said forcefully, and she strode forward alone.

"Wait …!" Karl called after her. "We go together … slowly and carefully!"

As they approached close to the open gates of giant polished shell, between its two halves, a single figure walked slowly past the twin golden statues of sphinxes. They stopped to stare at it; the figure was a child, in a long dress made of such a fine weave it was translucent, almost invisible. She was naked under her dress. She looked to be a young girl, perhaps twelve, but her body from the waist down was covered in short, thick fur, white with patches of brown, and her strange legs were bent backwards.

"A faun …!" Elaina gasped.

"A pan …!" Alarika gasped at the same time.

"A satyr …!" Henry exclaimed.

Seeing them, the strange girl startled, too, yet she recovered soonest. Her eyes looked red, as if she'd been recently crying. She nodded to them, and spoke in Egyptian.

"Please come in," Alarika translated, "and be welcomed."

"Welcomed …?" Eloise asked.

"Ask her who's screaming," Karl said.

"Don't you know …?" she asked in English. "Oh, you're not Egyptians."

"I am," Alarika said.

"Who's screaming?" Eloise asked.

"Perhaps I'd better show you," she said. "Please, don't be afraid."

She waved them forward, and the companions hesitantly entered through the iridescent shell gates.

Fountains spraying water filled the inside of the city, and many flowers floated in each pool. Voices reached them, and figures similar to the young girl appeared; men and women, half-human and half-goat, walked calmly about.

"What may we call you?" Eloise asked the girl.

"Menes is my name," she said. "We're pans … although we've other names in distant lands."

"We're happy to meet you, Menes," Eloise said.

"I envy you," Menes replied. "Here, happiness is rare."

Her goat-legs didn't seem to bother her walking, and her tiny, furry tail twitched against the inside of her translucent dress as she led them into the presence of the other pans. As they passed into the shadow of the great tree's branches, the dim starlight was cut off, but torches flared on many walls, some pans carried oil lamps, and the flickering glows of a bonfire reflected from the giant leaves above them. Other pans appeared fully grown, most shorter than Eloise, but all bore expressions of great sadness. They didn't act surprised to see the companions, but nodded respectfully … with welcoming civility.

The monuments that dotted this city were different than in the City of Thoth. Most of these statues showed a beautiful woman, usually holding bent sticks, and sometimes depicted with a beard. Othertimes she wore a tall crown, or a helmet fashioned in the shape of a cow's head.

"Isis," Alarika whispered. "This is the City of Isis."

"Queen of the Gods…?" Roselyn asked.

"The wife of Osiris," Alarika replied. "She Who Mourns Forever."

Under the vast tree, the screams of agony grew louder.

Menes led them past lantern-lit monuments of a reed-boat, a full-sized golden cow, and large, fearsome dogs carved of dark stone.

"The dogs of Nephthys," Alarika whispered.

They passed more fountains filled with the same white and blue flowers, each with a yellow bloom in the center, and some pans carried silver bowls of water in which blossoms floated.

"What are the flowers?" Sister Aspertine asked, looking closely at them.

"They are lotus," Menes explained. "These flowers are sacred to our goddess. The blue water lilies open up each morning, their golden center shines amid the blue petals, imitating the sky that once embraced our sun. Alas that it is always night, or you would see them in their fullness. They mirror the story of creation. The white flowers are the prettiest, but the blue flowers release the strongest scent, and we hold both as honored religious icons."

Elaina felt overpowered by the exotic, otherworldly aroma of lotus flowers. She loved flowers, and the sweet scent of the lotus reminded her of a Dutch Hyacinth, which grew even in Norway. Yet the sheer numbers of them seemed oddly threatening, and the pleasantness of Menes' company worried her; so far, the threats of this world were purposefully unobvious.

Menes led them toward the base of the giant tree, whose trunk was flickering with the flames of a huge fire, which was pouring black smoke into its leaves. As the fire came into view, they saw the screamer: a young human boy, barely ten, was floating in the center of a great flame emitting from the nostrils of a silver statue of a great cow, set right below him. Hung inside the flames, the boy's skin was blackened, and he writhed as he screamed.

Menes led them to a tall pan, an older woman holding a small silver bowl in which floated a single white lotus. She was openly weeping, tears running down her face, dripping into her flowerbowl.

"This is Amosis," Menes said, speaking loud to be heard over the screams.

"Thank you, Menes," Amosis said. "Welcome, strangers, to the City of Mourning."

"The City of Isis," Alarika said.

"Isis is our goddess," Amosis said. "Here you may rest and recover … and we will care for you."

"We can't stay," Karl said. "The Duat …"

"You may rest safely here," Amosis said. "Only the Prince of Byblos may allow you to exit this city, and to ask him, you must first cap the flames of Isis and set him free."

"How …?" Karl began, but she waved him silent.

"Menes, take our guests to a house, feed them, and let them rest," Amosis said. "See to all their needs. I will come when they are ready."

Menes bowed deeply to Amosis, and then started to speak, but a sudden loud wail from the burning boy overwhelmed her soft voice, so she merely gestured, and led the companions away.

The City of Isis, beautiful except for the torment of one boy, was larger than it seemed from the outside. Menes led them a long way down wide, smooth streets to a lovely building surrounded by rows of splashing fountains, all filled with lotus. The house was a single large room, with open doorways on all four sides, lanterns brightening the colorfully-painted carvings engraved into its inner walls, divided by rows of their strange writing. Pillowed couches, beds, and chairs filled the ornate room, and a still pool lay in its very center. Beside the pool lay large water basins.

"Rest here," Menes said. "Bathe, sleep, and recover. I'll bring you food."

"Thank you," Karl said.

"You honor us with your hospitality," Eloise added, and Menes bowed deeply and departed.

"And we slept on sand …!" Elaina scoffed, and she hurried to the rectangular pool.

"At least they're not harpies …," Phil said, casting a glance at his brother, and Nate blushed.

"Might as well be," Sister Aspertine scowled. "Those … see-through dresses …! Why do they bother…?"

"Beauty is a gift from our gods," Alarika said. "In ancient days, it was considered a sin to hide beauty."

"Well, I'm about to show some beauty," Roselyn said, also approaching the pool and unbuckling the small belts of Hel's armor. "Any man can watch … but it will cost him his eyes …!"

Roselyn continued her unstrapping, and all the men turned away.

"Perhaps we should wait outside …?" Henry suggested, and the men quietly fled.

Bathing was luxurious, laying amid the floating lotus blossoms. All of the women bathed, although pressed against the sides and corners, careful not to touch each other.

Elaina noticed their silent, hateful stares and sighed. Eloise and Roselyn hated each other over Karl, both hated Sister Aspertine, who despised them for their pagan beliefs, and none trusted Alarika, who'd tried to betray them in the Field of Wheat.

Even the cool lotus waters couldn't soothe their animosities.

Menes arrived, entering through a different door, leading a troop of pans. Some were men, but they seemed insensitive to the women's nudity, even as Sister Aspertine covered herself with her hands and dipped as low as she could. They carried in trays of colorful fruits, breads, bottles and cups, thick towels, and translucent dresses such as they wore, but sized to fit the companions.

"You'd better not expect …!" Roselyn began, but Eloise cut her off.

"Grateful as we are, we hope you understand that we prefer our own clothes," Eloise said.

"Your comfort is our only desire," Menes said as the pans laid their gifts on the tables and couches. "If we have anything you desire, ask and it is yours."

"Why is that boy in the fire?" Roselyn asked.

"I think I can answer that," Alarika said. "After Set killed Osiris, the Lord of All, the pans brought news to Isis that she was a widow. In her grief, Isis cut off a lock of her hair and forever adorned herself in garments of mourning.

"Afterwards, Isis sought for the body of her dead husband, traveling the expanses of many lands, and finally heard that his spirit had floated underground. In the City of the Dead, the spirit of Osiris had mated with Isis' sister, Nephthys, the Queen of Death. From their union sprang Anubis.

"Jealous of her husband's infidelity with her younger sister, Isis grew enraged, and young Anubis fled into dark tunnels for fear of Isis. Determined to avenge her honor, Isis used the dogs of Nephthys to sniff out Anubis … yet, upon seeing him, she saw in his face a reflection of her lost husband, his father Osiris, and her anger quelled. Isis accepted Anubis as a second son, a half-brother to Horus, and she made him her guard and attendant.

"In gratitude, Anubis told Isis that the chest of Set, containing the body of Osiris, had been carried by the waters of the Nile to Byblos, where it had floated into the roots of a Tamarisk tree. That tree fed upon the nobility of Osiris, and from his majesty the tree grew so vast that it entombed the chest deep inside its thick trunk.

"Admiring the giant tree, the King of Byblos had it chopped down, and made its trunk into the central pillar of his hall. Isis begged the king to release her husband's body, but the King of Byblos refused. Instead, he demanded that Isis nurse his newborn son, that the milk of the goddess would grant his son immortality. Furious, Isis was forced to agree, but when no one was watching, she held his child into the hot flames every night. Then, during the day, Isis transformed into a swallow to fly about Byblos and mourn her husband.

"One night, the Queen of Byblos saw Isis roasting her son. She screamed, and thus the immortality of her son was destroyed. To prevent Isis from carrying her mortal son into the fires again, she cut open the great pillar and drew from it the chest of Set. Isis took her husband's body, still inside the chest of Set, and fled, determined to reunite Osiris' body with his spirit … and bring him back to life."

"You speak with wisdom," Menes said to Alarika. "Isis brought Osiris' dead body back to Egypt, but she couldn't find his spirit. Then Isis wept many tears … as do we."

"But … wasn't that boy an infant …?" Eloise asked.

"Yes," Menes said, "but that happened long ago."

Menes bowed and departed, and the other pans left with her. Lost in thought, Alarika, Elaina, Eloise, Roselyn, and Sister Aspertine finished bathing in silence, then arose and shook out their clothes before redressing.

When done, the women stood outside while the men bathed … before they ate … to the women's unanimous insistence. The men bathed quickly, and then they all feasted on the many exotic fruits, which Elaina was beginning to appreciate.

"How can this be?" Henry asked, after Alarika retold her story. "The boy we saw was alive, in the fire, but in your story, he'd already lost his immortality. Also, if that big tree is the Tamarisk tree that the king cut down …"

"Like the City of Thoth, this place is a construct," Roselyn said. "Gods placate their ego; everything here is a reflection of her story."

"If we don't solve the test of Isis, then we'll never escape," Eloise said. "The solution will probably involve her story."

"Master, I find it hard to believe that the City of Isis will be any easier to escape than the City of Thoth," Henry said.

"We'd best know all we can about Isis," Karl said. "Alarika, would you …?"

Alarika sighed, then took a cup of wine and sat down, as if preparing for a long speech.

"To speak of Isis, I must first tell you of Atum, the Creator," Alarika said. "In the beginning flowed only a great waters, which we call the Nu, the Swirling Chaos. Out of the Nu arose Atum, the First One. Atum was created by his own wise thoughts, and only Thoth equals his wisdom. Seeing only waters, Atum wished for a place to stand, and thus he created the first hill, upon the very spot where the Temple of Heliopolis exists today. Afraid of the hill, the Nu receded, exposing all the lands of Egypt, the First land, and the receding waters of the Nu became the Nile River.

"Atum stood alone, lonely, and so he made a union with his shadow. Into his shadow, Atum spat forth his son, Tefnut, the Rain, who created the 'Principles of Order', and then Atum vomited his daughter, Shu, the Void, who created the 'Principles of Life'. The 'Principles of Order' and the 'Principles of Life' combined to establish the first social order, to which both men and gods instantly became subject. Yet the children of Atum were endlessly curious; Tefnut and Shu departed from Atum, to explore all the new, distant lands, and they journeyed far from Egypt.

"Atum had only one eye, the Udjat eye. One day, he removed it, and sent his eye in search of his children. Years later, Tefnut and Shu returned with the Udjat. At this reunion, Atum wept tears of joy, and where these tears hit the ground, the first men and women grew.

"Shu and Tefnut married, and became the parents of Geb, the Earth-god, and Nut, the Sky-goddess. Geb and Nut married and gave birth to Osiris, Isis, Seth, and Nephthys. Yet, still eager to seek new lands and learn all, Tefnut and Shu sailed away again, and thus they again separated from their father, Atum, who mourned them deeply. Tefnut and Shu vanished with the receding chaos of the Nu."

*"Brother and sister … married …?"* Sister Aspertine sneered.

"They were the first-borns, and no others existed," Alarika scorned her interruption, and then continued. "When Osiris was born, a great voice spoke over all the lands and the Nu, proclaiming that Osiris was the true King of the World, but Isis proved that she was equally worthy. Isis was wise and inventive; she created wheat and barley, divined the secret of grinding their grains, and began the art of cooking. Isis invented the first words of healing, and once Egypt became civilized to the 'Principles of Order' and the 'Principles of Life', Osiris departed to bring order to the rest of his domain. While Osiris traveled to civilize lands distant and unknown, Isis ruled Egypt wisely and well."

*"A woman ruled …?"* Sister Aspertine asked.

"A goddess ruled," Alarika scowled. "As I ruled my army of thieves …"

"Is there anything else?" Karl asked, overspeaking Sister Aspertine's retort.

"Isis was the mother of Horus," Alarika said. "Horus is the greatest of all warriors, always victorious. When Horus was a boy, he became angry with his mother, Isis, and cut off her head. Too wise to die, Isis replaced her severed head with the head of a cow, until she could heal herself. This is why Isis is often sculpted with cow horns in her headdress."

Amosis arrived the next morning, shortly after they awoke. With her came half a dozen pans, and they placed new bowls of fruits, baskets of breads, and pitchers of irep on their table. Menes was one of these pans, but at a polite 'thank you', Menes and the other pans bowed and fell silent.

"We welcome you to a new day in the City of Mourning," Amosis said to the companions.

"How can you tell it's morning?" Henry asked, yawning, but then he cupped his hand over his mouth.

"Morning restarts our time of sorrow," Amosis said.

"Why is this a City of Mourning?" Eloise asked.

"Isis is in eternal mourning for Osiris," Amosis said.

"But Isis brought Osiris back to life," Alarika said.

"Yet Osiris must wear the wrappings of the grave, and so Isis wears only vestments of mourning," Amosis said. "We, the servants of Isis, share her eternal mourning."

"Great lady, what must we do?" Karl asked.

"On the far side of our city is a wide lake, the Nuaap, and in its center lies an island," Amosis said. "On the island is a temple to Isis, and inside the temple lies a golden helmet. Only a golden helmet can completely seal the silver statue of the great cow and extinguish the flames emitting from its nose. This alone can free the Prince of Byblos from his torment, and he alone can grant you exit from the City of Isis."

"What guards the golden helmet?" Roselyn asked.

"Only one guardian protects the temple," Amosis said. "A mad cow rampages upon the island … and will slay any who comes near its horns."

"A … mad cow …?" Karl asked. "Surely it's more than a normal cow …"

"My friends, you are wise," Amosis said. "You know that the cities of the gods are tests to prove your worth. I've told you all you need to know to accomplish your goal. I can't reveal more … or what kind of test would this be? Yes, more than one challenge awaits you, but this, and all else, you must devise, if you would succeed."

"We thank you, Amosis, Mistress of the City of Isis," Eloise said, and she bowed respectfully. Amosis returned her gesture.

"We wish you all blessings … for both victory and safety," Amosis said.

"How do we get to the island?" Henry asked.

"Those who are worthy of Isis will know," Amosis said.

They ate quickly, and left behind most of their gear, which the younger pans insisted would remain untouched until their return … or their deaths.

Dressed and ready, they followed Amosis outside, onto the wide streets, and in the light of the dim stars, torches, glowing lanterns, and the fire in which burned the Prince of Byblos, they marched through the city toward the Nuaap.

Many pans stopped to watch as the companions paraded past them, some mostly hidden in the dim starlight filtering through the leafy branches of the giant tree. Other pans carried glowing lamps, illuminating their sad expressions. The companions proceeded past more immaculate dwellings; not a stain or mark of disrepair marred the City of Isis. The distant screams of the Prince of Byblos could be heard, but they were moving farther from the boy in the flames.

Then the city opened up, and the buildings gave way to a gentle slope of grasslands leading to a huge lake. In the center of the lake rose an island; their destination.

The island was wide. Tall, sandy dunes covered it, divided by deep, narrow ruts. No trees grew upon it, but over the dunes rose the ornate top of a white marble temple in its center.

"That's our goal?" Karl asked.

"Inside that temple you'll find what you need," Amosis said.

"Where's the mad cow?" Eloise asked.

"You needn't seek him," Amosis said. "He'll seek you."

Long before they reached the water, all of them stopped, even Amosis. In gaps through the tall reeds, dozens of huge crocodiles lay resting in the water near the shore.

"How do we cross?" Karl asked.

"I've given you all I can," Amosis said. "Here I and my pans must leave you. Remember: you must bring back that token which alone can cap the flames that consume Prince of Byblos. Farewell, and good luck!"

With a polite bow, Amosis slowly retreated, and the nearby pans followed her.

"How …?" Phil began, but Alarika cut him off.

"This is easy," Alarika said. "To search for the lost parts of Osiris, Isis fashioned of boat of papyrus, from which all crocodiles feared and fled."

"Paper …?" Eloise asked. "How can …?"

"In Egypt, papyrus is made of reeds," Alarika said. "See these reeds? All the puzzle pieces are here; knowledge of Isis is all that we need."

"How do we make a boat of reeds?" Nate asked.

"Harvest and tie them in one great bundle …

shaped like a ship," Alarika said. "It's a poor man's boat, but I've seen many sailing the Nile."

"Reed boats are common in many southern climes," Henry said. "They sail like any other ship."

"Isis invented many things," Elaina said. "We should be able to build this."

"We'll need a huge boat," Karl argued.

"Master, there are eight of us," Henry said. "A boat that can carry all of us would be a challenge. But … if the crocodiles do flee from it, I could ferry us in several trips, so our boat needn't be big …"

"Durability is what we need," Roselyn said. "Getting there may be easy; we also need to get back."

"Need we all go?" Sister Aspertine asked.

"Henry can take us across in pairs," Karl said. "Roselyn and I will go first; we're best qualified to kill a mad cow. Eloise and Alarika will follow …"

"The lake isn't too wide," Elaina said. "If you need us, just signal."

"Master …!" Nate objected.

"Master, we should be there!" Phil said.

"Stand ready," Karl told his squires. "You'll be Henry's third trip, if we need you."

"Hel's sword can kill any cow," Roselyn said.

"If it can be killed …," Eloise reminded her.

Roselyn and Eloise exchanged furious expressions.

"Begging your pardon, Master," Henry said. "If our boat can carry more, we should. Fewer trips, and more to deal with threats …"

Karl nodded. "Good advice."

"We should get started," Elaina said. "We won't know how many our boat can carry until we build it."

Under Alarika's instructions, Karl, Roselyn, Phil, Nate, and Henry cut several hundred long reeds and carried them up to the women. Eloise, Elaina, and Sister Aspertine sorted the reeds into three piles, based on their thickness. Then Alarika spread out the thickest reeds to form the bottom of their boat, and divided the middle reeds to be its sides. Once done, she drew a knife and split the thinnest reeds, which she peeled apart, and then she twisted a pair of them into a thin cord. She used this cord to tie a fistful of reeds in their very center, and she pulled hard to bind them tightly. Then she pressed a second fistful of reeds against the bound ones, and began tying them together.

As Eloise, Elaina, and Sister Aspertine watched, Alarika wove new split reeds into her cord. She showed them how to twist the cords properly, and soon Eloise took over, working the cord and binding more reeds.

Sister Aspertine borrowed Alarika's knife and began splitting more thin reeds. Alarika began on the other side of Eloise, and soon Elaina was able to replace her. Following Alarika's example, the women kicked off their shoes and used their bare feet to push against the tough reeds as they bound them tightly.

When they had enough reeds, the men joined the women, barefoot, tying up the next row, only a handspan thick, to the one beside it. Roselyn, who admired this new skill, worked hard and fast, and Henry joined Sister Aspertine, splitting thin reeds and twisting them into more cords so that the others wouldn't run out.

At first, it seemed an impossible task, but as several hours passed, they made a sturdy base, and began lifting the outer edges as they bound their ends; the shape of a boat began to be evident.

"Fast is better than perfect," Alarika insisted. "We just need to get to the island and back. As long as we float, it won't hurt us to get a little wet."

It took longer than Alarika expected, such that Karl walked back to talk to the pans watching them, and then returned smiling.

"Amosis says that there's no hurry," Karl said. "We can feast and rest in the house tonight, and sail to the island tomorrow."

The companions cheered weakly, and several almost smiled. When they finished, Alarika took back her knife and sliced off the loose, untied stalks just above the last laces on both ends. Yet no one wanted to leave their boat untested, and Alarika said that letting it soak in water, then dry overnight, would swell the reeds and make it more water-tight.

However, the waters were full of crocodiles, so they approached with swords drawn. Their reed boat was surprisingly light, with everyone helping to carry it, and they hoisted it and proceeded down to the shore. As they'd hoped, once the front edge of the boat touched the water, the crocodiles instantly drew back, as they had in the story of Isis.

Carefully, they slipped the boat into the water, Phil and Karl keeping a firm grip on it. It did float, and when Henry climbed aboard it, it sank only about halfway into the water, bearing his full weight.

"Well, I'll be damned …!" Henry exclaimed, balancing with one foot on each side. "Water's leaking in, but it's buoyant!"

"Let's take it out," Karl said. "We'll sail across tomorrow, fresh and rested."

Wet, their reed boat was considerably heavier. Streaming and dripping water, they carried it as far as the first building, where they found Menes among the pans watching them. She insisted that they could leave their boat there, and that no one would touch it. All of the companions thanked her, and she escorted them back to their house, where they again bathed before feasting.

The men slept on one side of the room. Karl slept apart, disdaining both Eloise and Roselyn, which Elaina thought wise, but which engendered glares from both his wife and his immortal lover. Yet Nate's expression seized her attention; frowning, his jaw tight, Nate intently watched Sister Aspertine shake out her bed-roll, lay down, and cover herself … carefully avoiding looking at him.

Elaina awoke first and arose while the others slept. Barefoot, she slipped out the back door. There stood a nice garden, with a sandy walk around another raised stone pool, in which floated blue and white lotuses. The flowers' exotic scents filled her nostrils, quite invigorating, and the coolness under the dim starlight tingled her skin.

She hadn't slept well. To have come all this way through a land of dead gods was the thrill of her life, but if the companions angrily separated, driven apart by their rivalries, then she doubted if any of them would survive. Irritated by the tensions within the company, Elaina needed a dance.

Quick, smooth footsteps automatically flowed from her soul, and she opened her mind, but then the disharmonies of the distant screams stabbed into her ears. She faltered. His anguish washed over her, and yet she wondered; *was he real? Was any of this real?* The entire Egyptian afterlife seemed to be a series of tests, to prove one's worthiness to … *what?* To live with the gods of Egypt …?

Elaina knew of many gods: Norse, Christian, Druid, Greek, Roman … and now Egyptian. In their stories, every god acted petty and vain. Most were lecherous, some openly distrustful, and a few outright cruel. Why anyone would worship gods … or desire to join with them forever, mystified her. Gods existed only to satisfy their own opinions of themselves … and punished mortals for even questioning their greatness.

*Who would want a god for a friend …?*

She tried to open her senses, to feel the heart of the city; the distant crackling bonfire, the light breeze wafting through the smoky, giant leaves of the monstrous tree, and the whispers and heartbeats of the many pans that lived here … but the screams of the prince penetrated all else.

Then Elaina realized it; *his torturous screams were the heartbeat of this city.* Reversing her efforts to block them out, Elaina embraced his cries. Her bare feet stepped hard, slapping the ground. Her arms struck out, and her lithe fingers tightened into fists. Elaina danced an angry dance, wild and hectic, hammering herself in harmony with the City of Isis. Her fury of her companion's petty disputes stomped, and her frustrations with their immaturities pounded like clubs upon the taut drum-skins of their selfish hearts. Elaina danced a fury, kicking sand and swatting aside leaves and blossoms, and she rose onto the stone edge of the pool and danced as she would upon a serrated blade. Rage exploded from her, and Elaina screamed so long and loudly that she drowned out all other sounds.

Suddenly … her music had ended. Elaina was standing flat-footed upon stones around the lotus pool, her chest heaving, bathed in sweat. Resentments such as she'd never felt before radiated from her flesh. Tensions struck outwards like lightning from her hair and skin, and she forcibly closed her eyes, luxuriating in her turmoiled release.

When Elaina opened her eyes, every one of her companions was standing in the doorway, staring at her in newly-awoken, but fully-awake, horror.

Elaina gulped deep breaths, and wondered what she could do to regain her dignity, when her eyes met theirs. Her companions, even Henry, who was closest to her age, were all children compared to her. They weren't to blame for their immaturity. They were still growing, and many years would pass before they grasped the understandings that she possessed.

Elaina sighed and absently stepped down onto the sand, stopping to appreciate the beauty and fragrance of the many floating lotus blossoms.

"Well …?" Elaina smiled coyly at their aghast faces. "Shall we eat breakfast?"

*"Mother …?"* Eloise started to ask, but Elaina waved her silent.

"When communing with the universe, seers must struggle against the immaturity of those around them," Elaina said, and to their surprise, she walked right through their midst, amused at how they stepped back to give her room. She strode right to the table covered with breads, dates, bananas, and melons, and lifted and drank from the first bottle that she reached.

An hour later, followed by many pans, the companions paraded through the city to find their reed boat exactly where they'd left it. The reeds had swollen as they'd dried, and their boat seemed stiffer, more fixed in its shape.

They carried their boat back to the crocodile-crowded shore, and Elaina wondered how they'd ever reach the water. Yet, as the legend of Isis predicted, the fearsome crocodiles again grudgingly gave way, crawling overtop each other to escape the reed boat that they carried. They waited, and gave the crocodiles time to depart on their own, although they received many angry hisses, and huge mouths snapped deadly-looking teeth at them. Slowly they slid the reed boat downhill, and soon the small beach and the waters before it cleared.

They set the boat onto the water and slid it out until it floated, much higher than it had rested upon the waters only yesterday. The nearest crocodiles slapped the water with their tails and swam away, winding through the water as snakes slither through grass. Henry jumped onto the reed boat and it barely sank at all. Karl stepped aboard. Karl reached to assist Roselyn, but she drew Hel's sword and jumped aboard, making their ship tilt hard.

"Enough of that," Karl said. "We take no chances unless …"

"I can kill a cow," Roselyn scowled.

Karl nodded, and Henry lifted up a stout pole and pushed them away from the shore. They floated off … and Elaina watched them apprehensively. The goddess Isis had devised this test; she suspected it wouldn't be as easy as Roselyn believed.

The crossing wasn't long. The lake wasn't deep, and Henry's long pole seemed to reach the bottom the whole way across. The swimming crocodiles seemed offended by their presence, and scattered from their path, although Elaina suspected their fear wouldn't last if the reed boat capsized. Roselyn and Karl disembarked, and then Karl pushed the boat away from the shore to help Henry get it started back across the water.

Once Karl and Roselyn stood beside them, the dark ruts between the tall dunes looked even larger. Elaina and the others watched Henry pole back to them. As he neared the shore, Alarika and Eloise moved forward, prepared to embark, when a fierce bellow broke the quiet and startled them.

*"Mmmmmoooooooo!"*

Out from a shadowy rut charged a huge cow, bucking and braying, thrashing about wildly. It wasn't a giant cow, but it was large. It lowered its horns and charged, and Karl and Roselyn scrambled to get out of its way. It focused on Karl, and he dodged out of its path just in time; the head of the cow slammed into the side of the rut where Karl had stood, and its impact shook the island.

Alarika and Eloise jumped onto the reed boat even before it reached the shore … and Nate and Phil joined them.

*"Hey …!"* Eloise complained.

*"Karl needs us!"* Phil shouted.

The boat lowered in the water, but it didn't sink. Henry leaned hard on his pole, but the reed boat barely moved.

Unwilling to be left behind, Elaina jumped on after the boat began moving. It rocked, and they all grabbed each other to keep from falling over.

"It'll take longer to pole us all!" Henry complained.

"Eloise, push us across!" Elaina shouted.

A dawning comprehension brightening her face, Eloise pushed back her sleeves, then stepped to the front of the boat and lifted her arms. Suddenly the waters beneath them rose, lifted the boat, and hurled them forward.

The crocodiles had cleared their path, and their boat sped faster than any pole could propel it. Elaina glanced back only once; alone, Sister Aspertine had knelt on the bank and was making the sign of the cross. Elaina hoped that she was praying for them to win … and not for the cow.

After its miss, the mad cow jumped around, kicking and thrashing its head, and finally it focused on Roselyn. Roselyn stood unmoving, Hel's sword raised, but as the cow charged her, she turned and ran. The cow ran her down, but a second before its horns reached her, Roselyn jumped straight at the sandy wall of a dune, leapt high, ran two paces up it, and then she flipped backwards through the air. Its horns rammed into the dune, so hard that the cow buried its head into the wall of sand. Sword-first, Roselyn landed right across the back of the cow, sitting upon it as if it were a steed, and she drove the long blade of the Norse Goddess of Death deep into the cow's spine.

The cow brayed madly, deafeningly, and thrashed so hard that it flung Roselyn off its back, yanking her sword out as she was tossed. She landed ten feet away, where she expertly rolled and rose facing her foe, Hel's sword poised to strike again. The mad cow only bucked and shuddered, flailing in its death-throes.

Then a blinding green glow enveloped it. Suddenly the cow moved again, repeating every buck and flail that it had just demonstrated, but in reverse, as if time itself were moving backwards. The cow shoved its head back into the sandy dune wall, into the shallow impression it had left. The ground shook again, and then it exploded outwards, running backwards, every movement exactly opposite that it had done before. Then it stopped, and the blinding green glow faded, and the cow resumed normal time, thrashing madly about, kicking and braying, no longer wounded.

"It's healed!" Karl shouted.

"We have to kill it completely!" Roselyn shouted back.

"Wait for us!" Phil shouted to them.

Pushed by the water, the reed boat sped closer.

"Don't let us crash into the shore!" Henry cried. "Our boat will be broken!"

Eloise lowered her arms, and the boat slowed suddenly, drifting almost to the bank. It also sank halfway underwater, so that water splashed over all their shoes and boots and soaked into the women's skirts. Yet Eloise jumped ashore as soon as she could, closely followed by Phil and Nate. Elaina jumped to join them as the cow noticed their movements, stopped thrashing about, and charged them.

"Push the boat out!" Phil shouted to Nate.

Phil drew his sword and ran to the side, waving to keep the cow's attention on him. Nate did as ordered, although he shouted his brother's name.

The cow lowered its horns and charged straight at Phil. Elaina froze, terrified; *she had no power to stop a mad cow's charge, and even Hel's sword had failed to wound the magical beast.*

At the last second, Phil dove aside onto a growth of reeds. No tall dune rose behind him; the cow's momentum carried it splashing out into the lake. Henry poled hard to get away from it, and the cow resumed thrashing its head and kicking, as if it could splash all the waters out of the lake.

"Climb the dunes!" Nate shouted. "It can't reach us there!"

Phil clambered to his feet and, with silent agreement, they ran to the nearest dune. Roselyn met them at its base, and lifted them with ease.

"I'm strong again!" Roselyn said. "The Water of Life is restoring me."

"I feel it, too," Karl remarked. "When we get back, we should all drink as much as we can."

Roselyn hesitated when it was Eloise's turn, yet after a moment of reluctance, Roselyn seized and helped lift Eloise, who placed one foot upon Roselyn's bent thigh, lifted a foot to her shoulder, and then was pulled up by the others. Elaina went next, displaying acrobatics that needed no assistance; using Roselyn's armored body like a series of steps, she bounced up with ease. Karl came last, and he and Phil pulled Roselyn up to join them.

From atop the dune, the island looked like a maze, deep ruts where the cow had trampled and dug its way into twisting paths, possibly worn away after centuries, leaving narrow mounds of sand. Some of the mounds had crumbled, and some were no wider than a few feet, but most were small hills, strong enough to walk upon. In the distance, they spied the top of the silver temple; their goal, but it looked a long way away.

"Here it comes!" Phil warned.

The mad cow splashed out of the lake. It brayed angrily and snorted fiercely. Then it saw them … and charged.

"Hold on!" Karl shouted, and they grasped each other seconds before the cow crashed into the dune beneath them. Their whole hill shook, and they flailed for balance. Karl and Phil jumped backwards as part of their dune crumbled beneath their feet. Then the cow drew back and steadied itself for another charge.

"This won't work!" Roselyn shouted. "It'll take out the dune beneath us!"

"Let me …!" Eloise said, trying to push forward.

"Get back!" Roselyn shoved her back. "I'll …!"

"Let Eloise try!" Karl shouted. "If she can stop it without taking risks …!"

Swapping indignant glares, Eloise pushed her way forward, then loosened her fingers by shaking them.

"Wait …!" Karl said. "Hold on …!"

The mad cow charged and rammed the sandy wall beneath them, almost shaking them all off the hilltop. Karl pulled Eloise back as another foot of cliff crumbled, and then the cow fell back, bucking and snorting.

Eloise cast her spell. The eyes of the cow were red and fiery, bulging, but a gentle cloud of sparkles appeared before them, like a flickering dance of fairies, and the cow hesitated. The eyes dulled momentarily, but then the head shook, the long horns slashed the sparkling cloud apart, and it dissipated and vanished; *Eloise's spell had failed.*

The cow charged again, and this time it crashed into the side of the dune so hard that three feet of it collapsed.

"Let me …!" Roselyn insisted.

"All right, but be careful!" Karl said.

"I'll help," Elaina said.

"You …?" Roselyn asked contemptuously.

"I move better than any of you," Elaina said. "I dodge faster; I can distract it."

"Can I trust …?" Roselyn began, but Elaina cut her off.

"If we stop trusting each other, then we might as well give up now," Elaina said.

The cow began to charge again, and suddenly Elaina jumped, bounced off the wall of the dune next to them, back to the wall of their own dune, and jumped onto the back of the charging cow. With one foot, she kicked off it, flipped, and landed onto her feet behind it.

The cow turned its head, slashing its horns at her without checking its charge. It slammed shoulder-first into the dune, making it shake. The mad cow stumbled, struggling to get to Elaina.

Roselyn dropped down, swinging Hel's blade as she fell. Her boots struck sand an instant before Hel's sword hacked; a mighty downward swing. Yet the horns turned unexpectedly, took the blow undamaged, and slashed hard. One sharp horn caught a black, skull-shaped scale of Hel's armor … and tore a rip in their pattern, leaving a bare rent over Roselyn's hip.

Screaming her outrage, Roselyn avenged Hel's gift; she jumped high and swung again. Her blade struck hard onto the back of the cow's neck, chopped deep, and completely severed its head.

The cow's head fell at Roselyn's feet as a splash of blood coated her, and its body collapsed a moment later.

Nate cheered, and a whoop rose from Henry, floating offshore, but none of the others spoke.

Roselyn grinned, a gleam of murderous triumphance, and Elaina paused, taken aback by the wicked smile of a victorious Valkyrie. The head and carcass were completely separated, undeniably dead. But then … slowly the blinding green glow returned. The mad cow's hide shined like emeralds, the severed body rose to its feet, and then the head popped off the ground and reattached itself. The cow's horns slashed in reverse, its shoulder slammed into the stout cliff-wall, and then it ran backwards to where its charge began.

"It's immortal!" Roselyn scowled.

"Get back up here!" Karl shouted. "Hurry, before it attacks!"

Frowning, and still covered in blood, Roselyn stepped beside the dune wall and gestured to Elaina, and she forced her fears aside, ran forward, and leapt onto Roselyn's outheld hands, shoulder, and up onto the cliff. Then Karl and Phil pulled Roselyn up while the cow madly jumped about and thrashed.

"We must split … and decoy it away," Roselyn said.

"I'll do it," Elaina said.

*"Mother …!"* Eloise gasped.

"Strength can't win," Elaina said. "I'm the most limber and balanced …"

"Elaina …," Karl began.

"I'm the decoy!" Elaina insisted. "If you children can't put your differences aside and go find the Helmet of Isis, then don't lecture me on cooperation!"

The cow stopped thrashing and seemed to remember that they were there. At once it oriented on them and charged.

"Hold on!" Karl shouted.

The cow rammed into the dune, shook them, and more sand crumbled beneath their feet. Then the cow drew back a step, and Elaina jumped toward it, bounced off its back, and leapt to the next closest dune-top. The cow snorted and flung its horns wildly to try and get to her, but she only laughed and called to it, and then ran away. Furious, the cow chased after her.

Leading the cow was easy. Lithe as she was, Elaina ran quickly down the dune-top. The ruts, she suspected, were gaps in the dunes which this mad cow had dug out and trampled, running in circles around the island. Where she could, she leapt to adjacent dunes, and she purposefully chose the tallest, so that she could map her best route. When the cow charged, and slammed into the dune-sides beneath her, sometimes she leapt over it, using its thrashings to boost her to the next dune. This infuriated the beast, and several times it bellowed angrily at her. She noted that the size and shape of the cow's head looked exactly like the silver cow statue under the burning Prince of Byblos, and suspected that the statue was made to resemble it. Yet she tried to stay focused on her task; where the cow struck the dunes, an imprint of the cow's head often remained … with deep holes where its horns struck.

Elaina frowned; she'd be impaled and crushed if caught between those horns and the sand.

Elaina led the cow farther away, and spied the others hurrying toward the temple. She meant to keep the cow distracted, but as it crashed into her thinly-piled dune, the dune collapsed. Elaina dodged aside as the dune collapsed beneath her, and watched as the mad cow drove through the sundered dune, and then emerged, covered in sand, and ran off down a long, narrow route, headed in the wrong direction. Elaina watched it run off, and then dashed back toward the others.

With ease Elaina jumped from dune to dune, lighter than ever. She felt stronger, freer, and wondered if she, like Roselyn, was feeling the strength and vitality of the Water of Life.

Arriving at the temple, Elaina found it surrounded by tall, thick pillars of stone, each pillar squared and covered with hieroglyphs. The gaps between the columns were too narrow to allow the cow to enter, yet Elaina easily slipped through. She found the companions standing before a series of hanging gold mirrors, all circled around … an empty marble stand.

"Where …?" Phil asked.

"Gone," Karl said. "Maybe someone took it …?"

"We'll hunt them …!" Roselyn started.

"No one took it," Eloise sighed. "We're being tested …"

"Maybe it's hidden elsewhere … or invisible …?" Henry suggested, and he waved his hands over the empty pedestal.

"Where would Isis hide it?" Nate asked. "It must have something to do with her story …"

"Isis had to search for the body of Osiris when it was whole, and then find all the pieces after Set cut him up," Alarika said. "She searched many lands …"

"Amosis said that we'd find the cow-helmet on the island," Karl said.

"No …," Roselyn and Eloise said together, and they exchanged nasty glances.

"Amosis said that the golden cow helmet would be inside the temple," Roselyn said. "So the cow helmet must be here."

"She also said 'that more than one challenge awaits us, but this we must … 'devise' was the word she used," Eloise said.

"Devise …?" Karl asked, scratching his chin. "Boys, search as best you can. See if you can find anything."

"I'll read the hieroglyphs," Alarika said.

Nate and Phil began searching the floor, the pedestal, and the columns, slipping between the six thin golden mirrors hanging all around, reflecting the empty pedestal. Alarika went to read the strange picture-glyphs on the columns.

"I doubt they'll find anything," Karl said. "In the City of Thoth, Nate had to deduce the solution."

"Devise …," Roselyn said. "That's an unusual word."

"Isis devised all sorts of things, like grain … and cooking," Alarika said.

"How do we devise a missing helmet?" Karl asked.

"Maybe there is no golden helmet," Roselyn said. "Maybe we need to forge one."

"These mirrors are gold," Eloise said. "We could fashion a helmet from them."

"We've no forge or tools," Karl said. "Even if we did, the helmet has to cap that statue, and we'd never get it sized and shaped perfectly."

Silently thinking, the companions stood perplexed. Nate and Phil found nothing, and Alarika came back and shook her head.

"These columns tell the stories of Isis, and praises to her, but they don't mention her helmet," Alarika said.

"Are there any carvings of the helmet?" Karl asked.

"Just the usual inlay," Alarika said. "A sun disk between the horns of a cow."

Eventually the mad cow found them, and came snorting and stomping outside the temple, but its wide bulk couldn't fit through the thick columns. It charged the temple, but always stopped before striking it, then blew through its nose and raged about.

Tired, Henry and Alarika sat and fumed. Nate and Phil seemed bored. No one could devise a solution … or deduce where the missing helmet could be.

Elaina pondered their circumstance; without a solution, a puzzle was only a trap. Yet these tests were designed to challenge the faithful, to prove their worth to join their gods. Somewhere on this island was a key to the missing helmet; they just had to find it.

Elaina counted the thick columns; eighteen, but that number held no significance to Isis that Alarika knew. Outside, three marble steps led to the ring of columns around them. The columns were covered with Egyptian writing, but so were many things in Egypt … and its afterlife. The pedestal was white marble, but displayed no obvious clues. Six golden mirrors hung from thin chains, each about three feet in diameter, and very thin, no thicker than parchment. She stared at the mirrors. *How could she …?*

*The mirrors were disks … disks needing horns …*

"I have it!" Elaina said. "I can make a helmet of Isis!"

"How…?" several voices asked.

"Take down one of those mirrors," Elaina said, and instantly Phil unhooked one and handed it to her. It was paper-thin and surprisingly light.

"Wait here," Elaina said. "This won't take long."

Elaina ran out of the temple onto the sand. Instantly the cow oriented on her, lowered its horns, and charged.

Elaina set aside the golden disk, waited until the last moment, jumped right toward the cow, placing a foot atop its head. As it threw back its head, the cow flung her, and she flipped over it, and let the cow run underneath her.

*"Mother . . . !"* Eloise screamed.

Elaina couldn't afford to be distracted by her daughter; she'd get only one chance at this. The momentum of the mad cow had carried it away; she had only seconds. She grabbed the golden mirror, ran to the nearest tall dune, and pressed the bottom of the golden mirror into the grains of sand. Securely she rested it against the vertical wall of sand, only a foot above the ground.

The mad cow stopped its thrashing and turned around. Elaina shouted at the cow, her usually soft pitch shrill and stuttered, and she waved her arms over her head. The mad cow brayed deafeningly, and then lowered its horns and charged.

Tensed, Elaina stood still, waving her arms and screaming to keep the cow's attention. The cow charged straight toward her. Eloise screamed, but Elaina ignored her. She waited until the very last second, then jumped as high as she could, over the lowered horns. She slapped both her hands against the beast's shoulders and vaulted heels-over-head above it. Behind her, the mad cow slammed into the dune wall, crashing into the golden mirror that she'd placed upon it.

Elaina bounced free off its rump, safely landing on the sands, and then she turned and looked at the mad cow. Horns-first, the cow had plowed into the sturdy bank of sand, and struck almost center of the golden mirror that she'd placed there. When the cow pulled free, the mirror came with it, and Elaina smiled; the thin gold disk had plated itself over the face of the mad cow, and was now stuck upon it. The cow thrashed and shook free; the golden disk, stamped with the impression of the mad cow, flew off to land upon the sand not far away.

Elaina jumped for it, snatched up the gold disk, and ran for the temple. The cow chased, but too late; she ran fast, and lithely slipped between the columns into the safety of its inside. As before, the mad cow stopped short of ramming the columns, snorting angrily.

"A golden helmet," Elaina said, and she held out the gold disk, now stamped with the image of the mad cow's head. It was off center, and one horn had punched through it, leaving a hole, but Karl smiled.

"Helmet or not, this should cover the statue under the Prince of Byblos," Karl said, and everyone smiled and thanked her. Roselyn especially praised Elaina's wisdom, skill, and daring.

"Except for divining the future, I never thought dancing was of any use to a warrior," Roselyn said. "No einherjar could've managed that; you're indeed worthy of Valhalla."

In an unexpected gesture of appreciation, Roselyn insisted on distracting the mad cow herself, so that the others could get back. This made their journey easy, and Roselyn proved no less adept than Elaina at the task; the mad cow chased her, and Roselyn slew it again, then used the moments while it was healing, moving backwards through time, to climb to safety. While Henry ferried all the others back to Sister Aspertine in two trips, and then came back for her, Roselyn led the cow on another merry chase, then darted back to the water. She and Henry were thirty feet offshore before the mad cow splashed into the waters, braying as if cursing their escape and challenging them to return.

Clutching their prize, they found Amosis standing beside Sister Aspertine on the shore.

"You've proven your worth," Amosis smiled, looking at the stamped golden mirror. "Come, and join in the celebration. Tomorrow you shall depart, with all the blessings of Isis."

They carried the newly-made helmet of Isis straight to the statue from which streamed the fire which consumed the blackened figure of the young man floating above it. There, Karl gave the helmet to Elaina. Avoiding the heat, she inched forward … and slipped the shaped gold disk over the matching silver horns and face of the mad cow. The imprint matched perfectly. The helmet slipped onto the statue like a mask, affixed to it, and instantly its flames were stifled.

The blackened figure stopped screaming, shook itself, an[illegible] blackness fell off him. It floated down, a fine, dus[illegible] Unburnt, the young Prince of Byblos smiled dow[illegible]m, and then he floated down to the ground and [illegible] deeply to Elaina.

"[illegible] new friends, let the feast begin!" he shouted.

The celebration of the pans was a wondrous party, and the companions drank, feasted, and danced until even Elaina became weary and had to sit and rest. The Prince of Byblos, a handsome young boy, danced some, but then he sat and drank with Karl, raising many toasts to him and all the companions. Karl tried to get the prince, or any of the pans, to tell him more of what they could expect in the next city, but they only laughed off his questions.

"You can't cheat gods," the Prince of Byblos said. "If I tell you what to expect, then when you arrive, the challenge will have changed. Trust your strengths and courage, and never waver in your devotion to seek our gods."

"Our gods are ever foremost in my heart," Alarika assured him.

They returned to their house, slept long, and when they arose, all the pans of the City of Isis lined their path and threw lotus petals at their feet. The Prince of Byblos led them back to the base of the huge Tamarisk tree, and there he swung out a section of bark that opened like a door, and directed them into the dark tunnel in the center of the tree.

"This tunnel will lead you safely out of the City of Isis," the prince said. "Your next destination isn't far. Farewell, my friends, and all blessings go with you."

The companions thanked the Prince of Byblos, Amosis, Menes, and all the other pans.

"A great goddess Isis must be to have such wonderful pans in her city," Eloise said.

The pans cheered the companions, and one by one, Karl leading, they waved good-bye, and stepped up into the opening of the tunnel, which led down a deep stone stairs. Menes gave Phil a lit torch, and he held it high as they walked out of the City of Isis.

## Chapter 4

## The City of Nut

# PHIL

As they walked, Phil held his torch high, its flickering flames dancing against the low sandstone ceiling. They needed its flames for light, but after they reached the base of the stairs, their tunnel was straight, smooth, and went on for miles.

Yet, the longer that they walked, in utter silence, the deeper Phil frowned. If they did make it back to England, would any friendships endure … or would jealousies and resentments have torn them asunder? Phil would risk any danger that Karl asked him to face, but he could only shake his head and say nothing when he imagined a Castle Bristlen where only antagonisms ruled.

When the tunnel finally began ascending, its grade was gentle. As expected, they emerged from the rocky tunnel onto barren sands under a barely-starred sky. Directly before them rose a huge, black city, hiding behind a towering obsidian wall, with tall gates of beaten gold.

Normally they would've camped, but a distant horn blew as they appeared, and figures upon the stone walls waved at them, so they marched straight toward it. As they approached, the priceless gates opened, and a crowd inside the gate cheered. The folk of this city greeted the companions warmly, with many smiles and waves.

The companions stood transfixed: before them stood a large crowd of men and women, all with skins of purest black, like darkness in the bottom of a cave. They looked tall, stately, and exceedingly healthy, yet the companions startled: not one of the inhabitants of this city was wearing a stitch of clothes.

One woman and one man approached them. Both were tall and shapely, and into their black skins were embedded countless tiny gems, of many colors, but mostly clear or white, shining like stars against their dark skin, so that both looked like the night's sky come to life.

"Welcome to the City of the Shape of the World," the woman said.

Phil stood stunned; of all the naked women, this leader looked the most like Alarika, tall and strong, with the same long, midnight hair and entrancing eyes. Her body was perfect, without blemish, and she stood without shame, justly proud of her beauty. She walked with royal elegance, like Eloise, and moved like Elaina, with a flowing sway, lithe and smoothly, almost mesmerical. The man beside her was clearly her equal, taller than Karl, with the same dark skin, and boldly he stood naked before them. His skin bore the same gems, looking like a shifting body of sparkling stars as his thick muscles flexed.

Sister Aspertine gasped and covered her eyes with her hands.

*"Can't you please wear clothes?!?"* Sister Aspertine shrieked, her hands squeezed tightly over her face.

"We are clothed as our goddess, skyclad," the man said. "Enter, good friends, and behold She Above and Below."

"Below ...?" Alarika asked. "How can the goddess of the sky be below ...?"

The crowd parted, and Alarika's question was instantly answered. Instead of being filled with countless monuments, the City of Nut was formed like a great coliseum. All of the tall, stark buildings were pressed against the insides of the wall around the city. The central floor, between the buildings, was flat and uncluttered. A great mosaic of the night's sky gleamed upon it, huge gems sparkling like mirrors of every glowing star that ever shined, set against smooth, black, even tiles. It was as if the brightest stars above the deepest deserts of Egypt lay floored in the city's center. The huge mosaic was arranged in the shape of a giant woman, in slightly-raised relief: Nut, Goddess of the Sky.

At the foot of the stairs before them shined the mammoth feet of the goddess, and her head lay in the distance, at the far end of the city, her arms stretched over her thick hair. The companions stared; the starry night's sky reflected the countess stars of the real world ... in defiance of the few stars shining upon the land of the Egyptian gods.

Even more amazing, if anything could be, were the floating people. Walking ten, or even twenty feet over the starry mosaic, across thin air, the people of Nut trod upon walkways that no companion could see.

"Be not surprised," the naked man said. "Shu, the Goddess of Air, upholds Nut, the sky, as Geb, the God of Earth, lies beneath. We are the children of Nut, her most devout followers."

"We thank you for your welcome," Karl said. "Please, tell us what task we must …"

The crowd laughed.

"Nut requires no task," the star-gemmed woman said. "No mission awaits you. No mystery must be revealed or puzzle solved."

Instantly Phil doubted this pronouncement, and his suspicious eyes scanned the unbroken line of buildings surrounding the mosaic. Suddenly, he realized what was missing.

"Master," Phil whispered from behind Karl, worry filling his voice. "Look at the far side …!"

Karl glanced about, from the beauty of the dark-skinned people to the buildings along the wall, and to the huge mosaic of Nut, yet he obviously didn't see it.

*"No door!"* Phil whispered back. *"No exit!"*

Karl startled and glanced again; no break showed in the wall or buildings surrounding the mosaic, yet the crowd only laughed.

"Worry about nothing here," the man said. "Being vanquished to the Duat is what all travelers fear, and we'll aid you to avoid it, if we can."

"The door that you seek lies before you," the woman said. "When you can leave, then you'll see your path. Until then, if there's any joy or pleasure that you desire, all that we have is yours."

The naked, gem-studded followers of Nut gestured them to enter, and the two who'd come forward led their way. Unlike the other cities, the City of Nut was dark, its wall, buildings, and paved floor carved of huge black rocks. Some buildings looked as if they were shaped from a single block. Many windows glowed from lights within, but the only other lights came from the countless gems in the vast mosaic of Nut, each of which glowed like a star.

As they approached the mosaic, they realized that countless thousands of gems lay before them. Most of the gems were tiny, small as a drop of water, while others looked as large as a fist.

The buildings of this city were different; every wall that Phil saw was flat and smooth, with no trace of hieroglyphs or ornate decorations, such as cluttered the cities of Thoth and Isis. Yet, Phil mostly stared at the people, especially the women, who walked on thin air, sometimes directly over them. All were naked, save for their many studs, and each was built of envious proportions. Every man was generously endowed, each woman exquisitely gifted. Even Phil, who'd always prided himself on his muscular physique, felt diminished, for in this city, his obviously superior attribute was common.

As in the City of Isis, the companions were led to a building seemingly built for guests. This dwelling held a spacious central room, with many small side-rooms, and a narrow stairs led up to other floors, through a rectangle cut into the ceiling. Each room was furnished with furniture made of ebony, softened by cushions of dark reds, greens, and blues, and floored with mosaics of obsidian and basalt, with lighter stones embedded in intricate patterns. The main room boasted two small pools; a few blue and white lotuses floating in them, not nearly as many as floated in the City of Isis. Small oil lamps and candles lit the darkest rooms, but no room seemed bright.

"Rest here," the woman said. "I'm Djehuti, and this is Hatshep."

"Call upon us for anything … at any time," Hatshep said. "If you have any desire, our greatest delight is to fulfill it."

"We're grateful," Karl said. "We must pass through your city, and seek your gods. We ask only for the knowledge of how we may do so."

"Your minds overflow with chaos," Djehuti said. "You may depart at any time, but first, you must overcome your chaos within. To depart our city, you must become one with Shu and arise to Nut."

"Fly …like your people …?" Elaina asked.

"Not fly," Hatshep said. "Our people walk with Shu, one with the invisible deity."

"We must walk on air …?" Eloise asked.

"Only the path of Shu exits the City of Nut," Djehuti said.

"Nut shall lead you to Shu," Hatshep said. "Our goddess Nut is wife and sister of Geb, and both were born of Shu and Tefnut, the children of Atum. Nut and Geb have four children: Osiris, Isis, Set, and Nephthys."

"Of all of the gods of Egypt, Nut is the Loving Mother," Djehuti said. "To her brother, Geb, Nut became the first mother goddess to bear more than two children, and thus she greatly strengthened the family of Atum. Nut loved her husband, but her beauty is so great that all who see her love her. Kronos, who Atum calls Keb, saw her, and despite her vows, wooed her into submission."

"Who's Kronos?" Eloise asked.

"Unaging Kronos is Eternity, the God of Everlasting Time, created by the joining of the Aether and Chaos, and self-born of a silvery egg, but little else is known of Kronos," Djehuti said. "Kronos alone existed before the Nu, and Kronos is said to have witnessed even the birth of Atum, although none can speak on this. The semen of Kronos was placed in the farthest recesses of existence, and it is said that from this was born the first pantheon of gods."

"First…?" Elaina asked. "Were the gods of Egypt not the first …?"

"Only foreigners to Egypt would ask such a question," Hatshep said. "Ask not again, for we don't disrespect our gods."

"They're race is young, their gods children," Alarika said. "I have told them of Nut, and how Re cursed her, so that Thoth created five new days during which she could give birth."

"The birth of Kronos extends beyond memory, even beyond that of Nu, the great waters," Djehuti said. "Before eternities of darkness, the mind of Kronos awoke, but nothing existed to see. Thoth alone knows what may have existed before Kronos, but Thoth doesn't share such secrets."

"Not even our gods know whose voice spoke in that hour when Osiris was born," Hatshep said. "It was someone's voice, powerful and commanding, declaring that Osiris was the Ruler of All, but such questions are unwise for mortals to ask."

"Best that we return to Nut," Djehuti said. "At first, Nut spurred Kronos, for she feared his secretive ways. However, Kronos defeated her, for she was wooed by his praises and looked not into his heart. You must learn to look inside your hearts, or like Nut, you will fall."

"Every dawn, after Ra defeats Aapep, our goddess Nut swallows the sun god, so that he may travel the sky through her," Hatshep said. "In this way, during the day, his brilliance blinds mortals to her starry beauty. Ra's nightly entry through the Akhet, Black Gateway to the

Duat, is death. Yet all who enter Nut … of their own will … come to life."

"Nut shares with all her protection, love, and fertility; for this, we of her city worship her," Djehuti said. "Yet Nut also welcomes the nine bows."

At this expression, all except Alarika looked confused.

"Egyptians call foreigners 'the nine bows', those who threaten pharaonic rule and the stability of Maat," Hatshep said. "Egyptians associate those of foreign nations with hostile deserts. We, and our gods, are deeply tied to the lands beside the Nile. At times, we've been driven to protect them."

"We offer no violence or ill-will," Eloise said. "We're here to help a friend …"

"Nut knows that," Djehuti said.

*"She knows …?"* the companions exclaimed.

"Few true believers now come to these lands," Djehuti said. "The arrival of strangers hasn't gone unnoticed."

"Can you tell us anything … about our friend?" Eloise asked.

"Only that he stands with our gods," Djehuti said. "You'll find him easily … if you can reach the throne of Osiris."

"Could you send us straight there … or send him a message …?" Karl asked.

"Nut knows of your quest, but she has no power over the other gods," Hatshep said. "We're instructed to aid you as much as we can."

"Thank Heaven!" Phil exclaimed, and then he fell silent as Karl glanced at him.

"What must we do?" Roselyn asked.

"You may leave as soon as you can travel the Celestial Path," Hatshep said.

"How can we walk upon air … I mean … walk with Shu?" Eloise asked.

"Only those whose hearts are light as Nut may explore the Celestial Path," Djehuti said. "Secrets, doubts, and fears are chains that bind mortals to Geb. To leave, you must lighten your hearts."

Phil bit his lip as the rest of his companions fell nervously silent. So many resentments filled their company that he couldn't count them all, and revealing their doubts would cause even more hate.

"How … how long do we have?" Karl asked.

"Many days … at least," Hatshep said.

"What happens then?" Eloise asked.

"When it opens, those who can't walk with Shu fall into the Duat," Hatshep said.

Djehuti and Hatshep stood as four other dark-skinned worshippers of Nut arrived, carrying hot bowls of steaming food, especially baked mushrooms in bubbling hot cream, which they set on the low wooden table in the center of the main room. All of the people of Nut looked different. One man, with exceptional muscles, was studded only with red gems, in countless short, straight lines, while one woman wore only swirling lines of green and violet. Djehuti and Hatshep moved like starry reflections of each other, in perfect harmony. When they turned to leave, Djehuti and Hatshep bowed to the companions.

"There's no pleasure of yours we wouldn't be happy to fulfill," Djehuti smiled brightly.

"That goes for your women as well," Hatshep nodded to the women. "Please, call upon us for anything you desire."

Djehuti and Hatshep departed, leaving most of the companions speechless.

*"Harlots!"* Sister Aspertine scowled. *"Sinners and … temptresses and … whatever men-sluts are called! Why can't they wear clothes …?"*

Phil said nothing, but he couldn't deny the attractiveness of the women of Nut. The way that their gems sparkled as they moved stole his thoughts and aroused the deepest parts of him. He wanted to chase after Djehuti … and test the truth of her offer. Yet, he couldn't help notice: two companions had averted their eyes as Djehuti and Hatshep had departed. Sister Aspertine's reaction was expected, but his brother …? *Phil was surprised that Nate wasn't already running after her.*

Nate had always been a sucker for any woman. As squires in Bristlen, like most castle guards, they'd found few opportunities with women except in Demril, where any man with coins could be seduced into an empty purse. Phil's first experience in Demril had taught him how hollow the compliments of barmaids proved once he'd spent his pouch; *he didn't like being deceived.* Yet Nate desired easy women; his morals could be bought cheaply, and he valued quick profits. Sometimes Nate's gambles earned him far more than Phil had ever owned, but then he'd lose it … gambling, or on sneaky plans that never worked.

Yet … the expression on Nate's face when he looked away from Djehuti; *Phil had never seen his brother look truly sad.*

Alone, the companions stared at the plentiful food, but no one reached for it.

"Secrets, doubts, and fears …," Henry repeated.

"Lighten our hearts …?" Eloise asked.

Evil glares darted from many eyes.

"Mad cows and harpies this company can defeat," Elaina shook her head. "Our greatest danger … has always been … us."

Finally Elaina reached for some food and began eating. The rest of them only watched her. Phil didn't dare move, although he knew that someone must. Long moments passed, and finally Phil managed the courage to step forward and join Elaina. She rewarded him with a smile, and he felt his face warm. He reached for some dates, almost overturned a small bowl, and blushed scarlet.

"Eat and rest," Karl ordered. "Tomorrow …"

Karl never finished his sentence. The companions ate in silence, and Phil cursed his clumsiness, the City of Nut, and … *honesty … the one enemy that they could defeat … but probably wouldn't.*

"Please, explore our city," Hatshep said to them as the same disciples of Nut brought them fresh fruits and morning bowls of clean water. "Go anywhere you wish."

"You must feel comfortable," Djehuti said. "You can't be expected to surrender your hearts in unknown surroundings."

*"Surrender our hearts …?"* Roselyn asked as if acid was burning her tongue.

After breakfast, the companions exited to find the city unchanged. In the dim starlight, their domicile looked like all the other buildings, tall, black, undecorated, and lined against the thick wall that ringed the city. More residents of the city stood about, and many nodded respectful greetings as the companions emerged. However, only a small number of inhabitants stood upon the ground; most hovered in midair, fully relaxed, floating motionless, walking, or stretched at an angle as if lounging on invisible pillows.

Sister Aspertine scowled and turned to go back inside, but Karl stopped her.

"We can't offend our hosts," Karl said.

*"Those naked sinners …!"* Sister Aspertine scowled.

"We've only a few days to learn to walk on Shu," Eloise interrupted her. "Remember the Duat that swallowed the Field of Wheat? If we can't learn quickly then …"

"I'll die and go to Hell before I become a sinner!" Sister Aspertine said.

"You won't reach Heaven or Hell from here," Eloise said. "It took a powerful seer to bring the Lady to Yggdrasil …"

"Blasphemy …!" Sister Aspertine said.

"Yet we're here …," Elaina interjected.

"If we die here, we'll be trapped here," Eloise said. "Spirits can't open a 'crack in the world'."

"Egyptians never die," Alarika said. "We live on Earth … or here. The City of the Gods awaits those who can reach it. The Duat devours all who fail."

"Naked people belong in their Duat!" Sister Aspertine scowled.

"They dress like their goddess," Eloise said. "You may hate their openness, but you can't deny their devotion."

"It's your choice," Karl said. "We all have to learn … Shu-walking. Those who can't float, the Duat will swallow."

With a tilt of his head, Karl motioned the companions onward. With wary glances, the rest of the companions followed. Phil disdained Karl's declaration

… but then he saw Sister Aspertine following them at a distance.

The City of Nut held no surprises. Each building looked almost exactly like theirs. When they explored the stairs of one building, its inhabitants welcomed them gladly, and they climbed to the top of a roof and looked out over the wall, down upon the familiar starlit land of endless gray dunes that stretched to the horizon.

"Why can't we see the City of Isis?" Nate asked. "We didn't travel that far."

"In Yggdrasil, locations and distances were uncertain, constantly changing," Karl said. "Maybe you can't map these lands, either."

The immense view offered no revelations, so they walked along the wall, and then descended through another building to the street. The residents of that house seemed equally delighted by their passage, and offered them food, but they politely declined and explored on.

Phil couldn't help but stare. The black women were beautiful; each was studded differently, their patterns exotic. Some wore their gems in random patterns, like the stars, and others in stunning arrangements. Their nudity seemed startling at first, but Phil quickly got used to it … and appreciated its beauty.

With bright smiles, the women willingly displayed themselves. Hands reached out to lightly graze Phil's arms as he passed. Winks flashed from many eyes, and eyebrows rose invitingly. Several women blew kisses at them, and Phil blushed, glad that he was wearing clothes.

Black men offered enticements to the women just as blatantly, and all the women reacted differently. Eloise nodded politely, acknowledging but declining their offers. Roselyn glared, and sometimes openly scowled. Alarika didn't smile at them, yet her eyes frequently widened … and lingered on several men as they walked past. Sister Aspertine ignored them entirely, and often bowed her head and shielded her eyes. Yet Elaina smiled and winked back at the men, and seemed coyly excited by their flirtatious touches.

Watching Elaina, Phil frowned and shook his head. She was noble, too beautiful and dignified to display her attractions so freely. These folk were like the barmaids of Demril, both the men and the women. He disliked their forwardness … and disapproved of Elaina's appreciation of their advances. Unfortunately, it wasn't his place to say anything.

Karl's reaction bothered him the most. Every few seconds, Karl obviously tore his eyes away from one naked woman … after a brief, hungry stare, to affix upon another. Every time that a new black beauty appeared, Karl's expression revealed his desires. Phil admired Karl in every way but this; *Karl was as bad as Nate, attracted to any woman.*

Nate seemed confused, willing to stare at every woman, but only momentarily, and then he'd look away. He never even blushed. He seemed to be torn; interested, but holding back.

Henry alone was obviously delighted, his smile as wide as it would stretch. He flirted with the ladies and welcomed their touches. His fingers softly trailed down many gem-studded arms, which freely extended toward him, and he kissed several hands. Phil envied him, and wished that he could act so friendly, but everyone would see … yet Henry was married; he had no more business staring at these overly-friendly women than Karl.

Phil swallowed hard. *He could never let himself be seen acting lewdly.*

Walking around the city, ignoring the folk walking on Shu only ten feet above them, the companions strolled out onto the mosaic of Nut. Touching it, the basalt stones beneath their shoes and boots felt cold, flat, and smooth, the beautiful gems firmly embedded in them. The gems shined from an inner light, a soft glow that shifted within them and made them twinkle like stars.

The gems were cold to the touch, most so small that one fingertip covered them entirely, while the biggest were too large to be covered by a single hand. Phil recognized some of the gemstones from seeing them on Eloise's crown: diamond, ruby, and topaz, but others were unknown to him, and a beautiful, translucent purple stone captured his attention, although he knew no name for it.

They walked across the elbow of the mosaic of Nut, and stopped at her jeweled ribs. There, they looked about. Around them, the City of Nut looked peaceful, its people floating in pairs or small groups.

"It's time that we got started," Karl said. "We should find Djehuti and Hatshep."

"Must we …?" Eloise asked.

"If we can't float … walk on Shu … when the Duat opens …," Alarika warned.

"We must learn to fly," Elaina said. "Our only path … is up."

"Master, may I speak?" Phil asked.

"Of course," Karl said.

"If you wish it, I'll stay … and fall into the Duat," Phil said in his most serious tone. "However, as a squire's duty is to protect his knight, I advise you … we must succeed."

Karl nodded.

"Where's Djehuti and Hatshep?" Karl asked.

"You believe in death," Hatshep said, sitting on a bench in their main room. "Death is the ultimate deception. To believe in death is to already be dead."

"Why is death to be feared?" Djehuti asked, seated on the edge of the pool of floating lotus. "Do you fear cessation … or the unknown? Both are illusions. Death only changes our existence. For Egyptians, mortal death slowly brings our spirits here. For those who turn away from the gods, their faithlessness limits their existence to the Duat. To fear death is to surrender to murder of your control over where you'll spend eternity."

"To truly live, you must embrace death," Hatshep said.

"That's a Valkyrie belief," Roselyn said. "Only warriors face death unafraid, for they may be chosen for Valhalla."

"Warriors kill … and break God's commandment," Sister Aspertine argued. "Only the followers of Christ enter Heaven."

"Once, the faith of Egypt embraced each of those beliefs," Djehuti said. "When Horus defeated Set, warriors led our faith. In our later days of peace, Ra dominated."

"Your faith changes?" Elaina asked.

"Our faith follows our gods," Djehuti said. "When they change, we do. Yet Osiris always rules, and he knows all the Lands of the Living and the Dead …"

"Isn't this the Land of the Dead …?" Karl asked.

"Your path hasn't visited the Palace of Nephthys," Djehuti said. "Having never experienced mortal death, you may be spared the ordeal of mummification…"

"Alarika mentioned 'mummification', but what is it?" Eloise asked.

"Mummification is the preparation of the body … that it may someday be rejoined with the Ba, the Ka, the Ib, the Ren, and the Sheut," Hatshep said. "As the body of Osiris was separated, the physical remains are blessed and wrapped in sacred, oil-soaked strips of linen, after the organs are removed and sanctified …"

"Heaven forbid!" Sister Aspertine exclaimed.

"The Palace of Nephthys lies underground, though not in the Duat," Hatshep continued. "If you travel Shu, then you'll ascend to the Celestial Path."

"Nephthys chooses the routes of all who come to her, but you entered through the wisdom of Hor-em-akhet," Djehuti smiled.

"We call it a 'crack in the world'," Karl said.

"That was my fourth passage through such a portal," Roselyn said. "The underground lake, the Mere of Mab, Bifrost, and Mistyhel; that's where I first entered your realm, but there I appeared trapped inside a great cavern … facing the Dragon of Winter."

Shock lightened the faces of Djehuti and Hatshep, and they stared at Roselyn.

*"You saw the Dragon of Winter …?"* Djehuti gasped.

Roselyn drew and displayed her blade.

"This is the sword of Hel, my Goddess of Death, which I drove to the hilt into the ice sheet covering that white mountain."

Djehuti and Hatshep exchanged another glance.

"Never has one so formidable visited us … nor anyone provided us news of such importance," Hatshep said.

"We must inform Nut," Djehuti said.

"Roselyn is also called Reginleif, a Queen of Valhalla, the Land of the Warriors of the Norse gods," Karl said, and Djehuti and Hatshep gaped in wonder. "We know many secrets valuable to your Egyptian gods … or goddesses …"

"We'd be grateful for all wisdom that you'd care to share," Hatshep said.

"But first, you must walk with Shu," Djehuti said. "Poor hosts we'd be to let those who bring us gifts tumble into darkness."

"Help us, and we'll tell you everything," Karl said.

"Why do you think we're telling you about death?" Djehuti asked. "Fear binds all five parts of the spirits to Geb. You must overcome those fears to arise."

"Valkyrie fear not death," Roselyn said.

"What do you fear?" Hatshep asked.

"Nothing," Roselyn said.

"How about stealing a husband from his rightful wife?" Eloise hissed.

"Not now," Karl snapped. "How about not finding the Seer … and never being allowed back into Valhalla?"

Roselyn glared at both of them.

"Hear the anger in your voices," Hatshep said. "While such feelings remain, none will arise."

"I fear our angers," Elaina said.

"And I," Phil added.

"You've endured much, and suffering exposes hearts to the fiends of Set," Djehuti said. "You must unburden yourselves …"

"I'll try first," Elaina said. "What must I do?"

"To start, look into each of your companions' eyes … and release your full truths," Djehuti said.

Elaina glanced warily at the others, and then bowed her head. "Maybe another should go first …"

"It won't get easier," Hatshep said. "Speak your heart."

"I've bared my heart before …," Elaina said.

"You forget where you stand, the nature of our cities," Djehuti said. "Our gods wish you to succeed."

Elaina hesitated, and Phil thought that she looked anxious, off-balance for the first time in her life.

Elaina turned to her daughter.

"Eloise …," Elaina spoke hesitantly, lowering her eyes. "I … didn't just come here for your sake. I … was never a devout follower of any faith. All seemed … imperfect. I came because I … wanted to see another realm with my own eyes, to prove to myself that other worlds existed."

"Look into her eyes," Djehuti said. "See the reflections of your truths inside her soul-mirrors."

Elaina swallowed hard, then looked straight into Eloise's eyes.

"Eloise, I love you so much, and I'm so proud of you, but … I was jealous of your journey to Yggdrasil," Elaina said.

"Mother …," Eloise began.

"Don't interrupt," Djehuti said. "Truths flow best when hearts drift free."

Eloise fell silent, and Elaina exhaled heavily.

"You … married a man … pledged to another," Elaina said, laboring for breath, forcing out each word. "I'm sorry, dear, but … you made Skafti's curse come true."

Eloise's jaw dropped, but suddenly Elaina turned to face Karl.

"Son-in-law, you married my daughter while loving another woman," Elaina snapped, her words gushing. "You're a good man, but not a leader; you're indecisive … which you should've gotten over before you married anyone!"

Karl looked shocked, but she gave him no chance to reply. Without waiting for another breath, Elaina's eyes flashed to Roselyn.

"You should've married Karl the day you became a Valkyrie!" Elaina sneered. "You're the strongest woman I've ever met, but … sending your one love into the bed of your best friend … that's the stupidest mistake I've ever seen a woman make!"

Roselyn opened her mouth to retort, but both Djehuti and Hatshep waved her silent, and she resigned to their will.

"Phil, you've impressed me the most," Elaina said, turning to him and meeting his eyes. "Your brother thinks faster than you, but you think deeper, and you're more … moral. In fact, you may be the most moral member of this company, including me."

She turned to Sister Aspertine.

"Child of God, only your youth excuses your unchristianity," Elaina snapped. "Repeatedly you've had the chance to act with humility and grace, and instead speak as if your choice of faiths gives you superiority over everyone. Look around you! Other faiths exist, and are just as real as yours! My only hope is that you'll realize, when you think back upon all this, that true superiority is shown by silent contemplation, understanding, and how much devotion one shows toward their beliefs … not by which faith they chose, but how they use their faith to help others … and not belittle them!"

Ignoring Sister Aspertine's stubborn glare, Elaina instantly turned to Nate, as if trying to get through her ordeal as quickly as possible.

"You … little frog … how could any woman desire you?" Elaina scorned Nate, who looked shocked. "You're neither as smart nor as attractive as you think you are, and cuckolding God is the dumbest thing I've ever seen a man do!"

Nate blushed pale scarlet, as if his face couldn't decide to be horrified or ashamed. Elaina whipped her face from him to Alarika.

"You would've left us for dead!" Elaina practically shouted the accusation. "If we didn't need you, then I'd have asked Karl to abandon you in the desert … before we reached the City of Thoth! You can't be trusted!"

Finally Elaina faced Henry.

"You …!" Elaina started, but then anger her dropped and she smiled. "You've been a loyal and good servant … and I hope that you'll always be my friend … even when you throw me overboard into the Mediteranian Sea."

Henry smiled at her.

Her breaths coming in gasps, Elaina inhaled deeply … and then exhaled heavily, as if all her deepest feelings were exuding from her. She looked exhausted, as if she'd faced a harsh challenge, and the relief that her challenge was finally over smoothed her pale face.

Slowly she lifted off the floor, rose a few inches into the air, and hovered there.

"Walk with Shu," Hatshep whispered.

Elaina gasped to see that she was floating … and descended back to the floor.

"Fear of Shu binds you to Geb," Djehuti said. "Let go … be not afraid to arise to Nut."

Elaina took another breath, then closed her eyes and again rose into the air, but only a few inches, and then she sank back down. Djehuti and Hatshep smiled.

"It's a first step," Djehuti said to Elaina. "You've far to go … but your journey to Nut has begun."

"Thank you," Elaina smiled.

"Who's next?" Hatshep asked.

No one volunteered.

## Chapter 5

## Trials of Nut

# PHIL

At Djehuti's suggestion, the companions stopped to eat lunch, and Hatshep departed to fetch food. Djehuti warned them not to speak to Elaina about her words toward them, but advised each that they should prepare for their turn. Phil tried not to blush, but reservations filled his mind. No squire could speak ill of his knight, nor of his knight's lady, and Roselyn would impale him for his thoughts about her. Yet, if he kept his secrets, would he fall into the Duat?

Their eyes screamed during their silent meal. Few would look at Elaina, who looked unhappy that she'd been the only one to speak. Even Henry seemed troubled, and he usually seemed the most relaxed, the most unconcerned, as if he'd follow Karl blindly no matter where he led. Phil would also follow Karl anywhere, but he had to admit … he was frequently restrained by overwhelming reservations.

An hour later, Phil was stuffed, but he reached for another banana, hoping to delay the inevitable. He wasn't the only one still eating, yet Djehuti and Hatshep returned, seeming aware of their purposeful delay.

"Let's begin," Djehuti said. "Who wants to be next?"

Only Elaina smiled; her devilish grin made Phil wish that he'd gone first.

"Alarika," Karl said softly.

Alarika looked startled, then sighed resignedly.

"I should've expected this," Alarika said to Karl. "I've no loyalty to any of you … and I've never had friends." Alarika glanced at all of them, her frown deep. "I've no need to lie; I don't like any of you, but I need to stay out of the Duat, so I'm helping … and that's it."

Suddenly she sat back, as if she'd finished her part.

"Have you opened your heart?" Hatshep asked Alarika. "Have you stared into the eyes of each of your companions … seen their reflections of your words … and let truth flow?"

Alarika scowled, and then she rose and stepped close to Karl, staring into his eyes.

"I've never seen a worse leader," Alarika snarled at Karl. "No one fears you. You don't command or inspire. My army of thieves would've carved you alive just to hear you scream. You can't even choose which woman you want; a desert leader would bed both. I can't guess why any woman would want you."

With a nasty last look, Alarika turned to Eloise.

"You pathetic weakling!" Alarika virtually shouted at Eloise. "You command desert storms … and then moon after this calf of a man!" She nodded her head at Karl. "With your power, I'd send my raiders to strike, hard and fast, and when my enemies marched against me, I'd raise the desert to crush their armies! All of Egypt would bow before me, and I'd be its greatest queen!"

Eloise started to argue, but Hatshep waved for her to say nothing. Eloise subsided, and Alarika turned to attack Roselyn.

"You … disgrace all warriors!" Alarika shouted. "Never have I seen a woman fight so fiercely … and have the heart of a mouse! No true queen would risk her crown for a lover … certainly not this weasel-leader!"

Roselyn glared back, but not a single hair twitched, only the hand resting on her hilt tightened its grip. Alarika turned to Elaina.

"Another witch … meek and obedient," Alarika scowled, looking disgusted. "Like mother like daughter. You divine secrets and weaknesses that you could exploit, if you had the courage … and arise to infinite wealth and a crown. Why seek power unless you plan to use it?"

Alarika turned to stare at Sister Aspertine.

"Bride of a deaf and blind god!" Alarika said, less angrily, but still forceful. "You pray day and night, on your knees, and not once has your god aided us! You demean others for believing their faiths, then sleep with a boy to violate yours! You're the basest peasant I've ever met, and if I could, I'd stomp you into the ground, which is all you deserve!"

Alarika spun around to glare at Phil, and he met her eyes.

"Snakes are also silent, but they'd bite you … even if you're trying to help," Alarika scowled. "There's honor in a loyal man, but only if he chooses his leader wisely. It's our choices by which we're judged, and I judge you small … and simple!"

Phil squared his jaw, ready to resist anything else that she said, but she abruptly turned away from him, as if he weren't worth wasting more words.

"You finally bed your desire … and then you whine about it!" Alarika scorned, glaring at Nate. "Men boast when they conquer … and revel in their victories! You mope like a whipped cur! Shame on any woman for bedding the likes of you!"

Alarika spun from Nate, as if in a hurry to finish. She faced Henry.

"You're nothing," she sneered. "You're not even worth insulting. You're a … blind follower … who seeks to be nothing better!"

Instantly Alarika dropped down onto a couch, her arms crossed, staring at the floor. Angry, the companions stared at her.

"Don't stop now," Hatshep said.

Alarika snapped her face to stare at him.

"I spoke to each …!" she insisted.

"You didn't," Djehuti said. "The person you need to speak to the most … is yourself."

Alarika stared. "How can I …?"

"Did you give anyone knowledge that they didn't already suspect?" Djehuti asked. "Why did you join them? Why did you come to these lands?"

"I … It was foretold!" Alarika said. "My father told me that strangers would come … and lead me to him!"

"You were a queen …," Djehuti said.

"It's not the same!" Alarika argued. "I didn't have power over my thieves … only their fear of my father … who was dead …!"

Djehuti glanced at Hatshep, who raised his eyebrows and shook his head.

"I had no choice!" Alarika insisted. "I had to open the sacred portal …!"

"Why?" Djehuti asked.

"It was my father's dream!" Alarika argued.

"Your father lives in the Duat," Hatshep said. "Why were you following his dream? What's your dream?"

"I don't have dreams," Alarika said coldly. "Dreams are for fools …!"

"Fools like your father …?" Djehuti asked.

*"You don't know what he did to me!"* Alarika sneered, her face twisted with rage. "No home, begging for food, taunted by other beggars, and fleeing every city when news of his murders spread …!"

"Then why reward him?" Hatshep asked. "Why fulfill his dream, if it wasn't your own?"

*"To prove that I'm better than him …!"* Alarika screamed, and she jumped to her feet. *"So I can …!"*

Alarika radiated hate, her teeth clenched, chest heaving, and muscles knotted as her fists clenched. Her hand shook as if aching for her khopesh; Phil wondered what he should do if she attacked Djehuti and Hatshep.

"Very good," Djehuti smiled. "Who's next?"

The companions stood stunned and speechless.

Alarika glanced at each, eager to vent more anger, but no one challenged her stare. Finally she snarled … like a desert wildcat … and then sat back down, bristling.

After a long wait, Karl broke the silence.

"Sister Aspertine."

Sister Aspertine's eyes flew open, but she took a deep breath and stood.

"I can't participate in a pagan ritual," Sister Aspertine said. "If it means that I must fall into the Duat, so be it."

"This isn't a ritual," Karl said. "No one's asking you to do anything but speak the truth."

"Only God speaks pure truth," Sister Aspertine said.

"Fine … be like God … as much as you can," Karl said.

Another heavy breath later, Sister Aspertine turned to face Karl, and looked up to meet his eyes.

"You're a sinner and a blasphemer," Sister Aspertine said. "I've prayed for you, but you live … sworn to evil. You led us here, away from God …"

"I thought that God was everywhere …," Roselyn sneered.

"Let her speak!" Karl snapped at Roselyn before Djehuti or Hatshep could object, and then he turned back to Sister Aspertine, staring into her eyes.

Sister Aspertine glanced angrily at Roselyn, but then she ignored her.

"The goal of every Christian leader is to lead others to God," Sister Aspertine said to Karl. "You abandoned your true wife, disgraced yourself … and condemned all of us to this pagan Hell."

Sister Aspertine slowly turned to Roselyn.

"You were highborn, a Christian, but you've been perverted by pagans," Sister Aspertine said. "You've lost every grace a woman should have: humility, innocence, silence, timidity, demureness … I've prayed for every companion, but for you I had the least hope. You're more demon than woman."

Sister Aspertine turned to Eloise.

"Baroness, your transgression is the worst," Sister Aspertine said. "Afflicted by one set of false, pagan gods, you refused both them and Christ … and embraced a witch, became her servant, and indulged in unholy practices. You can still come back …," she paused and stared into Eloise's eyes. "… but you won't. Your willful nature bars you from Heaven."

She faced Elaina.

"You condemned yourself the instant you accepted the word of any Viking prophecy … and abandoned your child," Sister Aspertine said. "Only God can curse mortals, and the worst curse of all is to be denied His grace." Sister Aspertine shook her head. "You … dance like an angel. Find your way back to the fold, and you'll be welcomed … but you must choose: dance on clouds … or in lakes of fire."

Sister Aspertine paused, and then she stepped toward Alarika, who was still sitting.

"You I feel sorry for," Sister Aspertine said to Alarika. "You were born a pagan, the daughter of a murderer … a murderer of children. You know nothing of the salvation you could've had. I'd hope to convert you, but this horrid land has entrenched your heathen beliefs. Even if they hadn't, you're a savage, murderous desert rat …"

Alarika grabbed her khopesh's hilt, but every companion's reaction started toward her, and she desisted.

"You poor, lost lamb," Sister Aspertine continued. "You've shown your heart … and only darkness fills it."

Alarika glared, but Sister Aspertine shifted from her to Henry.

"Every time that I've asked others to join me in prayer, you have," Sister Aspertine said. "Yet, every time Karl asked you to support his pagan quest, you've chosen Karl over God. Your duty to your baron should be nothing beside your duty to God. Repent, and beg for forgiveness … while you can."

Henry listened carefully, and then he bowed slightly, seemingly accepting her judgement. Sister Aspertine nodded back to him, then turned to Phil.

"Like Henry, you pray, but then you follow Karl," Sister Aspertine said. "All squires want to be knights, and I encourage that, but knights are the warriors of Christ. Your first duty isn't to your liege; it's to God."

Phil bowed to Sister Aspertine; she didn't seem finished with him, but she bowed back, and slowly turned to Nate. Their eyes met for the first time since the Field of Wheat. For long moments, she only stared.

"The Field of Dreams gave you … opportunity, but in your heart … you were already a rapist … of a Wife of God," Sister Aspertine accused.

Nate lowered his head, but kept his eyes looking into hers.

"My duty is to forgive all, but … what you did … to me … I may never accomplish my duty. You've ruined me; when I enter Hell, I'll be walking the path you laid. I see no forgiveness … for either of us."

To their surprise, Sister Aspertine turned to Djehuti and Hatshep.

"I don't know what you two are," Sister Aspertine said to both of them. "Are you mortals trapped here, demons created by your pagan gods, or lost souls who've never had access to the Truth? Clothe yourselves, if you have modesty! I'll stay here, if you ask it, and teach you of Christ, before whom your gods failed. I'll become a missionary in your pagan land … if you'll listen and repent."

Djehuti and Hatshep both looked surprised.

"You honor us," Djehuti said. "You offer us your wisdom, and we'd gladly accept, if we could. But you can't stay; either you succeed in your quest for our gods, or you spend eternity in the Duat. However, if ever we can sit in peace, we'd be glad to learn of your faith."

"Learning isn't enough," Sister Aspertine said. "You have to accept …!"

"We thank you greatly for your generous offer," Hatshep interrupted her. "Yet, like Alarika, you accuse, but your heart remains hidden. You stand in our world, and have braved many challenges; does your belief still deny our existence?"

Sister Aspertine stiffened, and took another deep breath.

"I can't deny that you … exist," Sister Aspertine said, an unusual softness to her voice. "I … I haven't the imagination to dream all this. I fear that … Yggdrasil … and the Elysian Fields … must also exist. I doubt if God made all these worlds just to test my faith, but I also know that I'll never turn from Him. Stand or fall, I am His.

"You … you ask me to open my heart … in my heart, I'm greatly saddened to know all that I've learned here. My mind overflows with blasphemies."

"What about your body …?" Djehuti asked. "You know how it feels to be a woman …?"

Sister Aspertine swallowed hard, and momentarily glanced at Nate.

"I must forget," Sister Aspertine said, and tiny tears leaked from her eyes. "I must … refuse …"

"Refuse pleasure …?" Djehuti asked.

"Refuse sin," Sister Aspertine said, and she wiped her tears away. "Hell, the Duat … what does it matter? To be without God is the greatest doom of all."

Djehuti and Hatshep exchanged a glance, and then both nodded to Sister Aspertine, who walked over to a bench, sat upon it, and bowed her head.

"Henry," Karl announced.

Henry nodded, then stepped forward.

"I've a confession to make," Henry said to Karl, and even Sister Aspertine looked up. "It happened in the Field of Wheat. I had my turn, out in the stalks, where you couldn't see." Everyone exchanged glances. "Thorkel, Dennel, and Samuel were my best friends. We watched them die, and when the power of dreams came to me, I summoned them back. They're good men; they didn't deserve death in foreign lands. When they appeared, I explained what had happened, and it took some doing to convince them that they'd died. Finally, they thanked me for bringing them back, and they would've stayed to serve you more. But I refused them. They'd sacrificed everything that any loyal servant could … even to you, Sir Karl; they'd done their service. I wished them all to Rishard's bedside … in Italy … and as far as I know, that's where they are."

Karl reached out and put a hand on Henry's shoulder, then pulled him into a hug. When they pushed apart, Henry stared into Karl's eyes.

"Baron Sir Karl, like every man of Demril, I've watched you since you were crowned and wedded Eloise. You practically killed yourself to protect us … your peasants. You offered to die at the hands of Sir Aledard to save us. Unlike my friends, I didn't die for you; that's why I stayed. I couldn't offer less than my friends did."

They hugged again, and Karl started to speak, but Hatshep loudly tutted, and both men only nodded to each other.

Henry turned to Alarika.

"I'm not nothing," Henry said flatly, almost a challenge. "I'm not one of the great, just a man of the sea, but at least my soul isn't empty. I've seen people like you, greedy, ambitious, and callous … living only to impress yourselves … since no one else is impressed. You're just as wrong about the rest of us. I followed Karl against Sir Lasky, when he saved hundreds of lives by taking all of the risk upon himself. Eloise is a perfect baroness, and she's as devoted to her barony as to her children. Roselyn's the greatest mortal warrior, and soon she'll be an immortal queen again. I know my place. I know I'll probably never see England again … but at least I'll die with honor; that you know nothing about."

Alarika glared, but said nothing. Henry turned to Eloise, and his expression softened.

"Baroness Eloise Elizabeth Domwin du Harmonn," Henry said with a smile. "I remember the day that you were born; all of Demril celebrated for a week. Every night, your father bought drinks for every man in The Bent Hook. He loved you so much! I'd never fault any of you, but if I did, I'd say that you, Karl, and Roselyn should've settled matters before any of you wed. Alas, nobility and peasants are alike made fools by love. I'm commanded to speak my heart, but I also speak with more years than I'd like, many spent watching empty horizons. Seas reflect souls, and so sailors see ourselves clearly. As loyal as I am to Karl, I hope you know, I serve you with equal love."

Eloise threw herself against Henry and wrapped her arms tightly around him. Long they held each other, and when they separated, Henry bowed deeply to her. Then he turned to Roselyn.

"I … stand humbled in your presence," Henry said. "I've always known what Norsemen said the Valkyrie are, but until I saw you and your sisters defeat that army, I didn't understand. I don't know if you're a goddess, a half-god, or something else; all I know is that I honor you, and what I've seen, since we became shipmates, has greatly impressed me … not because of your strength, but because of your restraint … despite superior abilities. I must give you the same advice I gave to Eloise. However, you … have my allegiance."

Roselyn stood imperiously before Henry, and never did she so completely resemble a queen. Roselyn raised a fist and rapped her armored chest above her breasts, then, with a rare smile, she tapped her fist against Henry's chest. Finally she shook both of his hands.

Henry smiled back, and then he turned to Elaina … and bowed deeply.

"You were my baroness long before Eloise, and I've … admired you … all my life," Henry said. "You … you're a treasure … and no angel could dance more beautifully!"

Elaina smiled brightly and curtsied to Henry with slow grace. Henry bowed again, and then he turned to Phil.

"Boy, if I hadn't taken to the sea, I'd have hoped to be just like you," Henry said, and he clapped a friendly hand on his shoulder. "You and I; we're more alike than any youth can understand. If I fall, I won't fear that Karl and Eloise will lack a loyal follower."

They warmly shook hands, and then Henry turned to Nate.

"Boy, you've done some fast growing," Henry said. "Abundance of wit makes being old easier, but it's been the downfall of countless boys. Don't despair; failures can be atoned, and better times await in England, if you can get back. Stay loyal to your knight … and let time heal."

Nate bowed to Henry … as if to a father.

Henry turned to face Sister Aspertine.

"Honored Sister, you're my inspiration," Henry said. "You share the foolishness of youth, but you've learned more than any church elder … in a too brief time. When age grants wisdom, you'll understand better. But … Nate was as much of a victim of the Field of Wheat as you. Your hearts committed no sin, whatever your bodies did."

Sister Aspertine's expression didn't react, but when he was finished, she dropped her head and made the sign of the cross.

Henry turned back to face Djehuti and Hatshep, and with his first step, he rose into the air. Quickly he flailed his arms and fumbled for balance, and these motions lowered him back to the ground.

"Some live closer to Shu than others," Hatshep said, smiling.

"Who shall speak next?" Djehuti asked.

"Phil," Karl said.

Phil gritted his teeth as a wave of panic washed over him. He'd known that his turn was coming, but knowledge never entirely quells fear. Still, he was honor-bound; his squirely oath left no room for refusal. He tried to look at Karl, and found himself jerking away.

"It's all right," Karl said. "Just … be honest."

Phil was good at being honest … he just didn't like talking. He coughed, stammered, cleared his throat, and faced his fears. He looked at his tiny reflection in Karl's eyes.

"My knight and master, I … I think you pay … too much attention to women," Phil said, and to his surprise, several applauded this comment. "You have a good wife, and … rightly so, not until death will you be freed. It's unchristian … for a married man … to think of other women … in a wifely manner."

Phil choked again, and Karl reached out and grasped his arm, met his eyes, and nodded approvingly. Phil felt sure that he was disobeying his squirely vows by criticizing his knight, but Karl said nothing, and he shook Phil's arm, as if urging him to continue.

"I can say …. no more against my knight," Phil said. "In my heart of hearts, I think I'm … lucky to have you for my liege."

Karl nodded and released him with a friendly pat on his back. Phil turned to Eloise, and she was already smiling at him. Phil reached out to take her hand, and then dropped to one knee before her.

"Baroness Eloise, I …!"

"Look into her eyes," Djehuti said.

He lifted his face to hers. His voice trembled, and suddenly Eloise clasped his hand in both of hers. She also nodded. "Baroness, I … love you. Not like a husband, or a brother … but … like I love Lady Seren … and my mother. You're the best of women, and you've made my knight … the luckiest man alive. I … do think you treasure … treasures … too much, and I mourn that you and Roselyn aren't close anymore. I feel … I believe … you should have trusted in God … and not turned to the Lady … *Oh, Baroness … forgive me!*"

Phil bowed his head to hide the moisture he felt in his eyes, and Eloise hugged and held him tightly. Long seconds passed before Phil regained himself, ashamed for having lost control.

Finally he whispered a mumbled apology. Eloise only smiled. She had tears in her eyes, and he felt them; as he stood, Eloise rose up onto her toes and kissed both of his cheeks.

Phil turned away and saw Roselyn frowning at him.

"Countess Roselyn, Queen Reginleif, Valkyrie," Phil bowed deeply before her. "Odin was a fool to banish you. I beg your pardon … I know you could kill me … but you stepped aside, and while Karl lives, I feel … all should respect vows made before God. I'm grateful for the training you gave me … you're the wisest swordmaster. When Karl goes to Valhalla, I hope that you'll … make him … as happy as he was in life."

Like eyes from a stone statue, Roselyn stared at Phil, and he felt certain that he'd soon die … murdered for speaking his heart. Yet … suddenly Roselyn burst out laughing, and she absently waved him away, as one might dismiss a jester.

Blushing, Phil turned his gaze upon his brother.

"Nate," Phil said, and an ill-humor filled his voice. "You think you're so smart … all you've ever done is invent paths to ruin. You're weak, small, and you estimate yourself equal to a king … or your knight, for which you should be beaten. You slept with a nun! You've disgraced yourself, our knight, and our family! When I tell father …!" Phil stammered, lost for words. "Only Karl keeps me from giving you the thrashing you deserve …!"

Phil turned away, not knowing or caring how Nate reacted. He found Henry facing him. Phil stared at him long, seeking to find true words.

"I like you," Phil finally said, and then he shrugged his shoulders, having nothing else to say. Henry smiled, and Phil turned to Sister Aspertine.

"Sister, I fear for you most," Phil said. "I've grown up surrounded by many faiths, but all this is so new, so different … I can't imagine how you're coping. I pray for you, Sister, and I … I'm sorry … about … my brother. However, you shouldn't condemn others for their beliefs. You're the light that we need here, but … you must trust your … illumination … to shine upon others, not dim theirs."

Meeting his eyes, Sister Aspertine nodded, and her frown flexed, as if she were trying to smile. Close up, Phil couldn't help admire how pretty she was, young and smooth-skinned, but …

He glanced around, certain he'd missed someone, when he spied Alarika. He didn't really want to talk to her, but he knew that the Duat would swallow him if he didn't.

"Alarika, you're … untrustworthy, unreliable … and … unworthy of respect," Phil said. "You're only helping because of your half-snake father. Given the chance, will you betray us … again?"

Phil clenched his teeth, trying to find something else to say. Yet he couldn't, so he turned away, and walked back to stand beside Nate.

A silence fell, and Phil wondered if all of them were angry at him.

"Phil," Karl said, "… *Elaina …?*"

Phil startled; he'd forgotten her. *Why did he always make himself look stupid when he spoke in front of others?* He glanced at her, then lowered his eyes. He wanted to speak to her least of all.

"Baroness Elaina …," Phil mumbled.

"Meet her eyes," Djehuti said.

Phil hesitated, then shuffled forward. Reluctantly he looked up and saw her eyes, as bright as Eloise's, but filled with wisdom. Phil's throat caught, his mouth drier than the endless deserts.

"B-b-beautiful …!" Phil forced the word out of his mouth, and then he turned away, unable to say anymore. He retreated to his brother's side … and stared at the floor. Eternities of reprimands and self-recriminations flew past, and his cheeks felt as red as apples.

"Nate," Karl said with a light chuckle to his voice, and Phil felt relieved; his burden was over. It was his brother's turn.

Unexpectedly, his brother stepped right in front of him first, and Phil glanced to see his brother's eyes staring right at him.

"I hate you," Nate said to Phil. "You've been picking on me all our lives. You're not as dumb as I thought … of course, you never could tell the dangerous end of a sword. You act like you're better, morally superior, as if that justifies mistreating …! Acting saintly doesn't make you a saint, and silence can't hide stupidity. Centuries of kneeling can't cure over-bloated self-impressions … or teach you why!"

Phil's teeth gritted, and his muscles tightened, but Nate turned away, giving Phil no time to react. Instantly, Nate dropped to one knee before Karl, looking up at his face.

"My knight, my rightful liege," Nate said. "I've done everything I can to earn your respect. I've failed many times … but I keep trying! When I do succeed, then you'll see what I've been trying to do. You're my lord; you decide, I support. I know my place, but I think … I believe that you want me to rise as high as I can … and eventually I will."

Nate said all this very quickly, unlike Phil's slow speech, and he stared clearly into Karl's eyes as if he didn't care if he offended his knight. Phil thought him disrespectful, but Karl nodded approvingly. Then Nate rose, bowed slightly, and turned to Eloise.

"My baroness, with all due respects, like your husband, my eyes can't fail to notice beauty … such as yours," Nate said, and he dropped to one knee and reached out to take her hand.

Phil stood aghast, but Eloise reacted warmly, with a smile and sparkling eyes.

"It's not my place to judge you, Karl, or Roselyn. I respect each of you … to mind your affairs without my opinions. I just hope that you understand that Karl's loudest command to my brother and I, even though he's never spoken these words, is to protect you first and foremost, at any price, even above his life, and certainly above ours. Since we met you, his every action has issued this command to me as clearly as if it were scribed on his forehead. I'm honored to obey; I hope you know that."

Nate bowed deeply, and Eloise reached out her other hand to squeeze his, and Nate drew both of her hands to his lips and kissed them. Phil was outraged, and almost shouted at Nate, but startled to find that all of his other companions seemed to approve Nate's indecency.

Slowly Nate stood and faced Roselyn. Boldly he saluted her with a clenched fist across his chest and a slight bow.

"Queen Reginleif, my sword is yours," Nate said. "I stand beside you always, and great honor would it be to lay down my life for you. You're the supreme warrior, the mightiest woman, and no greater trust could I have than to know you're defending my back. Your slightest whim is my command. Test me, if you wish. Now, or as an einherjar, I'm honored to serve."

Roselyn looked imperiously down upon Nate … and nodded her thanks.

"You're also … an eternal and unparalleled beauty," Nate added with a grin.

Phil thought that Roselyn would draw her sword and cut Nate in half. Instead, Roselyn half-smiled, failed to decapitate him, and then Nate turned to face Elaina.

"My stuttering brother spoke most-truly to you, oh, Beauty of the North, mother of Eloise, wisest of us all," Nate said. "You don't need visions; your dances are the most magical feats I've ever witnessed. My service is yours for the asking."

Phil seethed … *how dare he?!?* With difficulty, he clenched his hilt and started forward … to beat his brother to a pulp for insulting Elaina, who was so beautiful and queenly that Phil could barely speak to her. Yet, his first forward step was noticed by Karl, who quietly waved him back. Phil glared at his sibling … *Nate would pay for this insolence!*

Nate turned to Alarika. She met his glare forcefully, but Nate only smiled at her.

"You and I are a lot alike," Nate said, and Alarika looked surprised. "That's not a compliment. We're quick, decisive, and acquisitive, but you undervalue us. Trusting the wrong person proves fatal, but look around you; you're the only one here who'd turn against a friend. Your biggest problem, besides your overpowering beauty, is that you don't realize how lucky you are. You claim that Thoth weighs the hearts of all; you should quail before his judgement. There's no evil I could do to you to equal what Thoth will."

Alarika stared, looking confused, but after a long moment, she stood, reached out to Nate's outstretched hand … and shook it.

Nate walked up to Henry and clapped his hands on both of his arms.

"Nothing …?" Nate laughed. "The top of a mountain owes everything to its base, and you, Henry, and your fellows, are the foundation of this company. Our places aren't far apart, but just because we're born somewhere doesn't mean that we need die there. You're just a sailor now, but if we make it back, you'll be the sailor who traversed the lands of the Egyptian gods! And, God willing, you'll have me there, to verify your stories … and share the endless drinks that everyone will buy us …!"

Henry burst out laughing, and Nate clapped him again, and then he turned to face Sister Aspertine.

She looked up at him, half angry, half fearful. For a moment, Nate seemed frozen, and then he lowered himself to both knees, folded his hands, and deeply bowed before her.

"Sister … Aspertine," Nate said, and for once his words were slow, and even more slowly he looked up into her eyes. "Nothing excuses … what has passed between us … but I wouldn't change it if I could." Several gasps sounded, yet Phil, astounded by his brother's audacity, couldn't glance aside to identify their sources. "I … have quick eyes, and a mind that never stops, even when I try to sleep. I'm mesmerized by beauty. I'm drowning in this company, for beauty immeasurable exists everywhere. But I … no longer see any woman … as anything … but a pale reflection of you. I know what we did was … can never happen again. I'll never again enjoy … that which only I know. But … I love you, Sister Aspertine. I'll always love you. I just … you should know … I'll never stop dreaming of … of our brief moment. I'm sorry … but I can't regret … learning what love is … from you."

Nate stammered, for the first time unable to speak. No one broke the silence, and Phil stood stunned. *Was this another twist of his brother's deviousness? Was he play-acting, hoping to bed Sister Aspertine again …?*

Sister Aspertine looked shocked, frozen, as if she'd never move again. Slowly Nate bowed again, then rose to stand beside his brother. He didn't float, as Henry had, but looked doomedly glum.

Karl broke the silence.

"Roselyn …"

Roselyn startled, as if so lost in Nate's admission that she'd forgotten what was coming. Never slow, Roselyn boldly stepped forward and faced Karl. Yet, then she slowly glanced back at Nate and Sister Aspertine.

"I want that," Roselyn said to Karl, nodding to Nate and Sister Aspertine. "We once loved that way. Thrown together, outlawed, a runaway farmboy … and my father's broken pawn. I died for you. You swore that you'd do the same … and I'm still waiting. I don't know if we could ever … like we loved before. My return to Valhalla without you would be … an eternal disgrace. I don't want to … kill you …"

Roselyn slowly turned and looked at all her companions.

"You've no idea how lonely immortality is," she said to all of them. "I'm surrounded by sisters, Eric, Svenson, and millions of einherjar. I fight. I feast. I kill. I die. None of it matters. It's the endless moments between that immortals despise … waiting while your drink is poured … marching back to Elvidner after the battle … or coming back to life at sunset, watching your mortal wounds close … and remembering doing exactly the same thing yesterday, and knowing you'll be doing it every day until time crumbles …"

Tears moistened Roselyn's harden cheeks, leaking from eyes that had long lost softness.

"Hel spoke truly: there's no doom worse than loneliness."

For the first time that Phil had ever heard, Roselyn's voice cracked with emotion.

"Glororil and Silvana showed me that. Love, sharing your heart with another, is the only thing that makes eternity bearable."

Roselyn reached out her hand, and ran her fingers through Karl's short beard, grazing his cheeks. Expressions that Phil couldn't recognize shined from Karl and Roselyn; their eyes seemed locked, yet Roselyn said no more. She bowed her head, withdrew her hand, and turned away.

Roselyn stepped up to Eloise.

"You and I were closer than ever I was to my mortal sisters," Roselyn said to Eloise. "Now our rivalry is … unresolvable. You've born three children to the man I've sworn to love. No mortal disgraces a Valkyrie; if Karl abandons me, then I must kill him, and we'll never speak again. However, after Ragnarrok, if any survive, legends say that new worlds will rise from the ashes, and those of honor will be reborn. Then you and I … maybe we'll be friends again."

Suddenly Eloise and Roselyn were hugging, raining tears, too quickly to tell who moved first. Long they clutched at each other, and when they separated, Eloise wiped her drenched cheeks. Roselyn, of course, never acknowledged tears.

Roselyn stepped to the side to face Elaina.

"If you were a fighter, I'd make you a Valkyrie," Roselyn said to Elaina, who looked astounded. "You're noble, strong, and wise … I'd gladly take you to Alfhiem so that you could dance with others equal to your skill … and join you … in the Mere of Mab. My … division with your daughter … has hidden my admiration. You have my respect."

Elaina tried to smile, but surprise slowed her reaction, and so she performed a perfect curtsey to Roselyn, who saluted her with a clenched fist across her chest. Then Roselyn turned to Phil and stared into his eyes.

"Your fighting has improved, but you need practice," Roselyn said. "You're worthy of the einherjar. You could defend my back; in Valhalla, that's a great compliment. But, unlike your brother, your true strength lies in your heart. Find that strength … and you'll be unbeatable."

Roselyn turned to Nate.

"I'm greatly jealous," Roselyn said. "You've exposed your heart, yet your strength is your mind. You could be a devious fighter … a brilliant strategist. Youthful foolishness dies. Keep training … especially practice recognizing truth and lies in the eyes of opponents; there you'll find every advantage you need."

"Thank you," Nate said, and no one admonished him for speaking.

Roselyn faced Henry, who smiled at her.

"You're unworthy of Valhalla," Roselyn said, and his smile faltered. "You cling to your 'place' instead of putting others in theirs. Yet Njord, God of the Sea, hosts many sailors in his hall, and doubtless you'd be welcomed among them. You have courage, and proudly would I lead you to Njord's hall, to share drinks and pass the idle hours. I speak no ill; we've chosen different paths, and I wish you well on yours."

Roselyn and Henry bowed slightly to each other, gestures of allowance, if not acceptance. Roselyn turned from him, ignored Sister Aspertine, and stepped toward Alarika.

"Stand!" Roselyn commanded her.

After a delay close to being a challenge, Alarika rose to her feet and faced Roselyn, glaring defiance, but Roselyn only nodded.

"These words none reclining should hear," Roselyn said. "I don't like or trust you, but you're a worthy fighter, a strong woman, and a deep, ambitious thinker. When I told my sisters that you'd make a good Valkyrie, I spoke the truth. Yet, to be so, you'd have to surrender your faith and your will to Odin; this I know you'll never do. Therefore I give you this advice: any heart as cruel as a desert will betray itself. The fires of the Valkyrie burn in my heart. Yet … iron wills exist … to guard softness. When one is only iron, no fire warms you … not even your hottest deserts."

No nods or gestures followed; both seemed to know that Roselyn was finished. Alarika sat back down, but Roselyn remained, and slowly turned, as if reluctantly, to face Sister Aspertine. Her steps toward her were shuffles, as if the Valkyrie feared to face the nun.

"Wife of God, I … envy you," Roselyn said, and Phil almost stumbled, disbelieving his ears. "I was raised and raped a Christian, and no faith spared my suffering. I never sought to be a Valkyrie; my only choice was to be a queen in Valhalla … or rot in Niflhiem. You're traveling a realm like Yggdrasil … and still pray to God in Heaven; your faith has never failed. I know what awaits you, should you return; Catholics persecute all witnesses to powers beyond Christ. Remember, when your church excommunicates you, the solace that your God of Love has given you: I've been a fool; only a fool trades a loyal lover for an empty bed."

To everyone's amazement, Roselyn bowed to Sister Aspertine, who silently recoiled, her surprised mouth gaping.

"Don't mistake my envy for admiration," Roselyn added. "You're a most offensive companion."

Phil smiled; *that he'd expected.* Then, something happened that left them all speechless.

Roselyn took a deep breath, and shook herself, as if freeing herself from clinging hands, and then she stepped high … and rose into the air. Roselyn stepped again, as if ascending an invisible stair, and climbed into the air with confident ease.

"Shu be praised!" Djehuti and Hatshep exclaimed.

"Valkyrie always triumph," Roselyn said, stopping and floating high, her head bumping the ceiling. "How do I get down?"

"Shu is down here as much as up there," Hatshep said.

Roselyn closed her eyes, her expression void, and slowly she sank back down. As she reached the floor, Djehuti smiled.

"Few are brave enough to expose their heart so fully," Djehuti said.

"Valkyries thrive on challenge," Roselyn said. "This test … I'd have avoided, if I could've, but I do feel … lighter."

Hatshep smiled, and then he looked at Karl. "Are you next?"

"No," Karl said. "Eloise …"

Eloise sighed heavily, and then stepped forward. She glanced at Karl, hesitated, and then walked to stand before Roselyn.

"I've summoned Death, whom not even a Valkyrie could survive," Eloise said, glaring up into Roselyn's eyes. Roselyn looked startled, then matched her deadly glare. "You have millions of einherjar to choose from. Karl's my husband and the father of my children … you told him to marry me! If I have to suffer eternity in the Duat for my love, so be it."

Immortal enmity flowed in the silence following these words. Eloise's eyes burned upon Roselyn, who glared back. Then Eloise's expression softened.

"I miss … my sister," Eloise said, her voice cracking.

Slowly Eloise wrenched her eyes away and faced Karl.

"Little Eric, little Roselyn, and little Athelwynne await their father's return," Eloise said. "Without a baron, the king will sell me off to be raped, probably to Sir Aledard, and your children will end up as I did, fatherless, hated by a stepfather who wants only sons of his own … before he markets them like prized cows. Farmer Tiller, his friends, and all our folk, Bristlen and Demril, will lose everything that we've worked for since Eric killed Baron Theodolf. All in du Harmonn will suffer; that's our doom if you don't return."

Eloise glowered at Karl with fury equal to her rivalry with Roselyn. Karl met her glare passively, although he swallowed hard and his brows perceptively lowered. Eloise maintained her stare, and finally Karl looked away. Her stare ignored, Eloise turned upon Alarika.

"You're contemptable," Eloise said to Alarika. "Without us, you'd have been killed by your own army of thieves, and you never would've awakened the sphinx. Your heart's as barren as your Deshret. You're only hope is to change your faith, and abandon your gods … before Thoth tests your heart. As long as you serve Thoth, the Duat will be your doom."

Eloise didn't bother with a war of stares, but moved to face Nate. She stopped and stared at him, then passed him by to face his brother. Phil met her bulging eyes, alight with worry; her usually pretty face radiated rage. He feared what she might say, but then she dropped her eyes and moved on.

Eloise faced Henry, paused a few moments, and then moved on to Sister Aspertine. Phil expected Eloise to explode; she and Sister Aspertine had been feuding since Italy. Eloise looked ready to burst, and opened her mouth, but no sounds evoked, as if all words failed her.

Without speaking, Eloise ran into her mother's arms, and embraced her desperately, as if on the verge of sobs. Elaina wrapped her arms tightly around her daughter. Long moments passed, and then Elaina lifted her head.

"May I speak?" Elaina asked Djehuti and Hatshep.

"You may," Djehuti said.

Elaina clenched her daughter even tighter.

"Eloise, my love," Elaina said. "I know why you can't speak. Your heart's so heavy with bitterness that no room remains. You have to be stronger; I can't lose you to the Duat."

Eloise jerked back, as if her mother had stabbed her. Eyes blazing, she glanced around, took in all the companions … and suddenly stormed out of their building, stomping toward the mosaic of Nut.

Phil watched Eloise depart with deep regret. He understood her anger … *nothing infuriates like betrayal.*

"Boys, go after her," Karl said. "Give her all the space she needs, but … keep her in sight."

Phil nodded and turned to follow.

"Master, you haven't spoken yet," Nate said.

Phil hesitated … *why hadn't he remembered that Karl had yet to speak?* His younger brother was smart … *smarter than was good for him.*

Karl glanced at Djehuti and Hatshep, but they just looked at him curiously.

"I'll go later," Karl said. "First priority: the safety of every companion."

Nate nodded, and headed toward the door that Eloise had exited. With a frown, Phil followed his brother out of their dwelling.

Eloise marched straight across the jewel-studded mosaic. She only glanced back once, saw Nate and Phil following her, and hastened her footsteps. The boys followed her all the way across the city, where she barged into an occupied building, and at once ascended their stairs. The inhabitants seemed surprised, not angry, and both Phil and Nate apologized and begged pardon for their intrusion, and proceeded upstairs after Eloise. Phil was glad that every doorway was only thinly curtained so that Eloise couldn't lock herself inside a room.

Ascending to the very top, they found Eloise sitting on the edge of the high wall, her face turned to look out across the empty, starlit gray sands. Nate and Phil said nothing, simply stood and tried not to stare at her.

After an hour, a resident of the house below them suddenly floated up, outside of the building, to their height. He politely asked if he could perform any service, and if they wanted food or drink. Phil would've declined, but Nate thanked him and accepted his offer. When the man floated back down, Nate suggested in whispers that one of them should go back and tell Karl where they were. Phil insisted on staying with Eloise, so Nate vanished down the stairs, and Phil, left alone, simply watched his charge.

A tray of cheeses, also holding three clay cups and a bottle, were carried up to them, and Phil took them and thanked the floating man. He set the tray down on the roof, and Phil poured a cup full of a tart-smelling irep and carried it to Eloise.

"Mistress …?" he asked, holding out the cup.

Eloise turned her face from the shadowy desert, eyes full of tears. She saw the cup, took it absently, and drank deeply.

"May I sit with you, mistress?" Phil asked.

Eloise nodded, and Phil sat down upon the edge of the wall beside her.

"You know … I'm as loyal to you as I am to Karl," Phil said.

Eloise weakly nodded, a soft sigh escaping her lips.

"Even if it was my place to speak, I wouldn't know what to say," Phil said.

Eloise nodded again, and turned back to stare at the distant horizon. Phil followed her example, and shared the bleakness of the view and conundrum.

Eloise slept in an upper room of that house. Nate insisted on staying awake to guard first, but when Phil finally awoke, he found Nate asleep, and hurriedly checked to see that Eloise hadn't departed. Then Phil awoke Nate with a sharp kick.

When Eloise awoke, she approached a window and looked out upon the city of Nut. Phil stepped beside her and looked about the dark city; Phil longed to see the sun again … not the cruel desert sun of Egypt, but the warm, friendly sun of England.

"You don't know what to say," Eloise finally whispered to Phil. "I don't know what to do."

Eloise went back and sat on the edge of her bed. Phil struggled; he wasn't as good a talker as Nate, but he put more thought into what he said. He thought a long time, and then he approached and bowed to Eloise.

"Mistress, I don't mean to …," Phil began.

"Your advice is appreciated," Eloise said.

"If … any solution is possible, here might not be the best place to enact it," Phil said.

"He wants her …," Eloise said. "He's always wanted her …"

"No man could choose to lose his right leg over his left," Phil said. "I can't speak against Karl … and I've no wish to sound like Sister Aspertine, but I consider a vow made before God paramount to a vow made before Odin."

"I consider both inferior to a vow made to the Lady," Eloise said. "Yet I can't argue religious superiority without being a hypocrite. I chose to seek Druid powers … and lost my husband."

"Karl chose you when Roselyn sacrificed that child to open the portal …," Phil said.

"Karl hates making choices, and hates sticking with them even more," Eloise said.

"Karl seldom chooses what's best for him," Phil said pointedly. "Karl always chooses what's best for everyone … *everyone who's there at that time.*"

"How does that help …?" Eloise asked.

"Here, it works against you," Phil said. "Back home, what's best for everyone … includes what's best for your children … and for the people of du Harmonn."

Eloise's eyes opened wide, and a thin smile stretched her lips.

## Chapter 6

## The Doom of Nut

# PHIL

Eloise gave Nate a carefully-worded message and sent him back to deliver it. The residents of the building invited them to join them for a hot meal, and Eloise gratefully accepted. A steaming, roasted pheasant was provided, surrounded by nuts, along with sweet breads topped with coriander seeds, boiled cabbages, figs, and barley soup with diced radishes.

Sitting among them, they fell into casual conversation, asking if the companions liked the City of Nut, and what challenges they overcame to get there. Eloise praised the city, and asked Phil to relate their stories, but he deferred; Nate was a far better storyteller than he. Finally one woman of exceptional beauty stood up, a line of silvery gems swirling around her, and Eloise could keep her question unspoken no longer.

"How can you be naked all the time?" Eloise asked.

The night-people smiled.

"You arrived as a group … and we're commanded to help you," the woman said. "In olden days, when these cities were often used, Egyptians arrived alone … and quickly accepted our offers. Many preferred endless pleasures … rather than learn to walk with Shu …"

"They fell into the Duat," Phil said.

"Our cities are tests," the woman said. "Nut commanded us to help you, but we can only teach … you must open your hearts."

"Is there no way around that?" Phil asked. "If one can't walk with Shu, can the rest of us carry …?"

"Those who can't walk with Shu will drag down any that cling to them," the woman said. "If I may be so bold, the secret to honesty is to speak your heart without concern for consequences."

"Speaking is only half of your challenge," a man beside her said. "The greater part is listening; hearing and accepting … without taking offense. Mortals easily condemn the decisions of others … but seldom judge their own."

"No one can dwell in peace with our gods if they can't live in harmony with themselves," the woman said. "While your hearts remain troubled, you won't find Shu."

Phil and Nate followed Eloise into their dwelling. In the light of a small oil lamp, Djehuti, Hatshep, and the companions sat waiting. Eloise stopped and curtseyed to all of them, then marched up to Karl.

"You married a jealous woman," Eloise said to Karl. "She loves you so much it drives her crazy, and she can't imagine life without you."

Without hesitation Eloise turned to Roselyn.

"You're the reason I'm jealous," Eloise said. "I'm … jealous of you; you look exactly the same as when we first met. Odin chose well … you've always had a fighting spirit. If I could choose anyone to be my friend, it'd be you. I can't blame Karl for loving you; I do. But that doesn't change anything."

Roselyn looked speechless, yet Eloise turned away and faced Elaina.

"Mother, I'll never understand how you could abandon me," Eloise said. "I'm happy we're together again. I'm proud of you, and impressed with your magic. I couldn't ask for a better mother … except one that was there to mother."

Elaina looked as shocked as Roselyn, yet too late she opened her arms to hug Eloise; Eloise turned to face Alarika.

"I'd love to trust you, but I can't," Eloise said. "You're loyalty is grudging. You're openly resentful. I hope you do make it to the throne of Osiris; you'll regret his judgement. When you're in the Duat, remember … we could've helped you."

As if in a rush to finish, Eloise turned to face Henry.

"You're a good man," Eloise said. "The greatest joy a baroness can have is to care for subjects like you."

Henry started to bow, but Eloise turned to Sister Aspertine. She gazed at her long.

"You … gnat," Eloise hissed. "Everywhere we go, you buzz around, annoying everyone, the least holy … and needing to be swatted. I'm not going to repeat the advice of the others … you wouldn't take it from me, but if you don't heed them, then you're the stupidest woman I've ever met."

Sister Aspertine rose suddenly, as if she wanted to punch Eloise, but with a lingering glare, Eloise turned to face Nate.

"Your worst enemy is your mouth, but the worst I can say about you is that you're … like my husband," Eloise said. "You'll grow to be a man worthy of respect … someday … when you're worthy of accepting one woman's love."

Eloise stopped, and slowly turned to Phil, as if suddenly in no hurry at all. Eloise didn't just look Phil in his eyes, she grasped both of his hands, held them tightly, and stared beaming into his face.

"No god … or goddess … could find fault in your heart," Eloise said. "You're Karl's squire, but from this day on, you're Chief Advisor to the Baroness du Harmonn." Eloise pulled herself up high enough to kiss Phil's cheek. "I love you boys … and Edith … like my own children."

Eloise turned around, smiling brightly, and lifted her arms … as if expecting to rise. However, she didn't.

"Lightening the heart takes time," Hatshep said to her.

Only Karl looked unhappy. He didn't glance at anyone's eyes, but seemed to stare at the floor, as if confessing.

"I know that … I need to speak my heart … or I'll never walk with Shu," Karl said, and he scowled. "I'd prefer another life-and-death struggle. Yggdrasil taught me not to trust gods or believe in truths. Without believers, perfection fails, and all believers are imperfect. My heart is … a stranger …" Karl glanced up at Roselyn and Eloise. "I can't speak what I don't know."

Karl took a deep breath, then stepped up to face Roselyn.

"I love you," Karl said, staring straight into her face. "You're … perfect, the adventure … that no man wants to end. We could spend eternity together … but I'd forever miss Eloise … and my children. I want Valhalla … but I'll never know happiness without my family."

To Phil's surprise, and Eloise's shocked expression, Karl gripped Roselyn by her arms, drew her forward, and kissed her long and hard. When they separated, Karl nodded, and then turned to Eloise.

"I love you, wife … mother of our children," Karl said, staring straight into her face. "No greater joy could exist than to spend eternity with you … but I'd always miss Roselyn … and Eric. I want you … but I'd forever regret not being with them."

Karl kissed Eloise in the same manner, and then he stepped back and bowed his head.

"You each deserve better than I have to give … a better man than I am," Karl said aloud, and he turned away from both of their shocked expressions.

Karl sighed deeply, and then he faced Alarika.

"Alarika, your father's warning saved us," Karl said. "Otherwise we'd have fallen into the Duat. Your prayers let us enter and exit these cities. But you need us more than we need you; only the Seer could return you to Egypt before you face the test of Thoth. You need time … to change your ways. We offered friendship, but you must accept it … or you'll spend eternity hissing like your father."

Karl ignored her stare and turned to face Henry.

"Friend, you're faithfulness isn't just a godsend … it's an inspiration," Karl said. "You don't just serve me; we serve everyone. My trust is yours … forever."

Karl embraced Henry, and then he turned to Sister Aspertine.

"Sister, you've been a thorn in this company since you joined it, yet I doubt if we'd have survived Count Fernando's palace without you," Karl said. "Rafe will be proud to hear of your faithfulness. At first, I was worried that you might sabotage us, but … well, you wouldn't believe the religious tensions of travelling with Eric, Rafe, and the Seer; compared to them, you're a blessing."

Karl bowed slightly to her, and then he grabbed each of his squires by an arm and shook them roughly.

"Boys, you both have strengths … and weaknesses," Karl said, looking from one to the other. "Each of your strengths could make up for the weaknesses of the other, if not for your ridiculous rivalry. If you can't work together, you two may drop us into the Duat … or earn a year cleaning out Rafe's stable." Karl smiled widely. "Whatever happens, I'm proud of you … both."

Lastly, Karl looked at Elaina. Slowly he shook his head.

"I'd have done what you did," Karl said to her. "I could never bear to hurt my children, any of them, no matter what it cost me … even if I had to live never seeing them again."

Elaina nodded to Karl without smiling.

Karl stepped back, and looked down at his feet, as if expecting to rise.

"I do feel lighter," Karl said to Djehuti and Hatshep. "Why don't I…?"

"Opening your heart is only a first step," Djehuti said. "To arise is good, but to remain aloft is required."

"Now you must learn to live with your revelations," Hatshep said.

"We'll come back tomorrow," Djehuti said. "Remember; knowledge doesn't climb Shu … honest emotions do … emotions that don't fade."

Djehuti and Hatshep departed, promising to have fresh foods delivered soon. The companions stared at each other in silence, not knowing what to say; *they'd said it all.*

Elaina tried to arise into the air, and floated a few inches off the ground, but then she floated back down, despite flapping her arms. Roselyn fared no better, and most of them couldn't rise at all. When food arrived, they ate, and still none spoke. Phil wondered if their revelations would nullify their animosities … or spark open war.

After a long, sleepless night, they heard footsteps enter their dwelling, and emerged from their small, separate rooms to find new trays of food being delivered, and Djehuti and Hatshep awaited them.

"You've much to learn today, if you would journey with Shu before the Duat opens," Hatshep said as the companions began to eat.

"I can't fly anymore," Elaina complained.

"Your unburdening released you … for the moment," Hatshep said. "To walk with Shu, those feelings must be constant."

"Yesterday you opened your hearts to each other," Djehuti said. "Today, you must see into your own hearts."

"Each part of you is sacred," Hatshep said. "Names are most-sacred, for they give us power over the named."

"The whole of your body is called the Ha," Djehuti began. "The Ha is created by Khnum upon a potter's wheel, and inserted into the bellies of mothers. The Ha is your only physical essence, all of you that can die, so it is your Ha that must walk with Shu."

"Your Ha contains your Akh, the power of your mind," Hatshep said. "The Akh is your conscious mind and memory, composed of your Ka and your Ba. Upon mortal death, the Akh is separated into the Ka and the

Ba, which must be reunited in the House of Nephthys, where the Akh is reborn."

"I have instructed them on the Ka, Ba, Khaibit, Khu, and Sekhem," Alarika said.

"Excellent," Hatshep said. "Then they will easily understand the Ib."

"The Ib is caring," Djehuti said. "At conception, one drop of blood from the mother's heart bestows the Ib within her child. The Ib consists of two halves: Awt-ib, your happiness, and Xak-ib, from which comes all pains of loss and separation."

"The Ib is the vessel of all emotions and desires," Hatshep said. "Without the Ib, you can't walk with Shu, and the Test of Thoth can't be won. The Ib is most-closely examined by Anubis during the Weighing of the Heart. If the Ib weighs more than the feather of Maat, then it is hurled to the crocodiles and consumed by the monster Ammit."

"Your Ren is your birth-name," Djehuti said. "As long as your name remains within the minds of the living, your Ren strengthens and flourishes."

"Cartouches, the magical rope, surround every written Ren to protect it," Hatshep said. "The cartouche is the elongated form of the Shen Ring, which grants divine protection, so only godly names don't need it. Cartouches of evil men are often desecrated to drive their Ren from the minds of the living. To walk with Shu, focus on your Ren, for it contains all of you."

"You've opened your hearts to each other," Djehuti said. "Your instinct is to respond, to defend yourselves, but you'd only speak the one voice that you know. Before you reply, you must know each response within you. Listen again … repeat in your minds every word spoken to you … both the good and the bad … and hear which … of all the parts within you … refute those words … and which parts agree with them."

"Solitude is best," Hatshep said. "Dwell deeply upon all that your companions have said, and poll each part of your soul … separately."

"Go now, without speaking, and recall each word spoken to you, but take not too long," Djehuti said. "The Duat awaits."

In unison, Djehuti and Hatshep rose and gestured the companions toward the door. Each of the companions rose and, with worried expressions, they walked outside. Djehuti and Hatshep followed, and with a sweep of their arms, they gestured to the whole of their city. Without words, Phil and the others understood, and each walked away in a different direction.

Phil wandered back toward the gate, to the only solid doors that he'd seen in the city. The people of Nut smiled at him; he felt uncomfortable around the naked men, with their physiques matching his. He admired their arrays of colored jewel studs, but the women were breathtaking and mesmerizing, and several brazenly walked up to him and ran their fingers through his hair or across his mail, smiling sweetly.

"We're yours, if we may in any way please you," several said openly, not even lowering their voices to whispers.

One woman, an enchanting beauty, walked up without a word, squeezed her firm body against Phil's hard mail, and kissed him long and softly. Phil couldn't resist, and when she took his hand, he followed. She led him into a building, with many men and women turning their heads and smiling at them. Phil blushed, but he didn't pull away.

Two hours she pleased him, and Phil experienced pleasures that no slut of Demril could equal. Afterwards, she bathed him in a fountain, and he put his clothes and armor back on, watching her smile at him, and knowing that she'd never spoken a word.

"How … how can you … give yourself like that?" Phil asked. "You don't know me … you can't love me."

"The worshippers of Nut have no wants … no needs," she said. "We give and take freely, and are filled with happiness. What purpose would you have … without wants or needs?"

Words failed Phil. The City of Nut was a veritable Garden of Eden before Adam and Eve cast themselves out. *What purpose did Adam and Eve have before they lost paradise?*

Phil kissed her, nodded his thanks, and left, determined that the others must never know what he'd done. His problem was … *he was the problem.* He couldn't give freely … without sacrificing his wants and needs. He was plagued by human pride, shame, doubt, envy, fear, desire, and … lust … all parts of himself that Djehuti and Hatshep had named or described.

*Would true freedom make him more than human … or less …?*

He wandered until he found a lonely spot, and there he sat, trying to recall everything said to him … about him. No insights came … *maybe he should swallow his pride and ask Nate to explain it.*

Hours later, when Phil was starting to feel hungry, a tall man floated up to him.

"Your companions are gathering at their dwelling and wish your company," the man said.

Phil gritted his teeth, forced a frown, and started back … praying that the others wouldn't see the tiny light of joy his unnamed lover had ignited inside him … or his disgust that he wasn't as quick-thinking as Nate.

"You've heard the Ibs of each other," Hatshep said, once they'd gathered and eaten. "Now comes the greatest challenge of all, the strongest chain of Geb."

"You've echoed your companions' word to each part of your Ha," Djehuti said. "Doubtless, your tongues are full of spiteful retorts, rehearsed in your Kas, aching to be spewed. The challenge facing you now is … to release those words … unsaid."

*"What …?"* Nate exclaimed.

"Never voice your replies," Hatshep said. "Forgive … fully … or walk not with Shu."

All of the companions gaped, speechless.

"Being one with Shu isn't about others," Djehuti said. "Shu is a journey that each walks alone. Justifications don't help your community. Sacrifice your pride, and free yourself from the chains binding your Ha to the opinions of others."

"When we're struck, an illusion of our Akh creates our desire to strike back," Hatshep said. "Fulfilling that desire is pointless; no one grows from retaliation. Free yourself … and walk with Shu."

Phil stared, unknowing what to do.

"I don't just I forgive you, I agree with you … all of you," Elaina said to every companion, and before he turned to look at her, he could hear the surprise, joy, and the genuine smile in her voice. She seemed delighted … as if eternally relaxed. Then, suddenly, Elaina rose into the air, her shoes dangling below her.

"That's it?" Karl asked. "Forgiveness …?"

"Our worst ties are our bitterest truths," Djehuti said.

"Unwanted thoughts chain us to Geb," Hatshep said.

"I can … fly!" Elaina said, and with her dancer's grace, she floated along the ceiling in the direction of her gesture.

Suddenly, Henry rose into the air. Then, more slowly, Karl floated up. Roselyn never twitched a muscle, but she rose, frowning, into the air.

Hesitantly, jerking, and then making motions as if swimming, Nate kicked and swam into Shu.

Phil grimaced. He felt ashamed of his recent weakness … succumbing to the beautiful woman … which had led to the most exquisite two hours of his life. He was ashamed of countless things in his life, mistakes, stupid ideas, and failed attempts. Yet he'd done everything with the best of intentions. His primary weakness was … being human. He frowned; no human could be blamed for not always maintaining perfect control, yet somehow that didn't make it any easier.

*Was it supposed to be easy? Or … were his wants and needs making it hard …? All humans had needs … and made mistakes … and regretted both.*

*Why was he blaming himself for being human …?*

A lightness seized him, and Phil floated upwards. He waved his arms for balance, feeling awkward as he rose. No answer had saved him; *he'd needed to ask the right question!*

*"I'm sorry, Father!"* Alarika cried aloud, as if he could hear. *"I've failed you … not by what I've done, but by what I've become … what I allowed you to make me!"*

Slowly Alarika arose, still in her sitting position, as if an invisible chair had carried her into the air.

Eloise and Sister Aspertine sat, heads bowed, unmoving. Neither arose. Eloise lifted her arms expectantly, but no lightness came, while Sister Aspertine simply sat and said nothing.

Phil experimented, and found that he could walk in any direction, even climb like he was on an invisible ladder. Walking with Shu was easy, and just turning his head rotated him, and he could will himself forward … and slowly float in that direction. Yet walking seemed more natural, and although he felt no ground beneath his boots, he propelled himself faster with the motions of walking.

The other companions also experimented; Nate quickly mastered flipping heels-over-head, while Alarika remained sitting at ease. Elaina flew swiftly and smoothly in any direction that she chose, and she spiraled as if dancing in the air. Henry seemed content to float about, watching the others, and Roselyn rose until she bumped her head on the ceiling, but her posture remained stiff.

"Perhaps you should meet Shu outside," Djehuti suggested to Roselyn.

"Eloise …?" Karl floated down, gesturing encouragingly to Eloise. She closed her eyes and concentrated, and flapped her arms, anything to defy Geb, but she couldn't rise. Sister Aspertine didn't even try.

"You can't help them," Hatshep said to Karl. "No one can heal another's soul."

"Sister Aspertine, at least try," Karl said, but she only looked away. Finally he turned to their mentors.

"How long …?" Karl asked.

"A day … or maybe two," Hatshep said. "Sooner, if they give up trying."

At Karl's request, Phil, Roselyn, Alarika, and Henry floated out the door … Nate floated up the stairs and exited from an upper window. Karl and Elaina remained, and Phil hoped that they'd help Eloise and Sister Aspertine, if they could.

Outside, the citizens of Nut applauded their success. They could rise to any height, and soared over the mosaic of Nut, which looked exactly like Earth's night sky when he rose high enough. Phil asked if their powers would fail if he flew over the wall, out over the desert sands, and they assured him that he could walk with Shu anywhere on the Celestial Path. Phil tested their claim, and flew out over the wall, and then floated back.

Phil saw Roselyn holding Hel's naked blade, swinging her sword in practice, as if testing her fighting skills in midair. Nate was flying like a bird, his arms wide, flying up, then diving low. Henry and Alarika were hovering inches above the ground, talking to a group of people. Phil wafted down to join them, and then he understood; the novelty quickly wore off, and he felt more comfortable near the ground.

A low rumble sounded, distant, and the ground that they weren't touching trembled. Phil, Alarika, and Henry exchanged glances, but Nut's folk seemed undisturbed.

"The Duat," one said. "It will open soon."

"How soon?" Phil asked.

"None can say," the speaker replied. "An hour … or a week?"

They returned to the dwelling to find Eloise and Sister Aspertine enduring another speech from Djehuti and Hatshep; neither could rise higher than their toes.

"Afterlife is similar to mortal existence," Hatshep said. "Think of the two journeys of Ra. In the time of night, the Sun-chariot descends, and Ra enters the Duat. His dark road follows the River of Fire, and he faces constant challenges from demons. Down there, Ra keeps an eye open, always looking for the mummified reflection of Osiris, the Dead God, who knows all the secrets of Anubis. Eventually Ra shines his Light of Life upon Osiris, and Osiris empowers Ra with the calmness of his faith. Girded with the faith of Osiris, Ra faces Aapep, the ultimate death, the final consummation of the many parts of the spirit. All of the deceased, those doomed to the Duat, rise against him, in bodies twisted by their absence of hope. They rise from their tombs to aid the great demon they serve, becoming whatever Aapep needs. However, none can deny the power of faith. Armed with the faith of Osiris, Ra drives back Aapep, and emerges from the Duat … to bring dawn to the world."

"All mortals carry the light of Osiris, which you call hope, and shadows of the Duat, which you call despair," Djehuti said.

"With the dawn, your Ba reunites with your Ka, as it does in the afterlife," Hatshep said. "Ra greets your arisal each morning with these words: '*Welcome, welcome, into this, your House of the Living!*'"

"Nephthys always loved Osiris, but when he married Isis, she married Set," Hatshep said to Eloise and Sister Aspertine. "Yet she gave Set no sons, and his godly anger raged … and thus he killed Osiris. Then, when Osiris came to the House of Death, Nephthys bore Osiris a son, Anubis, and under the jealousy of Isis, the evils of Set plagued Egypt. For his cruelties, Horus drove Set from Egypt forever; you must now do so … drive the evils from the collection of your Ha … or you'll never walk with Shu."

Food was served, and they again dined well, but despite suggestions and encouragements, Eloise and Sister Aspertine remained on the floor.

As before, when the companions began nodding, each left to their separate rooms. Phil was yawning before he pulled his blanket over him, but he awoke suddenly; a familiar face appeared at his window … *the woman he'd lain with!*

"*You …!*" Phil whispered, and without meaning to, he began floating off his bed.

She smiled at him, then reached her arm in through the window, and Phil grasped her reaching hand and let her pull him outside. Kisses pressed against his lips before his feet left his room, and her arms tightened around him.

"*We must be quiet!*" Phil whispered to her, and she giggled.

He didn't understand, but then she nodded, and Phil looked out across the City of Nut. Elaina and Alarika, each in the company of several men, were already halfway across the mosaic of Nut, floating in different directions, and Henry was emerging from his window into the arms of half a dozen beautiful women.

His beauty pulled him off to the side, away from the others, and they skimmed over rooftops, then floated down a stairs into an empty bedroom.

"May I please you again?" she asked. "Or … perhaps you'd prefer another … or many …?"

"No," Phil said. "I … I seek only one … but I would prefer … to join with her forever …"

"I'll serve you, even beyond these walls," she said. "If you wish it, I'll be yours forever, but my mortal body is here, and I can't return to the lands of the living. Nut wouldn't allow it, for my wisdom of Nephthys is too great. Besides, Nut wishes you to arise upon the Celestial Path, and her will is mine. I'd rather you didn't enter the Duat, which you will, if you choose to stay. If you reach the throne of Osiris, and still desire to return to me, only then could we share eternity. But you'd have to swear all of your soul to Nut, and be bound to Her service, as I am. I'd gladly kiss you forever, if you wished it, but I don't think that your endless happiness lies here."

"At least tell me your name," Phil said.

"The secret of a name is its power over the named," she said. "Nut alone rules me. Call me what I am: *your dream ... your every desire.*"

Their lips met, and Phil's hands found her soft, gem-studded flesh, and amid her soft moans, Phil's Akh faded to paradise.

The next morning, Phil awoke to infinitely-warm kisses, and he opened his eyes to find himself back in his room.

"Your friends will awaken soon, so I brought you back," she whispered into his ear. "I must go ... or your friends will find us together."

"I ... thank you," Phil stammered, wishing that he could spout flowery words like Nate. "I wish ... I could do something for you ..."

"Think you that I took no pleasure while pleasing you?" she grinned sweetly. "You've given me all you could, and I'll enjoy you every night ... forever ... in our shared dreams."

She kissed him again, and then she floated toward the window with grace as gentle as Elaina's dancing. Yet, before she reached the window, both heard soft giggles come from outside. Phil rose to look, but she stopped him with a gesture.

"You're too noble to deny others the privacy that you desire," she said. "Farewell, my love. I'll always desire you as much as you desire me."

She blew Phil a last kiss, then floated out the window. He watched every inch of her perfection as she departed from his vision, until her black toes slipped out of sight, and then he sighed heavily. He wanted to rush to the window, to watch her even as she floated into the distance, but her last words stayed him; he knew that he'd always dream of her, but also that … someday … he'd find a woman to love … one woman … and become all that she dreamed …

Others were awakening as he emerged, fully dressed in the clothes and armor which his lovely lover must've had help carrying back. He tried not to smile, but he couldn't help but notice that Henry, Elaina, and Alarika all joined them for breakfast with irrepressible grins.

*If he'd arrived in the City of Nut like any other Egyptian, would he have learned to walk with Shu … or lain with her in ecstasy until the Duat opened beneath him?*

Phil tried to push the question from his mind … and felt a sudden heaviness weigh him down.

*He didn't know … but given a chance to escape the Duat … he'd have lain in her arms forever.*

The truth lifted his heaviness … which evaporated like fears in her arms.

Djehuti and Hatshep arrived with more food, and while they ate, the ground rumbled and shook again.

"It won't be long," Hatshep said. "The Duat is coming."

All eyes fell on Eloise and Sister Aspertine. Eloise scowled.

"I tried," Sister Aspertine confessed, despair heightening her voice. "Tell … Master Sir Rafe … that I fulfilled my charge as long as I could … and ask him to pray for me."

"Ask him yourself," Karl said. "You can't wait any longer. Whatever's holding you down, let it go. We can't stay."

"You can't stay for my sake," Sister Aspertine said.

"I don't want to stay!" Eloise said, halfway between pleading and growling.

"We've given you all we can," Djehuti said. "We've no power to make your souls speak."

"Open all the hearts of your community," Hatshep said. "Speak every truth, and maybe your mouths will voice feelings you're unaware of …"

Eloise tried to speak, but no words emerged, and tears of frustration filled her eyes.

Sister Aspertine knelt down, folded her hands, and bowed her head to pray.

"Is there nothing else we can do?" Elaina asked Djehuti and Hatshep.

Both shrugged gem-studded shoulders.

"You've heard your companions," Hatshep said. "You've heard all that we said."

"Not all secrets are revealed by conversation," Djehuti said. "Our deepest secrets we reveal only to ourselves … alone."

"Gather your belongings," Hatshep said. "These buildings will collapse when the Duat opens."

Fifteen minutes later, the companions emerged into the dim light of the stars and the radiant gems of the mosaic, carrying their packs and botas. Those who could tested their skills, and with differing abilities; each stepped into Shu. Eloise and Sister Aspertine remained aground, frowning at their impotence.

"Say nothing to them," Karl said to the floaters. "Give them space. But …" he turned back to the earthbound, "before the Duat opens, we'll be back."

Phil said nothing, although he held grave reservations. Eloise could've used a night like he'd enjoyed, but she was a married woman … although Karl loved Roselyn, and Roselyn … Phil pushed it from his mind; now wasn't the time to weigh himself with burdens that he couldn't carry.

Several hours passed, and all of the people of Nut emerged from their buildings in anticipation of the coming Duat. Far more people lived here than Phil had realized, and he stared at the beauty of them, studded with shining gems, twinkling in the starlight. Among them, he spied the woman of his dreams, but she merely smiled and winked at him, before she disappeared into the crowd.

Hours later, the ground shook again, harder, and the rumble roared.

"We're done waiting," Karl said, and all the companions converged on Eloise and Sister Aspertine.

*"I can't speak truths I don't know!"* Eloise shouted as Karl approached her, raising her voice above the churning roar. *"I'm a trained Druid priestess; I should be able to do this!"*

Sister Aspertine stayed on her knees, praying, but she shifted herself to keep from falling over as the ground shook. The inhabitants of the city rose higher, but the companions descended, hovering only a foot above the mosaic.

"We'll carry them," Karl announced.

"Nut's folk said that we couldn't," Elaina said. "Come, daughter, you can tell me anything…!"

*"Mother ….!"* Eloise began, but again, words failed her.

"Sister Aspertine, please arise," Nate said. "Try … you must …!"

She looked up at him, masked with anguish, then bowed her head and resumed praying.

"Maybe it's both of you," Alarika said. "You two can't arise … maybe it's the arguments between you that's holding you both."

Phil looked at her, surprised; he hadn't expected Alarika to help anyone, yet he doubted if their religious animosity was chaining them to Geb. Eloise and Sister Aspertine exchanged a sideways glance, and seemed to come to the same conclusion.

The ground shook harder, and the buildings all around them began to crumble. A few walls toppled, and cracks appeared in the mosaic of Nut.

"Grab them!" Karl shouted, and he reached down and seized Eloise's arms. Elaina flew forward and grabbed her other arm.

*"No!"* Eloise shouted, trying to shake free of them. *"I won't let you sacrifice …!"*

*"No one's giving you a choice!"* Roselyn shouted, and she floated down behind Eloise and reached under her arms from behind, locking her hands over Eloise's chest.

No one knew what to say, but Nate wrapped his arms around Sister Aspertine in exactly the same manner, and Phil and Alarika descended to help him. Sister Aspertine flinched at each touch, but seemed too terrified to fight back. Henry floated low between them, ready to help whoever needed it the most.

The mosaic of Nut cracked open, and sulfurous fumes hissed out. The roar grew louder. The floating companions clung to their friends, but Eloise struggled to push Karl and her mother away, and finally grabbed Roselyn's hands and tried to pull them apart. Yet her puny strength failed before the grip of a Valkyrie. Eloise twisted; Roselyn's face was pressed against the side of her head, the closest that they'd been in eight years. Eloise turned to look at her face … and met the indomitable determination of a warrior.

*"You …!"* Eloise shouted, and then she turned to look at Karl. *"Why her? Why always her? I've loved you more than any woman, given you everything, my body, my heart, children … why can't you love me most? Only me …?"*

With a power of mind that her companions couldn't match, Eloise blasted them back, away from her, with the force of a desert whirlwind. Karl, Elaina, and Roselyn flew backwards into the air, unable to resist the power of the Lady. Henry jumped to grab her, but her magics shoved him away. With a will equaling the Seer, Eloise seized them all with her Druidic powers, lifted, and hurled them higher, away from the vents of the Duat.

Clenching her tiny fists, Eloise stood … and suddenly screamed, long and shrill, her frustrations screeching even above the roar of the opening Duat. She kept screaming until her lungs emptied.

The huge mosaic cracked apart. The stones and gems beneath their feet shook loose and fell, opening a deep hole to reveal a glaring red light.

*"No!"* Karl shouted, and he flew downwards just as the stones beneath Eloise collapsed.

Incredibly, Eloise didn't fall. Her scream, her bellow of rage and frustration, seemed to have burst the chain holding her. The Duat gaped open, bathing her in infernal light, yet Eloise didn't fall. She stood … upon the fumes arising to Shu … and hovered.

*"You did it!"* Karl shouted, and as he reached down to her, she rose toward him.

Sister Aspertine screamed.

The mosaic crumbled, and its gemmed stones fell down into the gaping maw. Nate, Phil, and Alarika struggled to hold Sister Aspertine aloft, but even together, they couldn't lift her. Her feet lowered as, beneath her, the gemmed stones fell and splashed loudly into the molten red river snaking through the wide, black Underground; *the Tunnel of Everlasting Torment.* A deafening roar arose as the City of Nut slowly cracked apart and crashed down into the widening pit, overwhelmed by screams from every mouth.

Karl released Eloise, who floated in midair, and flew to help. He grabbed Alarika by her arms, whose hard Egyptian fingers clutched deeply into Sister Aspertine's habit, and he pulled. Roselyn came right behind him, and she seized Phil by the back of his leather swordbelt, and pulled with all her might. Elaina came next, having pulled her daughter upwards to safety, she descended to join the others, pulling on Henry's arm. Lastly, Eloise swam back downwards, slowly, still awkward and uncertain about how to fly. She lowered herself down to join the pull as Sister Aspertine started to drag everyone down, below the level of the ground that had fallen away, into the hot vapors rising from the red river. Eloise managed to grab on, one hand grasping her mother's ankle, and her other hand on Roselyn's boot; both hovered inverted, straining to keep Sister Aspertine from falling into the doom below.

Beneath them, pungent fumes arose, stinking and steaming, as if the Duat were breathing, a living tunnel, blasting them with acrid breaths. All of the companions resisted, but they couldn't help but glance down. The red river was molten lava, as they'd seen beneath the giant scales in the City of Thoth, only thicker, with flaming, blackened boulders floating in it.

On both sides of the river, the walls and floors of the wide Duat looked cavernous, darkened by smoke and soot, and there awaited hundreds of half-human, half-creature demons, staring up at them, snarling, hissing, squawking, and roaring … *hungrily.* Ravenous eyes met theirs; *the companions could never survive there.* If they weren't torn apart and devoured, then they'd turn into monsters, like Alarika's father, unable to resist.

Inhuman eyes glared up at them, and the companions pulled even harder. Yet they couldn't lift Sister Aspertine. Slowly, she pulled them down … into the Duat.

The screams of the people of Nut reached their ears as the roars of the opening of the Duat slowly ceased.

*"Release her!"* they cried.

*"Save yourselves!"*

*"Each must fly on their own!"*

The Duat seemed equally determined. Gases spewed directly upon them, as if blown by evil gusts. As they descended, a cloud of noxious vapors enveloped Eloise and Elaina; both choked and coughed, gasping unbreathable fumes, and were finally forced to let go. Mother and daughter turned and swam upwards, coughing and hacking, thrashing against the poisonous air, and Henry followed them, gasping and wheezing.

Then a blast of fire burst from the molten river, enveloped in a cloud of burning black smoke, struck Karl and Alarika. While he choked, she screamed. Forced to let go, the smoke buffeted her long hair and scorched her lungs as, with her hands, she beat out the tiny flames burning her garments. Suddenly another gust, hurled by the fury of the Duat, blew Alarika upwards. Karl, his fingers locked around Alarika's arm, tried to push past her, but the stinking gusts of the Duat struck and threw them both upwards, away from Sister Aspertine.

Phil struggled, but an acidic mist struck him … and his flesh burned. Yet he squeezed his eyes shut as fire seemed to engulf him and agony shot through every inch of his exposed flesh; his face, his neck, and his hands burned and stung, and yet he tried to hold on. Sister Aspertine would be lost if he failed, but his torments flamed. Blisters rose all over his cooked flesh, and Phil's burning fingers slipped, scrabbling for a new hold. Finally his grip broke free. Blind, he felt only pain and Roselyn tugging on his belt, and then a searing blast of scalding wind blew both of them upwards.

Sister Aspertine descended deeper into the Duat, closer to the flaming river, only Nate still clinging to her. Both were screaming. His cheek lay pressed tightly against hers; any breath that struck him would burn her, too.

*"I won't let go!"* Nate cried. *"If the Duat claims us, we go together!"*

*"No!"* Sister Aspertine screamed, and tears flowed from her eyes as she tried to push free of his grip. *"Let go!"*

*"I can't!"* Nate shouted, and they descended lower. *"I love you!"*

*"I can't love you!"* Sister Aspertine shouted. *"I can't …! I can't …! I wish that I could …!"*

Suddenly both ceased descending, only feet from the molten river of fire, hovering, baking in its heat. Not far away, a hundred hungry, half-creature demons stared at them, licking beaks, muzzles, and fangs, eager to reach them.

*"You wish that you could love me!"* Nate shouted. *"That's the truth! Keep speaking! The truth will make you rise!"*

Sister Aspertine glanced down, at the red doom boiling just beneath her shoes, and at the hungry half-beasts all around them, and then she looked back at Nate. She reached up, and grabbed his arms, tightly clenched around her chest, and clung to him.

*"Your touch … haunts me … every night!"* Sister Aspertine confessed. *"I … love … and I hate you … I'll never feel free … never be free of you!"*

Slowly, Nate and Sister Aspertine began to rise.

*"I can't be with you!"* Sister Aspertine cried. *"My faith … my faith before my life; that's what my vows mean to me! I've been praying to be free of the memory of … your … feelings … and I know that I never will …!"*

Tears dripping on both of their faces despite the sweltering heat, Sister Aspertine and Nate rose up out of the Duat, and he pulled her even higher.

*"I knew my future … and I was content,"* Sister Aspertine cried as they rose. *"Now …uncertainty …confusion …damnation! I can't have what I want … to deny what I've seen …what we did … what I feel …!"*

Nate and Sister Aspertine rose above the Duat, back to the level where the city had once stood, although not a brick remained of it. Desperately they clung, holding each other.

Below them, the Duat roared again, and then suddenly, like a giant maw, it closed with a thunderclap like the snap of giant teeth taking one last bite at them. The *crash!* blasted them, strong gusts blew back their hair and clothes … and then it slowly died.

The huge, starry outline of Nut appeared below them, the jewels in her black-stone mosaic restored, and her city reappeared out of the thick columns of dissipating smoke … as if it had never crumbled.

"Let her go," Djehuti smiled at Nate. "She's learned to walk with Shu."

Hesitantly, Nate released Sister Aspertine, who floated by herself upon the air. Her expression was incredulous.

"Go in peace," Hatshep said. "You've escaped the Duat … and so met the challenge of Nut. Now you can move on. Find your next city, and rest there before you face its challenge."

"We … thank you," Karl gasped, still coughing and hacking.

"Nut the Wondrous blesses you," Djehuti said. "We thank you, for your victory is her will."

"Go with the love of the people of Nut!" Hatshep said. "And go with healing, for such we can give."

Phil's stinging eyes burned like every inch of his flesh, so badly that he could barely see, but as Hatshep waved his arm in a wide arc, Phil's pains vanished, his blisters healed, and he could breathe again. All around him, the coughing and agonized whimpers of his companions ceased. As his eyes cleared, he saw the other companions healing, too, although Alarika's thickly-layered skirts still showed scorch marks where it'd been burned.

"You best hurry … before dark thoughts return," Djehuti said, and she looked up at the dim stars and waved both of her arms.

Out of nothing, a great silvery ribbon of sparkling lights appeared, descending down to the City of Nut. With many twists and turns it fell down from the sky, thin, but wide. The companions looked up; *their route was clear.*

"Behold the Celestial Path!" Hatshep said.

"Hurry, before it dissipates," Djehuti said. "Walk lightly, and all our blessings go with you!"

"We'll go," Karl promised, still breathing hard, and he gestured to the companions. Taking hands, the better fliers pulled the weaker, and as one, they rose quickly, up onto the sparkling, silvery path.

"Again, thank you!" Karl shouted.

The people of Nut waved as the companions walked across the sky, their feet brushing the intangible path of tiny silver stars. Phil couldn't believe that he'd almost lost his brother … *how could he explain his death to their mother?* … and he was astounded that his brother would willingly sacrifice himself for Sister Aspertine … *did this mean … that their love was real …?*

Phil looked down, searching the floating crowd for the face of the one woman whom he'd secretly loved, but too many waved back at him, and he'd never known her name. A twinge of regret sparked inside him, so he blew a kiss at all of them, at all the people of Nut, hoping that she'd know that his kiss was meant for her, and then he hurried on, before dark thoughts dropped him back down.

They'd survived the City of Nut, with great help, but who knew what terrors the monstrous gods of Egypt had yet to throw at them?

# Chapter 7

## The City of Osiris

## ELOISE

*I'm losing my husband again,* Eloise thought, but then she pushed that pain from her mind … *that thought felt heavy, and they were too high to survive a fall.*

For hours she walked, or floated, between Phil and Henry, in the middle, climbing the sparkling path of silvery stars … as far from either edge as she could get. Eloise didn't like heights, and her few glances down filled her with horror. Below, the desert seemed an endless dark swath, too distant to recognize any features. The City of Nut was hidden from her view by their floating path, and possibly lost from sight, but she didn't dare venture close enough to the edge of their silvery path to peer over.

*Karl,* Eloise thought again, but she couldn't let dark thoughts weigh her down. If the Egyptian afterlife boasted clouds, then she suspected that they'd be above them.

*Not even the Seer could survive a fall from such a height.*

Eloise felt exhausted, but not enough to stop and rest on this flimsy sky-walk. Then a clear voice spoke up.

"The City of Osiris …!" Alarika exclaimed.

Eloise tilted her head back; floating above them on a wide, silvery base, their starry path led straight to the gate of a magnificent floating city, with low walls of white stone blocks, over which many temples and monuments arose. Two tall towers, the most impressive that they could see, flanked its entrance, which seemed to be an unbarred entryway.

"How do you know it's the City of Osiris?" Karl asked.

"See the snake-head ornaments?" Alarika asked. "Atop each tower? Those are asps, cobra-heads, the symbol of Egyptian royalty, and the tops of those buildings are shaped as the traditional crowns of Egypt; only the Ruler of All would decorate his city so."

"Is this it?" Roselyn asked. "Will we find the Seer here?"

"I expect that the City of Gods will be dedicated to all of them, not just one," Elaina said.

"Shouldn't the throne of Osiris be in his city?" Nate asked.

"The throne of Osiris rests before the scales of Thoth, where the final judgement happens," Alarika said. "We may find a throne, as we found a scale in the City of Thoth, but I doubt if we'll find the Ruler of All seated upon it."

"We should rest …," Karl said.

"Not until solid ground supports me!" Eloise insisted.

No one objected, so despite their weariness they kept walking. Features of the city grew more distinct, and flashes of gold, silver, and bronze twinkled in the starlight. The floating city seemed to be a great palace, a monument to the majesty of Osiris.

Their last few miles seemed the steepest and hardest, but their starry, silvery path ended at its grand entrance, which was flanked by two silver statues of a mummy in funeral wrappings, wearing the crown of Egypt topped with a cobra, each holding a sharp spear pointed at the metal flagstones comprising the entrance's platform. Seated upon a throne, each massive statue was half the height of the tall, ornate, snake-headed towers behind it. Grand temples and monuments crowded the city behind the towers. Its entrance was unbarred, with no gate or door, just a welcoming platform of solid gold plates, but the absence of any guard seemed ominous.

"Where are they …?" Roselyn asked, peering inside.

The others followed her gaze, yet saw nothing but the impressive tributes to Osiris.

"No people," Roselyn warned. "No guardians … no doorwards."

"Is that a bad thing?" Sister Aspertine asked.

"Nothing's as deadly as the unknown," Roselyn said.

`"Everyone, be careful," Karl ordered.

"We can be careful inside!" Eloise snapped.

Warily, they entered the city, many sighing with relief as their weight met firm footing. Nate tested his footing, then rose up, floating several feet above the gold platform.

"We can still fly," Nate said.

"Phil, watch behind us," Karl said. "Henry, watch to the left. Alarika, watch to the right. Nate, go straight up, to the height of these towers, and keep your eyes peeled. Then come back down … and tell us what you see."

With ease, Nate rose higher as the others obeyed.

"Sister Aspertine, watch right in front of us, while we watch Nate," Karl said, glancing cautiously behind them. "I don't want harpies or anything else attacking without warning."

Nate rose to the tops of the towers, then slowly descended.

"Nothing," Nate said. "Monuments, rooftops, gardens, and walkways … but no one … anywhere."

"Nut knew that we were in her city," Roselyn said. "Doubtless all the gods are aware of us …"

"They could be inside the temples …," Elaina said, but without much conviction.

"Phil and Nate, guard duty," Karl said. "We rest here."

Before them stood a black-stone obelisk depicting a painted engraving of Osiris, seated before his court, surrounded by retainers. They sat on the gold flagstones before it, far enough from the gate that Eloise felt safe from the abyss.

"Alarika, what can you tell us about …?" Karl asked.

Alarika gestured to the painted engraving of Osiris, wrapped in bands of sacred linens, seated upon his throne, surrounded by godly retainers and servants.

"This is Osiris," Alarika said. "The two goddesses behind him are Maat, and they always stand there, one upon his left and one upon his right, and they speak wisdom into his ears."

Roselyn scowled and irritably turned away.

"What …?" Alarika asked her.

"Nothing," Roselyn grumbled.

"Something we should know …?" Karl asked.

"No," Roselyn said. "It's just … the first of their gods is Atum, but it's Osiris, his great-grandson, who's the king of their gods. In Yggdrasil, Buri was the first of the

Vanir, but it's Odin, Buri's grandson, who rules the Vanir and the Aesir. I've seen Hugin and Mugin, Odin's ravens, who sit on his right and left shoulders, and whisper wisdom in his ears. Osiris has two goddesses of Maat … who speak wisdom into his ears. Odin hung himself until he was dead … and came back to life. Osiris was murdered … and was brought back to life. When Norse gods die, they go to Hel, a woman, the Norse Queen of Death. When Osiris died, he went to Nephthys, a woman, the Egyptian Queen of Death. In battle, Odin wields his magic spear, Gungnir. Fighting Aapep, Ra wields the Amsu-staff. Thor, Asgard's mightiest warrior, is Odin's son, while their mightiest warrior is Horus, Osiris' son. Loki is the Evil One, and the brother of Thor. Here, Set is the Evil One, and the brother of Osiris. All nine worlds of my people were created in Gunningap, when the ice of Niflhiem was melted by the fires of Muspell into a great waters … and the Nu is a great waters … from which the lands of Egypt arose …!"

"Tremendous similarities …," Elaina agreed.

"All pantheons of gods have similarities," Eloise said. "On the Isle of the Druids, we learned about Greek and Roman gods, so similar that many think them the same. Countless deities share the same birthdays, the same histories, and indulge in the same infidelities …"

"We're here to rescue the Seer, not become scholars … or wizards," Karl said. "Alarika, continue your tale … anything about Osiris might be useful."

"It would be useful if you accepted that my gods are older … and truer … than yours," Alarika said.

"Blasphemy …," Sister Aspertine shook her head. "God … if any of your nonsense is true … survived His Winter, and Alarika's gods didn't …"

"Now you blaspheme …!" Alarika snarled.

"We're not here to argue!" Karl overspoke them all. "None of us could've survived the challenges we've faced, and gotten as far as we have, alone. We need to work together …!"

"I agree," Elaina said. "Alarika, please …"

Alarika sighed, glared at them all, and then resumed speaking.

"As you know, Nut conceived Osiris, but she couldn't give birth to him until the five sacred days were created by Thoth," Alarika said. "Osiris was her first-born … and as he came into being, a voice echoed across the lands that the *'Lord of All was born'*. Thus he is named Osiris Unneferu, the Sahu of the Gods, the King of Taa-urit, the Prince in Amenta, the Lord of Abydos, the Lord of Forces, the Most Mighty, Lord of the Atef crown, the Crocodile, the Lord of Amu, and the Master of the Amsu-staff.

"By Atum, Osiris was crowned king of Egypt, and he became the father of laws and civilization. He labored hard to perfect Egypt, until all his people were joyous, and then Osiris departed to civilize distant lands. While he labored among the barbarians, Isis, Osiris' sister and wife, ruled well and wisely upon his throne. In his absence, Isis banished evil and suffering from Egypt, so much that Set, the Evil One, the Father of Serpents, who is also called Typhon, knelt helpless before her.

"Beautiful, dark-eyed Nephthys, Isis' younger sister, was Nebt-het, the Lady of the House of the Dead. For this, Nephthys wears a hat resembling a tiny house, often atop of a pair of horns. Nephthys loved Osiris, and was jealous of his love for her sister. After Osiris married Isis, Nephthys married Set. But she never bore Set a son, and when Set learned of his wife's love of Osiris, hatred filled his heart such that all else was expelled.

"Set journeyed far from Egypt and Nephthys, and gathered unto him a great following of evil hearts from distant lands. His hatred and jealousy of Osiris consumed him, and long he plotted against his brother.

"When Osiris finally returned from his duties elsewhere, Isis greeted him with all the love and devotion of a true wife. To celebrate her husband's return, Isis commanded a great banquet be prepared, and every Egyptian rejoiced. When Set arrived for the feast, Osiris greeted Set, his brother, with great delight, and welcomed his company.

"Set presented Osiris with an extraordinary gift to celebrate his homecoming: a sarcophagi, a great wooden chest, massive and beautifully carved, with the shape of Osiris resting upon its top. Osiris was delighted, and amazed not only by its craftsmanship, but by its immensity. Set confessed to Osiris that he'd hoped to construct it large enough that Osiris could lie within it, but he also claimed that he feared that, from such a comfortable position, Osiris might never willingly arise. Osiris laughed at this, and to dispel his brother's fears, Osiris opened the sarcophagi of Set and willingly laid down inside it.

"Set slammed shut the lid of the sarcophagi, and by secret locks, sealed his brother inside. Thus Set trapped the Lord of All, and instantly swept him from the feast while all the gods cried out. Then Set carried the sarcophagi far away.

"Isis led the gods on a long chase, but the allies of Set, the evil hearts that he'd befriended, distracted the gods, and thus Set escaped and vanished into hidden caverns and unknown lands.

"Set sank the sarcophagi, and drowned Osiris, near the Mouth of the Nile. Immediately the Ba and the Ka of

Osiris flew underground to the house of Nephthys. There, besotted by her sister's husband, Nephthys seduced Osiris, and soon bore him a child: Anubis. In his mother's house, Anubis grew and became strong … but also wise in the secrets of death and darkness.

"While Anubis grew, the sarcophagi of Set floated downstream, into the roots of a Tamarisk tree, which fed upon Osiris' godly glory, and grew to a vast thickness, such that it encased the sarcophagi. Impressed by its magnificence, the King of Byblos cut down the mighty tree, and used the thick trunk, containing Osiris' body, to support the roof of his greatest hall.

"As you know, Isis begged the King of Byblos to release her husband, but he held the body of Osiris hostage, and ordered her to nurse his infant son each day, that his child would grow immortal drinking the milk of the goddess. Isis relented, but she burned the child in large fire every night, which only her milk allowed him to survive. Yet the Queen of Byblos saw her, and screamed so loudly that her son's protection failed. To spare her son, the Queen of Byblos cut open the great pillar and drew forth the sarcophagi of Set. Thus Isis abandoned the young Prince of Byblos and carried Osiris' body back to Egypt.

"Isis and Horus hid the sarcophagi of Set, and then sought to return Osiris' spirit, but they couldn't find him, despite long searches. In their absence, Set found and dismembered the body of Osiris into fourteen pieces, and hurled the sections to many distant lands. In a reed boat, Isis journeyed long to gather the scattered pieces of her husband.

"Jealous of his wife's infidelity, Set refused to allow Nephthys to help resurrect Osiris. When all the pieces of Osiris were collected and assembled, Set attacked Isis, but by then her son, Horus, was fully-grown, and he challenged Set. The whole Earth trembled from the violence of their battle, which lasted many days. Horus finally triumphed, and Set crawled before him, and thus was Set imprisoned.

"While Set languished, Isis despaired that she'd never find all the parts of Osiris' spirit. While Horus was away, Set promised Isis that he'd return her husband's spirits in exchange for his freedom. Torn by grief, Isis released Set.

"Enraged to find Set escaped, Horus tore from Isis her precious Diadem, the jeweled crown of Egypt. Such was his fury that Isis' head was broken in two, and she would've died, but she replaced her head with the head of a cow, to last until she could heal herself. To aid her, Thoth adorned her with a magic helmet in the shape of a cow's head, and thus her life was saved.

"Horus hunted Set, and when they met in battle for the second time, again the ground shook beneath their blows, but both retired from the field undefeated. Soon they met again, and the world trembled, but neither triumphed. Upon their third meeting, Horus arose victorious. Set fled to distant lands and never again came to Egypt.

"In Set's absence, with the secrets of Anubis, Isis restored Osiris to life, and he reclaimed his rulership. Yet, his unjust murder by his brother dismayed him, and thus Osiris remained in his linens of the grave, and Isis thereafter wore only her white garment of mourning.

"Osiris is the possessor of Maat, and he subsists upon it. Osiris also possesses the Vase of the Water of Renewal, containing the divine, life-giving sap of the Tamarisk tree. The fetish of Osiris is an animal's skin hanging from a stick, although this is also a symbol of

Anubis. The eyes of Osiris reflect the Sun and the Moon, and he forever wears the Diadem, the jeweled crown of Egypt."

Alarika stared at each of them in turn.

"You don't believe," Alarika scowled. "You stand here … in our afterlife … and deny what you see. You only seek our history …"

" … So that we can rescue our friend," Eloise finished.

"That's what we do for friendship," Karl said.

"That's why they entered Yggdrasil … when I was a kid," Nate spoke up. "Back then, they were helping Eric, who remained there."

"You … expect me to remain …?" Alarika asked.

"Eric wished to remain," Karl said. "Once we find the Seer, we'll help you get that palace …"

"The Seer could probably give it to you," Eloise said.

"The soul of the Seer still lies in the memory box of Anubis," Roselyn said. "Celebrations should be planned after victory."

"We can't fight Anubis," Alarika said. "Mortals can't win."

"We've heard that before … from gods still in their prime," Karl said.

"Young gods," Alarika said. "Wisdom is the only true power … known by gods a millennia older than your deities."

"Your gods know that we're here," Karl said. "They're making us walk this path. The gods of Egypt are real; we wouldn't be here if they weren't, but I've seen a lot of gods … and none have impressed me. They all seem motivated only by their desires. When I see gods seeking to reduce the suffering of the humans that worship them, then I'll be impressed."

"We're supposed to be resting," Elaina reminded them.

"It's been a long climb … float … whatever," Karl nodded. "Sleep if you can. Phil, Nate; wake Henry and I when you tire."

Eloise wasn't tired, but she laid quiet to let the others rest.

Hours later, suddenly her mother awoke her.

"Anything …?" Eloise asked her mother.

"Nothing," Elaina said. "No movements, no sounds."

"Perhaps the city is abandoned," Roselyn said, and she flexed her shoulders and rubbed her arms, then uncorked her bota. "I ache; the Water of Life is wearing off again, and we can't get more. Alarika, you said that Osiris has an urn of sacred water …?"

"The Vase of the Water of Renewal," Alarika said.

"Keep an eye out for vases," Roselyn said to everyone.

After they ate, and shared a mouthful each of their dwindling supply of the Water of Life, Roselyn drew Hel's sword, hefted it, and then led the way.

Past the twin, mammoth statues of golden Osiris enthroned, each holding a long spear pointed down at their path, they followed Roselyn into the city. Alarika stared at the etchings of funeral accoutrements, whose depictions squeezed between countless lines of hieroglyphic writing.

"Anything important to us …?" Karl asked.

"Little that I didn't already tell you," Alarika said.

Hours they searched every jewel-bedecked temple, every giant statue, behind every monument, everywhere. Except for them, the city seemed abandoned.

All the widest paths converged on a great garden, in the center of which lay a pool of water. Floating upon the water stood a huge silver throne, shaded by tall palm trees. The garden bore countless ripe berries of many kinds, and yellow bananas hung long and thickly against tall trunks. Floating upwards, Nate and Phil retrieved dozens, and between the bananas and berries, they ate well. Several pools and fountains provided fresh water; they wouldn't starve. Yet they saw no one … and no other gate, nor clue of how to depart the city.

"Elaina …?" Karl asked.

Elaina nodded and slipped off her shoes. She chose a wide, stone-floored platform, a low monument, which looked like it could be the base of a mammoth statue, but nothing stood atop it. It made a good stage, and as Elaina floated herself up onto it, Eloise began to sing.

Eloise wasn't a great singer, but she knew many songs, and sang notes for her mother's dance. The others joined in; Phil knew the words to her tune, but most just hummed the song. Henry and Sister Aspertine joined Phil, and Roselyn and Alarika clapped their hands to match their tempo.

Elaina danced to their song with expert abandon, never faltering, never off-balance. She spun and leapt, capered, and waved her arms like rolls of surf sliding toward the sand. Soon her feet left the platform, and Elaina danced up into the air. Flying, her grace seemed magnified, floating in swift circles, or changing direction unexpectantly, but always with perfect timing, seeming eternally practiced, although all knew that she'd never danced like this. Eloise envied her mother's rhythm and coordination. Eloise recalled dancing with her mother in Castle Bristlen, and how she'd briefly cavorted with her mother's skill; *the magic of dancing had made her feel happier than any Druid spell that Eloise had ever cast.*

Elaina circled outside them, in ever widening rings of Shu, staring out at the temples, fountains, and monuments. When done, she floated back, and ended with a dramatic flourish, curling into a ball, then slowly budding like a flower until she floated, tall and smiling, her arms open wide as if drinking the starlight.

"They're here …!" Elaina said, just above a whisper. "They're all around us …!"

"Hiding …?" Karl asked. "Invisible …?"

"I don't know," Elaina said. "Yet … I sense them."

"Let's look again," Karl said.

They began searching anew, more diligently, touching surfaces, and looking under outcroppings. Still they found nothing.

Finally, Eloise found a small, grassy knoll, overgrown with flowers. Waiting until the others wandered away, Eloise slipped in among the thick yellow blossoms, squatting down so she wouldn't be seen, pulled up her skirt, and slid down her undergarments. Relieving herself, Eloise tried to hurry, so that she could catch up to the others without being missed.

Then a soft wind wafted the bright petals around her, and a softer voice whispered in her ear.

*"They will betray you."*

Eloise almost jumped, and glanced over each shoulder twice; nothing but blossoms, stalks, and leaves hung behind her. She finished faster than usual, although not nearly fast enough.

*"Karl …!"* Eloise cried.

She was barely out of the flowers when the others came running back to her.

"I heard them!" Eloise shouted.

*"Where …?"* Karl demanded, and Nate and Phil drew swords and pushed into the flowers.

"They're not there," Eloise said. "I heard someone … a man … speaking right in my ear, but I was alone …!"

"No one here!" Nate shouted.

"No tracks!" Phil added.

"I heard them, I swear!" Eloise insisted.

"What did they say?" Roselyn asked.

Eloise hesitated before speaking. "They said … *they will betray you.*"

"Exactly like that?" Roselyn asked. "Did they repeat the first word … or stutter?"

"Neither," Eloise admitted. "They spoke softly, smoothly, like a … whisper on the wind."

"Trust no words unless you know who said them," Roselyn said. "Einherjar will say terrible things, insults, lies, and even offer to betray their kin, before they stab hidden knives into their enemies."

"That's dishonorable," Phil said.

"Norsemen live for honor, but fight for victory," Roselyn said. "A loyal einherjar may sacrifice honor to insure that his allies triumph."

"Let's all be quiet," Elaina suggested. "Maybe they'll speak again."

They stood amid the yellow flowers, listening, waiting, and finally gave up.

"What do we do?" Eloise asked.

"They don't seem in a hurry to speak to us," Karl said.

"Exactly," Sister Aspertine said. "Us … Eloise was alone."

The companions glanced at each other, and then Karl nodded to Sister Aspertine.

"It's worth a try," Karl said. "I'll …"

"Master, you should let Nate or I try," Phil said.

Karl frowned deeply. "If we were in Castle Bristlen, I'd box your ears. Go, both of you. Don't wander too far, or too far apart. Separate, be careful, and come back soon."

Sharing one glance, Nate and Phil headed off in different directions, Nate toward the garden with the giant silver throne floating upon the water, Phil to an ornate temple that they'd already explored. With glances back to make sure that they were being watched, Nate walked around the small pool, behind the throne, and Phil entered the temple. Only minutes later, both emerged and walked back, Nate looking behind him at the silver throne.

"Well …?" Karl asked.

"A woman's voice," Phil said. "She said that I'll never escape the City of Osiris."

"I had a man's voice," Nate said. "He told me to sit on the silver throne."

"Probably not a good idea," Roselyn said.

"What do we do?" Eloise asked. "We don't know who to trust …"

"We trust nothing," Karl said. "No one's been hurt; that's the main thing. We need to separate, but not too far apart. Let's hear everything they have to say …"

"They may never tell us anything useful," Roselyn said. "They could keep delaying us … until the Duat."

"The purpose of these cities has been consistent," Karl said. "Test the faithful, but don't deny them a fair chance. Until we have evidence that the rules have changed, let's assume that these voices speak clues."

"Alarika should study the hieroglyphs, in case our assumption is wrong," Roselyn said.

"I can do both," Alarika said.

"Fifteen minutes, then come back and report," Karl said.

With worried expressions, the companions divided. Eloise headed toward an obelisk over fifteen feet high, made of gleaming alabaster, with painted depictions of a gray-skinned woman and a man with the black head of a jackal standing over a bearded mummy with a tall hat decorated with a golden cobra. The far side showed a goddess that she recognized from the city with the mad cow: Isis, and beside her stood a young man holding a bolt of lightning; it must be Horus.

*"There's nothing hiding here,"* a woman's whisper echoed in her ear.

Eloise jumped; even though she'd been expecting it, the voice from nowhere was startling. She glanced around, but none were nearby. She paused, waiting to see if any more whispers would come, but they didn't.

Then Eloise explored inside a temple. It had ornate doors that opened wide, a tall ceiling, and large depictions of Osiris, again with the two figures of Maat behind him.

*"Your friends have abandoned you."*

Eloise kept moving, ignoring the unreasonable fears that stabbed like needles; she knew that they'd never abandon her. Yet the voices were unnerving.

*"Roselyn will kill you!"* a man's voice whispered.

Eloise paused. *How could they know?* She couldn't remember anyone speaking Roselyn's name since they'd arrived.

Eloise continued, past tall, round posts upholding the ceiling, carved hieroglyphs encircling their stones. Many hieroglyphs lay inside loops, the magical rope that protected names; cartouches, but Eloise couldn't decipher one glyph.

Before the back wall, on elegantly-painted stands, lay large treasures on display. A golden songbird as big as a vulture, a monstrous bronze crocodile, a huge white feather, and a giant silver hand; these looked like holy relics, and Eloise was careful not to touch them.

*"Karl will never enter the Elysian Fields."*

Disgusted but convinced, Eloise walked back to join with the others.

"It's us," Eloise said as she walked up to Karl, who was standing beside Elaina, Henry, and Nate. Phil and Roselyn were still approaching, and Alarika was standing before a distant monument covered in hieroglyphs.

"What's us?" Karl asked.

"The voices," Eloise said. "Either they can read our minds, and know our fears, or they simply give voice to our fears. Either way, what they say comes from us."

"One of mine said something …," Elaina said hesitantly. "They said *'Your daughter hates you in her heart'*."

"I don't …!" Eloise began.

"Yes, but how did it know that you … any of you … were my daughter?" Elaina asked.

"I heard a similar message … about me sailing the sea," Henry said. "But another said *'You will find nothing here'*."

"One of mine said *'Nothing is hidden here'*," Eloise said.

"*Your search will be fruitless*," Roselyn said as she and Phil walked up.

Each repeated their voices for Roselyn, but when it became Phil's turn, he looked around.

"Where's Sister Aspertine?" Phil asked.

"She went that way," Nate pointed at the main garden.

"Find her," Karl ordered, and they all went looking.

Nate found Sister Aspertine on her knees, weeping. As the others hurried to join them, Nate reached out to comfort her, but she recoiled from his touch.

*"I've betrayed God!"* Sister Aspertine screamed.

"Those voices …!" Eloise began.

*"They're the whispers of the devil!"* Nate overspoke her. "They'll trick you, if you let them. They lie! Don't listen!"

Sister Aspertine looked up, as if wavering between the devil who'd whispered in her ear and the devil who'd violated her body.

"They know our fears … and use them against us," Phil added.

Sister Aspertine shook her head, and then made the sign of the cross.

"I hate this place," she said.

"We'll all be glad to leave it," Karl said.

"The Seer's our only exit," Roselyn said.

They didn't leave Sister Aspertine alone again. The others took turns wandering off, stepping out momentarily of sight, and then returning to report the words of the voices. Yet no insights came. Whenever Eloise stepped away, the voices whispered fears that stabbed into her, but she knew to disregard them.

*"The Lady of the Druids scorns the priestess that denied her."*

*"You will die before the dead gods of Egypt."*

*"Your children will never see their mother again … they'll die believing themselves abandoned."*

Other voices spoke of the recent revelations of her companions.

*"Nate lusts for you!"*

*"Afflicted by one set of false, pagan gods, you refused both them and Christ … and embraced a witch."*

*"You married a man pledged to another, but it's your mother who cursed you!"*

Some spoke so clearly that she could identify their sex, while others whispered softly, like a gentle, buffeting breeze. Eloise ignored them all, but one sparked her curiosity.

*"Your companions will rend your body. Under the green lotus your legs will lie forever!"*

When they gathered, Eloise related this one, and heard two others equally perplexing.

*"The head of your company shall be pierced by the Amsu-staff,"* Henry reported.

*"Your body shall lie in the deepest pool forever,"* Roselyn quoted.

"Body parts," Alarika said. "Set cut Osiris into fourteen parts. Isis traveled far to gather the parts, and she put them back together."

"Could it be that simple?" Phil asked. "We find the parts …"

"None of the other cities were this easy," Elaina said.

"I saw a big silver hand," Eloise said, pointing. "Inside that temple, on a stand near the back wall."

Eloise led, and soon the companions stood inside the temple, before the silver hand.

"Should we touch it?" Elaina asked.

"What choice do we have?" Roselyn asked, and without waiting, she reached out and picked up the silver hand, under whose weight she staggered; the hand was solid silver, at least thirty pounds.

Somewhere in the city, a great noise rang out, a metallic crash, but unlike a bell, it maintained a single, unbroken note, rolling like thunder, until it faded in the distance.

"Either we're on the right path … or we just offended Osiris and alerted his guardians," Alarika said.

"Phil, Nate; draw swords, flank the door," Karl said. "Don't go out."

Both boys obeyed, but after long minutes passed, Eloise suspected that their preparation was unneeded.

"Better wasted caution than a fool's death," Roselyn said, and she gave the heavy silver hand to Henry, drew Hel's sword, and slowly braved the starlight.

"We need to find the green lotus," Eloise said. "Most are white or blue, so it shouldn't be hard."

In a corner of the city, near a small, empty house whose tiny windows they'd peered inside, stood a pool of water upon which floated a hundred green lotuses. Elaina brushed the water with her hand and swept back the blossoms, but in the dim starlight, the water looked dark and forbidding.

"Anything could be down there," Karl said.

"The easiest path usually leads to a trap," Roselyn said.

"We can debate forever," Eloise said. "Phil, you have the longest reach …"

Phil nodded, then held his hand out over the water.

"Be careful!" Elaina cautioned.

Phil took a deep breath, then plunged his arm into the water, drenching his sleeve. He hesitated, then bent over and reached deep, the water was up to his shoulder.

"Nothing," Phil said. "I feel the side of the well, but no bottom."

"Disarmor," Karl said.

Nervous glances exchanged as Phil disrobed until only his trousers remained. Sister Aspertine took his wet gambeson and tunic, before he piled them atop his armor, and wrung the water out of them as best she could.

Watching her, Eloise smiled, and Sister Aspertine gave her a puzzled look.

"You remind me of Lady Seren," Eloise said.

"Master Sir Rafe's wife …?" Sister Aspertine asked.

Eloise nodded. "She's a good Christian."

"Swords out," Karl said, and he drew his sword with one hand and grasped Phil's wrist with his other. "Don't go any deeper than you have to. If we see you thrash, we're coming in … swords first."

Phil nodded, then sat on the low ledge and dipped his feet in. Then, lowering himself slowly, he slipped into the dark water … to his waist … to his chest … and then his head vanished with a soft splash. Almost instantly Phil resurfaced, shaking water from his hair and eyes.

"I felt something," Phil said. "With my toes. I'm going to have to go deep."

Karl frowned. "Don't stay under long."

Phil inhaled deeply, then vanished under countless ripples. No one spoke, each full of worry, and then Phil splashed back up.

"Legs," Phil gasped and sputtered. "Metal, and huge; they match the silver hand."

"Can you bring it up?" Eloise asked.

"No," Phil said. "Solid silver … must weigh hundreds of pounds."

"How can we …?" Elaina began.

"I'm going down again," Phil said. "Now that I know what I'm feeling, I may be able to find out more."

Phil took another deep breath, then vanished underwater with a '*plop!*'. He stayed under more than a minute, then resurfaced, and pulled himself up onto the ledge. The others helped, and soon he stood, splashing water onto the flagstones.

"I don't think anything's holding it down," Phil said. "If we had a strong rope …"

"So far, no task has been impossible," Karl said.

"No task has been easy, either," Eloise reminded him.

"Divide up," Karl said. "Roselyn, Henry, Nate, Phil, Alarika, and I will find a way to pull it up. Eloise, you lead Elaina and Sister Aspertine; find the other pieces."

Eloise nodded.

"How …?" Henry asked, looking at the well, as Eloise started to walk away.

"My people built the pyramids," Alarika said, looking at the dark water. "We should be able to lift this."

Eloise didn't know where to search, but she needed to look confident. Elaina and Sister Aspertine followed her, walking about.

"Where do we start?" Sister Aspertine asked.

*"The head of your company shall be pierced by the Amsu-staff,"* Elaina repeated. "The head … we should look for the staff."

"It could be anywhere," Eloise said. "Staffs are made of wood; let's start among the trees."

Many small trees grew in rows of planted spaces lined with smooth stones, and in several wooded areas they grew wild. Around the silver throne grew the tallest trees, but none looked like a staff. They searched the temples again … with the same result. Then they examined the monuments, and looked at all the drawings surrounded by hieroglyphs.

"We should've brought Alarika," Eloise said, looking at an elaborate drawing. "Maybe this writing says where the staff is."

"Is that a staff?" Sister Aspertine asked, pointing at a painted relief carving.

"That's a spear … held by Ra," Elaina said. "He's the god with the head of a falcon, with the sun over him."

"Doesn't Ra fight with the Amsu-staff?" Sister Aspertine asked. "Isn't it … a weapon?"

Eloise and Elaina exchanged a surprised look.

"The Amsu-staff … is a spear …!" Eloise exclaimed.

"I think I know where it is," Sister Aspertine said.

Sister Aspertine threaded through the monuments and around the temples … all the way back to the entrance. As they neared it, Eloise saw it.

*"Mother of Loki!"* Elaina exclaimed.

Near the gate stood the mammoth golden statues of throned Osiris beneath which they'd rested. Twin spears hung, one in the left hand of one statue of Osiris, the other in the right hand of the opposite statue. The spears of the flanking statues, guarding the gates, both pointed to the same spot: one of the golden plates that floored the entryway.

All three girls hurried to it, and with a little pushing, managed to move one of the heavy gold plates that floored the platform inside the gate. Scrabbling, and with all of them straining their hardest, they lifted one edge of it onto a nearby plate, and then they pushed with their feet to slide it out of their way.

Below the flagstone lay a rectangular space filled with sand. They dug; buried in the sand they uncovered the giant head of a silver statue … layered with horizontal bands … like metal-cast mummy wrappings. The only parts missing were its eyes; empty sockets stared sightlessly.

"How do we get it out?" Elaina asked.

"It must weigh a hundred pounds," Sister Aspertine said, and she reached out a hand and pushed against it.

"The men can carry it," Eloise said. "Let's tell them that we found it."

"Should we cover it up?" Elaina asked.

"Why?" Sister Aspertine asked. "No one's here."

"Something whispers to us when we're alone," Elaina said.

"Mother's right," Eloise said. "I'll stay. I can at least do magic, if I must. Get the men … and hurry back."

"Are you sure?" Elaina asked.

"Voices don't bother me," Eloise said. "Go … and don't dawdle."

Elaina and Sister Aspertine exchanged a glance, then hurried off, and Eloise sat down and slid her fingers across the smooth, cold metal of the statue of Osiris' head. This much silver would restock the treasury of Castle Bristlen … and buy another castle just like it. Yet she'd seen vastly more wealth than this in the treasury of Utgard-Loki, guarded by Heid. The wealth of Earth paled before the riches of Yggdrasil and the Egyptian afterlife.

She needed to take some back with her. Perhaps Athelwynne could …?

*"You'll never return to Castle Bristlen. You'll die in the Duat."*

"Stop it," Eloise spoke aloud, not sure if the voices could hear her or not. "According to the disciples of Nut, no one dies in the Duat. The fallen are transformed, but still alive. So, either you're repeating my fears … or telling lies."

Moments creeped by, and then …

*"Jump over the ledge, now, while you can …!"*

"Don't be silly," Eloise said.

*"Osiris is the dead god. If you reassemble Osiris, he'll crush you!"*

"I doubt that," Eloise said.

*"Isis spent centuries looking for the fourteen parts of Osiris. Mortals can't live one …"*

"We've found three sections in just a few hours," Eloise said. "Why don't you just tell me where the others are?"

*"In the end, Osiris shall desire you to join him … in death."*

"I've disappointed gods before," Eloise said.

*"The Seer can't help you."*

"Then I'll help him," Eloise said.

*"You'll fall into the Duat."*

"Either tell me something I need to know … or go to the Duat," Eloise said.

*"Assembling the parts of Osiris isn't enough. Saxons can't solve this."*

This voice sounded like a child. Eloise waited, hoping they'd say more.

*"Osiris is dead and buried, and you can't awaken him with a statue,"* spoke the voice of an old woman.

"These cities are tests, not traps," Eloise said.

*"This test wasn't meant for you."*

Eloise shook her head. No single person could lift the heavy silver legs from the pool; this statue could only be assembled by a group. Someone had chosen this test for them.

*"Karl will leave you. Rafe and Seren are old. Your mother won't live long after them. You'll end up facing death alone."*

Panic tingled in the back of Eloise's mind, but she forced herself not to react. She'd looked into the face of Death … and into the eyes of the Lady of the Druids. She'd felt Her goodness, and become Her priestess. She was looking forward to arriving at the Elysian Fields. Yet … *growing old alone* … Eloise shuddered involuntarily. She didn't let it show, but she felt certain the voices knew that they'd affected her.

Nate, Phil, Henry, and Alarika walked up with Elaina and Sister Aspertine. Eloise stared at them, alarmed, and then jumped up.

*"You left them alone …?!?"* Eloise cried.

Everyone froze.

"Who …?" Nate asked.

*"Karl and Roselyn!"* Eloise snapped.

"They're … working," Elaina said.

"Only Hel's sword can cut the beams, and only Karl knows how to shape the end-braces," Nate said.

"Braces …?" Eloise asked.

"We need a scaffold …," Nate said.

"Here's the head," Eloise pointed.

Minutes later, Eloise led the parade shouldering the huge silver head back to the pool of green lotuses. Karl and Roselyn were both working hard, chopping and shaping the rough trunks of the trees that they'd cut down, but both stopped to look at the silver head when the companions set it next to the silver hand.

Nate and Phil resumed splitting reeds, while Henry and Alarika returned to weaving their split-reeds into a thick rope. Nate explained how they needed the beams to lift the legs of the statue out of the well. Karl had learned these methods on his father's farm, and used similar beams to repair the gates of Castle Bristlen.

Eloise, Elaina, and Sister Aspertine left them to their work … to search for more sections of the silver statue of Osiris.

*"Your body shall lie in the deepest pool forever,"* Sister Aspertine repeated Roselyn's quote.

"Do we really need to swim in every pool?" Elaina asked. "I'd rather dance than swim."

To keep the others from disturbing them, they found a distant open space, and there Elaina began dancing with her usual mastery, but soon she was leaping past monuments, skipping the length of temples, and they followed her. Finally she stopped before a dark lake surrounded by thin palms.

"How deep is it?" Eloise asked.

"No idea," Elaina said.

"I don't understand," Sister Aspertine said to Eloise. "In the Valley of Thieves, you made fire dance all over you. Couldn't you … make the water dance … somewhere else?"

Eloise and Elaina exchanged glances.

"You … are suggesting that we use magic …?" Eloise asked.

"I need to get back to the land of God," Sister Aspertine said, seeming exhausted.

Elaina smiled at Sister Aspertine, but Eloise frowned. Since leaving the Field of Wheat, her attempts to use magic had usually failed. Even the Seer couldn't sense the Lady from Yggdrasil, and his mental focus excelled anything that she could accomplish. Normally, Eloise only felt the Lady in her deepest ceremonies, and she hadn't done that since she'd summoned Death. Yet water, like fire, could be her friend, except that Eloise hated the idea of swimming in the dark, starlit lake.

"I can try," Eloise said, and she stepped toward the lake.

While Elaina and Sister Aspertine watched, Eloise stopped at the water's edge, lifted her hands, and gazed at the few stars.

*"Lady of Light*
*Hear my plea*
*Your blessings bestow*

*Your disciple see*
*Your servant awaits*
*At your call*
*Unto your will*
*I submit all."*

Nothing. No tingles, no dizziness, and no sudden elation filled her. Eloise tried to force herself to believe that the Lady could hear her; *belief strengthened bonds.* On the Magic Isle, surrounded by equally-eager novitiates, deep in the woods under a full moon, she could almost feel the Lady's embrace. Alone, without any fellows, trapped beyond a 'crack in the world', and facing the threats of foreign gods, Eloise had only herself.

Eloise dipped her fingers into the lake: *cold.* Eloise didn't like swimming because she didn't like cold. She preferred warm water; hot baths were her favorite. Being a baroness held many advantages; hot baths were a luxury that peasants seldom enjoyed.

Fire; Eloise liked fire. Flames were warm, friendly, and playful. Eloise looked askance at the dark lake; *cold water wasn't fun.*

Eloise cleared her mind and focused on the chant she'd learned from the Seer's diaries.

*"Blessed Lady, goddess divine*
*Heed now this will of mine*
*Blessed Lady, eternal love,*
*Send now help from above,*
*Blessed Lady, burning fire*
*If my will be your desire*
*Blessed Lady, glowing light*
*Grant to me your godly might*
*Blessed Lady, for eternity*
*As you will, so mote it be!"*

Eloise focused within, deeply, reaching inside. Insights, understandings, and sympathies powered magic more than divine intervention. Eloise had to control her thoughts and emotions; not deny them, but explore them, diving into their depths and causes. *Magic lies within, where few seek it. The hearts of light and darkness coexist in our deepest passions. Only the bravest look into both …*

Eloise knew herself … at least, as deeply as she needed. The first stage of magic depended on her summoning of simultaneous opposites, not of thoughts, but of feelings. Conflicting emotions began the bridge to join the contrary worlds of magic and reality. This stage was different for everyone, and Eloise had long identified her triggers.

Delicious foods were her favorite triggers. Eloise especially loved treats, but she hated their effect, and had struggled after the birth of each child to regain what she could of her youthful figure. Her simultaneous feelings of love and hate, as she recalled her favorite sweets, helped trigger the magic inside her. Her strongest trigger was Karl, whom she wanted more than she could say, yet his endless infatuation with Roselyn frequently fueled a desire to punch him. She loved the beauty of a perfectly-woven spiderweb, but spiders made her recoil. On the Magic Isle, she'd identified numerous evokers of duality, and she mentally stepped through each, then cleared her mind of all conscious thought, and letting only conflicting emotions wash over her entirely.

Holding contradictory emotions simultaneously was difficult, mastered only after years of practice. Eloise dove into and unbound her emotional turmoils, using her new trigger: the Egyptian gods. Eloise reveled in the accomplishment of finding and entering a second 'crack in the world' and facing an entirely new godly pantheon.

Yet she also hated this land, not only because she might lose Karl to Roselyn, but because her magics didn't seem as powerful here. Doubt weakened magic, and she worried that even the Lady of the Druids couldn't hear prayers from a divine realm that was passing into antiquity as the Elysian Fields were being born.

Conscious thoughts faded. Her emotions washed over her, unbound, and slowly unfamiliar emotions crept in. Standing nearby, her mother's love flowed into her, yet Sister Aspertine's regrets and despair splashed against her like foam on rocks. Both felt horribly weary.

Disdaining their feelings, Eloise delved farther. Her other companions, working at the distant pool, registered faintly, but she sought the Lady, her only real connection to the divine. Eloise opened her mind wider, exploring her sensitivity, her vulnerability, seeking the familiar sensations of She Whom All Druids Worshipped.

She continued through the remaining steps of spellcasting. Reality faded until only endless desires welled, where willpower subordinated, and only sensations dominated. She touched the schism of the *mundus imaginalis*, where reality wavered … and only madness lay beyond. Gently Eloise leaked her newest desires, to let her will flow into both tenuous worlds, not as a force, but as bait, a novelty upon which to spin reactions. She flexed her fingers, and reached out to the nearby waters of the lake, felt its cold wetness rise up to join with her hands … and felt its touch instantly drench her sleeves. She yearned to draw it closer, to welcome the water, to play with it, as she'd invited the warm flames in the Valley of Thieves. But the water's chill repelled her, its sopping disgust dissuaded her, and both plunged her back to reality. The cold waters fell back, and when she peeked, her hands were soaked but empty; *she'd failed again.*

Exhausted by the effort, Eloise staggered, then lowered to sit upon the grass. All magic was draining, but magical failures fed frustration, weakening the caster even farther. She heard Elaina and Sister Aspertine approaching her from behind, having witnessed her botched attempt. Eloise flushed, embarrassed.

"What happened?" her mother asked.

"It … didn't work," Eloise admitted.

"Perhaps you're not surrendering enough …," Elaina said.

"Surrendering …?" Eloise asked.

"When dancing, hearing the music is only the beginning," Elaina said. "Dancing isn't just movement; it's combining yourself with the flow, the essence, of all there is. By joining with the music, and surrendering to the dance, dancers become the magic."

"Like surrendering yourself to the will of God," Sister Aspertine said. "The magic is in His love."

Elaina smiled at Sister Aspertine. "Hard to believe our magics are so similar."

Sister Aspertine sighed and looked away.

"Druid magic exploits the schisms that exist in nature," Eloise said. "We bring harmony between disparate realities."

"That lake doesn't look harmonious," Elaina said.

"It's cold," Eloise said. "And it's big. Even if I could coax it out, where would I put it? It'd simply flow back in."

"Why move the lake?" Sister Aspertine asked. "We want to move the body of the statue, not the lake."

Eloise and Elaina exchanged glances.

"It's worth a try," Elaina said.

Eloise turned back to the lake, doubtful, but trying to clear her mind, preparing for her next attempt.

"Surrender to the rhythms of the lake," Elaina said. "Surrender to its flow … and become one."

"Surrender to the divine," Sister Aspertine said. "Miracles are gifts of God."

Eloise frowned, irritated by their conflicting advice. Magic existed to work one's will … *or else what worth had it?* Her magics exposed the pure emotions around her, and strove to feel for their ways, to turn them to her will. To surrender one's will was to become a tool. Besides, what needs could a lake … or a statue … have? Joining with or submitting to the inanimate couldn't enhance a spell. When she loved fire, fire responded, but her affections sparked its reaction, not any consciousness of the flames.

Yet … *what wonders could combining the magics of Druids, Norse, and Christians produce?*

Eloise pushed away their interference and focused on her chant. As before, she recited the words, then began blurring her thoughts, summoning her triggers, and exploring the dualities of her emotions. Yet nagging thoughts kept popping into her mind.

*Join …? Submit …?*

*How could those help?*

Slowly her conflicting emotions abridged the contrary worlds. From her reality, sensations of magic wavered, dim and shadowy, almost imperceptible. Eloise focused on each sensation, drew it to her, and exposed it. She reached out her hands; she needed to push her will, to mold and shape its insubstantiality, to force her desires.

She extended her perceptions, and felt the cold, moving depths of the lake. Slowly she opened her eyes. The lake was beautiful, reflecting the few stars, and shadowed by the palm trees around it. Quiet and serene, the gentle breeze wafted small ripples, visible only as the starlight danced upon it. Peaceful; Eloise desired peace such as this lake had. She delved deep, then shared with the lake the love of peace she held in her heart. She spread her arms, offering her love freely. She sensed the lake respond, as did all things that cherished love.

However, the lake never moved. She'd accomplished nothing.

Eloise redoubled her efforts … to no avail. All elements respond to love but, as pretty as it was, Eloise held no love for this cold, dark lake.

*If only it was hot …!*

That dim thought pierced her will, her ability to maintain feelings without thoughts. Pushing her disdain away didn't help; it only weakened her spell.

*Only love brings true warmth …*

Yes, Eloise loved warm water. She changed her focus, filling her mind with the sensations she fondly recalled. *Warmth, cleanliness, relaxing, luxuriating, bathing … a world of peaceful pleasures in water … of drifting off to happy dreams …in wonderful, steaming water …*

Fiery yearnings raged, followed by pleasant sensations.

"Look …!" Sister Aspertine gasped.

"Quiet!" Elaina hissed.

Despite her training, Eloise opened her eyes. Lights glowed from the bottom of the lake, pale, pink, and growing. Eloise kept watching, consciously spurring her love for the lake, willing it warm, and the lake responded. Long minutes passed, and brighter pink lights started to shine upwards from its bottom. Little bubbles rose. The bubbles grew denser, larger, and wisps of steam appeared, illuminated by the pink radiance. Eloise felt confused, reducing her connection.

*Was her love of the lake being reflected back at her?*

*Or … was she feeling the love of the lake …?*

*'Surrender to the rhythms …!' Her mother had said.*

*'Surrender to the divine …!' Sister Aspertine had said.*

Eloise surrendered herself … and become one with the steamy lake.

The lake rose in a sudden, splashing wave. Warm water cascaded over her, suffused her clothes … and her heart. Eloise raised her hands in triumph; she'd always loved warm water … but this was the first time that warm water had loved her back. Their communion was warm as a hug, intense, wondrous, and … bubbly. Her mouth was spared; the water had no desire to hurt her. She felt streamed upon by loving emotions, drenched by a perfect waterfall, splashing upwards rather than down. Floating in warmth and indulgence, her love of the water rose to a connection greater than she'd ever experienced. Eloise felt hot, liquid, and able to flow in all directions.

Slowly Eloise blinked her eyes. The water flowed back into the lake, steaming, and still softly glowing. Tiny bubbles danced in the pink light under its surface. She was soaked to the bone, dripping, her hair and clothes streaming warm water.

Elaina and Sister Aspertine look shocked, almost frozen, and equally drenched in steamy water. Puddles pooled around them, and little rivulets flowed through the tiny grasses back toward the lake. Both looked aghast, but neither was looking at her.

Eloise glanced down; on the edge of the water, at her feet, lay a huge silver chest, the piece of the statue from the bottom.

*"Why …?"* Sister Aspertine demanded, her voice hoarse with misery. *"Why include me …? I don't want to feel … like that …!"*

Fatigued, Eloise stood dumbfounded, still gasping.

"That was just a taste," Elaina said calmly to Sister Aspertine. "The love of God, when you reach Him, will excel the love of this lake. Don't be afraid. The more you understand love, the deeper that you'll experience it … when you share it with God."

Sister Aspertine stared at her, bewildered.

"You mean … as I felt … from Nate?" Sister Aspertine asked.

"In a sense," Elaina said. "True love permeates all."

Eloise smiled as realization dawned upon Sister Aspertine, but her arms drooped, weary after spellcasting.

"Let's go get the others … all of them," Elaina said, reaching out a hand to support Eloise. "Leave the statue here … our lake will protect it."

"I … felt like I was dancing … while standing still," Eloise said.

"It felt magnificent," Elaina agreed. "Like I was motionless … and the universe was twirling around me."

Mother and daughter embraced, but Sister Aspertine turned away.

*"I … can't be part of spells …!"* Sister Aspertine complained.

Elaina reached over and hugged Sister Aspertine. Then she reached out, grabbed Eloise, and drew her in. All three hugged deeply.

Still dripping, their hair plastered flat, they approached the men in time to see the huge legs lift out of the water. They rushed forward, grabbed the end of the rope behind Alarika, and helped pull. The heavy, dripping legs rose higher as the hewn braces strained, and then Karl and Phil pushed from the other side, titled their log-tripod, and eased the silver legs over the stone lip of the pool. The metal legs tilted onto the grass.

"What happened to you?" Alarika asked, staring at the drenched three once the silver legs stopped rocking.

"We saw the pink light, but we couldn't stop …," Karl said.

"We have the chest, and it's heavy," Eloise said.

"Eloise did it," Sister Aspertine said, fighting to hide her disgust from her voice. "She cast a spell … and the lake gave up the statue's chest."

Sweating and still gasping from their labors, the exhausted companions turned to stare at Eloise.

"I couldn't have done it without mother's wisdom … and Sister Aspertine's faith," Eloise said.

They had no spare clothes, so they lit a fire from the many wood shavings that Roselyn and Karl had cut. Henry coiled and shouldered his rope, and then he and the others went on a quest to find more sections of Osiris while Eloise, Elaina, and Sister Aspertine stayed behind. Once the companions were out of sight, they stripped, wrung out their clothes, and held them close to the fire to dry them.

"Couldn't you dry us with magic?" Sister Aspertine asked Eloise, holding her deep blue habit up before the high flames.

"I'd rather be soaking in hot waters again," Elaina said.

"It's strange," Eloise said. "Usually I'm exhausted after casting a spell that powerful, but I feel … weak, but invigorated."

"You touched true love," Elaina smiled. "Love always gives back more."

An hour later, the girls heard shouted warnings, and Roselyn and Alarika came around a corner, carrying a silver arm. Loose clothes were held up to shield the nakedness of the women, in case the men should follow.

They set down the silver arm beside the hand and legs.

"Buried in tall weeds and thorny vines," Alarika said. "We'd never have found it if not for the voices."

"We found the chest, but it was closer to the garden than to here," Roselyn said. "We think that the statue has to be assembled on the giant empty throne, so we carried it there."

"We'll come when our dresses are dry," Eloise said.

"Don't bother," Roselyn said. "We're all tired. Keep the fire going; Phil got a clue to where another piece might be found, and whether we find it or not, soon we'll need to rest. We can try again in the morning … such as it is."

Roselyn drew out the sword of Hel and hacked into one of the discarded logs. Quickly the godly sword chopped a section free, and Alarika piled it atop the flames.

"That should last until we get back," Alarika nodded, and she and Roselyn walked back to the men.

"We'd better dress," Eloise said, although their clothes were still damp.

When the companions returned, most of them had armloads of fruits from the garden. Phil carried a silver snake.

"It's part of the Crown of Egypt," Alarika explained.

"One less thing to search for tomorrow," Karl said.

"We should save these beams," Henry advised, looking at Karl. "We'll need them to assemble the statue."

Karl nodded. "Nate, Phil; after we eat, scavenge for firewood."

Morning never came, and Eloise was the last to awaken. She frowned at the dim stars and wished for sunlight, and then slowly arose. The others were eating again, and Elaina handed her a huge orange.

Afterwards, they began searching for more sections. The voices seemed to have surrendered to the inevitable. Before they needed to eat again, they found the other silver hand inside a hollow monument, one foot buried in a garden, and the other hanging behind a thick row of coconuts in a tree. The other arm hung on a wall, holding a huge sword, the sword so impressive that no one had noticed the arm. The eyes were imbedded in a wall amid painted decorations, and easily removed, once spotted. A bent rod that looked like a scepter was on display in another temple. The crown itself looked like a display stand, on top of which was a small golden scorpion. They moved all fourteen parts to the garden, which grew around the massive empty throne resting upon the pool.

As Isis once did to the real Osiris, the assembly began. They erected their beams on the platform and lifted the legs to sit on the great silver throne. Their reed rope strained and creaked greatly, but it held. They set the feet in place, and then lowered the legs onto the seat, where it pinned the feet in place. The chest proved hardest, but Alarika showed them methods of adjusting their beams, which slowly lifted the heavy weight. Karl, Phil, Nate, and Alarika finally climbed atop the throne to settle the chest atop the silver legs. The rest of the pieces were easier, and seemed to attach naturally; their seams sealed when pressed together correctly. Once the head was attached, they added the arms, crown, scepter, and snake, and lastly they inserted the eyes.

Finally the statue was complete. The companions moved the beams aside, then stepped back to admire it. The throne and figure of Osiris looked like a single monument.

"What now?" Nate asked.

His question went unanswered. The statue never moved.

"Take a walk," Karl said. "Let's hear what the voices say."

However, the voices had fallen silent. They all quickly returned. Not one voice had spoken to any of them.

*"Assembling the parts of Osiris isn't enough. Saxons can't solve this,"* Eloise quoted, and she looked at Alarika. "You're the only one of us who isn't a Saxon."

Alarika paused, then stepped before the statue of Osiris, raised both hands, and spoke loudly.

*"Hail to thee, Osiris Unneferu,*
*Son of Nut and eldest son of Seb,*
*The Great One who proceedeth from Nut,*
*King in Taa-urit, Prince in Amenta;*
*Lord of Abydos, the Lord of Forces,*
*The most Mighty, Lord of the Atef crown in Suten-hunen,*
*Lord of Power in Taa-urit, Lord of the Mansion,*
*Most-powerful in Tattu, Lord of Administration,*
*and the many festivals in Tattu."*

From the water of the pool sprouted a single lotus flower, and from the flower glowed large images of four children.

"It's the sons of Horus: Imesety, Duamutef, Hapi, and Qubehsenuef, the grandsons of Osiris," Alarika whispered.

Two other figures rose, guards in gleaming armor. One stood on each side of the throne of Osiris, and their fingers glowed like a red-hot iron fresh from a forge. Alarika stepped back, gesturing the others to retreat.

*"Hurtful fingers!"* Alarika cried. *"The attendants of Osiris!"*

The companions all drew back, and Alarika kneeled before the six newcomers. The attendants seemed appeased; each turned to the statue, reached out with one hand, and touched the silver throne. Their fiery touches seared the metal chair, which absorbed their glow, and in the radiance, the silver statue of Osiris flexed and breathed.

"Heed the Oracle of Osiris, the Sleeping God," the voice of the statue boomed. "I know you, and the distant lands from whence you came, which I civilized ages ago." His silver eyes lowered to Alarika. "Arise, my brave and wise daughter; I am the mouth of your god, not Osiris himself."

"I kneel to honor you … as I would honor him," Alarika said, and she bowed deeply, and then rose to her feet.

"The Seer of the Lady of the Druids stands before the true Throne of Osiris in the City of the Gods," the oracle said. "His soul is trapped in the memory box of Anubis, who will not surrender it. The Seer brings light to our darkened land, such as has not brightened our Winter since the glow of the Chariot of Ra failed. The gods enjoy the light, which reminds them of days when their lands were the height of civilization.

"Your accomplishments have earned renown, but not all of the gods favor your presence," the oracle warned. "Hope abandoned them long ago, and your approach restores their misery. Yet the Sleeping God allows you to continue. The Celestial Path from my gate now leads to the next city. However, I can return you to Egypt, if you wish. You may end your journey now … and spare your lives. Ask, and I shall comply."

Karl started to speak, but Alarika gestured, and he fell silent, but glared at her warningly.

"Oracle of Osiris, we thank you, and are humbled by your offer," Alarika said. "Before the City of Nut, greatly I desired that which you offer, but no more. The troubles of Egypt, since your Winter began, had hardened my heart, and made me unworthy to join the gods. Now I see through the eyes of others … and regret the weighty darkness which has filled my Ka and Ba. I would see my friends to their goal 'ere I submit to the trial of Thoth."

"Anubis now leads the gods," the oracle said. "When the light of Ra failed, Osiris returned to the peace of Nephthys. But what of your companions? Would they proceed … or return to the lands of the living?"

"They won't surrender their friend," Alarika said.

"Loyalty delights Osiris," the oracle said. "The Sleeping One grants you continuance."

"Great Oracle, could I ask a question?" Karl asked.

The silver statue nodded.

"Is there any way your Celestial Path can lead us straight to the City of the Gods?" Karl asked. "Your tests are challenging, but we're only here to rescue a friend."

"The gods chose your path, not their oracle," the statue said. "Only Nephthys could grant this request; thus is the City of the Dead denied to you."

"We thank you, Oracle of Osiris," Eloise spoke up.

The oracle nodded, then resumed its original position, ceased all movement, and became a silver statue again. The images of the sons of Horus vanished, and the guards removed their red-glowing fingers from the throne. As the companions watched, the guards both faded into white smoke and blew away.

The companions looked at each other … and Henry smiled.

"Welcome to our company, Companion Alarika," Henry said.

## Chapter 8

## The City of Horus

# HENRY

On the entry platform, they rested and ate before the twin golden statues, then shouldered their refilled food packs and bota bags before beginning their next trek. The sparkly, silver road from the sole gate now flowed in a different direction, leading farther up into the starry blackness.

Atop the silvery sparkles they walked for an hour, saying nothing, single-file, staying far from either edge of their narrow road. Far below, the desert looked flat and peaceful, but Henry doubted if even walking on Shu would help if he slipped and fell miles to his death.

*Not that it would matter …*

Nate experimented, floating upwards, above the path, as they had in the City of Nut, but Karl ordered him back down and to *'stop horsing around'*. Henry thought this good advice.

They walked skyway toward a shining gleam that grew from one of the twinkling stars. Slowly it manifested into a great shape, that of a silvery bust, the head and shoulders of a great man … wearing a golden pharaoh's crown … like a helmet … surrounding the silver face of a hawk.

"Horus," Alarika said.

"The son of Osiris and Isis …?" Elaina asked.

"You learn well," Alarika said.

"This could be trouble," Karl said. "Horus was their god of …"

"… is our god of …!" Alarika corrected him.

"Horus is a warrior-god," Karl nodded respectfully, and Alarika subsided.

"An Egyptian Thor," Roselyn said. "This could work in our favor. Of all Odin's children, Thor is the Son of Earth, who is his mother, and he has the most in common with humans."

"We don't know how closely those comparisons run …or how much we can trust them," Eloise said.

"There's no point arguing," Karl said. "Alarika, we know that Horus fought Set. Is there anything else that we should know?"

Alarika swallowed hard.

"Horus has many names: Avenger, the Eternal One, Horus of the Two Horizons, and …," Alarika hesitated. "Horus, the Prince of the City … of Blindness."

*"Blindness …?!?"* half of the companions shouted.

"Upon his brow Horus wears the red diadem of the South and the blue diadem of the North," Alarika said. "He is the master of both, the look-out of Ra's ship, and at his sides stand Thoth and Maat. So great are his deeds that his presence illuminates even the Duat, shining into their sepulchers, and dark souls cower before him.

"Invisibly, Horus may walk unseen when he chooses, and not even a god may be aware of him. With his fingers, Horus casts bolts of death. Before Horus, all adversaries are overthrown and slaughtered.

"You know that Horus, when he was young, struck off the head of his mother, Isis. You know also that Isis sought Horus to help her search for Osiris' spirit, upon the boat of papyrus that she made, which was feared by all crocodiles. In their first combat, Horus met Set, triumphed over evil, and made Set his prisoner. When Set escaped, using lies, Horus hunted him, and again they fought, twice to a standstill, and then so frightfully that Set fell, fled from Horus, and never again came to Egypt. Thus was evil banished from our lands …"

"Until the Winter of your gods began …," Roselyn interrupted, but Karl silenced her with an angry hiss.

"Horus also wears armor invulnerable to evil, and often carries the Amsu-staff, the Staff of Pharaohs, and Horus casts lightning from his fingers …"

*"Lightning …?"* Roselyn scowled.

"Look, if you don't …!" Alarika began.

"Don't argue!" Karl said. "That's another similarity; Thor is the Thunderer, the God of Lightning …"

"Let's just get there," Roselyn said. "I can't bear another similarity."

As they approached the prodigious city, shaped like the head of Horus, they saw that his sharp beak crowned a great gate, and the features of his hawk's face were formed of parts of tall monuments. As their road ended upon a bronze platform, they stared into a city seemingly constructed entirely of metal, whose every surface gleamed as if freshly polished.

As they stepped onto the solid bronze platform, two growling voices greeted them in unison.

*"Welcome, Guests of Horus!"*

From out of the shadows came two large, slim, black and tan dogs. Their ears were sharp and pert, and canine heads stared with looks of undisguised intelligence.

Henry smiled; *he'd always liked dogs.*

"The hounds of Horus!" Alarika exclaimed.

"We comprise that honored title," one of the dogs said, speaking clearly. "For centuries before mortals walked we have served our master."

"We are sent to welcome you," the other dog said.

"Horus knows that we're here …?" Karl asked.

"Of course," said a dog. "Horus delights in your coming, for he detests the darkness of Winter."

"We'll do all we can," Karl said. "Gladly … and if you could send us straight to him …"

"That we can't do," said a dog. "The son of Osiris and Isis can't offend the youngest daughter of Geb and Nut, Nephthys, nor deny the right of her offspring …"

"Anubis?" Karl asked.

"The jackal-god," the dog said. "We speak no evil of Anubis, for jackals are canines, close cousins of ours."

"Anubis welcomes you not," the other dog said. "Anubis was born in the house of Nephthys, and is the Master of Darkness, which holds no secrets from him."

"Anubis owns the memory box which traps our friend," Karl said.

"All the gods know that," a dog said.

"Well, since Horus wishes us to succeed, may we pass your city without enduring your test?" Karl asked.

"All mortals must prove their worth to pass the City of Horus," a dog said. "However, since Horus does wish you well, he has made your test simple."

"What is our test?" Karl asked.

"Destroy Set," a dog said.

*"Set is a god!"* Alarika exclaimed. "Mortals can't kill a god, and even if we could, even Horus didn't kill Set; he defeated him, and Set fled."

"None knows where the true Set hides," the dog said. "The Set we speak of is not the god, but one of his great evils, a symbol of Set, with whom Set colluded to capture and steal Osiris."

"A serpent," Alarika said.

"A vast serpent … with powers of its own," a dog said. "Defeat it, kill it, or drive it away, and you'll have proven to Horus that you're worthy of his approval."

"This shall prove your warrior's courage, the Badge of Horus, with which you may depart in honor," the dog said.

"Where's this serpent?" Karl asked.

"Inside the city … somewhere," said the dog. "You won't need to hunt him …"

"We'll be hunted," Karl translated.

"We will attend you, but we'll be of little use," the dog said. "We can't assist you … or we would."

"Can you tell us what *'powers of its own'* this serpent has?" Karl asked.

"That would be an assistance," the dog said.

"We can guess," Alarika said. "Horus fights with lightning and walks with invisibility … one or both."

"You're a wise woman," the dog said.

"We'd best think up a plan of attack before we enter your city," Karl said.

"You're a wise man," the other dog said.

"The sword of Hel can slay any serpent," Roselyn said.

"But you have to be able to see it, and not be struck by lightning," Karl said.

“Height,” Nate said. “We can fly up … see what we can.”

“We don’t know how big the serpent is … how high it can reach,” Karl said.

“I could dance, but I don’t know what to ask,” Elaina offered.

Karl nodded, then addressed his squires.

“Nate, be careful,” Karl said. “Phil, keep close … don’t let him out of your sight. Stay near something, a building or monument, and then come back.”

Nate grinned, then stepped into the air, and kept walking. Phil frowned, but he followed right behind his brother. They arose, floating close to the wide golden shaft that formed the inside rim of the helmet of Horus, and then they slipped out of sight.

“Roselyn, guard one side, and watch for anything,” Karl said. “Alarika, watch the other side. I’ll take center. Henry, you watch behind. Shout if you see or hear anything … or if you suddenly see nothing; I don’t like all this talk of blindness.”

“What can we do?” Eloise asked.

“You and Sister Aspertine aid Elaina,” Karl said. “Elaina, I don’t know what to ask, but any information is better than none …”

Elaina nodded, and slipped off her shoes. Eloise and Sister Aspertine looked at each other, then started clapping a simple rhythm. Elaina matched their rhythm with her first step, and then began to dance.

Henry drew his khopesh and held it ready. He wasn’t a fighter, and everyone knew it, although his training sessions with Roselyn had taught him to think like one. He was too old to be a great fighter, almost as old as Elaina, a man whose strength had been spent in years fighting the sea. He’d survived mostly by luck which, like all sailors, he knew to take seriously. Yet, with each glance, he watched Elaina dance with less joy than he'd previously felt; luck eventually runs out, and Henry felt they'd already enjoyed an abundance of luck. So far, their luck had been purchased by the lives of Thorkel, Dennel, and Samuel. If their luck ran out again, Henry knew that he'd be expected to pay its fee … like his fellows had done.

Elaina danced with her usual artistry and abandon, demonstrating her perfect physique and coordination, such that even the dogs of Horus sat and raptly watched. Henry recalled her youth, when she'd been the beautiful baroness, envied by every maiden as she'd cradled her infant Eloise to her breast. Every man in the barony had loved her. Yet those days were long ago. Eric Bjornson and King Svenson Two-Sword had stolen her from England … the brightest star that had ever graced their land. Henry gripped his khopesh tightly; if he was to die, then he'd be glad to give his last breath defending her.

Suddenly, Elaina fell … hard … and screamed. Everyone started to run to her, but Karl shouted for them not to surrender their posts. Eloise and Sister Aspertine were already holding Elaina, trying to lift her.

"I'm … alright," Elaina gasped. "I … felt it … evil … desiring only … murder …!"

Nate and Phil came suddenly floating down, both with frantic expressions.

"Did you see it?" Karl asked.

"Couldn't miss it," Nate said.

"It's huge," Phil said. "It could wrap around Castle Bristlen and crush it."

"Its body could barely squeeze through the castle gate," Nate said. "It's pale white, and as long as the trail to Demril."

"It has scales like … metal shields … and a hood like a tent," Phil said. "Its mouth could swallow all of us … and that's not the worst …!"

The companions fell silent, expectant …

"It sparks … lightning," Nate said. "Bolts flash between it and nearby surfaces."

"If we get struck …!" Phil began.

"How close …?" Karl asked.

"It can't get here," Nate said. "Not without sliding over the tall spikes that fence it in."

"Pointed pillars, like a cage," Phil said. "It seems to be trapped inside it."

"That cage is bigger than the whole rest of the city," Nate said. "It's just a huge, open area … no barriers, nothing to hide behind."

"We fight exposed …?" Karl frowned.

"We can't fight such a monster!" Elaina gasped. "It's … pure hate …!"

"Horus wouldn't give us an impossible challenge," Alarika said.

"If we approach it, we'll get struck by lightning," Phil said.

"We can't defeat it by staying away," Nate said.

"Could we strike … fast enough … to kill it … before it kills us?" Karl asked.

Phil shook his head.

"Roselyn might, but I …!" Nate spread his hands helplessly.

"Then I will …!" Roselyn said.

"You'd need three swords of Hel to sever its head," Phil said.

"Can a Valkyrie endure a bolt of lightning …?" Karl asked Roselyn, but she only frowned.

Karl turned to the dogs, who sat watching them.

"You said that we didn't have to kill it, but how could we drive it away …?" Karl asked.

"That's for you to decide," one of the dogs said.

"Could you give us … good advice?" Eloise asked.

The dogs exchanged glances, and both gave very human shrugs.

"Take your time," the first dog said. "Consider all options."

"Plan well," the second dog said. "Even the reflection of Set kills."

At Nate's suggestion, the companions slipped through the thick maze of monuments to Horus. They found the tall metal pillars, of gold, black iron, steel, silver, and other metals, reaching to the sky.

Beyond the spikes lay a horror that Henry had never imagined. Here was a monster the like of which he'd expected since arriving; eyes as big as wagon-wheels, a mouth like a tunnel, and a hood like a ship's sail. When it sensed them and reared. It bared fangs like spears, dripping with glutinous poison. Its head rose above them like a castle tower, glaring down. Never before had Henry seen anything so terrifying, so ultimately formidable.

*How could they kill that …?*

With the dogs walking beside them, they slunk back toward the gate. There they sat, silent, just staring at each other. Henry tried to break the silence, but horror consumed his thoughts.

Hours later, Elaina and Sister Aspertine started passing out food and bota bags, and still no one spoke. Elaina bowed to the dogs.

"I fear we have only vegetables and breads, but you're welcome to some …," she offered.

The dogs seemed amused.

"We thank you for your generosity," one dog said. "We have duck, pheasant, goat, ox, and mutton, if you'd care …"

"Please …!" Nate interrupted. "I can't remember my last taste of red meat."

"Your kind offer is most appreciated," the other dog said. "Horus delights in kindness."

"I thought Horus was a warrior," Sister Aspertine said.

"Horus is the Warrior, the Mighty, and the Undefeated," the first dog said. "Kindness is essential to warriors; it's the one quality that separates warriors from killers."

"Kindness is the heart of Osiris, the father of Horus," the other dog said. "Kindness is the purpose of civilization; without kindness, strength has no greater purpose, no need to create rather than to destroy."

"The gods of Egypt must be great, if such goals they emulate," Elaina said.

"We speak no evil of any gods," a dog said. "Yet our gods are older and wiser than yours; they recognize their imperfections. Set is a god of Egypt, no less than his brother Osiris. Yet Set is an oasis of maliciousness, the poisoned flood of our gods. Other pantheons deny the evil among them, or claim perfection which their actions deny."

"Evil flows from imperfect hearts," a dog said. "The Ha, the Ka, the Ba, and the Ib know this, and are bound to the lightness of the Ren or the darkness of the Sheut."

"Even for an immortal god, to change the heart is no small effort, yet it is the greatest triumph of any warrior," a dog said.

"Mortals are blameless for the heart with which they were born," the other dog said. "It is by the heart with which they die that all are judged."

"And only truth reveals a heart," Alarika said. "That's why Thoth tests the heart, and weighs it against the Feather of Truth."

"No secrets hide from the Feather of Truth," a dog said.

"Then prove your civilized ways," Karl said. "Share with us your truth."

"What truth?" a dog asked.

"The truth …!" Karl gritted his teeth to keep from shouting. "We don't have the power to slay Set … or that giant token of him. It must have a … weakness … a secret …!"

"To conquer a weakness is to be the greater strength," a dog said.

"But we're not …!" Karl said. "We'd all have to be Reginleifs, and …!"

"That's it, isn't it?" Roselyn said, looking at the dogs. "That's what Horus wants …?"

"Great is the power of secrets," a dog said.

"What …?" Karl demanded.

"The Fighting Secrets of the Valkyrie," Roselyn said. "That's why Horus chose a giant serpent … which Horus himself could endow with lightning. Only a troop of Valkyrie could defeat it."

"Horus respects the younger gods, but he also envies them," a dog said. "Over a thousand years ago, when our gods weakened, our protections over our people failed. The legions of Jupiter invaded Egypt, and slew our staunchest believers. Weakly flows the faith of followers whose deities are condemned to Winter. Each arrival is a momentous occasion, taking precedence over all else. Yet a true warrior never fails in hope … or preparation."

"Horus is indeed a warrior," Roselyn said. "If I share this, will he aid us against Anubis?"

"Horus and Anubis are brothers," a dog said. "Would you turn against your sister … for the secrets of a stranger?"

"If I share the Fighting Secrets of the Valkyrie, how do I know that Horus won't use them against us?" Roselyn asked.

*"Roselyn …!"* Eloise scolded. *"We're in his city …!"*

"Any warrior would ask that … and understand," a dog said to Eloise.

"You must trust Horus … and his desire for Spring," a dog said to Roselyn.

"Spring …?" Karl asked.

"The people of Osiris once enslaved the people of Yahweh," a dog said. "In his youth, Osiris traveled to civilize distant lands … and found mortals of great faith, but whose god he couldn't find. Our gods knew not their elder faith, but they see it now, rising again, driving out the gods of Yggdrasil and Elysia. Never before has any pantheon survived its Winter … but if it's possible, then Horus will fight any enemy to be reborn."

*"Christ!"* Sister Aspertine exclaimed. *"You mean Christianity!"*

"For this we were sent to Yggdrasil," Eloise said. "The Lady of the Druids sent us to the afterlife-lands of the Norse gods … to summon Her there … that by mingling their wisdom She might someday escape Her Winter."

"Horus would end our Winter," a dog said.

"The Fighting Secrets of the Valkyrie are … not weapons," Roselyn said. "They're a philosophy … for attaining victory … at any cost."

"Small wonder why the champion of our gods desires them," a dog said.

"Give me a moment," Roselyn said, turning away. "Let me think …!"

Roselyn walked away, facing the edge of the bronze platform, at the gate, from which the Celestial Path still sparkled and descended back to the City of Osiris. Henry felt relieved; Roselyn was stubborn, but not stupid: *she'd share her secrets.* Roselyn wanted to rejoin her Valkyrie sisters, and she might violate her oath to them if she revealed their secrets. Yet, if she kept her secrets, then they'd all die, and she'd never rejoin her sisters.

Horus had baited this trap well, far better than the other gods, for he'd profit from their victory. Yet Henry didn't care; he'd been afraid that their only hope would be to decoy the great serpent with bait … *and as the only real expendable person in the party, he knew whom they'd choose to be the bait.*

Karl started to rise, but Henry grabbed his arm, and when Karl looked surprised, Henry shook his head.

"Trust a man twice your years," Henry whispered to Karl. "Roselyn must decide this alone."

Although he frowned, Karl nodded and sat back down.

An hour later, Roselyn returned.

"The Fighting Secrets of the Valkyrie don't guarantee survival," Roselyn warned, her tone hard and blunt.

"We are the ears of Horus," the dogs said in unison.

"Sacrifice; that's the Fighting Secret of the Valkyrie," Roselyn said. "War isn't about gain. You can gain forever after your opponents lie dead. War is about your opponent's loss, which must be complete and eternally-irreversible. True victory removes even the smallest morsel of hope from your enemies."

Roselyn's eyes shined, her teeth gritted, and she glared like death.

"Winning is all that matters," Roselyn said. "Victory is everything, your only goal. Your condition after the battle is equally meaningless. Better that both sides die than your enemy survives to force a second war. Cast aside all conditions that could lessen your chance of ultimate victory … even if those conditions would save your life … or the lives of those you love. If you can't sacrifice all that you love for victory, then your chances of victory are diminished."

Roselyn paused for a breath.

"Warriors must know evil," Roselyn said. "Evil has no desires, no cares. Evil seeks only destruction. Loki isn't evil. Set isn't evil. Only Black Surt, who would burn down all the nine realms and cast them into ruin … even his own … that's evil. Evil destroys for the pure pleasure of destruction. And, when you face true evil, then you must fight with no greater purpose than evil … or evil will turn your purpose against you."

"Sacrifice is our most-powerful weapon," Roselyn said. "True evil can't sacrifice itself without defeat. Most evils, lesser evils, won't sacrifice themselves at all. Evil must defeat its enemies and survive.

"But we, the Valkyrie, we can sacrifice. Good seeks to defeat its enemies at any cost, and death is acceptable, if by our sacrifice others may survive. So we can take chances that evils can't, and brave risks that evils wouldn't dare, because our only goal is evil's death. Even if all the Valkyrie sacrifice themselves, survival isn't our goal. If our sacrifice can weaken our foe to where the surviving gods and the einherjar are assured victory, then the Valkyrie win … even in death."

"With this mentality, Valkyrie always win," Roselyn said. "We brave what others can't. We risk what others won't. We push harder for victory than our opponents. We stop at nothing but complete victory."

Roselyn surveyed the eyes of her listeners, even pausing on Henry, who took in each word as carefully as he could … fearing that his heart would give out.

"Valkyrie don't sacrifice lightly," Roselyn continued. "To fight like a Valkyrie, you must be willing to sacrifice yourself to save one of your sisters, but only if your sacrifice insures overall victory; otherwise, you save yourself and keep fighting … even if it means watching her die. She's sworn to do the same to you. Valkyrie take these oaths very seriously.

"To fight like a Valkyrie, you must become True Terror, and force the hesitation of fear into your enemies' eyes. Become Death, and charge forth to claim those whose lives are rightfully yours. Fear nothing; no pain is too great if you drag all of your enemies with you into oblivion.

"To fight like a Valkyrie, you must starve for glory, be ravenous for it, and suck in every taste and smell of glory for yourself alone, and thereby deny even the slightest hint of glory to any enemy, especially the glory of killing you," Roselyn said. "Even life is secondary to honor, for life can end, but honor lives eternally. Honor supersedes life. Rota swears that, from the ashes of the old, all of exceptional honor are reborn in each new world. As all worlds are doomed to eventually fall, and others rise in their place, honor alone grants immortality. The greater the glory, the greater the honor, and no honor is greater than final and indisputable victory … the total destruction of your foes.

"An enemy is dead only when they can never again attack you, not after their hearts have stopped beating," Roselyn said. "To fight like a Valkyrie, you fight until each enemy is fully dead. Once dead, ignore them and attack elsewhere; slay the badly-wounded only after the battle is won, or when you're too wounded to continue fighting.

"Don't love killing," Roselyn said. "Valkyrie never pause to relish a kill while any enemies stand. The best time to attack another enemy is when your blade has just penetrated their comrades' heart. Killing is an art. The Valkyrie are artists of victory."

"In life or death, Valkyrie must win," Roselyn said. "When your limbs tire, when the effort to strike another blow threatens to tear your muscles from your bones, then that's what Valkyrie do: we tear our flesh from our bones. We never stop. We never give up. While thoughts exist, and fury burns in our hearts, we push our bodies to any requirement, no matter the pain, no matter the resistance.

"Becoming a Valkyrie requires training that only immortals can endure," Roselyn said. "None learn the lessons of death except by death. But, when you have an undefeatable enemy, a foe that you can't beat … then each of you must willingly sacrifice everything you have … everything that you are … everything that you love … and, most importantly, sacrifice all of your fears … for victory."

"Aren't …?" Nate began, but he swallowed hard and fell silent.

"Ask," Roselyn commanded him.

"What … what if victory … is impossible?" Nate asked.

"Does that matter?" Roselyn asked. "If victory is possible, and you give it everything that you have, all your strength and determination, all your wits and dedication, solely to attain victory at any cost … then you win. If victory is impossible, and you give equal share … then you did all you could, and honor shall still be won."

"What about timing … and strategy?" Karl asked. "Sometimes victory can only be won by tactics, not by marching headlong into death."

Roselyn snickered.

"Tactics and leadership are the crowning arts of warfare," Roselyn grinned. "Until you've celebrated your 5,000th battle, no einherjar cares what your opinions are. Luckily, we don't need complexity; giant snakes don't use subterfuge. I might be able to take out its eyes, but if I'm struck … Valkyrie aren't invulnerable to lightning … then someone will have to back me up … with possibly a second. We could all strike at once, but what if we're all struck? We can't guarantee that we'll win today, but unless the lightning strikes all of us simultaneously, some of us should score snakeflesh. If I fall, then one of you must take and use Hel's sword … it's got the best hope of killing … after you've struck with your own. Eyes are usually a weak point, and its brain is right behind its eyes, but attacking its eyes brings you closest to its fangs, and those looked poisoned.

"There are two likely diversions we could use: visual and rear. A visual attack might distract it, and give us some control over which direction it's facing, but again, its eyes are near its fangs. A rear attack is more-likely to be successful, but only to divert its attention, and send it in an unpredictable direction. Unpredictability is a threat to victory; a good plan controls your enemy's movements, so we'll need a simple controlling advance with multiple side-assaults, backups, and a deception. Afterwards, simple attacks should provide the best chance of victory."

Henry stared at Roselyn blankly, then looked at the others companions' faces; their confused expressions matched his.

*"Simple …?"* Eloise asked.

"By Elvidner standards, yes," Roselyn chuckled.

"Roselyn, you decide strategy," Karl said.

"First, you talk," Roselyn said. "Hearing that speech, even as many times as I have, can only help a little. It has to be understood and accepted; instinctive and automatic."

Roselyn turned to the dogs.

"Was that enough for Horus?" she asked.

Both dogs stood, on all fours, and faced Roselyn. As one, they lowered their heads in a deep and respectful bow.

"Horus is pleased … and honors your wisdom," they said in unison.

"Do we still have to fight the snake?" Karl asked.

"Horus would be honored if you'd demonstrate your abilities," the dog said. "Words may not impart your full meaning."

"You'll be rewarded for victory," the other dog said. "Horus can't openly defy the other gods for mortals, but he can gift you greatly before you leave."

"Gifts to aid in your journey," the first dog said.

"We accept … since we have no choice," Karl said.

"Begin your discussion," said the other dog. "I will summon food."

Dinner was a feast, mostly of rich, hot mutton and swine, cooked to perfection and layered with Egyptian spices. They discussed every fighting secret of the Valkyrie, and sidetracked onto similar topics, sometimes repeating conversations they had in the desert while searching for the army of thieves.

"The challenges of the mind are far different than the challenges of the body," Roselyn said. "Both must be mastered in every fight. The challenges of the mind are to be aware only of your opponents, to wash all other thoughts out of your mind. Watch his weapons, staying aware of his every move. Watch his body as he swings and anticipate where each blow will land. Watch out for fakes and practiced attack-combinations, which may be repeated. If you see a comrade fall, note how they were killed, so that you don't succumb to the same attack. Never stare at a target. Know the range and threat of your opponent's weapons, and stay mindful of hidden dangers. Know your terrain."

"The challenges of the body are; breathe in through your nose, out through your mouth, and fill the deepest bottoms of your lungs. Tighten your whole body for rapid movement, but don't tense up or you'll stiffen, making your movements rigid. Shift your defense to anticipate your opponent's attacks, not your opponent himself. Strike whenever possible. Move your feet in wide, rapid successions to establish and maintain optimum range. Stay balanced, always ready to leap forward or back. Defend to equal your opponent's weapons …"

"But … we're not facing an enemy with weapons," Nate said.

"Fangs are weapons," Roselyn said to him. "Crushing weight is a weapon. You can't equal the Valkyrie without repeated deaths, but you can begin to think like us, which would vastly improve your skills."

They discussed these challenges throughout dinner, and after dinner, ranging into other areas.

"Focus overrides distraction," Roselyn said. "The punishment of the body is the victory of the mind; if you can't push your body to its limits, then you'll never expand those limits."

Discussion lasted long, and even the dogs joined in … until heads were nodding, and then Roselyn ordered them all to sleep … to gain the rest that they'd need.

Henry hated looking at their enemy; monstrous, towering, and hissing. The colossal cobra slithered slowly, its massive coils undulating over the smooth, shallow bowl of its monstrous cage. At random intervals, from its countless wide, smooth snake-scales, a sudden glow erupted, and then a yellow blast exploded, arcing across the cage with a concussion of thunder. The floor or metal bar where the bolt struck sizzled, sparked, and smoked.

Roselyn gestured the companions close to her.

"Normally I'd say to maintain a sturdy, mobile defense, but our only defense against lightning is speed; attack fast and hard before you're struck," Roselyn said. "Charge in without fear. Keep your eyes on its fangs, and better to let it strike your body standing, and knock you back, than to fall and get crushed beneath its coils. Stay fast, loose, and agile, and flee with equal speed when your task is done.

"Take your positions and wait for my signal."

Roselyn nodded to them, and Nate and Phil rose, floating into the air.

Henry headed off, as instructed, circling widely. He didn't like Roselyn's plan; he'd be the first to risk his life, but he had no choice. Either they'd defeat the lightning-cobra … or they'd fall into the Duat … and from their height, that'd be a long fall.

Henry kept his khopesh tight in one hand, a borrowed spear in his other. He carefully peeked to make sure that the eyes of the serpent weren't facing him, and then he ran forward to hide behind the next monument. There seemed to be no end of monuments; silver statues of serpents, some locked in battle with a golden Horus, and others just tall walls and arches covered in hieroglyphs, as if their writing had been cast upon their metal surfaces. Sweat ran down his face as thunder echoed about him; the *boom!* and *crackle!* of each bolt filled his ears. The farther that he got around to the back of the snake, the safer his job would be. However, he had to be ready to strike … when the signal came, no matter the danger.

*Bam! Bam! Bam!*

Henry had spied his next hiding place before the first signal came, but his time for anxiety was over. Three hits; *he had to attack now.*

Henry clenched his teeth and ran toward the tall row of spikes. He'd long given up wondering why he was doing this; his duty was clear. He ran behind the nearest spike, hearing a loud hiss, and seeing the cobra's eyes dart as it twisted its huge, hooded head in every direction, tightening its coils. Their eyes met, and the huge mouth opened and lowered toward him, malevolently hissing, almost spitting its poison. Henry tried to hide behind the wide metal spike, which wasn't nearly wide enough. Then a flash blinded him, followed by a shower of white sparks falling all over him, and a deafening thunderclap. Henry's skin tingled, and he feared that he'd breathed his last, when he heard the second signal.

*Bam! Bam!*

Hel's sword-flat hammered against a metal surface, clanging loudly. The huge cobra-head slammed into the metal spikes just above Henry, and its gaping mouth snapped, but its vast bulk couldn't get through the narrow gap. Then Henry heard voices shouting; Roselyn, Alarika, and Karl were shouting loudly. Henry prayed, and then he heard the angry hiss move away; *they were distracting it from him!*

Even the vastness of its cage couldn't enclose the length of Horus' electrical cobra. Yet the head moved with startling speed, darting forward to strike at the others. Henry had only seconds; *he had to go now!*

Still tingling, every hair on end, Henry dropped his khopesh and ran out between the tall spikes. The massive coils of the serpent flexed and slid overtop each other as its head struck the far edge of its pen, against the spikes behind which hid Karl, Roselyn, and Alarika. Each coil was wider than several ships that he'd sailed.

The nearest coil was moving away. He ran straight at it, and then he heard another thunderclap, of a distant lightning bolt, arcing from the snake … *Henry hoped that none of his friends had gotten fried!*

His boots slapping the metal floor, Henry ran forward, inside its pen, his spear gripped in both hands. He raised it and rushed at the wall of living snake taller than he, looking for a gap in the shield-sized scales, which were too close already, and threatening to crush him. As Roselyn had predicted, no gap appeared, so he followed his instructions: where the giant muscles flexed, he spied a ripple of rising scales, and ran to stab upstream of the sliding wall. Targeting a single spot was impossible, as the massive coils slid so fast, but Henry couldn't wait for a bolt to strike him; Henry jumped and stabbed, and his sharp speartip struck a smooth scale, scraped along its edge, and slipped into a gap. Snakeflesh met the point, and Henry stabbed with all his might, suddenly showered in spewing cobra-blood.

The coil struck like a giant's hammer, smashing into him, flinging Henry away. Henry flew through the air, helpless, and fell rolling, finally sliding to an agonized stop. A huge coil hammered the ground right behind him, bouncing him upon the metal floor, and shaking the spear-shaft still stabbing out from between its giant scales. The lightning-cobra was thrashing, violently writhing, venomously hissing its fury and outrage. The giant head turned to face him, glaring eyes locking upon him, its hood spread to its widest. Then the head was flying at him, mouth gaping, long fangs gleaming.

Henry jumped to stand, but fell back; his leg wasn't working. *This wasn't part of the plan!* He glanced to see his leg, twisted and bent, not at his knee. The vast jaws shot toward him like a boulder from a trebuchet; *the approaching maw of Death.*

*I knew that this was going to happen!*

*I knew that I'd die … be sacrificed like my fellows …!*

Suddenly flames burst all around him. Henry screamed, engulfed by fire. He saw the tall flames rise, covering him. *Had he been struck by lightning?*

The murderous head swooped aside, avoiding the flames. Henry gasped to realize: *he wasn't burning!*

*Eloise! These were Eloise's flames!*

His consuming pain screamed from his broken leg, not the fire. Henry rolled, gritting his teeth, and trying to ignore his useless limb. Onto his chest Henry flopped, and then he began to crawl, clawing at the smooth metal, dragging himself inch-by-inch from the thrashing coils hammering the floor behind him. He could still get crushed, and the safety of the tall spikes that walled the snake's cage seemed a mile away.

The long scream startled him, and Henry looked to see Elaina dancing, her pale arms waving wildly. The third signal must've sounded … and he'd missed it. They were distracting the snake again, controlling it. Elaina possessed timing and coordination excelling his; he'd been the first distraction, and the most risky. He needed to disorient their enemy with pain, to draw its head toward the back of its cage, and now Elaina could draw it forward, closer to those who'd attack it directly. Elaina had to cut her encounter far closer than he, for they needed the snake to strike at her just as she jumped outside its cage. However, as Henry continued to crawl, the cobra's attention seemed too wrapped in attacking its enemy …

Thunder exploded, deafening Henry, and the crackle and sizzling sounds near him overwhelmed even the cobra's horrible, enraged hisses. Henry was blinded by intense white, the metal ground beneath him stung with every touch, and his beard smoked; *lightning had struck him!*

Henry collapsed, unable to crawl.

The pale coils of the snake tumbled closer, an avalanche rolling to crush him, but the closest coil suddenly lifted and smashed into the spikes that encaged it, just over Henry's head. Henry was amazed to see how close it really was, but when he tried to pull himself toward safety, the pain staggered; *his body was ruined.*

The hooded head shot towards Elaina, and through Eloise's illusion of fire, Henry's view of Elaina became lost behind the massive body, which moved startlingly fast.

Henry fretted; *Elaina was too beautiful to die in the belly of a snake!* He heard its head crash into the tall spikes.

*Had Elaina escaped …?*

A cloaked figure appeared, sliding out between the spikes, not far from the snake's head. Behind it, Sister Aspertine gave the figure one last push, and then she turned and ran for safety, back behind the spikes, having exposed herself for only a second, but far too long for one unaccustomed to courage.

The lightning-cobra hissed and dove upon the cloaked figure, striking with its long, spear-like fangs, biting deep and hard.

No scream came; the cloaked figure was one of the many golden statues of Horus … hidden inside Elaina's cloak.

Roselyn's battle-cry screamed, and she, Karl, and Alarika leapt into view. At the same instant, Nate and Phil dropped out of the sky. All converged on the massive head, aiming at its eyes. Thunder boomed and lightning flashed, but none heeded it; they attacked as one, all swords stabbing at its most-vulnerable targets. The snake had three attacks: its crushing coils, its deadly fangs, and its lightning. No strategy could defy the massive coils save confusion, and no tricks could deflect lightning. Yet its fangs, its surest weapon, lay driven through a thick cloak covering a metal statue, which filled its mouth. Its deadliest threat entangled, all who could charged forward, for if one succeeded, they'd all win.

The lightning-cobra thrashed more wildly than ever, such that Henry was certain that he'd be crushed. Again he tried to crawl to safety, but he couldn't; his muscles wouldn't obey.

Dimly, Henry heard a cry of triumph, and then he heard no more.

The sea confused him. Above, white clouds and a clear sky shined blue and bright … from the glorious sun that he hadn't seen since he'd last sailed the Nile River from Giza. Everything looked calm, peaceful, and perfect. Below him, the sea raged, deep swells and giant breakers, dark green under heavy shadows, spattered as rain fell heavily. Above, not a single gray cloud marred the perfect, sunny day. Beneath, a tempest stormed.

A rhythmic whisper, soft and gentle, permeated his confusion.

*"Dearest Lady, Goddess divine*
*Restore with all the power thine*
*Bright your healing powers shine*
*Flesh now mend, wounds bind."*

Eloise's voice sang, a melody flowing through him. Pain, anguish, and suffering washed away. Sleep wafted like a fog, seeping into his very core, warmed by an immense fire that seemed to be burning inside him. Henry yawned and stretched … like he was waking up after a long, deep sleep.

He felt strangely hungry.

A soft hiss, not like the angry hiss of a snake, met his ears, as if someone were trying to attract attention.

"Henry!" Elaina exclaimed.

Eloise's song ended, and Henry opened his eyes. Eloise hovered over him, kneeling by his side, her arms wide, while Sister Aspertine knelt on his other side, her hands folded in prayer. Henry hesitated, confused.

*Hadn't he died …?*

"Thank God!" Sister Aspertine exclaimed.

Eloise flashed a glare at her, but the nun didn't notice.

"Wha … what happened …?" Henry breathed.

"We thought you were dead," Elaina said, and other faces swam into view.

"Henry!" Karl's voice rang out. "You're back!"

"Eloise has been casting healing spells on you for days," Elaina said.

*"Days ...?"* Henry asked.

"Five days ... or at least, we've slept five times," Karl said.

"I dreamed ... of the sun," Henry said.

"I wish that would come true," Karl said. "Can you sit up?"

"Slowly!" Eloise ordered Henry. "The power of the Lady flows weakly in these lands."

"Everyone ... safe?" Henry asked.

"I'm alive," Nate said, holding up a heavily bandaged arm.

"Nate and Alarika were also hit by bolts, but not as badly as you," Elaina said. "They're healing; it's you we were worried about."

Henry struggled, feeling strangely weak, and hands reached from all around to lift and steady him. He sat up, and lifted his hand to his dizzy head. His other arm was bandaged with thin white wrappings, the same kind that Nate wore, and his leg was bandaged with a splint made of six golden rods. A bota bag was forced into his hands, and Henry drank greedily of the Water of Life, realizing that his throat was parched.

"How do you feel?" Eloise asked.

"Like a seasick sailor ... on his first voyage," Henry gasped after handing back the bota bag. He looked around; Alarika limped forward, but she wore no bandages. On each side of her walked one of the hounds of Horus.

"We rejoice to see you awake," a dog said.

"The … cobra …?" Henry asked.

"Dead and gone," the other dog said. "Your companions fought with bravery equaling your own. Horus is pleased, and considering forming a new regiment to become his personal Valkyrie."

"And your reward is almost ready," the first dog said. "Horus has delayed the Duat, so there's no hurry. We'll present your gifts when they're completed, and you may remain here … safely … until you're ready to go."

They unbound Henry's leg, which was so weak that it buckled under his weight, but Henry could stand by leaning on a spear. The dogs suggested that he attempt to walk with Shu, which greatly helped, but it was days before he could walk on his own.

To Henry's delight, their daily feasts were magnificent, with hot roast pork, fresh quail, beef legs, and lamb, and each day brought a surprise. Within a week, he'd feasted on crocodile, hippo, monkey, lion, and numerous other beasts of Egypt that he'd never before tasted. Henry found that Horus had summoned human servants especially for them, and a great outdoor kitchen now sat just inside the area that had once housed the snake.

The companions rested by a wide pool from which a stream of fresh water spewed, surrounded by monuments to Horus. A large fire burned before them, for those who desired warmth, and the wood beneath their fire never seemed to need replacing.

Nate soon gave up wearing his bandage, although a shiny red spot remained where the lightning had struck his forearm. Alarika slowly mended, and her limp became noticeably less. Eloise used her magic on both of them every day, although Alarika had to be treated in private, for her wound prevented her from sitting comfortably, and she'd sworn to bleed anyone who commented on it.

Alarika insisted that Eloise focus her energies on Henry, whom they'd feared would die. Henry gave Sister Aspertine equal time to pray over him, although she seemed more healed by her prayers than he did. When Eloise was elsewhere, Henry joined Sister Aspertine in prayer, and she appreciated his company.

A week passed in lazy comfort, and Alarika gained much skill in reading hieroglyphs, for some of these monuments were scribed from texts written when only Thoth understood writing, and their styles had varied over the centuries.

Finally the day of gifts came. The companions awoke to find, upon the ground beside each, a new set of armor, gleaming of gold and silver, and new weapons of divine origin.

"Look at this!" Nate exclaimed excitedly, holding up a helmet of exceptional craftsmanship, layered with gold and studded with precious gems. "Have you ever seen anything so perfect?"

To answer him, Karl, Roselyn, Alarika, and Phil all picked up and displayed equally-magnificent helmets.

Sister Aspertine gasped and recoiled, but only slightly. Her armor was a gown of thick linens, of many layers, deep blue, with thin armored plates seeming more for decoration than to withstand battle. Her gold breastplate was a wide, decorated cross, gleaming, almost shining, as if blessed. Her helmet was a spotless new white wimple with a wide ring of silver, like a halo, with white gems like stars, and small crosses between, which made her look like a champion of Christ.

Eloise had a similar outfit, but hers was dark green and flowing, of fewer layers, and her breastplate was silver, bearing a great flowering tree.

Karl's armor matched hers, trimmed with dark green, and on his chest he bore a gold lion's face, snarling and fierce, which matched the smaller lion's faces on each of his greaves and vambraces. He drew a sword so long and bright that it reflected every light, and whose pommel was a single, giant emerald. His helmet looked like a lion's mane, and small spikes like lion's teeth projected down from his forehead and up from his chin.

"Mine's a lion, too!" Nate said, pointing at the bronze cat on his breastplate, although his trim was black.

"That's a panther," Alarika said. "Panthers are wildcats of darkness, who hunt by moonlight."

Nate smiled wider.

Also trimmed with black, Phil's armor bore ravens, with huge beaks, wide wings, and sharp talons. Phil frowned at his token until Roselyn whispered to him.

"Ravens are tokens of wisdom … the favored birds of Odin," Roselyn said.

Henry's armor was just as impressive as any other, ocean blue, and decorated with images of dogs, the same breed as the hounds of Horus. Henry felt honored.

"Dogs are loyal … the greatest virtue," Henry said.

Roselyn eyed her new, red-trimmed armor carefully, examining each plate and strap, which bore none of the dents, scratches, and rents of Hel's damaged armor.

"Excellent craftsmanship," Roselyn said. "Equal to anything that the Valkyrie forge. I like the Norse designs."

"Horus commanded his personal smiths to please each of you," a dog said.

Undoubtedly, Alarika's armor was the most impressive. Trimmed with gold and lion's fur, her token was a golden hawk, the same as Horus.

"The Master of Battle senses greatness in you," a dog said to Alarika. "Impressed with you, daughter of Egypt, is he. Even if you survive and return to the land of the living, some day you'll return here, and undergo the Test of Thoth. Should you succeed, Horus offers a place for you."

"A … place …?" Alarika asked.

"Horus sees not why Odin should have a troop of women warriors … while Horus doesn't," the other dog said. "Horus is minded to create a troop of women, like the Valkyrie, but sworn to him. Should you survive the Test of Thoth, he would like you to be his first Hawklass, his personal, elite guard of sword-women."

Alarika stood silent, her mouth agape.

"She's a worthy choice," Roselyn said. "She has the favor of the Valkyrie, and would make a great leader of the Hawklasses of Horus."

Alarika turned to stare at her, dumbfounded.

"I agree," Eloise spoke up. "Consider her vouchsafed by a priestess of the Lady of the Druids."

"And by a bride of Christ," Sister Aspertine said.

Alarika glanced at each of the companions; all bowed or nodded.

"I will … strive to be worthy," Alarika said, and she formally bowed to the dogs.

"Horus is delighted," the dog said. "Now, are you ready to …?"

"Tomorrow, if we may," Roselyn overspoke Karl before he could reply. "Never begin a journey in new armor. New straps rub wrongly."

"Tomorrow, after we eat," Karl agreed.

Both dogs nodded.

"We welcome your company for another night," one dog said.

"Tomorrow we shall speed you on your way with the blessings of Horus," the other dog said.

At Roselyn's insistence, the companions all walked around the City of Horus, getting used to their new, fancy armor. The dogs promised to build a new monument displaying the damaged armor of Hel, to honor it forever, but Roselyn kept Hel's sword in addition to the new, smaller sword that came with her armor.

The dogs also promised Roselyn that four monuments would eventually be added to the numerous tributes already filling the city; one to Hel, the Norse Goddess of Death, one to the Valkyrie whose fighting secrets inspired Horus, one to the company that brought Horus even a faint hope of escape from Winter, and one to Alarika, if she should someday join the gods of Egypt as the first Hawklass.

The next day, Karl suspected that the dogs would refuse, but during their last meal together, he invited both dogs to join their company, if Horus would allow it. As expected, the dogs politely declined, but both wished them all luck and blessings, and then they escorted the companions back to the gate, where the Celestial Path awaited, its silvery trail leading upwards.

## Chapter 9

## The City of Ra

# ROSELYN

Although delighted with her new armor, Roselyn sulked as they marched away from the City of Horus. The afterlife of the Egyptians was as twisted as Yggdrasil and made just as little sense. Undoubtedly these cities held histories older than Odin, but she had to complete her mission or she'd never see Valhalla again. These tests infuriated her.

*Couldn't they just pass one test and get taken to the City of the Gods?*

The more tests that they were forced to endure, the more likely that they might fail one, and then her mission would never be accomplished. Roselyn couldn't live without being Reginleif again; even the torments of the Duat would pale if she failed to rescue Athelwynne.

The Celestial Path rose even higher; the desert far below only a hazy, indistinct sheen of shadows. Around them, stars twinkled bright and clear, as if they could reach out and touch them. However, even Nate didn't stray near the edge. Single file they walked; this silvery path seemed longer and steeper. They had to sit and rest several times, although resting comforted no one. Their breaks were brief, barely enough time to catch their breaths, and then they continued.

One star stood out from the others, and as they approached, it began to glow gold. The closer that it loomed in the dark sky, the brighter it shone, until its shape was clearly revealed.

"A chariot!" Karl said. "The whole city … rests inside a chariot!"

A monstrous golden chariot floated before them, hovering among the stars, and their silvery, sparkling road led straight to its rear. Wheels of immense dimensions hung upon either side, each larger than the crenelated wall around Castle Bristlen. Upon that chariot, where a gigantic god's sandals might stand, rose buildings, monuments, and a huge gate that radiated a light so blinding that they soon had to shield their eyes.

Warmth radiated from the light, like Egyptian sunlight in the morning before it became too hot. The companions smiled, for the first time in this land of eternal night feeling true warmth upon their skins. Long poles extended behind the chariot, beyond its front, as if awaiting a giant steed to be mounted to the city. The golden front and sides of the chariot looked like huge walls towering over and encircling the sides and back of the city, its top-edges shaped like solar rays shining forever skyward.

One man stood at the gates of the city, a large, powerfully-built man, who wore a tall, wide headdress, which glowed too brightly for the companions to see his face. As they neared the golden platform upon which he stood, which abutted the end of the sparkling Celestial

Path, they saw his garments were purest white, almost translucent, revealing his muscular figure in earnest, so blatantly that Sister Aspertine slapped her hands over her eyes when she spied it. Instantly Nate seized her arm to keep her from blindly stepping toward the edge of the silvery road.

Upon the stranger's masculine, human body, and under the shining, radiant orb upon his headdress, which was encircled by a living cobra, steely black eyes stared from the feathered head and face of a falcon.

Alarika gave a tiny shriek of surprise, then fell to her knees and splayed her arms wide, her face pressed against the sparkling Celestial Path. Roselyn stared at her, guessing that only one terror could spark this reaction.

Eloise and Elaina startled, then glanced at each other … and performed matching curtseys, showing respect to the falcon-headed man. Following their example, Karl stopped and bowed deeply, and Nate and Phil imitated their knight. Henry matched their gestures, and then dropped to one knee.

Roselyn laid her right hand upon the hilt of Hel's sword, tucked into her belt, and her left hand upon the hilt of her sword which came with her new armor, which lay inside the scabbard gifted to her by Horus. She bowed deeply before the sole figure.

"Hail to thee, Khepri, Kheperi, Khepera, Aten, Ra, Re, Atum Re, Raet-Tawy, Helios, God of the Sun!" Alarika shouted, unable to hide the tremulations in her voice.

The falcon-head nodded, and then its beak opened, and it spoke in plain English, with a voice high-pitched, but as threatening as an angry falcon's shriek.

"Arise, Flower of the Desert, most-honorable child of Egypt, Alarika, daughter of the Mad-Hermit, Warrior favored by Horus, Sage, and Queen of the Valley of Thieves."

Alarika lifted her head, her expression incredulous.

"Arise and welcome, Warrior Maiden, Valkyrie, Reginleif, Queen of Valhalla, Kin of the Gods, Countess Roselyn, daughter of Eorl Sir Guldwin, Champion, and Lady," the falcon-head spoke, and Roselyn hesitated … and then bowed even deeper.

"Arise and welcome, Eye of All Things, Seeress of Frigg and Freyja, Priestess, Elaina du Harmonn, Scholar, Baroness, Lady, Elder, Mother, and Dancer With All," Ra said, and Elaina rose to her full height, then nodded respectfully.

"Arise and welcome, Heart of Bravery, Lord, Knight, Baron Sir Karl, General, Soldier, Husband, Father, and Farmer," Ra said.

"You honor me," Karl arose, and then he bowed again.

"Arise and welcome, Monarch of Death, Priestess of the Lady of the Druids, Sorceress, Baroness Eloise du Harmonn, daughter of Josepha and Elaina, Scholar, Healer, Wife, Mother, and Lady," Ra said.

"At your service, Great One," Eloise arose, and she curtseyed again.

"Welcome, Bastion of Faith, Wife of God, Christian, Nun of St. Dunstay, Sister Aspertine, Elsbeth, Lady, and daughter of Rolf and Paulette," Ra said.

Nate shook her arm gently, and Sister Aspertine clumsily bowed, her hands still clamped over her eyes.

"Arise and welcome, Seafarer, Sailor, Elder, Henry, son of Helga, Friend, Confidant, Husband, and Father," Ra said.

Henry said nothing, but repeated his deep bow, still on one knee.

"Arise and welcome, Arm of Valor, Warrior, Servant, Squire Phil du Harmonn, son of Michael and Sarah," Ra said.

Phil partly rose, then bowed again.

"Arise and welcome, Lightning Thinker, Warrior, Servant, Squire Nate du Harmonn, son of Michael and Sarah," Ra said.

Nate mimicked his brother's reaction, keeping a grip on Sister Aspertine's arm, yet suddenly smiling.

As they watched, the tiny-feathered skin to either side of the deadly falcon-beak shifted, and rose, in the unmistakable fashion of a smile.

"That was well-done," Ra said. "You mortals can't imagine how much I enjoyed that! Enough gestures of respect; arise, and enter my city!"

Roselyn glanced at the fantastically-ornate gate, mostly gold and gems, and the fanciful ornamentations of other metals within the city, but she'd seen enough temples and monuments and focused entirely upon Ra.

"I beg your godly pardon, Great One," Eloise said. "Enjoyed … *what?*"

"Enjoyed greeting strangers to my city!" Ra said. "I could've sent servants to welcome you, but since our Winter began, the lives of our people seem purposeless. Even we gods stand bored and idle. Cut off from your world, having already perfected our own, we simply endure endless waiting. I welcome even the smallest distraction, and your coming is of great importance. The appearance of Athelwynne the Seer in our afterlife is our happiest event in a thousand years."

*"You've seen Athelwynne …?"* Roselyn gasped, stepping forward.

"All who live here know of Athelwynne," Ra said. "Large fires pale before the light of Athelwynne, which is the brightest glow to shine in these lands since my chariot was denied access to your realm."

*"Can you take us …?"* Roselyn began, but a wave from Ra's yellow-gloved hand silenced her.

"Friends all, I will answer your every question," Ra said. "Come, enter my city, and join me at my table. There we may speak."

The City of Ra seemed smaller in diameter than the other cities, but the walls of the chariot towered above anything in the other cities, and many of its monuments and obelisks rose nearly as high. Gold was predominate, and countless disks shined with blinding, godly light. Sunflowers grew out of wide planters all over his city, and as Ra walked, the wide yellow blossoms turned to face him.

Ra led them to a great, oval, oaken table layered with platters of bread, quail, pheasant, bowls of rice, and many other dishes that Roselyn didn't recognize, and a dozen tall bottles of irep resting in bowls of cooled water.

"Sit and feast with me, my friends, for this is a joyous moment, worthy of celebration," Ra said.

"Master, I am unworthy," Alarika said, bowing again.

"Daughter, come to me," Ra said, and he held out his hand. "Join me."

Alarika gasped, then stepped forward like a frightened petitioner. Ra took her hand firmly, then drew back a chair for her to sit beside the golden throne that was obviously his. Obediently Alarika sat, and the others took chairs as Ra gestured them to join her, and then he sat upon his throne.

"Eat and drink, honored guests," Ra said. "Eat, Alarika. Fear not this form."

"Form …?" Alarika asked.

"My child, do you truly believe this is my only form?" Ra said. "I have a voice that can boom across every desert of Egypt, eyes that can travel far and see all, and throne rooms so vast, so magnificent, that your minds would cringe and shrivel before them. I could shine with light so brilliant that all sights would be burned from your eyes forever, no matter how you tried to protect them. I could tower over you, taller than the mightiest giant, in shapes so tremendous and terrifying that you would throw yourselves off the Celestial Path for fear of my presence."

Ra laughed, a brief, bird-like chuckle.

"Such displays once amused me," Ra said. "Before the arising of the young gods, especially Jupiter, Zeus, and Wotan, I enjoyed those displays. No more. My lifespan excels many times that of the beautiful Lady of the Druids, whom I knew in the days of her virginity. Time is my burden, for I bear the weight of immense eternities, whereas your younger gods suffer only eons, and the new gods, being born as we speak, know only centuries. Only the Returned One, the Christ of Sister Aspertine, alone of all pantheons, has seen more history than I, and yet … many pantheons existed before He arose, and now lay trapped in eternal Winter, or else have fallen to self-destruction, forgotten gods unwilling to continue without hope. Their lands lie cold and dead, empty realms where once light and life shined."

Roselyn said nothing, but sat uneasy; *here was a god who watched Yggdrasil sprout!*

"Your coming is a fresh wind to our lands, which blows new hope to us," Ra said. "For this I welcome you, for no goal is dearer to my heart than change. Even the young gods can't understand the anguish of a thousand years of Winter, enduring against all hope. I know Athelwynne, and several of you, were involved in uniting the realms of Yggdrasil and Elysia. I seek the same. The Christian God once endured his Winter, and while he suffered, my people enslaved his. Now, I would be reborn, to restrengthen my people, as the Christian God did."

"The best person to help you is Athelwynne," Karl said. "We came to free him, and will do all we can to aid you, and we'd be grateful if you could help us."

"Surely Odin and my Lady would be honored to converse with you," Eloise said.

"So I believe, and so I am glad," Ra said. "But forget not our Winter; the strength of all gods fail with their followers, and our realm is consumed in darkness. After Horus defeated Set for the final time, Set fled, and thus did Egypt enjoy centuries of splendor. Then came our Winter, our darkness, and Anubis slowly arose as our new power, for he is the Master of Darkness, who now holds dominion over all these lands."

*"Anubis ...?"* Alarika exclaimed. *"But ... Osiris is the Ruler of All ...!"*

"The throne of Osiris sits empty," Ra said. "Osiris has returned to the sarcophagus of Set, a dead god in a dead land. All have tried to awaken him, but none have succeeded. Even Thoth knows no way, for it is by the will of Osiris that he sleeps. Osiris refuses to live in a land without hope."

"But ... aren't we hope ...?" Eloise asked.

"Osiris hasn't awakened, so many believe that you're a false hope," Ra said. "We suffer the weakness of our diminished faith ... as our followers are now few. Still, a great celebration is every Weighing of the Heart, and wondrous is our joy at every welcoming."

"What can we do?" Karl asked.

"If I had my way, you would've come straight here, and I'd carry you to the City of the Gods myself," Ra said. "I've done all I can: I insisted on being appointed for your path, and I've shortened your route, for only one city now lies between you and your goal. But that is the City of Anubis, and I can't control what happens there. However, in my city you face no test, and I'll give you all I can to prepare you to face Anubis."

"What about the Seer?" Roselyn asked. "How may we free him from the memory box of Anubis?"

"According to Thoth, not all the remaining gods of Egypt can revolt against Anubis and hope to win," Ra said.

"Remaining …?" Karl asked.

"Ours is a struggle that mortals don't comprehend," Ra said. "Mortal lives are so brief that you see gods as eternal. Our lives are more complex than your own, and infinitely longer, but not even gods are truly immortal. We're born, and can die, yet eternities may pass between; we seem infinite to mortals who know us only for a moment. Sometimes we choose multiple paths, and walk different routes through time, simultaneously existing as two or more, or multiple gods may combine to become one, greater than we were individually. Sometimes our unions fail, after hundreds of years, but worshippers lose faith when they see changes in their gods.

"For centuries I was worshipped as myself, as Ra, but then our Fall came, and I merged with Atum, and we became Atum-Re, and together we sought to prevent our Winter. Then, when Winter came, our union failed. I am Ra again, yet some still worship Atum-Re. Those fool mortals who believe that we gods are perfect accept no changes to their beliefs, and often kill each other to gain our favor, unwilling to accept that they worship changing incarnations of imperfect gods."

"What gods have we not seen?" Eloise asked, and Ra gestured to Alarika.

"There are many," Alarika said.

"Can the daughter of the Mad Hermit name those whose cities you haven't visited?" Ra asked.

"Ammit," Alarika answered hesitantly. "Ammit is a demon with the head of a crocodile, the torso of a leopard, and the hindquarters of a hippopotamus."

Ra nodded, and then he gestured for Alarika to continue.

"Bast, or Bastet, is the Goddess of Cats," Alarika said. "Mafdet is the God of Justice, Executioner of Unlawfuls, and Protector of the King's chambers. Amunet is the Goddess of Creation, the wife of Atum. Ptah is the God of Creation. Anhur is Ruler of the Daytime Sky. Hapi and his wife, Anuket, are the God and Goddess of the Nile.

"Hathor, also known as the feline lion Sehkmet, is the Goddess of Love. Heket is the Goddess of Frogs. Amun is the God of the Wind, who charges forth horned as a mighty ram. Kebechet is the Goddess of Purification. Maahes is the Lion-headed God of War. Nekhbet is the Vulture Goddess. Pakhet is the Goddess of Motherhood. Apis is the Bull-God, worshipped heavily in Memphis. Apophis is the God of Snakes, War, and Chaos, who is also called Aapep, who dwells in the Duat. Babi is the God of Baboons. Bes is the Dwarf God, the God of Pregnant Woman, Newborns, and Families. Gengen-Wer is the Goose God. Anput is the Goddess of the Seventeenth Nome and Mother of Kebechet. Qebui is the God of the North Wind. Qetesh is the Goddess of Fertility. Seker is the Falcon God.

Serqet is the Goddess of Scorpions. Tawaret is the Hippopotamus Goddess. Wadjet is the Goddess of Protection. Wadj-wer is the Goddess of the Mediterranean Sea. Seshat is the Goddess of Writing and Measurement, and Sobek is the God of Crocodiles and Alligators."

"Well spoken," Ra said. "You're truly a scholar. Yet, you should know, some of those you named were temporary mergings of others, and no mortals know the most recent children of the gods. Our numbers change slowly, but change blesses all … except the dead."

Alarika bowed as respectfully as she could in her chair.

"I never knew that there were so many," Karl said. "Glad that we don't have to visit all of their cities."

"The Path of Cities was abandoned long ago," Ra said. "I suspect that Anubis asked Nephthys to restore it for his sake … that you would have to pass through the one realm where he rules supreme. I don't think that Nephthys was pleased, so she made his city your last stop."

"How do your people approach the Test of Thoth, if not through your cities?" Eloise asked.

"In the end, I ferried them," Ra said. "In our Fall, the House of Nephthys delivered the faithful to the Gateway of the Duat, and if they knew the prayers to board my ship, then my light led them safely through. This is where I learned to befriend humans, as I met so many worthy Kas. I fought and drove back Aapep, and removed all barriers to their passage except the Test of Thoth. Then Winter approached, and my power to escort our people faded. Now only a long, painful path remains open, and only the most-faithful can follow it. Each success strengthens us, but our hope diminishes with their infrequency. Without their faith, our people fall to hopelessness, and their hopelessness further weakens us."

"And the more that you are weakened, the more of your people lose faith," Elaina said. "Yet … I don't understand how Winter comes … or can be so bleak. I've been to the Realm of Dreams; surely gods as ancient as you have been there, too."

"We call that land 'The Forge', for all things begin there," Ra said. "To mortals, what a sweet realm it is: all dreams, no substance. However, times come when dreams are insufficient, when the needs of your people multiply too great, and gods must seek achievement, actualization, and attainment. Then must we drag our dreams back here, and force them into reality; no small task … even for gods."

"Yet this we did. While Osiris civilized all the other lands of men, Isis made Egypt a paradise, and I blessed it with light, and Horus protected it. We succeeded at everything, and our powers knew no equal, not even from the pantheons preceding us. Egypt grew into the most cultured, advanced, educated, artistic, powerful, and spiritually-elevated civilization ever to exist."

"What happened?" Karl asked. "How could such greatness fall?"

"The Realm of Chaos," Ra said. "Perfection exists only in the Realm of Dreams, and to reach or return from there, you must pass the Realm of Chaos. Seeds of destruction fall into all exposed to its infernal machinations, and thus, once brought into being, all things are doomed."

"I passed through the Realm of Chaos," Elaina said. "Twice, and I bear no seeds."

"Mortals are born bearing seeds of destruction; else they'd never grow old," Ra said. "Even gods aren't immune to seeds of destruction. Gods begin in the Realm of Dreams, Thoth says, and many pantheons of gods willingly existed only as dreams, thinking perhaps that they might endure forever. Yet no god has ever done so, for the pleasures of dreams are greatest in their fulfillment, and such pleasures do all gods seek. Thus do all pantheons of gods bring about their own Winter … else they would live forever unfulfilled."

"The gods of Egypt have treated us well," Elaina said.

*"What …?!?"* half of the companions cried.

"Our tests have been difficult, even brutal," Elaina said. "Yet they've been fair. Gods are under no obligation to be fair, and thus I assume that it's their nature …"

"Maat requires fairness," Ra said. "She is balance, like the scales of Thoth, or the stability between humans and animals, which mirrors our favored appearances."

"However it happens, we're still alive … in a land of death," Elaina said. "I assume that any god could've slain us, if they'd wished."

"In the City of Anubis, the will to keep you alive won't be enough," Ra said. "It's a dwelling of darkness, where Anubis is the only master. To him, you're thieves come to steal his new treasure, and his challenge to you shall be harsh."

"Can Anubis be defeated, or at least, his city …?" Karl asked.

"That depends upon his challenge," Ra said. "If Anubis wishes to kill you, he's quite capable …"

"We defeated Loki, the Norse God of Mischief," Roselyn said.

"We defied him … and his daughter … several times," Karl corrected her. "We didn't kill Loki, and his strongest opponent was the Seer, not us."

"Anubis isn't Set," Alarika said. "We're hoping that he honors us with a fair test …"

"The Seasons of the Gods are the ultimate fairness," Ra said. "How would new divine pantheons arise if the old never weakened, never lost the worship of their people? Alas! Greatly pleased were we to arise, watching elder gods fall, but unhappy we were to suffer in our turn. Yet, all is for the best. Even for mortals, for the new to arise, the old must fall, and thus do worlds grow."

"Can we … awaken Osiris?" Elaina asked.

"We've tried for centuries," Ra said. "Even Isis has failed …"

"Surely there's some way … a legend … or a prophesy …?" Eloise asked.

"Willingly Osiris succumbed to his sarcophagus, saying that all hopes had failed," Ra said.

"But we are hope …!" Eloise said. "With our return, news of your existence would spread among the peoples of Egypt, and contact with Elysia and Yggdrasil may offer hopes never realized …!"

"Each failed hope drives us closer to oblivion," Ra said. "I hope, but Anubis claims that despair drives me to grasp at impossibilities."

"Would Anubis obey, if Osiris ordered him to release the Seer's soul?" Eloise asked.

"Think no ill of Anubis," Ra said. "None knows darkness as deeply as Anubis. Only because of him have we survived this long."

"What about …," Alarika began, but her voice stammered. "Forgive me, Great God of My People, and please ignore me if I speak of what's forbidden."

"Speak, my daughter," Ra said.

"What about … his Secret Name …?" Alarika asked.

Ra stiffened … and his eyes flamed.

"I see why Horus favors you," Ra said. "You're indeed brave."

"I would never knowingly offend …!" Alarika pleaded.

"To mention a divine weakness before … before the very god who suffered this indignity …!" Ra's falcon-voice deepened, and sharpened, and his glower enhanced.

"Forgive me," Alarika bowed her face toward him.

"I can't condemn," Ra said. "This reminder grates at my soul, but a warrior looks to all paths for victory. Anubis alone knows his secret name, and he would never reveal it; no god will risk my fate."

"Fate …?" Karl asked.

Ra scowled.

"They know not this story," Alarika said.

"Let them understand," Ra said, but his birdish tone belied disgust.

"You command, I obey," Alarika said.

Ra said nothing, just nodded to Alarika, and she acknowledged his gesture with another deep bow of her head, her nose almost touching her arm. Then she looked at her companions.

"I haven't told you the full story," Alarika said, glancing fearfully at Ra. "The greatest power of any god is their secret name, and all once feared the might of Ra. Isis desired his strength … and sought to steal it.

"Ra's explorations of all lands grew wearisome. One day, weakened from his exertions, Ra drooled, and his divine spittle fell upon the ground. Isis took his dirty spit and formed a sacred mud, and kneaded it in her hands. She shaped the mud into Uraeus, the Fanged-One, and so Isis invented the cobra.

"Isis hid the cobra in the tall grass. As Ra returned from the mortal world, weary from battling Aapep, he stepped upon it, and the cobra bit Ra's foot. As its venom filled his blood, his cry echoed across all worlds, and then its poisons stole Ra's voice; he could speak no words of healing.

"The other gods raced to his aid, but Ra couldn't speak; his lips opened silently. He trembled, and Egypt shook, as the fiery venom consumed him, and the other gods wept.

"'*I could purge this poison,*' Isis said, '*… but my healing requires your secret name.*'

Ra struggled, and finally found his voice.

"'*I am the Maker of Heaven and Earth,*' Ra gasped in agony. '*I am the Builder of Mountains. I am the Source of Waters. I am Light and Darkness. I am the Creator of the Nile. I am the Kindler of Fire. I am Khepera in the morning, Ra at sun-high, and Tum in the dusk.*'

"'*All know these names,*' Isis said. '*Reveal to me your secret name … lest this poison end your existence.*'

"'*Promise me that you'll share my secret name to no other, save only your son yet to come, whose name shall be Horus,*' Ra said. '*And bind him first with such oaths that my name he will never speak nor reveal.*'

"Isis pledged her oath to Ra, and he whispered into her ear his true secret name, and thus Isis gained Ra's power.

"*By the Secret Name of Ra, I banish this poison!*" Isis cried.

"At her command, the venom vanished from Ra's veins, and all pain left him. Yet Ra thanked her not, for he perceived her treachery. Angry at his weakness, Ra abandoned the Earth, and arose upon the sun-disk of Thoth, to make his home in Nut, where he would sail across her each day. Yet his freedom bore a terrible curse; each night Ra must pass through the Underworld of Amenti, through the twelve divisions of the Duat.

"Thus Osiris armed Ra with his faith, and Horus gave to Ra the Amsu-staff, that he might each morning fight and drive back Aapep the Unslayable. With these, Ra could pass through the Duat safely, and each new dawn celebrates his victory over evil. This is why Ra is always honored first by mortals, for he would ferry the dead, and was named the Friend of the Lost, the Ferryman of the Fiery River, and the Savior of Spirits."

Alarika cast a worried glance at Ra, but he only stared forward, his beaked-frown deep.

"Three eternities have passed since that day, and still my shame continues," Ra said. "Isis now regrets her betrayal, but we were young, fearless … and foolish. Now we understand the hidden threat of our fearlessness. With wisdom comes the seed of Winter. Without change, stagnation grinds all to pointlessness. Stagnation alone can defeat Time, the ultimate failure of hope. Thus stands Maat, the balance of Time versus Stagnation, which forces the Seasons of the Gods."

Ra closed his eyes. For a long time, he sat unmoving, and Roselyn wondered what he was thinking. The companions shared wary looks, but none dared speak or move for fear that any sound might disturb the thoughts of Ra. Then the Sun God sighed, opened his eyes, and smiled.

"Forgive your host, my mortal friends, but what is to you only moments are to me eons of anguish," Ra said. "Yet this is not my will, to burden our feast with sorrow. Speak, any of you; if in you questions dwell. As best I may, I will answer."

The companions glanced at each other.

"What is the memory box of Anubis, and how may the Seer's soul be freed?" Roselyn asked.

"The chest that you speak of is small and square, only two handswidths wide, and no thicker than your clenched fist," Ra said. "Decorations cover it, painted runes forgotten by all but Thoth, and tiny mosaics of gems and sacred stones, gleaming of many colors. Two holes, shaped like eyes, open from one side of its edge, and inside it lay horrors old when the Nu was young, terrors to trap and devour the spirit of any who gaze into its depths. Some say that they are the dreams of Lost Gods, whose names were forgotten in the destruction of the last epoch, in a time of which not even Thoth recalls, in realms before the Earth was born.

"To free the Seer, you need only open the box, which no mortal shall do. Anubis will never surrender his memory box, so either he must open it … or it will never be opened."

"Can it be destroyed?" Roselyn asked.

"Can you slay a dream?" Ra asked. "The box itself can be destroyed, but the wrath of Anubis not even a god would brave. Someday our dark land will fail, and with that, then shall the Gods of Egypt fall and join the forgotten pantheons that thrived 'ere our birth. For a god to slay a god would only hasten our doom, and possibly cause our final light to dim and fade."

"That's why you don't anger Anubis," Karl said.

"Only our combined wills protect we Gods of Egypt from oblivion," Ra said.

"Great God, may I speak?" Henry asked.

"Speak freely, I command," Ra said.

"Well, it's obvious that true power comes from wisdom," Henry said. "Every divinity reports that. But wisdom only comes from knowledge, and the more we learn, the more chances at wisdom we get. We obviously can't defeat Anubis, but the more that we learn about him, the wiser our choices may be."

"Well has wisdom blessed you," Ra said. "Speak again, my daughter. Share with all … your wisdom of Anubis."

Alarika bowed again.

"You honor me, God of Gods," Alarika said.

Alarika took a deep breath, and then began.

"I've spoken of Anubis before," Alarika said. "He's the Guardian God, who rules the Gateway to the Duat. Anubis cuts the heart from the body and places it upon the Scale of Thoth, to face the Judgement of Osiris. Those hearts who balance not Anubis hurls into the Duat, where they are consumed by crocodiles.

"Anubis is the ill-begotten son of Osiris, the Dead God, and his youngest sister, Nephthys, the Goddess of Death. Anubis was born and raised in her House of Death, and the dead have no secrets that Anubis does not possess. Isis once hunted Anubis, jealous of her husband's infidelity, but the goodness hidden inside his darkness softened her ire. Seeing him, Isis forgave Anubis for being a living symbol of her shame, and Anubis named her 'Isis the Just and Merciful', and vowed that he'd serve and defend his step-mother forever. At her side, Anubis used his secret arts to help revive Osiris, and thus was the Ruler of All brought back from death."

Alarika paused, and glanced worriedly at Ra, but then continued speaking.

"Many believe that … the death of Osiris … was a first great weakening of Egypt," Alarika said.

"It was an age of terror," Ra said. "Osiris civilized all the lands, even to the most-distant, and when he fell, so too fell many civilizations. Evil thrived, and consumed much that was once good. As Osiris lay dead, whilst we fought with Set, none passed judgement upon petitioners, and countless devout worshippers undeservedly fell into the Duat. In this, we gods failed. Now Anubis passes final judgement, and grim are his verdicts, for each soul that passes not into the City of the Honored Dead weakens us."

*"Honored Dead . . . ?"* Roselyn exclaimed.

"We Gods of Egypt honored our dead before Valhalla existed," Ra said. "Think you that Odin knows not all my titles, save only my secret name, and the names of all my fellows? If so, then you underestimate your liege."

Roselyn swallowed hard; *if Odin knew of these gods and their afterlife, had he made her human again . . . knowing that she'd find an entrance to their lands? Had he sent her here to accomplish some hidden purpose . . . or to insure that she might never return?*

"Has Anubis assumed the throne of Osiris?" Elaina asked.

"Only in the Final Judgement," Ra said. "All the gods welcomed his assumption of this post, lest more worthy subjects fall to an undeserved doom. Thus it is that all other activities cease when a petitioner arrives for judgement, for nothing is more important to any God of Egypt than the welcoming of a devout follower into our company. For these rare moments do we live, for the wisdom of Thoth has foretold: when the doom of our last petitioner is declared, so too shall our doom fall."

Once more a silence fell, and then Henry spoke again.

"Pray tell, if you will, Great One," Henry began, "what became . . . of your boat?"

Ra's beak lowered, and for the first time, Ra looked angry.

"My boat burned," Ra said. "At horrendous cost, I snatched it from the River of Fire, and labored long to repair it. I have it here, and can show it to you, if you wish. But only in my prime could I sail the River Infernal; in our Winter, I can travel neither the Heavens nor the Underworld. Winter has weakened all faiths in our realm, even Aapep, yet the journey to face him would so weaken me so that even the Amsu-staff might fail to drive him back, and his evil can't be destroyed."

"If we survive the City of Anubis, how may we travel to the City of the Gods?" Elaina asked.

"The far gate of the City of Anubis opens upon a pathway of gold, not of silver," Ra said. "Should you succeed, the City of the Gods will welcome you gladly."

"Ra, I beg forgiveness for what I must ask," Roselyn said. "If I speak blasphemy, I do so out of ignorance, with no intent to offend." Ra looked at her, but withheld any reply. "As a Valkyrie, I seek every advantage in battle. I carry the Sword of Hel, Goddess of Death, and many times only by its strength have we survived. Yet I fear that even a weapon of the younger gods may not defeat Anubis. I must ask, with all humility: can a Valkyrie wield the Amsu-staff?"

Elaina gasped, and even Sister Aspertine looked shocked, but Ra only laughed.

"Only Atum, Shu, Geb, Thoth, Osiris, Isis, Horus, and I can lift the Amsu-staff," Ra said. "Even Maat can't lift it, for the Amsu-staff isn't a weapon of balance."

"Like the hammer of Thor," Elaina said. "Another similarity."

Roselyn cast Elaina a black stare, but neither said anything more. Roselyn fumed; the similarities between the Egyptians and the Norse gods infuriated her. The followers of every pantheon of gods claimed that theirs were the only gods, or the strongest gods, or the first gods. Yet the sheer number of similarities hinted that each pantheon was following a pattern, a plan beyond the grasp of any god or goddess.

*Was she, and all the Valkyrie, being manipulated by a pattern of similarities?*

Roselyn didn't mention the other similarities that only a Christian-born Valkyrie would notice; Thor, Horus, and the Horned Hunter were the greatest warriors. Thoth, Odin, and the Lady were gods of wisdom. Autm, Buri, and the Lady were the first-borns, founders of their races. Odin, Jesus, and Osiris all died and were reborn kings of all lands on Earth. Freyja, the Lady of the Druids, and Isis were the most-worthy, wisest, and kindest goddesses. Set, Loki, and the Horned Hunter; how different were they? Yet … if there was a pattern, a secret plan that each pantheon followed, didn't that imply … *something greater than any god existed … a core pantheon that started it all…?*

*How could she know …?*

*How could even a god know …?*

None of the companions asked another question, so Ra asked Karl for their story of Yggdrasil. Karl insisted that Nate was their best storyteller, and Nate spent the rest of the evening regaling them all with their story, which he called *'The Birth of Reginleif'*.

Roselyn quickly lost interest in the familiar tale, trying to focus on their next challenge. *Would Ra really let them leave without testing them?* He'd said so, but Roselyn wouldn't trust even a god without proof. Whether or not he did, soon they'd have to face Anubis, and then … deal with whatever he intended. Roselyn knew better than to look too far ahead. They'd survived so far because, however challenging, the tests of each city were designed to be beaten. Yet, if Anubis was like Loki, then the next city that they faced might have no path to success.

After Nate finished his tale, Ra sent them to a beautiful palace to rest, and there they slept upon soft feather quilts layered thickly over beds of gold.

"I shall be gone when you awaken, but you must not tarry," Ra said. "As our Winter deepens, your path lies onward, and I wish your completion … for good … or unto the worst of all ills."

# Chapter 10

## The City of Anubis

## ALARIKA

After hours of walking, Alarika froze mid-step; the sparkling Celestial Path suddenly sloped sharply downward … and at its end they spied the City of Anubis. Its gate was a giant head of a black jackal floating on a thundercloud, beyond which many buildings seemed to rise, so lost in shadow that their shapes were hard to see. The sight of the City of Anubis felt threatening, worsened by the realization that the jackal's head wasn't built of black stone, black metal, or black wood; its edges wavered, like smoke, shifting, flexing like a living thing. Whatever secrets lay inside the City of Anubis, the massive head was pure shadow, a construction of solid darkness laid over the city to conceal its nature.

Lightning flashed in the churning thundercloud under the city, from which a peal of thunder boomed. All the companions stopped as they saw the jackal-head, staring at the forbidding city.

"What are we waiting for?" Roselyn demanded.

"We can't beat Anubis," Elaina said, her eyes locked on the city.

"Standing idly changes no fate," Roselyn said, pushing to take the lead. "Fear insures defeat."

Alarika sighed and followed; *Roselyn was right.* She actually liked Roselyn. Of all her companions, only Roselyn seemed driven, fearless, but with a cautious respect for enemies. In the desert, Roselyn was the only companion, other than herself, that she knew would survive.

*Karl was a fool for choosing Eloise over Roselyn!*

As they marched forward, the slope of the silvery Celestial Path became treacherous. Their momentum slowed and they started to slip.

"Walk on Shu," Karl said.

Alarika stepped up, but felt no resistance. Shu seemed intangible. She paused, hearing the grunts and stumbles of the companions, and Roselyn waved her arms for balance.

"I can't walk on Shu …!" Nate exclaimed.

All of the companions glanced at each other, and several others, including Karl, raised a foot to step onto thin air. Alarika expelled her heavy thoughts, then tried to step up again … but no resistance met her foot.

*"Anubis!"* Eloise hissed. *"Anubis won't let us walk on Shu!"*

Suddenly Alarika slipped, and a tiny scream escaped her lips; their path was too steep. If they slipped off the edge, then they'd fall to their doom. Yet the Celestial Path felt softer, smoother, and as Alarika slipped upon its sparkles, she started to slide forward. Instantly she grabbed at the only object in her path, Roselyn's leg, but her grasp only pulled Roselyn down, and they began to slide together.

Roselyn cursed and kicked her leg free, then whipped out the Sword of Hel and, using both hands, she stabbed it downward, into their sparkling path, using it as a rudder. The blade penetrated, but with no more effect than slicing through air. Yet Roselyn's slide never faltered, and Alarika glanced at the edge, seeing it slip ever closer, amid mixed screams of terror.

However, as Alarika neared the edge, a powerful gust of wind, like a solid wall of air, pushed against her, forcing her back onto the path. Her speed increasing, the slope steepening, Alarika recognized it for what it was; a ploy of Anubis. She looked back, unsurprised to see all the companions, screaming, eyes wide, sliding right behind her.

*"Don't fear!"* Alarika shouted to the others. *"This won't kill us! Anubis wants us to arrive afraid!"*

Roselyn glanced at her, and her dawning comprehension stretched a smile across her lips. Roselyn pulled out the Sword of Hel and held it up high, shouting a warrior's challenge as they slid ever faster.

None of the companions fell off, although Sister Aspertine and Eloise never stopped screaming. All the time, the giant shadow-head of the jackal, the City of Anubis, loomed closer and larger. Finally they reached the bottom, where the slope of the Celestial Path grew level, and they slid forward as if on ice.

They stopped before a man wielding a heavy pole-axe, standing before a dark archway of black marble. He was tall, and his skin, hair, and even his eyes were black, but bearing none of the starry-gems or friendliness identifying the faithful in the City of Nut. His face was human, but he wore a thick linen shift held up by a wide leather belt, and upon his head rested a tall golden helmet shaped like a jackal, its gleaming muzzle protruding just above his forehead.

"Welcome to Death," he said. "I am the Doorman of Anubis. Arise, and obey his will."

The companions struggled to stand, helping each other to their feet.

"We didn't come here to die," Karl said.

"Our Lord Anubis is the Guardian God, who rules the Gateway to the Duat, and your existence in our afterlife defies his wishes," the doorman said. "Those who defy Anubis suffer dual death."

"Dual death …?" Eloise asked.

"Mortals can't deceive Thoth, yet they must reach him … if they can," the doorman said. "Your doom is certain … not to die, nor to reach Thoth, but to suffer eternally."

"But … what's dual death …?" Eloise asked.

"All mortals live two lives," Alarika explained. "Each man and woman lives a physical life … and a social life. All physical life is fed with the fruits of the Earth, and social life is fed by the respects of others. Life is best while both endure; to live physically but not socially bears the doom of loneliness and shame, and to die physically while living socially is to celebrate popularity but be unable to enjoy it."

"So … dual death must mean both deaths … or true death?" Henry asked.

"Only young faiths believe in true death," Alarika said. "Once an Egyptian inhales divine breath, both lives begin, and death can't slay the divine. After dual death, both lives are weighed by Thoth, once judged by Osiris, but now judged by Anubis. Those found worthy have all their parts rejoined and live forever with the gods."

"You shan't be so lucky," the doorman said. "Our lord and master knows of your journey … and impressed is he that you have thus far succeeded, but He Born In Darkness won't surrender the precious light he's captured. Seldom has his city ever appeared to mortals, for of all who enter, none exit."

"None …?" Eloise asked.

"Never," said the doorman. "When the God Born of Death wishes you no success then your journey ends."

"We'll see," Roselyn said, and she raised her long blade. "This is the Sword of Hel, Goddess of Death, from the lands of Yggdrasil."

"No threats!" Karl hissed. "To exit, we must first enter …"

"The door of Anubis is always open, here … and in the Duat," the doorman said. "Enter … and face doom, or stand … and await doom."

"We bring hope!" Karl emphasized. "At least a chance …! You must tell Anubis …!"

"Others have brought promises … which later failed," the doorman said. "Anubis holds no faith that your promises are any different."

"All we ask is for an audience," Eloise said.

"Anubis refuses …," the doorman said.

"What about you?" Karl demanded. "Forget Anubis. Don't you want to see daylight fill the sky again?"

"My desire is the will of Anubis," the doorman said. "His city awaits. Enter."

Alarika glanced at the archway of black marble. Inside, a dark tunnel led back as far as the starlight could penetrate. Beyond that … nothing but mystery.

Karl leaned forward and stared into the dark tunnel.

"We'll need torches," Karl said, but the doorman only sneered at him.

"I can make fire, but without something to burn …," Eloise said.

"We'd best get started," Karl said, and he stepped toward the archway of black marble. "At least, let's go deep enough to discover what awaits us …"

"I'll go first," Alarika held out an arm to stop him.

"We need you …," Karl argued. "No one else can read hieroglyphs, speak Egyptian, or knows your stories …"

"We're companions," Alarika said. "None of us are expendable."

Alarika met Karl's quizzical stare undaunted, but his sudden smile disarmed her.

"Glad to hear that," Karl said.

Alarika scowled and turned to face the tunnel. Frustrations swarmed inside her, tightening her stomach. She'd always been solitary, even as a child, living with her father. She'd never had real friends. As a woman, she'd known better than to trust anyone, and survived through strength and self-reliance … and then these pagans arrived. She'd used them, as she'd used everyone else, to escape her weakening control over her army of thieves.

*She still couldn't believe that they'd opened the Temple of Osiris … after all the times she'd watched her father fail …!*

She didn't trust smiles. Suspicion was comforting and familiar, while acceptance felt unaccustomed, like taking a needless risk. Smiles didn't come easy, yet snarls and frowns, which had supported her former life, now seemed awkward and inappropriate.

Although she would've preferred to remain separate, Alarika could no longer deny that she was part of this … bizarre collection of strangers of dissimilar faiths. Her lips felt mushy, smushed at odd angles, almost a smile, and she couldn't allow that. Yet Karl nodded to her, and stepped back to allow her to pass first … as if he trusted her.

*Had he tricked her into walking first into a trap …?*

*How could anyone suddenly trust someone who'd once betrayed them…?*

Warily, Alarika drew her khopesh and stepped forward, into the lightless tunnel. The passage was narrow; two might walk abreast, if they squeezed together, which would leave no room for swinging swords. The walls and floor were made of the same black marble, swallowing the last of the light behind them.

"Eloise …?" Karl whispered.

A sudden glow appeared behind her, not clear enough to see, but enough to cast dim shadows, which allowed her to navigate the tunnel. Eloise was holding a small, glowing white stone, perfectly round, but Alarika ignored it and focused on the darkness, wary of threats. The glow of Eloise's stone wasn't bright enough to see clearly, but it helped. A deeper shadow appeared to her left, and Alarika waved her khopesh through it.

"Side-tunnel," she whispered. "Do we take it?"

"No point heading straight to our doom," Karl said. "Don't bother whispering; Anubis knows we're here."

Alarika silently snarled, rebuking herself for taking pointless cautions, and slipped into the dark passage. She stepped slowly, holding her khopesh before her, barely able to see …

and then …

Alarika slashed at the figure and struck, but her khopesh rebounded as if she'd struck a wall.

*"Back …!"* Alarika shouted, both a warning to her companions and a challenge to the tall, unknown figure.

Yet no one moved. No retreating footsteps broke the silence behind her, and the shape before her didn't advance. Alarika stared at its shadowy outline, and then soft shoes scraped the stone floor, and Eloise stepped up beside her.

Peeking from the white stone ball in Eloise's cupped hands, the dim glow illuminated a statue; Anubis, carved from a single tree, seven feet tall, upon a pedestal of the same wood, painted and gilded. The statue stood in a wide crossways, which none of them had known that they'd entered. Beyond the statue, two other dark, doorless entryways opened to unknown destinations, and to their right a winding stairs arose from below and proceeded onward to the next level.

"Just a statue," Eloise whispered, and the other companions gathered around it. The statue of Anubis stared blankly forward, on its arm a deep gash of aged, inner wood showing where Alarika's slash had chopped through its black paint.

"Well, that should please Anubis," Roselyn scowled. "It's wood; we might as well go all the way."

"No," Karl said. "There's got to be some wood around here that isn't a desecration to burn."

"Here," Nate said, and he reached down, lifted the rotted ruins of a small broken table, and held it up to Eloise.

"Wait," Elaina said, looking at the wood. "This isn't right."

"What …?" Karl asked.

"Why would a god furnish his city with broken furniture?" Elaina asked.

The companions exchanged nervous glances … *no ruins had existed in the other cities.*

"Light the wood … and go upstairs," Karl said. "Whatever's here knows about us. We need to see it."

Eloise ceased her white stone's glow, then waved her hand over one end of the broken leg of the ruined table, and it burst into flame. With Nate following, holding their torch, Roselyn joined Alarika, and they led the way up the wide stone stairs. The steps were straight but cracked, and some broken fragments shifted beneath their feet. They climbed several flights and emerged into a large room, empty save for a few broken monuments to Anubis, one of which lay on its side, fallen onto the floor. Upon the far wall, they spied a row of tall windows. Karl gestured for Nate to extinguish their torch, and they approached the windows and peered out.

Near them, the City of Anubis looked crowded, packed with shadowy buildings and grand temples squeezed between narrow streets, wider than any city they'd yet seen. The dim starlight poorly illuminated the many towers and flat roofs. The city looked deserted. Not one window or doorway glimmered with a spec of light.

However, the far half of the City of Anubis held no structures, only rubble of what had once been towers and temples. The whole far side looked as if it'd once equaled this half, but only stones and broken beams remained, as if a giant's feet had stomped all its buildings into fragments. No lights shined in the city save at its farthest point; in the distance, a series of torches burned in sconces mounted upon the back wall, reflecting across the massive piles of broken rubble. The burning torches illuminated a large golden gate; their goal … the exit from the City of Anubis, which they all knew that the God of Darkness never intended for them to reach.

Alarika shook her head. *Did her companions really believe that they could defeat Anubis?* Most likely, the lights of the burning torches were the lure … and the golden gate was the trap.

Slowly her eyes adjusted, and she saw the complexity of the countless temples and monuments, packed into the half of the city closest to them. *Why had Anubis given them this dilapidated city? Narrow streets and empty buildings would make hiding easy!*

The entire far half, the piles of rubble and ruins, lay exposed, and would be difficult to traverse without being seen. Her eyes swept across miles of total destruction; not a single temple or monument remained standing, but many half-walls remained, the lone remnants of buildings crushed and torn asunder. She stared confused, for in no city that they'd visited had they witnessed anything but polished monuments and well-tended gardens.

Then a distant movement startled her. A whole building, or a massive hill, rose up, and seemed to move across the ruined section. Elaina gasped, and Sister Aspertine screamed.

"*Crocodile* …," Karl whispered, horror filling his voice.

Alarika's eyes widened as she recognized their death. The moving shadow was huge, too vast to be a living thing. Then they heard a crashing rumble, as if a thousand stone blocks were being crushed into pebbles, followed by a thunderous echo. The rumbling continued, as if four monstrous feet were crushing everything beneath them … as it crawled on its path of destruction.

Suddenly a head, the size of their red boat with golden sails, rose up, into the dim starlight, with eyes the size of covered carriages, and yellow teeth like tall bales of hay, pointed like thick stalactites. A vast snout extended, fully as long as a four-cart caravan. The head of the crocodile of Anubis excelled any terror they'd yet seen. Its huge body, if it matched its head, must exceed a hundred feet long, ranging from tunnel-sized nostrils to the tip of a long scaly tail.

*"Curse of Loki!"* Elaina exclaimed.

*"God save us!"* Sister Aspertine prayed.

*"How can we fight that …?"* Nate demanded.

"The Lightning-Serpent of Horus was a worm compared to that," Henry said.

"Everything has a weakness," Roselyn said. "Thor killed giants and dragons. The secret is to know the weakness of your opponent. The larger they are, the bigger their weakness."

"Thor had Mjollnir," Eloise said. "Maybe … if we had the Amsu-staff …"

"Look at the distance we have to cover!" Karl interrupted her. "Even running our fastest, we'd never reach the gate with that chasing us."

"Distraction …?" Phil suggested.

"Maybe, but what?" Karl asked. "Without one of us staying behind … letting that chase them … while the others ran to safety …!"

"Only the temples nearest the gate have been ruined," Elaina said. "Why there … and not the whole city …?"

"It's a guardian … defending the exit," Henry said. "Like a dog chained outside your chicken coup … to keep foxes away."

"It may not come closer, but we don't know that," Karl said. "If we could lure it …"

"Crocodiles are swift, even on land," Alarika said. "Egyptians can outrun most crocodiles, but look at that! At twenty feet per pace, it could catch a cheetah!"

"Anubis wants us to fail," Eloise said.

"We can't fail," Karl said. "Eloise, the Seer helped us escape from Loki and Hel with an illusion …"

"Only the Seer could do that," Eloise said.

"What about the dancing lights he created in Grusshire, to distract the Wolfqueen …?" Roselyn asked.

Eloise shook her head.

"I can create those lights, but they take all my concentration," Eloise said. "I can't run while I'm casting … or send them wandering."

"Every trap has a weak point," Karl said, and more rumbles of giant feet crushing fallen stones echoed in the distance. "Elaina, could you dance … and find us a weakness …?"

"I can try," Elaina said. "Here …?"

"We don't want Anubis' crocodile to know where we are," Karl said. "Can you dance in the dark … quietly?"

"Very quietly, begging your pardon," Henry said. "We don't know if that monster is our only threat."

"What greater threat could Anubis need?" Alarika asked.

"It wouldn't hurt us to stand guard while Elaina dances," Roselyn said.

As Nate and Phil stood watch on opposite sides, Elaina began her dance in the dark, a shadowy figure illuminated only by the dim starlight reflecting in the windows. Her khopesh gripped in case of trouble, Alarika watched … and envied Elaina. *Elaina's victories were assured;* dancing bore no risk, as Elaina neither had to approach nor fight any opponent, and powerful enemies could be overthrown just by knowledge of their secrets. Used right, dancing-magic could accumulate wealth and power, and would've cemented her control over her army of thieves, which would've swelled to rival the legions of Egypt.

She sighed heavily. Although years younger, Alarika could never match Elaina's grace.

Elaina screamed and fell, so suddenly that all of them startled. Alarika started forward, then stopped and glanced behind to make sure that nothing was sneaking up on them. Her desert skills knew only how to hurt; *best leave healing to the others.*

Like her, Roselyn, Phil, and Nate had stayed in their assigned places. Karl, Eloise, Sister Aspertine, and Henry ran to help Elaina.

"Jackals …!" Elaina gasped. "They were coming at me … from all sides … and … Anubis' voice … laughing at me …!"

"Anubis planned this whole city to thwart us, even in visions," Karl said.

"Are you hurt?" Eloise asked, kneeling before her mother.

"Just scared," Elaina said. "Anubis protects his secrets … *I failed …!*"

"None of that," Karl said. "We'll find a way. Let's explore more …"

"… and conserve our supplies," Henry added. "We may be looking for a long time."

Searching revealed numerous ancient temples, long plundered and stripped of any riches. Empty stands stood. Alcoves lay vacant. Chairs crumbled when touched. Stone benches bore deep cracks. Fallen statues lay broken. Alarika frowned; Anubis may prefer a dark city to celebrate his nocturnal glory … but not ruins. This city was an inescapable trap, designed to cement Anubis' dominion over the other gods … as their once-bright realm, trapped in endless Winter, slowly died.

Alarika couldn't blame Anubis for doubting the companions. Enduring a thousand years of Winter, Anubis possessed no hope.

Alarika looked about the city with disgust. *No weapons …or materials to make them,* Alarika thought. Anubis may not be as wise as Thoth, but he was devious; *he was giving them nothing that they could use.*

Upon the abandoned temples and monuments, rows of hieroglyphs lay destroyed by age, carvings eroded, and paint peeled. Clay pots crumbled, and wooden archways lay collapsed.

Some temples were one huge room, and others filled with labyrinthine passageways, upper floors, towers, and lower depths that looked like dungeons, entered by black stairways where no light of Ra had ever shined; they left those unexplored. Dust lay thick everywhere, undisturbed, without a mark to show that another living soul had ever walked there.

At Roselyn's insistence, they frequently climbed into towers to peek at their jailor. The monstrous, massive crocodile crawled slowly over the distant ruins. Echoes reached them as the grinding crashes of its clawed feet crushed to rubble the remaining brick walls that it had long torn down. As the hours passed, the companions slowly explored eastwards … what Henry's guess by the stars was eastwards … hoping to find a path of which the crocodile might not know.

Yet their hope failed; the temples and monuments ended a stone's throw from the city wall, which rose smooth, undecorated, and equally ancient, in some places partially broken down, gouged by giant claws scraping deep rents into its thick stones, or knocked over entirely. Where they could see through the gaps in the broken outer wall, nothing existed outside the city, only a deadly fall through a thundercloud, miles down to the hard sands of the gray desert.

"We have to kill it," Roselyn said.

"We can't," Karl said.

"Attack its eyes … like the snake," Roselyn said. "Decide on a gathering place. Waving torches, Eloise, Elaina, and Sister Aspertine draw it between two towers; as it gets close, they flee into the temples. We shoot arrows at the eyes, and if those fail, we drop down off the towers onto its back. The first to reach its eyes stabs deep. Blinding one eye should be enough to stop it; most badly-wounded beasts retreat. Reunite at the gathering place, and if we deem it safe, then we run for the golden gate."

"Anubis knows that we defeated Ra's lightning snake," Karl said. "Do you really think he'll allow us victory?"

"What about fire?" Henry asked. "Some of these temples have wooden roofs. If we could draw it into a ring of buildings and ignite them …"

"Torches swinging on ropes before big windows would create moving lights," Nate said. "In this darkness, moving lights would attract anything."

"My father once used a sandbag with a hole in its bottom," Alarika said. "As the dry sand poured out of the hole, its weight lessened, and the rope, snaked through a pulley, slowly lowered a burning torch into a wooden bucket of olive oil, which sparked a huge fire. This gave us ten minutes to escape before the distraction began."

"Let's eat," Karl said. "We should rest, and then decide on which plan we'll use. We may only get one chance …"

Alarika glanced toward the darkness so that the others couldn't see her expression. *What good would even their best attempt be … against Anubis?*

"Master, may I speak?" Phil asked while they sorted through their food-packs.

"Of course," Karl said.

"I suggest reconnaissance," Phil said. "I could sneak closer …"

"No," Karl said. "We stay together."

"Knowing what we're facing …," Roselyn began.

"We can't separate," Eloise said.

"We might see a weakness …," Phil said.

"We only need to know its weaknesses if we're fighting," Karl said. "If we can distract it, and avoid detection …"

"Karl, I'll do whatever you want," Henry said, "but if we try to cross those ruins … and fail, what then?"

"Then a crocodile, from which even the strongest army would flee, catches us without defenses out in the open … on its hunting ground." Roselyn said.

"The gods of Egypt aren't fools," Karl said. "Their cities are masterfully planned, their challenges perfectly designed. They've tested our strength, our determination, our cleverness, our morality, our ability to learn, our willingness to comply … everything that you'd want to know about someone beside whom you might be forced to spend eternity. Anubis is infinitely wise and cunning. Also, he's had weeks to watch us, to study us. I can only surmise …!"

Suddenly Roselyn burst out laughing. The companions all stared at her.

"You sound like Athelwynne!" Roselyn sniggered.

Eloise joined Roselyn in laughing, but none of the others did.

"How many times did we kill that Mad Cow of Isis, and it kept restoring itself?" Karl asked. "We killed all of the harpies of Thoth, the six that we knew of, and afterwards they flocked to us without a scratch. What if we attack its eyes … and our swords pass through them like smoke, or they're made of a metal that no blade can cut? What if nothing can pierce its hide, not even the Sword of Hel?"

"Crocodiles hides are softer … underneath," Alarika said.

"If you kill it from below, then a beast as big as Castle Bristlen falls atop you," Karl said.

"It could be worse," Nate said.

"How?" Karl demanded.

"There could be two …," Nate grinned.

No one laughed at his joke.

"Countess Roselyn … Queen Reginleif," Phil began, "What do the Fighting Secrets of the Valkyrie say about … when you know that you can't win?"

"When all hope of victory fails, and escape is impossible, then make them rue all," Roselyn said.

"I hope it won't come to that," Elaina said.

"Anubis has blocked our every avenue of survival," Karl said. "We must do something … unexpected."

"If we can't fight … and we can't evade … couldn't we deceive?" Sister Aspertine asked.

"Deceive …?" Karl asked.

"If the … monster … and Anubis … thought that we were dead and eaten …," Sister Aspertine said, "perhaps they'd stop looking for us."

Alarika burst out laughing.

"You wish to deceive the God of Darkness, child of the Dead God and the Goddess of Death, born and raised in the House of the Departed, who knows the hidden Secrets of the Dead … with nine false deaths?" Alarika sneered.

"It was a good thought … even if it won't work," Roselyn said, and she turned to Sister Aspertine. "I'm surprised that it came from you."

"Your companionship has … infected me," Sister Aspertine said, and Roselyn snickered.

"We must do something," Karl said. "If we do nothing, eventually the Duat will open beneath us."

They found a temple with exits on all sides and sat on its floor to share food and the Water of Life, of which their supply was running low.

"As we're in his city, is there any way that we could summon Anubis … and force him to talk to us?" Karl asked Alarika.

"Mortals can't force Anubis," Alarika said. "His will is our doom."

After eating, they again searched the city, seeking ideas. Alarika purposefully stayed slightly apart, lagging behind. She was now part of their company, but she was also an Egyptian, loyal to her gods.

*If Anubis wanted her dead, how could she deny him?*

Yet Ra and Nut wanted her alive.

*How should mortals choose when gods argue?*

Her spine still shivered as she recalled the Duat; watching her father be yanked into its yawning, all-consuming pit, which had swallowed the entire Field of Dreams. Seeing the Duat open beneath her, as she'd walked on Shu in the City of Nut, feeling its hot, reeking gusts blow against her skin, had sent chills through every fiber in her body. The thunder of its opening, the shaking of the ground beneath her, and the echoing *crash!* as it snapped closed, like biting teeth, haunted her nightmares … when she could sleep at all.

Alarika's best hope was to stay with the company. If Anubis wanted them dead, then she had little faith that his will could be defied. Yet she said nothing, and kept her distance, avoiding the eyes of her companions.

Whenever they ascended to a high window, they peeked out. The giant crocodile stayed on its half of the city, laying still … or slowly clawing its massive bulk over the huge stone blocks that cracked and crumbled under its weight.

"Maybe it's trapped there, next to the only exit," Phil said.

"What could restrain that?" Nate asked.

"The will of Anubis," Phil answered.

"Anubis wants us eaten," Nate argued.

"Enough," Karl silenced them. "Anubis probably doesn't care how we die. If the crocodile doesn't eat us, the Duat will. As long as Anubis controls this game, we lose."

After many fruitless hours, traveling west, they reached the far wall, and then they rested and ate again. Upon awakening, Karl led them back to a huge temple.

"Why here?" Roselyn asked.

"Large windows … wooden floors and ceiling," Karl said. "Plenty of wooden furniture. If we start a fire here, it'll burn for hours. The bigger our fire, the bigger our distraction. Nate, Phil; carry more broken wood up here. Pile it high … enough to set this roof on fire."

Nate and Phil nodded, then left to gather wood.

"Be quiet, and stay out of sight of windows," Roselyn hissed after them.

Sister Aspertine and Elaina were posted to watch the crocodile. The others carefully searched every room for anything burnable. Before the windows, they moved slowly, carefully, and secured every item before they stacked another on top of it. Within a few hours, most of the space before the windows was filled with broken tables, chairs, chests, and benches, and in each corner they stacked a pile as high as they dared.

"Any higher and it'll see us," Karl said. "Let's rest again. Nate, you guard first. No sleeping! Wake Phil when you start to nod. After a good sleep, we'll eat, and then light our fire."

"Which direction?" Elaina asked.

"Eastward," Karl said. "That beast's too big to walk between the buildings. When we get to the far wall, we'll look to see what's happening. We'll only run for the exit if we think we can make it."

While the others slept, Alarika watched Nate … and rose when he fell asleep. She glanced out the window and, in the distance, saw the huge crocodile. Shaking her head, she placed her hand firmly over Nate's mouth, preventing him from crying out as he startled awake.

"Go wake your brother," Alarika whispered in his ear. "I won't tell …"

Blushing, Nate thanked her, then slumped away. Alarika peeked out at the crocodile again, wondering if it slept. Anubis had prevented Elaina from dancing … and stopped all of them from walking on Shu; she doubted if his crocodile would ever tire of hunting them.

Phil approached, peeking out the window.

"Do crocodiles see well?" Phil asked in a whisper.

"Ask a crocodile," Alarika shrugged.

Phil hesitated, then asked: "Do you think this will work?"

"Mortals can't defeat Anubis," Alarika whispered.

They ate when Karl awoke, and drank deeply.

"We'll leave our provisions by the East wall, except the Water of Life," Karl said. "While we run, I want us as unencumbered as possible. If we pass through that golden gate, we'll find ourselves near the City of the Gods. If we don't, we'll never need food again."

"If we're forced back here, then ...?" Elaina asked.

"Then we'll be lucky to have not gotten eaten ... but not lucky enough," Karl said.

"If we're trapped, we fight!" Roselyn insisted.

The others exchanged hopeless glances.

"Eloise, save your strength," Karl whispered. "Henry, start the fire."

Henry nodded. They'd piled several small starter-places, filled with broken and rotted wood, certain to catch quickly, with thin slats and chair legs hanging just over them, in the path of the rising flames. Insisting that they were unlikely to need it again, Roselyn cut up all of their rope except one thin coil, and wrapped loops around broken table legs, making makeshift torches, half of which they hung from poles stuck in the piles. Without flammable oil, they wouldn't last long, but they should help get their fires seen.

With ease, Henry struck his flints against Phil's steel vambrace, and the sparks caught in the rotten wood. Blowing gently, the sparks burst into tiny flames, and they fed it thin shavings until it caught for certain. As the tiny flames rose, they held torches over it, lighting them all.

"Hurry!" Karl whispered.

With lit torches, they dashed to the sides, shoving them into the spots prepared. Quickly their woodpile flamed up in a dozen places. Its light shined and illuminated the vast room. They lit the hanging torches and started them swinging.

A loud roar, scraping upon their ears like heavy furniture being dragged over a wooden floor, but deep, guttural, echoed across the city ... accompanied by a malevolent hiss. A loud crash, sounding like a building being knocked down, followed.

*"Run!"* Karl shouted.

Dropping their torches, they dashed for the stairs. Not bothering to muffle their footfalls, they thundered down the steps, then sprinted across the hall and through the door out onto the street. Hammering crashes and booms deafened them; the giant crocodile was nearing. Outside, they ran past tall obelisks and stone monuments, entered the building behind them, and raced to its exit on the far side.

Over a mile away, Elaina and Henry both stopped, and the others paused with them, all gasping for breath.

Behind them, the city shook with thunderous reverberations. Alarika and Roselyn sprinted to the edge of a building and peeked around its corner.

The buildings were more of an impediment than they'd thought. The massive crocodile had tried to crawl over them, only to have each building collapse under its weight, and crush into a tumble of broken stones and clouds of dust. The earsplitting roar of its passage into the heart of the city deafened them, even at this distance. As they watched, it scraped huge stone blocks backwards, entire sections of wall, and clawed deep grooves in the rubble, pushing its way forward.

The lights of their fire glowed brightly, illuminating the wide, snorting nostrils of the beast, and glinting upon wicked eyes reflecting the flames. Only a few buildings remained between the monster and their fiery distraction, which was now pouring a thick, black cloud above its flaming ceiling, although its cloud looked small compared to the gray billows of dust driven into the sky by the beast's destructive encroachment.

Alarika and Roselyn abandoned the view of their executioner and ran to join the others.

Walking as swiftly as Elaina and Henry could, they slipped deeper into the city, leaving the carnage behind. Louder came the coarse, guttural roars of the crocodile, and then an angry hiss; *their slayer had reached the fire.* The *crash!* of the flaming temple resounded, but they never looked back, hurriedly seeking the darkest, narrowest streets and passageways, staying out of sight.

An hour they traveled, until they reached the far wall of the city, then they had to stop. Karl let them catch their breaths, and then they edged along the tall outer wall.

At length they reached the edge of the buildings and looked out across the vast, uneven tumult. Over two miles it stretched, along the wall, to the glints of torchlight glowing upon the distant golden gate.

*That golden gate was their only hope.*

"Low; stay in the ravines," Karl said.

"Hurry!" Roselyn said. "That temple won't burn forever."

Dropping all their supplies save their two remaining botas of the Water of Life, they crawled onto the broken, scattered rubble, amid cracked blocks of stone and shattered sections of wall. Broken pebbles crushed into gravel slid and tilted beneath their feet as they walked. Behind the tallest piles they ducked down, scampering from shadow to shadow. Many small valleys opened before them, and they slid down short hillsides as much as they crossed them. Occasionally they found tracks of the monster's claws, grooves it had dug long ago. In places, uneven ground opened up, and their feet fell through into crevices and gaps in the loose rocks, and they had to pull themselves out.

Several deep openings lay dark and forbidding, and Sister Aspertine almost slid into one. Each was a tiny section of dungeon, the only intact remains of the buildings that had once stood there, subterranean chambers whose ceilings had escaped the footfalls of the crocodile. These they avoided, as they looked half-filled with rubble and led nowhere.

Nate and Phil scrabbled up to the summit of a heap and peered over it. Then they slid back down and reported; several buildings were afire, and the crocodile seemed to be attacking the flames, then backing off from the heat.

Almost hour passed, and slowly they crossed the broken field of ruins. On the rises between valleys, they saw the golden gate coming closer. At last they reached the gate … only to gape dumbfounded.

The golden gate rose fifteen feet, almost as tall as the black-stone wall, and was ten feet wide. It was pure gold, priceless, gleaming, reflecting the flickering torches and the lights of the distant fire.

However … it wasn't a gate. No gap split it. No edges marked it. Its huge hinges, on both of the tall doors, and the frame that it was set in, were all one solid piece of gold.

*It wasn't a gate, it was a decoration …!*

*No gate … no exit …!*

"Hurry!" Roselyn said, and she picked up a large block of stone and set it against the gate.

"What …?" Karl asked.

"Build a ramp!" Roselyn said, grabbing another stone. "Stack the stones … until we can climb!"

"We should go back!" Eloise argued.

"Back to what?" Roselyn asked. "Where are we to go?"

"If this is an exit, then the Celestial Path will be on the other side," Nate said.

"What if it isn't …?" Eloise demanded.

"We won't get another chance to find out," Karl said, and he seized and lifted a large stone.

Built by desperation and fear, their pile quickly grew. The strongest lifted heavy stones. Elaina and Sister Aspertine poured handfuls of gravel in between the bigger stones, to fill any gaps that could allow shifts. Eloise attempted to use magic to draw the stones toward them, but in the City of Anubis, her efforts succeeded no more than Elaina's dancing. Quickly she gave up, and began shifting gravel by hand.

In the distance, the crocodile hissed and roared, its head still facing away from them, its thrashing tail knocking ever more bricks from crumbling walls.

Good rocks became hard to find, and had to be carried from farther away. Phil uncovered another hidden dungeon near them when he almost fell into it.

Their pile, against the fake gate of gold, grew higher. Yet, the taller that they piled their rocks, the wider they had to make their construction, and the slower it rose. Still they kept working, until it stood eight six tall.

"Enough!" Roselyn said, and she climbed atop it. "Hurry, climb up!"

At her gestures, Karl, Alarika, Nate, and Phil climbed as high as they could. Karl pulled Roselyn up beside him onto the rough summit of their pile, and as they scrambled for footing, Phil and Nate joined them.

"Alarika, climb up onto our shoulders," Roselyn said. "See if you can reach the top."

Alarika complied; she and Nate were the lightest of the fighters, and she was taller. She climbed them, her feet upon their armor, their hands gripping her boots.

Soon her hands splayed against the cool, solid gold of the false gate, and then she reached up to touch the black stone ridge. Finally, hands lifted her entirely, and pressed beneath her boots, and pulling with all her strength, Alarika clambered up, all the way to the top … and peered over the edge.

Instead of silver, a golden Celestial Path met her eyes; their final road to the City of the Gods.

*They were succeeding!*

However, as she looked, the whole city suddenly shook. The glowing Celestial Path never moved, but the entire city shifted and slid across the sky, far from the closest golden sparkles … leaving an empty gap of fifty feet between them and the Celestial Path.

*Anubis had thwarted them!*

*He'd moved his entire city!*

Suddenly a light glowed from below. Alarika glanced down; the entire golden gate was suddenly glowing brightly, shining like a navigational beacon. From the sky over the city came a loud, booming, sadistic laugh …

*The laughter of Anubis …!*

Distracted by the shaking of the city as it had retreated from the Celestial Path, the crocodile thrashed from side to side, and either spied the brightly glowing golden gate or heard the booming laughter of Anubis. At once it forgot the burning temple and turned to face them, knocking more buildings down, and clawing to get at them.

*"Down!"* Alarika cried, and she dropped to join the others, climbing down them. *"There's no exit here!"*

*"We must fight!"* Roselyn cried.

*"Nate! Phil!"* Karl cried. *"Get the others to that crevice, into that underground chamber!"*

*"I'm fighting with you!"* Nate argued.

*"Get them to safety, then come back!"* Karl shouted.

Nate and Phil both complied, and with their help, soon Eloise, Elaina, and Sister Aspertine had slid down the rubble into the hidden chamber.

*"Henry, go with them!"* Karl shouted. *"If we die, protect them as best you can!"*

Looking surprised, Henry paused, and then seemed to come to his senses. With Nate and Phil each holding one of his arms, they lowered him to join the women.

The giant crocodile finally fought its way to turn around, and then came charging. Its bulk moved frighteningly fast, and its eyes seemed locked on the yellow light from the glowing golden gate. It charged, its claws hurling rubble into the air behind it.

Nate and Phil reached the foot of their pile and began to climb.

*"Stay down!"* Roselyn shouted at them. *"Stay close, one on each side! You're our distractions! When I shout, run off along the wall. If it comes at you, keep running! If not, come back! We'll jump atop it … and go for its eyes!"*

*"No matter what happens, keep attacking!"* Karl said. *"Some of us must survive, even if others die!"*

Alarika stared at the crocodile, disbelieving.

*She'd known that Anubis wouldn't let them escape!*

*She'd known that his city meant death!*

Karl drew and lifted his sword.

*"Valkyrie!"* Karl shouted.

Roselyn paused and looked at him, and a thin smile softened her face. Then Roselyn raised her godly blade.

*"Mist!"* Roselyn shouted. *"Hrist! Skeggjöld! Skögul! Hildr! Prudr! Göll! Herfjötur! Hlökk! Geirahöd! Randgríðr! Róta!"*

*"Odin!"* Nate shouted from below.

*"Jesus!"* Phil cried from the other side.

Alarika tensed. *The crocodile would be upon them in seconds!*

*"Osiris!"* Alarika cried. *"Horus! Ra! Isis!"*

*"Nate … Phil … NOW!!!"* Roselyn screamed.

Despite the pounding crashes of the monstrous feet, Alarika heard more than saw the boys dash away, in opposite directions. Suddenly the crocodile, aware that it was about to slam into the golden gate, stomped onto the rubble with all four feet, skittering huge rocks like hail, and skidded to a near-stop, its mouth opening wide. As big as a valley, its mouth opened; before Alarika yawned a gullet that could swallow whole elephants, surrounded by dark-red skin, a hideous tongue, and wide, thick yellow-brown teeth longer than spears.

Roselyn's hand on her shoulder shoved hard, and suddenly Alarika was falling, pushed off their pile. She gasped, and instinctively turned her khopesh to strike Roselyn, but then saw her shoulder Karl off on the other side.

The head of the crocodile shifted, following their movement, but its momentum drove it on. As Alarika fell, she saw the massive muzzle of the crocodile slam into the golden wall, right where they'd been. A second before it hit, Roselyn leapt high, bounced off its huge nostrils, and then she dropped down, as its muzzle slammed into the golden gate.

The decorative gold dented, and the wall above it crumbled.

Alarika screamed, but then she heard a fierce cry, and saw Roselyn run straight up the snout of the crocodile … as another might climb a steep hill. She reached the huge globes of its eyes, steel flashing. With the Sword of Hel in one hand, and her Sword of Horus in the other, Roselyn stabbed hard and deeply, one sword into each eye.

A deafening cry of pain erupted from the huge, horrible gullet.

With its wounding, a jerk of its massive head flung Roselyn away. Raising her khopesh, Alarika cried out a savage yell, then jumped forward and slashed at its massive throat.

Hearing shouts, she looked under it to see Karl and Nate strike upon the far side, driving their swords into its left-front leg. Phil, on Alarika's side, ran up beside her and jumped, stabbing with his long, straight sword inverted, impaling the beast's neck to his hilt with all of his weight.

The thrashing head flew to the other direction, pulling Phil off his feet on the shifting rubble, and then jerked back, low and hard. Just as Phil was jumping back up, raising his bloody sword to strike again, rough, thick hide struck Alarika and knocked her into Phil so hard that both flew backwards and skidded across rough stones.

Scuffed and stunned, Alarika struggled to get her feet, pulled up at last by Phil.

*They'd wounded the giant crocodile!*

*It could be hurt!*

*It could be killed!*

A sickly green glow emanated from the huge crocodile. Suddenly the head reversed, and the crocodile jumped forward. For a second time, its nostrils slammed against the dented golden gate, above the now-vacated pile of stones which they'd stacked, and then it slid backwards, dragging its feet away from them, claws raised.

At first this made no sense, and then they all realized it: *time was moving backwards.* Magic was healing the crocodile, as the Mad Cow had repeatedly healed itself, even after being killed.

*The giant crocodile couldn't be hurt!*

*The giant crocodile couldn't be killed!*

*"Into the pit!"* Roselyn's voice shouted, sounding strangely weak. *"Hurry! Go!"*

*"Why?"* Karl demanded.

*"Nowhere else …!"* Roselyn shouted.

Alarika glanced at the tiny pit inside which Eloise, Elaina, Sister Aspertine, and Henry had hidden. *There was no escape there …!*

*There was no escape anywhere!*

The mammoth crocodile was running backwards, away from them, and glowing green, even as the Mad Cow of Isis had done. Soon it would restore itself … and come at them again.

*"No!"* Roselyn screamed, a definite note of pain in her voice. *"Leave me!"*

Nate and Karl appeared in the growing, swirling cloud of dust. Between them hung Roselyn, still gripping Hel's sword, but not standing; her legs were dragging behind her.

*"Go!"* Karl shouted at them, but Phil ran forward to help. Together they carried Roselyn's broken form toward the gap.

Alarika slid into the tiny remains of the room. It was low-ceilinged, or so filled with rubble that it was almost full, but only Elaina and Eloise were there. Peering into the darkness, Alarika spied a dark doorway, from which Henry and Sister Aspertine were watching them.

*"Here!"* Karl shouted as Phil jumped in, and he and Alarika took Roselyn's injured legs and helped lower her onto their shoulders. Then Nate and Karl jumped in.

*"This way!"* Eloise shouted, and she led the way to the doorway.

Only blackness lay within.

*"Eloise, make light!"* Karl shouted.

*"No!"* Elaina shouted. *"Light will attract it!"*

*"That monster will be back in moments!"* Karl shouted. *"We have to see . . . !"*

Suddenly light flashed; Henry was scraping his flints against the stone wall. In the brief flashes of sparks, they saw another door.

With haste they ran inside, Henry first, and they carried Roselyn with them. She was grunting, her teeth clenched, but not crying out.

*"Let me die fighting . . . !"* Roselyn shouted.

Alarika glanced up expectantly, seeing Henry's flashes illuminate the next room, only to have darkness conceal them all a second later. Henry was running along the wall. He reached the right wall, and then ran along it, striking sparks as fast as he could.

Then the sparks stopped.

"Where's the door?" Karl demanded.

"No door," Henry said in the darkness, his voice filled with regret. "Sorry, Master … no door."

*"This is it . . . ?"* Elaina said. *"There must be . . . !"*

*"We're trapped!"* Roselyn seethed between gritted teeth.

"No way out," Phil said.

Sparks returned, but they showed only Henry standing helpless, repeatedly dragging his flint across the bare, back stone wall. Alarika glanced about, too stunned to accept it, but seeing no exit.

"Anubis … wins," Alarika said.

Suddenly the crashes of giant footfalls returned; the crocodile was racing toward them.

*"No light!"* Karl hissed, and darkness fell again. *"Everyone, be quiet!"*

Yet the light wasn't needed, nor voices. Loud breathing echoed, just outside their dungeon. Then they heard a distinct snuffling, followed by a deafening grating. Shadows blocked the starlight behind them, and the huge snout of the crocodile pushed in.

Not daring to make a sound, Alarika froze. Fear paralyzed her, but the wide nostrils sniffed and snorted through the first doorway, a horrible stench blasting back her hair. Then it pressed, one nostril shoving through the too-small door, its wide snout breaking apart the wall, driving aside the rubble, filling the outer room, and blocking out the light.

Loud scrapings sounded, and the second stone wall cracked; the crocodile was clawing its way in, widening the gap, trying to get to them.

*Once it tore the roof off their dungeon …!*

*"Henry, light!"* Karl shouted, and at once more sparks flashed, but they showed only the wall caving in around the doorway. The companions edged away from it, until they stood pressed in the farthest corner.

*"It's coming in!"* Phil shouted.

*"There's nowhere to go!"* Nate shouted.

Several screams followed, but Karl's voice shouted above them all.

*"Anubis!"* Karl shouted. *"You win! We quit! We're through seeking the City of the Gods! Done! We go no further! Our quest is ended!"*

Suddenly the whole room shook. Stones fell from the wall where the massive crocodile had pushed into the doorway, but suddenly the huge snout withdrew. Starlight filled the other room, brighter than before, and reflected into their dead-end chamber, which began to shake harder.

The massive head was retreating …!

*"Karl, what have you done?"* Eloise cried.

*"We're going there anyway!"* Karl shouted. *"Better directly … than through the stomach of that crocodile!"*

Beneath them, the floor cracked open and the red light of the Duat shined upward, making them all glow like blood.

*"Hold on to each other!"* Karl shouted. *"Stay together!"*

Bathed in red light, the floor of their subterranean chamber cracked, crumbled, and opened … and they fell into the Duat.

# Chapter 11

## The Company Falls

## SISTER ASPERTINE

The darkness vanished with the floor. The bright red glow of the molten, fiery river of the Duat, directly below them, shined upwards as their footing dropped away … and they plummeted.

Sister Aspertine screamed as she fell, unsure which companions she was grasping … or whose hands were grasping her. Directly below them flowed the flaming river of lava …

*At least they'd perish together …!*

Waves of heat blistered her throat as she inhaled for a last scream, and burned her eyes as she stared downwards at the boiling river, unable to look away.

Suddenly long coils wrapped around them … and pulled hard. Sister Aspertine glanced up in surprise, and saw a horror eclipse the flames of the deadly river … the looming face of a large, long-fanged cobra … hissing … inches from her face.

Sister Aspertine screamed louder.

Jerked aside, they crashed, not into the flaming river, but onto the rocky bank. The force of their landing jarred painfully; they smashed down hard, piled atop each other.

*"Alarika …!!!"* cried a strangely-familiar voice. *"Alarika …!!!"*

Sister Aspertine turned her sore neck … and recognized … the Mad Hermit of the Valley of Thieves.

*"Alarika …!"* he shouted again.

The ground moved beneath her … no, she was lying atop her companions, most of whom were groaning. The coil seizing her slid free, and coils encircling the others withdrew, with a hissing, hooded snake's head topping each.

*"Father …?"* Alarika weakly called up from the bottom of the pile.

Sister Aspertine slid onto the rocky floor, rolling off her companions, and landed near serpentine feet. With a brief scream, she jumped up and away from the Mad Hermit, too close to the river's edge. As she toppled into the fumes wafting above the smoking lava, a snake-coil snapped out and wrapped around her waist, pulling her back. Sister Aspertine screamed again, and the Mad Hermit glanced up at her.

*"Stop that … and help me!"* the Mad Hermit shouted. *"I don't have hands!"*

Still quaking, Sister Aspertine looked down; all of her companions looked hurt. Despite her fear, her holy calling came first, and she bent and took Eloise's arms and lifted her off Henry, who looked unconscious. Beside him lay Roselyn, unconscious, with one leg obviously broken. Beneath Roselyn lay Nate and Elaina, both groaning, with Karl, Phil, and Alarika on the very bottom.

One by one, Sister Aspertine pulled each off the others. Only Nate and Elaina seemed slightly aware, merely stunned by their fall's impact. Finally, Phil and Alarika opened their eyes, but each seemed dazed, unaware of where they were. Blood spewed from a nasty gash on Karl's head, and Sister Aspertine couldn't awaken him or Henry.

"I'm sorry," the Mad Hermit said. "I've been tracking you this whole time, trying to stay underneath you. When I saw you fall, it was too fast; I just grabbed everyone, but you were too heavy …"

*"They need healing!"* Sister Aspertine said.

"I'm no healer!" the Mad Hermit exclaimed.

Sister Aspertine bit back her first instinct, but she couldn't hold it in. Reluctantly she knelt beside Eloise.

"This one," Sister Aspertine said disgustedly. "She's a … healer."

Eloise took some time to restore to consciousness. Her left cheek was badly bruised, both eyes blackened, and she had a deep gash cut across her right forearm, which had bled badly, soaking her sleeve. Cursing herself for her blasphemy, Sister Aspertine lifted an almost-empty skin and forced some Water of Life into Eloise's mouth. By the time that her eyes fluttered open, Nate had awakened, and was caring for the others.

Elaina tried to lift her head, but she couldn't; her breath was shallow, and she clutched a hand to her ribs with a pained expression. When she tried to stand, she wobbled and fell.

"Don't move," the Mad Hermit begged her. "You'll only make it worse."

In the eternity that Eloise took to focus her eyes, Sister Aspertine looked around at the bleak, barren Duat. In the fiery light of the river's red glow, only the smoke-black walls of the huge cavern shone, as if polished smooth. Sweat leaked from her pores; waves of hot fumes rose from the lava, which looked as it had in the pool under the giant scales in the City of Thoth. The wide cavern's ceiling had sealed itself after they'd fallen through, blocking any hope of escape back to the City of Anubis. She was glad that the giant crocodile hadn't fallen with them; its body would fill the cavern.

She saw several ominous tunnels leading off into darkness on both sides of the river, but otherwise, they were alone.

However, strange animal noises, grunts, clucks, and howls, filled the cavern … and were growing louder.

The Mad Hermit looked the same; his pupils were slitted and long fangs extended from his mouth. His red, raggedy robe looked unchanged, and where his legs and arms should've been, long coils of serpents still rose, topped with the heads of hissing cobras.

"I don't mean to rush you, but they won't remain hidden for long," the Mad Hermit said.

*"They …?"* Elaina gasped.

"You be quiet; you need rest," the Mad Hermit said to Elaina, and then he turned back to Sister Aspertine. "This tunnel is usually full, but they run whenever the ceiling opens over the river … sometimes lava splashes widely when a newcomer lands in the flow."

*"Eloise …!"* Sister Aspertine urged.

Her eyes wavered … as if struggling to open.

"Don't move," Sister Aspertine ordered Eloise. "You're hurt … we're all hurt. Alarika's father … saved us … sort of … but we're in trouble. Something's coming … soon."

Myriad animal noises issued from the tunnels, coming closer. Between the confused cacophony of low roars, piping bird-twitters, and angry squawks, Sister Aspertine clearly heard … the moo of a cow.

"What …?" Sister Aspertine began.

*"Look out!"* the Mad Hermit cried.

Out of the nearest cavern flew a winged shape, larger than a hawk. It dove toward them, but the Mad Hermit rose up; his arm-serpents struck and bit into its wings, one on each side. It looked like a huge bat, but it had the face and body of a man. The angry bat-shape shrieked at them, a piercing, high screech emanating from its fanged mouth, and then the Mad Hermit flung it into the lava, where it splashed in, screamed, and briefly thrashed as black smoke engulfed it. Finally it collapsed, completely burned, and sank into the fiery river.

"Here they come!" the Mad Hermit warned.

A figure stepped out of the tunnel into the light, shaped like a man but covered in bristly brown hair, yet his face wasn't human, his head equally covered with short brown fur. He had a pig's snout and tall tusks, curling upwards, stuck out from both sides of his mouth. A panther with the head of a woman walked on all fours beside him, and a monkey with human arms and legs followed. More hybrid combinations followed, each stranger than the last. They came slowly, cautiously peering out of the dark tunnel, however, once amassed, and seeing the companions, they rushed forward across the wide cavern.

The Mad Hermit rose against them, all four of his snake-heads hissing furiously, but suddenly a stream of fire leapt from the lava river and streaked between the Mad Hermit and the hybrid-creatures emerging from the side-caverns. At once, the half-beasts screamed, shrieked, howled, and twittered, and finally fled, escaping back into their tunnels. The Mad Hermit watched them flee from the flames, then looked back at Sister Aspertine, his expression confused.

Disgusted, Sister Aspertine looked down at Eloise.

"You did that, didn't you?" Sister Aspertine asked.

Despite an expression of complete exhaustion, Eloise smiled.

An hour later, Eloise had a bandage on her arm, Karl had his bleeding head wrapped, and Eloise had done her best to heal him. He hadn't awakened, but his blood no longer flowed. Henry had responded well to healing, and now was tending Elaina. Alarika had awoken under the care of her father, but she'd been on the bottom of the pile when they'd landed, and she ached all over. Yet she was awake and talking, so Eloise let her be. Phil had awakened, but he remained groggy and couldn't stand.

Almost everyone needed some healing, including Eloise, but she was weak, and had to retain enough strength to call upon the friendly fire if the half-creatures dared to return.

Nate and the Mad Hermit stood guard, watching the side entrances, from which numerous creatures occasionally peeked. Roars and shrieks frequently echoed throughout the vast tunnel. Sister Aspertine sat holding Karl's head in her lap, and shuddered at the repeated loud caws of a raven-headed man that came from the other side of the river. Fortunately, he had the body and feet of a huge black bird, but his arms remained human, so he couldn't fly over the lava.

"At least you can rest now," the Mad Hermit said.

*"Rest …?"* Nate asked.

"You can't rest in the lands above … or on the Celestial Path," the Mad Hermit said. "Now that you're in the Duat, there's no hurry."

"Great …!" Nate scowled. "Now we're only trapped in an underground demon-world for all eternity …!"

"At least your Ha didn't have to die," the Mad Hermit said.

"Is there no way out?" Eloise asked.

"There's only one exit, and the demon Aapep guards it," the Mad Hermit said. "Nothing has gotten past Aapep since Ra last sailed the Fire River, and he needed the all-powerful Amsu-staff to drive Aapep back."

"Then … we'll die," Alarika said weakly. "Without food or water …"

"There're fresh-water streams in the tunnels, and … food," the Mad Hermit said.

"Demon-meat …?" Eloise grimaced.

"The chicken half tastes like chicken," the Mad Hermit said.

"We'll grow old … or transform," Alarika said. "Father, we have to escape …!"

"Without the power of Ra, no one gets out of here," the Mad Hermit said.

Four days, without moving, they sat beside the fiery river. Both of Roselyn's legs were broken. Eloise cast healing spells every day, but Roselyn mended slowly, and healing quickly tired Eloise. However, under her healing, Alarika and Elaina soon recovered, and they helped Nate and the Mad Hermit defend them from the denizens of the Duat, which was difficult, as they were so exposed. Several times each day, one or more tunnels full of creatures came warily forward, creeping on claws, pads, talons, and feet, while the winged flew above them. Yet Karl and Roselyn couldn't be moved, so the companions stood ready. When she had the strength, Eloise called forth the friendly fires, to leap from the river and surround them, and drive back the half-beasts.

Quietly, Eloise confessed that her wall of flame couldn't hurt anyone unless they willingly stood inside it, and perhaps not even then. Yet the Mad Hermit explained that all the humanity and memories of these creatures had been lost long ago, and for thousands of years they'd feared nothing but Aapep and splashings of the Fire River. Those two fears now dominated them.

Sister Aspertine tried to assist them to drive back the demons, and she even bared the long dagger that Horus had provided with her new armor, which she was slowly starting to like. At first, her armor's weight had startled her, and she'd wondered how she'd walk in it. Since then, she'd come to appreciate its beauty, especially the ornate cross decorating her golden breastplate, which was the only token of Christianity that she had left. Her armor resembled her old nun's habit more than the articulated suits of the others, which were clearly made for combat. Her tiny plates, shaped like four-pointed stars, which covered her blue skirt, made her feel strong, although she knew that she was far from invulnerable. Yet she mostly assisted Eloise, caring for Phil, Karl, and Roselyn.

By the next day, Phil was much recovered, but he coughed blood, and Eloise spent many hours working on him, although he showed no physical wounds. Karl's deep gash swelled to a thick lump on the back of his head, had to remain heavily bandaged, and Eloise cried out each time that she worked her godless healing upon him. Yet Sister Aspertine helped, upholding and encouraging Eloise, assisting her in casting her devil's magic. She had no choice; Jesus himself would've aided those injured.

Karl finally awoke, but he seemed confused, and they made him stay down, as he'd pass out if he sat up. Roselyn refused to lie uselessly, and on the sixth day, she shakily rose to her feet, ignoring Eloise's insistence that she remain still. Yet Roselyn had taken only a few steps, then returned to laying down, cursing her injuries.

Eating was a silent affair. Drained of the Water of Life, the Mad Hermit had taken their few bota bags, and as the demons of the Duat were driven back, he slipped in amongst the half-beasts, into the tunnels, no more regarded than any other demon. He also took a sword, wrapped in snake-coils, and on the second day, he'd returned with a large slab of meat. None of the companions dared ask where he'd gotten it, but hunger drove them to eat it.

They cooked the meat upon their swords, holding it over the Fire River, and drank freely from their bota bags, but it wasn't the Water of Life. On the twelfth day, both Karl and Phil could stand up, and walk about, and Roselyn also walked … with stilted steps and gnashed teeth.

They limped to a new place, not far away; an alcove, barely a dent in the wall of the cave, but less open to attack. The demons were growing bolder, attacking more often, and their crowds seemed denser.

"How long are we going to lay about here?" Roselyn demanded, pushing Eloise's hands away.

"Forever," the Mad Hermit answered. "You couldn't defy Anubis. What makes you think that you can defeat Aapep?"

"You can barely walk," Karl said to Roselyn. "We need a plan before we make any attempt …"

"Yea, our last plan worked so well …," Phil scowled, and then he glanced up from staring at his feet. "Oh … sorry, Master."

Karl waved off his apology.

"Our last plan worked," Alarika said. "Anubis moved his city to thwart us."

"Plans won't work against Aapep," the Mad Hermit said.

"What is Aapep?" Elaina asked.

"He's never the same," the Mad Hermit said, holding up his four snake-limbs. "You've seen us and our gods; men and women … each mixed with one animal. Aapep is all things, simultaneously, and huge. He stands before the Black Gate of Dawn, beside a chamber called Aapep's Den, and blocks all passage. Those whom he devours become part of his nightmare form … and make him stronger."

"Are there any side-passages, or secret tunnels …?" Karl asked.

"None," the Mad Hermit said. "The first creatures to arrive have spent four thousand years searching for an escape."

"If any exit exists, I'll find it," Elaina said.

"If we find one now, it might move … or be blocked … before we reach it," Karl told her. "Wait until we're healed …"

"I'm healing as fast as I can," Eloise complained.

"We're all grateful," Karl said to Eloise. "Better the discomfort of waiting than we face the master-demon at less than our best."

"Many times, the countless creatures of the Duat have stampeded Aapep, hoping that some would get out," the Mad Hermit said. "None have ever succeeded. Aapep is the ultimate evil; some say he's worse than Set."

"How can we fight a foe that can simultaneously defeat every creature here ...?" Sister Aspertine asked.

"That's easy!" Nate said, standing beside Henry, guarding the entrance to their alcove.

*"How ...?"* they all demanded.

"What would Eric Bjornson do?" Nate asked with a grin.

Phil shook his head, but Eloise laughed, and Roselyn grinned wickedly.

"That's the spirit," Karl said. "Eric wouldn't back down."

"Neither will we," Henry affirmed.

Nate got wounded when the demons next rushed their alcove; gored by a woman with the head of a rhino while a man's head on the long neck of a giraffe was trying to bite his face. After summoning fiery help, and then sending the friendly fires back to the lava river, Eloise tended Nate, adding him to her remaining list of patients. She even tended a snake-head emerging from the Mad Hermit's left shoulder, which had gotten bitten by the head of a giant pinch-bug on the body of a dark-skinned woman.

"Is there any chance ... that you could heal me ... entirely?" the Mad Hermit asked, and all four snake-heads turned to look at him.

"I wouldn't know where to begin," Eloise said.

"Athelwynne will ... if it's possible," Roselyn said.

"He's your best hope ... and ours," Eloise said.

"Our only hope," Alarika said. "If we get past Aapep, then we'll be facing my gods, and against them ...!"

"I won't fight our gods," the Mad Hermit said.

"Fight only your current battle," Karl interrupted. "How we'll fight the gods won't matter … if we can't escape the Duat."

After Eloise had finished healing everyone, they waited another two days for her to recover her strength. She obliged them by summoning fires to drive back all the creatures so that some of them could return to the river to cook the new meats that the Mad Hermit had acquired; Karl wanted some spare food to carry, not certain when they'd get a chance to find more. Fully-healed, Roselyn trained their fighters harder than ever, and lectured them endlessly on the Fighting Secrets of the Valkyrie, repeating her former speeches, and each day their discussions lasted hours.

Finally Elaina arose to dance. While the companions clapped a steady beat, the Mad Hermit sang a song in Egyptian; unlike his harsh speaking voice, he sang wonderfully. His snake-heads softly hissed all the while, and the sound of their music echoed throughout the Duat.

By the glow of the River of Death, Elaina's dance proved especially mesmerizing. Despite Eloise's flame-fence, many creatures emerged from the tunnels to watch, as if some vestige of humanity remained in their half-animal forms. Prancing musically, Elaina skipped across the smooth, rocky floor of the cavern with fantastic grace and poise. Where she neared the fence, Eloise's friendly flames rose, as if eager to dance with her. Elaina laughed, and lightly waved her hands through their magic flames. To everyone's amazement, the flames leapt upon her, not consuming, not searing, but caressing her skin. Tongues of flame danced upon her arms, as the fires had once danced upon Eloise in the Valley of Thieves. After waving her unharmed hands, enveloped by friendly fire, Elaina danced directly into the wall of flames, and the fires arose around her like a vaporous hug, embracing her with flickering love.

A blazing spirit, Elaina danced wonderfully, mesmerically, and when she finished, she skipped toward the river, and the warm fires gladly streamed off her, returning to their origin. The crowd of creatures suddenly cheered and applauded, and Elaina bowed to them, free of fire and burns. Even her silver-streaked blonde hair was unsinged.

Yet, as Elaina looked back at the companions, she gave a slight shake of her head, and they all understood; *she'd found no exit.* None had really expected success, as none believed that a hidden exit existed. Their elation at her fantastic fire-dance quickly diminished.

They rested once more, and to their surprise, no half-creatures attacked. The demons seemed confused, staggered by Elaina's dance, as if briefly reminded that each of them were once human. When the companions stepped out, abandoning their alcove, the demons drew back before them, as if reverencing their passage.

They set out, walking alongside the Fire River. Every demon stepped back, giving them room. Some actually bowed. Swords drawn, Nate and Phil led their way, followed closely by Roselyn, slightly limping, using the Sword of Hel as a cane, and the Mad Hermit slithering behind her. Alarika, Karl, and Henry walked rearguard, with Elaina, Eloise, and Sister Aspertine sheltered between them. Stalactites hung like stone fangs from the tall, wide cave's ceiling, and stalagmites rose from the soot-dirty floor. Sometimes the stone fangs met to form thick, sloping columns. The endless red glow bathed everything in bloody light, save where it failed to penetrate the deep tunnels that led off from the main river chamber, which were filled only with demons and darkness. Their main tunnel wound left and then right, but it always sloped slowly downhill, as if they were gently descending into Hell.

Sister Aspertine walked as quietly as her armored habit allowed. The half-demon creatures no longer frightened her; *she pitied them.* Their faithlessness in life had condemned them, and no hope remained in their hearts. Most of the beings of this land, including those living in the cities upon the desert and floating amid the Celestial Path, were half-human, half-animal. The only difference between their gods and these poor, doomed souls were that the gods possessed the intelligence of their humanity, enhanced by eons of memories, while the minds of these sad fools had diminished even as their bodies had transformed, losing their intellect to the limitations of their animal's nature. Each looked fearsome, and fought savagely, yet Sister Aspertine knew that someday she'd pray for them.

What frightened Sister Aspertine most wasn't the changes in any of the others, but the changes in herself. Once she'd have screamed in horror at the sight of any monster, and now she passed by squid-men and albatross-women with barely a glance. Before, she'd have dropped to her knees and prayed to be saved from illusions of damnation, and now she was a part of their company, helping to distract a giant lightning-cobra, walking beside a man with arms and legs of snakes, and holding Eloise so that she could cast pagan healing spells.

*Where was her faith?*

*What had become of her devout, subservient nature?*

Her new armor bore a brilliant, golden cross upon her chest, yet when danger threatened, her hand now reached for her dagger.

*Was she changed … too changed to be worthy of her sacred calling …?*

*Too changed to be allowed into Heaven …?*

Sister Aspertine didn't know how to be meek any longer. She was becoming … like Roselyn, strong and confident, concepts that she'd never really understood. She was walking in a land of a divine pantheon older than her own, toward a City of Gods that defied every word written in the Bible. The very existence of Egyptian gods, Norse gods, and Eloise's Lady defied everything that she'd ever believed. Yet … she'd met Ra … and seen too much to return to innocence … or ignorance, which now seemed to be the same thing.

*How could the Bible be wrong …?*

*Faith …!!!*

Faith was her last and only answer, but faith could be misplaced.

*Could everything that she believed in be wrong …?*

Or … was it all part of a grand scheme that she was only beginning to understand? Was she damned for possessing knowledge forbidden to mortals … *or would she be raised up and praised for her accomplishments in this unchristian Hell?*

Yet these fears only stabbed lightly. Her greatest wound was the memories that she tried to forget every night. Now … each time that Sister Aspertine looked at Nate, remembrances swelled powerful sensations … pleasures that she hadn't the courage to examine.

Intimate yearnings were improper for nuns. She couldn't allow memories of soft, longing touches … or the soul-warming heat of heaving passion … to impure her thoughts. Yet she'd known carnal desires, and no human could simply force unwanted memories from their minds; the more that they tried, the deeper those memories entrenched.

She couldn't change her past, her alarming situation, or forget the warmest feelings that she'd ever known … but she was no longer a woman tamed by weakness.

*The biggest change of all troubled her … the change that she'd not dared admit … not even to herself … but that she somehow knew …!*

The huge tunnel seemed endless, the side-tunnels moreso, and they left the crowd of demons behind, entering an area where only they walked. Occasionally some lost soul charged out of a dark tunnel, and Sister Aspertine let the others slay or drive back the half-beast.

The wavering glow of the Fire River shone brightly, constant, and as they walked through the hot, sweltering tunnel, miles seemed to pass by, and Sister Aspertine's resolution grew.

Sweating, they stopped for rest and food, and Sister Aspertine noticed a wide stalagmite not far away. Preferring privacy, she nudged Nate's arm with her elbow, and when he looked at her, she nodded towards it, and then walked away, as if absently wandering, and vanished behind the stalagmite. Moments later, Nate appeared.

"It's not safe to wander …," Nate began, but Sister Aspertine grabbed his arms, pulled him into a tight hug, and kissed his cheek.

Nate's eyes seemed to explode.

"I'll always be a nun," Sister Aspertine whispered to him. "I'm a Wife of God … and I shall remain so until the day I die."

Nate's expression ranged from shocked to confused … to sad.

"I don't blame you for what we did," Sister Aspertine said. "Powers beyond mortal will, supremacies of dreams, misled us, but we can't deny our … history."

"I love you," Nate whispered.

Sister Aspertine smiled sweetly.

"My precious Nate, I'll love you forever," Sister Aspertine said, and she brushed his soft, newly-grown scruffy cheeks with her fingers. "I hope that you'll always be close at hand. But, you know, what we shared … I can't repeat. I can't regret what we did; you made me a woman, and showed me pleasures that I'd never imagined. Yet, I … choose … vows before pleasure …"

"I just … want to be near you … and for you not to hate me," Nate said.

"I couldn't hate you," Sister Aspertine said. "We'll always be close … and we'll have a wonderful gift to share … to remind us of our love."

"Gift …?" Nate asked. "What gift …?"

"I can't say … yet," Sister Aspertine smiled, and she took and lowered his hand and placed it protectively over her womb, just below her gold-armored belt. "I can feel it, but I'll never regret it … be it your son … or your daughter."

The utter shock on Nate's face made Sister Aspertine smile, and she leaned forward, kissed him again, and then walked away, leaving him stuttering and stammering.

While she ate, Sister Aspertine cast sly glances back at Nate, who'd stood unmoving until Karl called him back, and then he waked with all the volition of a slug.

"Snap out of it," Sister Aspertine whispered sweetly, walking up beside Nate after they'd resumed their subterranean march. "You can't focus on fighting … and worry about our … mutual treasure."

*"B-b-but …!"* Nate stammered.

"Take care," Sister Aspertine said. "Now we're fighting to save our child's life."

"But … what will you tell the others … at your convent …?" Nate asked.

"Does it matter?" Sister Aspertine asked. "After all we've faced, do you really think I'll cower before a bunch of aged nuns?"

Suddenly a terrible laughter assailed them; a man with the head of a hyena emerged from a tunnel on the far side of the river, and ran toward them, stopping only when he reached the burning bank. Leaning over the rising waves of heat, he followed the companions, step by step, as if hoping that a bridge across the river would magically appear. Then an otter with the face of a woman joined him, scampering beside the bank. Shortly afterwards appeared a woman whose whole torso lay encased in large tortoise's shell, awkwardly scuttling on human hands and feet sticking out at odd angles, and a man with a large beetle's head raced up behind her, followed by a dog with human arms, adding constant barks to the irritating hyena's laughs. All of them crawled, paced, and slithered along the bank's edge, following the companions.

With a wave of Eloise's hand, a burst of fire rose up right before them, and the creatures screamed, hissed, and howled as they ran, scuttled, and crawled away.

"Enough," Karl said to Eloise. "Save your strength."

"The noise bothered me," Eloise said, but she relented.

A woman with the head, fur, and tail of a rat dashed out at them on their side, but Phil, Karl, Roselyn, and Alarika met her with swords slashing, and left her badly bleeding. An eagle with the screaming head of an infant flew across the vast cavern, from the far side of the river, but one snake-head of the Mad Hermit swatted it hard, and it fell shrieking into the lava.

A woman with the head of an antelope watched warily as they passed by, seeming paralyzed except for her frightened eyes, which followed the companions' every step. A man with the body of a spider watched from a tunnel choked with webs. A black jungle-cat with human hands and feet pounced from behind a stalagmite, and bit hard but uselessly upon Phil's armored forearm. Its fingernails scratched his face, which would've been claws, had its transformation been complete. They dispatched the cat and continued.

As they walked away from its still form, Sister Aspertine heard hooves clatter on stone, and turned to see dozens of demons following them at a distance, mercilessly falling upon the wounded half-beasts that they were leaving behind them.

"What becomes of them?" Elaina asked the Mad Hermit. "When they die …?"

"Nothing dies here," the Mad Hermit said. "Their Has may be destroyed, but the five parts of their souls remain, haunting these tunnels forever. Theirs is the ultimate anguish, for those living amid pain can hope for death, but for those without physical form, there's no relief, no hope of change. Eventually they become spirits of madness … and join with Aapep."

"Join with Aapep …?" Elaina asked.

"That you'll learn soon," the Mad Hermit said. "Most creatures never come here; few demons risk the hunger of Aapep. Fortunately, you traveled much farther above-ground than I'd expected. We haven't far to go."

"You expected us to fail …?" Alarika asked.

"Daughter, I taught you all that I knew, but here, I've learned how little I understood," the Mad Hermit said. "My journey above-ground was far shorter; the water-route to the gods was much like your Celestial Path, but with islands and wide lakes instead of cities."

"We would've died in the Field of Wheat without your warning," Karl said.

"Everyone gets warned," the Mad Hermit said. "I was your messenger. Not everyone can abandon their dreams, even when faced with certain death; those are the souls that the Field of Wheat damns."

"The gods of Egypt are fair," Alarika said. "They test … and judge justly."

"Anubis wasn't fair," Eloise said.

"In the City of Thoth, we weren't trying to kill Thoth," the Mad Hermit said. "Anubis rules the darkness of this land, and to attack a rulership is to attack its ruler. You can't blame a god for defending himself."

"We don't want to attack anyone," Karl said.

"You won't find it easy to convince Anubis of that," the Mad Hermit said. "Changing a mind a thousand times older than your own may be your hardest challenge."

# Chapter 12

## The Infernal

## SISTER ASPERTINE

The huge skull of a monstrous hippopotamus filled the end of the tunnel, its jaws wide, and the only passage further led straight into its mouth. The skull was so massive that its lower jawbone was embedded in a black flow that seemed to have solidified after leaking from the cavern beyond it. The lava river pooled before it, flowing rapidly through a wide gap broken in the jawbone, where three of its teeth were missing, each tooth as wide as an elephant. The upper jaw hung upheld by two massive tusks, like pillars, thicker than trees, stabbed into the floor. The tunnel itself ended, and the gigantean skull blocked all other avenues, looking cemented in place by the same black flow that had leaked between its teeth and spilled out to solidify, forming a thick ramp.

The molten river, streaming into the huge skull, lit its interior, making the cavernous eyeholes flicker from shadows to red.

*Stink …!*

They gasped and fell back, coughing and holding their noses. The fumes emitting from the next chamber reeked of death, a vile, putrescent odor that sickened them all. They halted, hacking and choking.

"Welcome to the Doorway of Aapep," the Mad Hermit said.

"What's that smell …?" Eloise complained.

"The final stench," the Mad Hermit said. "Beyond this gate lies Aapep … and death."

"Where's the exit?" Karl asked.

"Oh, you'll see the exit, once you enter there," the Mad Hermit said. "You'll just never reach it."

"Well, at least, let's go up and look," Karl said.

"If Aapep sees us, won't he attack?" Alarika asked.

"Aapep never abandons his post," the Mad Hermit said. "I've gone inside; it's safe … unless you approach him."

Despite the horrible fumes, they approached the monstrous hippopotamus skull and climbed up onto the hard, crusty ramp.

"This isn't rock …!" Nate said, looking beneath their feet.

"No," the Mad Hermit said. "It's dried blood."

"Blood …?" Sister Aspertine gasped, looking at the huge flow.

"The blood of a hundred thousand feasts," the Mad Hermit said, glancing up at the skull. "Legends say the gods made this monstrous hippopotamus to slay Aapep, but Aapep killed and ate it, and then wedged its skull to be his entrance."

Sister Aspertine gazed high at the upper jaw, far above her, propped up by it huge tusks, like ivory pillars stabbed into the ramp of dried blood. Matched tusks, equally large, rose from the lower jaw toward the ceiling, one with its tip broken off. Between two mammoth teeth was a gap big enough for pairs to walk side-by-side; the companions stared into the Duat's final chamber.

*Even the crocodile of Anubis paled before this horror …!*

Aapep wasn't as long as the giant crocodile, but its back towered higher. Aapep was surrounded by darkness, like an oily cloud constantly stealing back and forth, sliding across its many moving surfaces. Behind the shadows, huge, crushing claws waved on short arms, long feelers extended toward them, and a deadly, poison-leaking sting, longer than a spear, lashed about on a tail that could swat … and crush … a city. Above the deadly sting gleamed a second set of wicked eyes, as if the tail itself was a writhing snake. Aapep was a massive scorpion, standing atop its mountain of dried blood, the residue of its countless victims, glowing in the red radiance of the river which streamed lava into its domain and cascaded into a devilishly-wide pit that opened suddenly. The lava-fall splashed from a small pool over the brink, and down endlessly, pouring down unknown depths into a well beneath the Duat.

Yet, where the legs of the giant reptile should be, foreign limbs extended, and none of the legs belonged to only one creature. The tallest, and longest, was clearly a giant spider's leg. It reached from its scaly body out to the farthest wall. Another leg was short, and armored in layers of wide gray scales, with a relatively tiny foot, bearing long, yellowed talons. Another leg had a thick upper section, dull green, with a long, thin lower part, ending in a clawed wedge that dug into the mountain of dried blood beneath it, like the hind leg of a giant grasshopper. Another leg looked like a giant insect's leg, a thin, curved black pole covered in hairy spikes, bending under the multi-beast's weight.

The moving darkness receded, and Sister Aspertine screamed. The skin of the monstrous scorpion wasn't soft, or a hard shell, but enlarged faces of countless bugs, giant ants, flies, termites, roaches, spiders, and countless others; thousands of bulbous eyes, long, waving feelers, and snapping jaws and pincers, each the size of a large dog, combined to form the mottled skin of the monstrous scorpion. A loud clicking came from Aapep, where its monstrous claws scraped against its mismatched legs. Then the darkness returned … and Aapep grew even bigger.

Aapep's whole shape changed. When the darkness uncovered it, Aapep was neither reptilian nor insectoid, but twice as tall. The massive head of a lion roared, stretching out from the body of a giant rhinoceros. One forefoot was that of a gargantuan feathered rooster, with a sharp talon ending each enormous toe. The other foreleg was that of a moose, with a hoof that could crush a barn. One hind leg was a wrinkled gray pillar, immensely wide, like the thick leg of an elephant, and the other hind leg looked like a squat horse's leg, but striped white and black … where the oily darkness failed to hide it.

Aapep's skin had changed, too. Where countless insect-faces had covered it, now emerged the life-sized heads of myriad animals; elks, panthers, lambs, colts, beavers, monkeys, stags, wolves, and endless other types of animal heads, extended from its surface, as if each head were a single hair of the furry beast, and encircling the lion's head hung a mane of long snakes, the necks and heads of giraffes, squawking, long-necked swans, and other beasts uncounted, all glaring angrily at the companions.

"Behold the ever-changing face of evil, Aapep the Unslayable," the Mad Hermit said. "The Beast of a Thousand Forms."

A new wave of stench wafted over them, like a cloud of foulness emitting from its new form. Each stench was putrid, like rotting corpses, and stung every eye and nose, burning their throats as they breathed it.

"If anything could kill one form, Aapep would just assume another … and consume its attacker," the Mad Hermit said. "Even Ra couldn't kill it; wielding the Amsu-staff, armored with the faith of Osiris, Ra could only drive it back, into that wide alcove, off to the right."

"And there …" the Mad Hermit pointed one of his snake's heads, "at the end of the tunnel behind it; see the stars? That's your goal. That rocky mouth is the only exit from the Duat. Ra would sail his ship through there, and each morning bring a new dawn to the City of the Gods that lay just beyond it. In the last days, those petitioners who knew the spells to appease Ra were allowed to board his ship, and sail with Ra through that exit, and escape back to life. In no other way, by no other means, has any ever escaped; Aapep is the infernal, unsleeping jailor of the Duat."

Sister Aspertine stared, wincing as Aapep roared again, its lion's voice deafening her ears. She didn't need to be a warrior to know that no power of mortals could defeat, or drive back, this ever-changing beast.

*They were trapped forever.*

"Well …?" Nate asked. "What would Eric Bjornson do?"

Even Roselyn had no answer.

"I could dance, but what could I seek?" Elaina whispered.

"My powers could never thwart this," Eloise said.

"What are we going to do?" Henry asked.

"I didn't bring you here to fight Aapep," the Mad Hermit said. "I brought you here to help you understand … and accept … your doom."

"Father, we can't …," Alarika began.

"When it becomes human, then you'll see its true skin," the Mad Hermit said. "When the heads of all those it has consumed appear, all the fools who tried to fight it, then you'll see where you'll end up … if you attack Aapep."

Following Karl, the companions retreated to a small indention, not even an alcove, in sight of the giant hippo-skull. Then he turned to face the companions and opened his mouth, but no words came.

"Take your time," the Mad Hermit said. "Haste gets you eaten."

An hour passed, and then a day, and except for posting guards in a rotating schedule, so that they could all sleep, no one spoke.

Karl, Henry, and Elaina took one watch. Roselyn, Phil, and the Mad Hermit took the second watch. Eloise, Alarika, and Nate took the third. Sister Aspertine was excused from watch duty; she suggested that her time would be better spent in prayer, and none objected. They ate sparingly, and the Mad Hermit found a nearby web-choked tunnel leading to an underground stream, but he had to make his way past a hungry woman with no human limbs, but two long spider's legs sprouted from each of her shoulders and hips. Nate assisted him, scooping a small, glowing lump of lava from the river, on the flat of his Sword of Horus, and he used it to threaten the hissing spider-woman back into a crack while the Mad Hermit slipped past.

They also took turns watching Aapep. Their jailor became a giant octopus with strange tentacles that Henry described as belonging to many different ocean creatures, one of which was a giant sea snake. Its head was that of a massive shark and reeked of rotting brine. Then Aapep took the form of a giant vulture, with avian creatures sprouting like feathers from its vast wings, and a beak like a giant spike of death, which spewed forth a bitter, alkaline stench. It finally became what Roselyn described as a Norse giant with the head of a troll, and human faces of thousands of its agonized victims appeared on its skin, most of them screaming in agony.

They ate sparingly, but two days later, their food ran out.

"We've no choice," Karl said. "We must attack Aapep."

"It's what Eric would do," Eloise said softly, but no enthusiasm lifted her tone.

"We attack in two groups," Karl said. "One group approaches alongside each wall. If it focuses on one group, the other may be able to escape unseen. If that happens, then we draw back and wait; the group that escapes will enter the City of the Gods and free the Seer; only he is powerful enough to rescue the rest of us."

"What if neither group can escape?" the Mad Hermit sneered.

"Both groups will refrain from attacking directly, and retreat when threatened," Karl said. "Our goal is to distract only; the group that succeeds will allow the other to escape."

No one expressed any belief that this plan would work, but no one had a better plan. Their only alternative was to accept their doom … and become demons of the Duat.

"Roselyn, you and I are our best warriors," Karl said. "We'll each lead one team. Eloise and Elaina, you're our magicians; you must each be in one team. Elaina, you stay with me, and I want Sister Aspertine, too. Where Eloise can distract with magic, Sister Aspertine can make noise, and Elaina's dexterity can let her dodge most threats. Henry, you can carry Eloise, if she exhausts herself; you're with Roselyn." Henry nodded. "Phil and Alarika, you're with Roselyn; do as she says. Nate, you're with me."

Karl sighed, then turned to the Mad Hermit.

"What's your real name?" Karl asked.

"Qebehsenuef," Qebehsenuef said. "I was named after the youngest son of Horus."

"Umm …, I can't pronounce that," Karl shook his head. "Hermit, I'm afraid that I must ask something terrible of you. Whichever team doesn't make it out of here won't survive long without you. If I can, I hope to be the team that stays; both Roselyn and Eloise care more for the Seer than I do; he's most likely to respond to them. If they distract, if we're the ones who escape, then you'll need to retreat and stay behind with your daughter. Either way, you're one of us now: we won't all escape unless you do."

"I understand," the Mad Hermit frowned, glancing at his daughter. "We've one foe, and I won't fail my daughter."

"There's nothing else I can think of," Karl said. "We're at full strength; we've no point in waiting any longer. Everyone, be as careful as you can. Our goal is to not get killed."

"That goes for you, too," Roselyn said to Karl.

"That goes for all of you," Eloise said, glancing at her mother.

"What if this doesn't work?" Henry asked.

"When all hope fails, run back here," Karl said. "If we fail, then we'll try something else."

They took only their weapons, leaving all bota bags for those who'd stay behind. When they reached the skull, they entered between its teeth, and then split apart without a word. Roselyn led, and her team jumped over the narrow lava-fall, where the molten rock tumbled over the lip of the vast pit and fell into darkness.

Roselyn led them to the far left side. Karl led his team off to the right side.

Aapep stood before them, a vast bear with the head of a monstrous lizard, reeking of sulfurous fumes. Numerous animals roared, brayed, and baa'd from its skin, but as they neared it, the oily darkness slid over it.

"Back!" Karl hissed. "It could become anything!"

Aapep shifted, and the darkness receded. A giant elephant's head, with huge flapping ears and long tusks, cried out an echoing trumpeting blast, and the long snout snaked out at them. Its body resembled a monstrous rat, equal in size to the giant head, and covered with the smaller heads of other beasts. Its trunk lifted high, then smashed down, struck and cracked the floor of dried blood, deafening them and shaking the entire cavern.

Karl and Nate jumped to either sides of the trunk as it slammed the ground between them. The Mad Hermit snaked his way out of being crushed, and Elaina grabbed

Sister Aspertine and ran out from under it just in time. Then the long, massive tusks swung toward them and struck the cave wall, shaking the cavern and dropping stones from its shadowed ceiling.

*"Retreat!"* Karl shouted, and he ran to Nate, who was swinging his sword at a thick tusk that threatened to crush him as it swung back and scraped over the ground. Karl grabbed Nate and pulled, and together they ran back just as Eloise's scream mixed with shouts from Alarika and Roselyn. Sister Aspertine shrieked and dodged to the side, ducking under the thick tusk, but then the snout returned, reaching for her.

Suddenly Elaina leapt up onto a tusk, bounced atop the thick snout, and danced upon biting heads. Simultaneously, the Mad Hermit jumped toward Sister Aspertine, wrapped a coil around her, and slithered back toward the jaws of the hippo-skull, pulling her to safety. The huge trunk arced back to draw Elaina closer, but she jumped onto a tusk, then spun off and hit the blood-crusted floor running … to join the others. The elephant head erupted with another ear-splitting trumpet, making them all cover their ears as they ran.

They gathered beside the teeth and stared back. Nate had been injured; blood streamed down his vambrace, and Elaina had a long tear in her leather skirt and a gash on her calf.

"If we can …!" Nate began after the trumpet's blare ended.

"Look …!" Sister Aspertine pointed.

Henry was carrying Eloise, with Phil beside him, Alarika and Roselyn right behind them. All jumped aside as the head of a giant python dove at them. Yet a stream of fire suddenly burst from the lava-fall and flew across the sky, shooting into the python's wide mouth. As it landed, Roselyn and Alarika spun and struck with their swords at its eyes, but the head plowed past them. Phil grabbed Henry, pulled him down, and the sword-blinded python smashed its head into the wall, bounced off, and then withdrew.

"Here!" Karl shouted, waving.

"No!" Roselyn cried. "Wait! See what it changes to next!"

Almost an hour passed. The python head reached out to its full length, but the spear-long fangs of the massive snake's head stopped twenty feet short of Roselyn's team. The trunk and horns of the elephant also stretched towards Karl's team, threateningly, but never came close.

They examined their wounds.

"A goat-head was sticking out of the side near me," Nate complained. "There was another head; I've no idea what it was, but it had long teeth. When I dodged its bite, one of the goat's horns caught me."

"There were faces atop the trunk," Elaina said as Karl held her and Sister Aspertine examined her calf. "One caught my skirt in its mouth … so hard that it tore. Another beast-head spat something at me, like spines, from its mouth. My skirt caught most of them, but one got through the gap …"

"This isn't right," Sister Aspertine said.

"What …?" Karl asked.

"It's swelling, and very red, right around the puncture," Sister Aspertine said. "It might be venom …"

"Eloise …!" Karl said.

"No," Elaina insisted. "I can walk, and we need to get out of here."

"It could be poisonous," Sister Aspertine said.

"Eloise can cure me after we get out of here," Elaina said.

"Either they get out or we do," Karl said. "You and her won't …"

*"I won't let my daughter die in here!"* Elaina snapped. "If she gets out, then she'll free the Seer, and he'll heal me. If not, then we'll free him."

When the oily darkness swarmed over Aapep, the body slowly twisted into that of a massive orange ape, with the colossal head of a black cat, its ape-limbs ending in the feet of three different animals … and one human hand.

"Look out!" Phil shouted.

The orange ape reached with arms amazingly long. The giant human hand had skin covered with the heads of weasels, snapping turtles, cats, squirrels, fox, and countless other beasts, most of which Sister Aspertine couldn't identify. Karl and Nate charged just within sword-reach, swinging hard. Karl cut a long slit in one giant finger, and Nate slashed off a small rabbit's head, which fell to the ground, still twitching. The hand drew back, made a fist, then suddenly hammered the ground, cracking apart the dried blood and bouncing them all.

"Back!" Karl shouted as shards of dried blood shot at them.

"They're running!" Elaina shouted.

"Who …?" Sister Aspertine asked, but then she looked across the huge chamber, to the left. Phil was carrying Eloise now, and Alarika was helping Henry as he limped. Roselyn, facing behind them, held Hel's and Horus' swords pointed at Aapep.

Sister Aspertine glanced again at the orange ape as its cat-face snarled at them, then turned aside; sticking out of the back of its cat-face was the head of a sphinx, facing the other direction.

"Retreat!" Karl shouted, and they slipped through the gap between the huge teeth, out of the chamber of Aapep. A minute later, Phil appeared, carrying Eloise.

"What happened?" Karl asked.

"The sphinx's mouth had a serpent-tongue … that lunged at us," Eloise gasped, and they realized that her feet were dripping with blood. "It spit at us, and its mucus sizzled where it landed."

Phil set Eloise down by the giant teeth, and she began healing her feet.

Alarika and Roselyn helped Henry limp through the gap in the teeth. The dog's face on his golden vambrace was deeply dented with marks that looked like teeth.

"Something bit him, some creature with a mouth like a wolf, only much bigger," Alarika said. "It was flinging him about. I decapitated it, but when it cut free, Henry flew across the cave … and crashed into the wall."

"We failed!" Roselyn cursed, snarling as deeply as Aapep.

"We never expected it to have two heads, one facing each way," Karl scowled.

"We're trapped," Alarika said. "We're never getting out."

"We've got to keep up our faith that we'll succeed," Karl said.

"Three incarnations!" Roselyn shouted. "We never got close …!"

"There has to be a way …!" Karl argued.

*"Wait …!"* Sister Aspertine said, and she stepped away. "No … leave me alone … I need to think …"

Sister Aspertine stepped away, ignoring the others, lost in thought.

*Faith, Karl had said …!*

The words of Ra returned to her.

*'Weakly flows the faith of followers whose deities are condemned to Winter.'*

*'Armed with the faith of Osiris, Ra drives back Aapep, and emerges from the Duat, to bring dawn to the world.'*

*'Winter has weakened all faiths in our realm, even Aapep.'*

The words of others followed.

*'Over a thousand years ago, when our gods weakened, our protections over our people failed. Without their faith, our people fell to hopelessness, and their hopelessness further weakened us.'*

*'But forget not our Winter; the strength of gods fail with their followers …'*

"Faith is the power of gods … of all gods …," Sister Aspertine whispered to herself. "Aapep is one of them, a part of their pantheon …!"

Sister Aspertine stared at the red river, then glanced to the alcove where their bota bags lay, then looked up at the giant hippo-skull. Slowly she paced a while, noting that the others were watching her.

Their eyes screamed misery. Their expressions mirrored defeat.

"We can't lose faith," Sister Aspertine said. "We can't defeat Aapep with swords, but as Roselyn said, everything has a weakness. Aapep has a weakness, the weakness of everything in this land: Winter, which has weakened this entire pantheon, and has been further weakened by … lack of followers … their diminished lack of faith."

Their expressions remained unchanged … but she held their full attention.

"Don't you see?" Sister Aspertine asked. "Faith powers the gods … and everything in their lands. They live for new believers to arrive. This whole world is dependent on faith. That's the real weapon that Ra used, *'armored with the Faith of Osiris'* and what we need, to fight Aapep: faith."

All eyes widened with disbelief.

"Argue if you want," Sister Aspertine said. "Recall what Ra said, and everything we've learned since we came here. All the challenges that we've faced were tests of faith, to see if we'd give up."

*"Their faiths failed …,"* Elaina said, *"and their gods were weakened."*

*"Each arrival of a faithful subject … is to them a feast,"* Eloise said.

"You can't be serious," Karl said.

"Husband, you're many great things, but you've never been a believer." Eloise said.

"What are you going to do, walk up to Aapep … praying?" Roselyn asked.

"Yes," Sister Aspertine said.

"You'll be swallowed whole," Alarika scowled.

"Your warrior's attack failed," Sister Aspertine said. "Aapep is too strong for swords. You need something … all-powerful."

"The Lady of the Druids could only be brought to Yggdrasil by Mimir, a creature of Yggdrasil," Karl said. "We have nothing all-powerful."

"Both of those pantheons are still strong, enduring only their Fall," Sister Aspertine said. "The Gods of Egypt, and all in this land, are trapped … deep in their Winter. My faith stands in its Summer …"

"What if you're wrong?" Karl demanded. "You'll be killed and eaten!"

"What other hope do you have?" Sister Aspertine asked. "What weapon do you have that you haven't tried? How will you defeat Aapep … or stop from transforming into demons?"

The companions fell silent.

"I'll go with you," Nate said.

"Squire …!" Karl argued.

"I have faith," Nate said.

*"You've never had faith!"* Phil scoffed.

Nate paused, then faced his brother.

"I have faith … in Sister Aspertine," Nate said.

"Thank you … but I'll go alone," Sister Aspertine said. "Just remember: if I fail, the fault is mine. Don't lose your faith in God … because of me."

"Can't you wait …?" Karl asked. "Let's discuss this …"

"Discussion won't alter my faith," Sister Aspertine said. "I'm going now."

"We could stop you …," Roselyn said.

"You won't," Sister Aspertine said. "You can't defeat faith."

With a soft bow, Sister Aspertine folded her hands … and turned toward the gap in the teeth.

"We'll be right behind you, if you change your mind," Karl said.

"I won't," Sister Aspertine said, and she walked away.

"You'll be killed," Alarika snapped.

"You can't kill faith," Sister Aspertine said, and she continued forward.

"Sister Aspertine …!" Phil said loudly. "Lord Sir Rafe … will be very proud of you."

Sister Aspertine almost smiled, but she tried to focus on her prayers. *When all other hopes fail, faith remains.* She was a true believer; she'd been through a land of foreign gods, tormented by the company of witches and a Valkyrie … and a lecherous bishop. In some ways, her experiences, her learning of other pantheons, had strengthened her faith, not weakened it.

*If all this was real, how obvious was it that her faith equally existed?*

*How could she ever imagine that Jesus wasn't real … when she'd met and dined with Ra?*

The gap in the hippo teeth loomed tall. Sister Aspertine tried to keep an even pace, neither slowing nor hurrying. Yes, she'd be afraid of Aapep, but faith was stronger than fear. Besides, what doom could be worse than cowering in despair, slowly transforming, until … like the Mad Hermit … you became a demon?

*Was fear what caused their transformations …?*

Sister Aspertine had no desire to discover the truth of the Duat. If God didn't want her eaten by Aapep, then she'd rather submit to His will than endure an eternity knowing that her faith had failed.

Atop the thick layers of dried blood she walked, through the gap in the monstrous hippo-skull's teeth, and into the stench and sight of Aapep.

Its form shifted, and the head of a jungle cat faced her … upon the body of a giant wasp. Wings of some huge, terrible bird flapped over it, blowing a stinking breeze upon her. Six mismatched legs held it up, and a vast hive of buzzing reached her ears.

Taking a last deep breath, Sister Aspertine stepped closer.

A hand gently took hers; Sister Aspertine startled to see Nate beside her, walking with her. He gave her a reassuring smile, and together they walked forward.

Aapep roared, a fierce, horrible blast which echoed in their ears, yet they didn't stop. Sister Aspertine knew, even as her fear rose, that Nate's company strengthened her, and she couldn't depart now … not while he was endangered.

Aapep inched backwards, and they walked forward.

Suddenly the jungle cat leaped forward, and its mouth opened, big enough to swallow both of them. The long, gleaming cat's teeth dove upon them, and surrounded them, the giant rough tongue dripping so closely that they could reach out and touch it, but the huge jaws never closed, merely blocked their way.

A massive hornet's sting, a spike large as a battering ram, dripping poison, hovered against the ground underneath it, pointed at them.

"In the name of the Father, the Son, and the Holy Spirit, I banish you," Sister Aspertine said, and she made the sign of the cross. "Begone, demon, before the light of faith!"

Hot breath spewed upon them, but the deadly teeth never closed, and the sting never stabbed. Nate's hand in her grip tightened.

"We've no fear left," Nate said to Aapep. "Before us, your faith is weak …!"

The jaws withdrew, the head drawing back. Then it leaned forward and roared again, hissing spittle upon their armor, but they never stepped back.

"Clear is the path of the faithful!" Sister Aspertine shouted, and she took another step forward.

"Blessed are the faithful!" Phil said, and he stepped up beside them.

Sister Aspertine smiled, reached out, and grasped Phil's hand.

"We stand of many faiths, and our faiths are strong!" Elaina said, and she stepped up … with Eloise beside her. They were already holding hands, and Elaina took Phil's hand.

"The Lady of the Druids sends her servant!" Eloise shouted. "My faith is unwavering!"

"My faith has never faltered," Henry said, and he stepped up and took hold of Nate's hand.

"No trial has ever weakened my faith," the Mad Hermit said, and he slithered up beside Henry, and wrapped a snake's coil twice around his arm.

Deafeningly Aapep roared, echoing his fury down every tunnel in the Duat. The oily darkness enveloped him, and he reformed as a huge multi-headed serpent … a hydra … each head covered with the faces of a thousand reptiles instead of scales. Furiously he hissed … and spat a smoking, green poison onto the black ground before them.

As one, arm-in-arm, the line of the faithful stepped forward.

Oily darkness returned, and a giant crab appeared. Then Aapep became a monstrous ram, with massive horns, on the body of a horse, with legs like a centipede. Then it became a hippopotamus head on the body of a shaggy dog … with the fore-legs of a monstrous vulture and an elk.

"You lose either way!" Nate shouted at Aapep. "Few come here anymore. If you consume us, none may ever come again, and you'll guard nothing. Death will come for you when all believers cease, and this realm dies forever! Then you'll know fear!"

"The faith of the new God drives out the old!" Sister Aspertine shouted. "We are that faith, and we drive you back!"

Hesitantly, Aapep stepped back, and the companions pressed him. Roselyn lowered Hel's blade and stepped up to join them, Alarika at her side.

"By God in Heaven, Odin in Asgard, the Lady in Elysia, and Osiris, Ruler of All, we command you back!" Elaina shouted.

Aapep began changing, shifting without stopping, the oily darkness barely hiding any features before they appeared anew. Angry roars, grunts, hoots, squawks, hisses, and trumpeting filled the Duat, each new sound blasting throughout the length of the Duat before the last returned as an echo. A light seemed to glow from the gathered companions, a golden-yellow brilliance, which struck Aapep, and turned his roars of fury into cries of pain.

With screams unequaled, hurling the vehemence of eons, Aapep fell back. Step by step, the vast, undulating Eater of Souls, the God of Snakes, War, and Chaos, Lord of the Duat, the Terrible Evil, the Beast of a Thousand Forms, Aapep the Unslayable … retreated. Led by Sister Aspertine, the companions stepped closer, and the Great Jailor withdrew.

As it backed into its den, the oily darkness seeped over all of its skin, fur, coils, claws, teeth, eyes, wings, and all the heads and faces upon it. Soon it covered Aapep in total darkness, and concealed him entirely.

Before them shined the dim night's sky … through the long, cavernous exit from the Duat. Karl came running up behind them, and together they ran through the tunnel … toward the exit.

## Chapter 13

## The City of the Gods

# HENRY

Henry stepped up onto the rocky rim of the cave's mouth, the exit from the Duat, and gazed down upon paradise. Under the same dim starlight that had always crowned this realm, a road of paved gold led to a huge city beside the sea, shining with flowing glints, gleaming as small ocean waves cascaded toward it. Palm trees lined and shadowed the golden road, and a thin forest flourished around the outskirts of the most amazing city, more magnificent than Henry had dreamed that Heaven could be. Uncounted tall obelisks towered amid silver temple roofs and ornate jeweled palaces rose from lamp-lit streets, and a bright white light shined from its center, the brightest light they'd seen since leaving their world, beaming its brilliance high into the dark sky, making even the twinkling stars pale.

*"The light of Athelwynne . . . !"* Elaina exclaimed.

"That light . . . is the Seer . . . ?" Alarika asked. "The one we seek to rescue . . . ?"

"Let's go get him," Karl said.

Their rich path sloped down from the round exit beyond Aapep's lair. The company began walking, their footfalls upon the gold road, and the lapping waves of the sea, the only sounds that they could hear.

"Sister Aspertine," Roselyn said, mirroring his thoughts, "I owe you my sincerest apologies. Rafe couldn't have chosen us a better companion."

Sister Aspertine smiled sweetly.

"Lord Sir Rafe couldn't have selected for me better friends," Sister Aspertine said.

"Add my apologies," Karl said. "You've saved us all … again."

"You've proven your worth … and your faith," Elaina smiled.

Agreements rained, and many patted her shoulders. Nate alone didn't reached out to her, but he paused and bowed formally to her, and they shared a smile that Henry recognized as carrying secret meanings.

"The sirens were busy inventing songs about all of you," the Mad Hermit said. "Laments, of course, but now I suspect they'll compose happier tunes."

"We're not finished yet," Karl said. "They could still be laments."

A sparkling, golden ribbon reached down from the sky, and ended at a wide, golden bridge that spanned a river flowing toward the sea. Beside the bridge, from the edge of their road, golden steps led down to an ornate dock and patio at the water's edge.

"The end of the Celestial Path … and this must be the end of the Water Route," the Mad Hermit said. "If we'd succeeded on our separate routes, here's where our paths would have joined."

Past the bridge, the smooth, gold road led all three routes to a series of four tall gates, before each of which stood two guardians.

"Let me deal with this," the Mad Hermit said, and he bowed to the first set of guards and recited a prayer.

*"Thou goest round the sky,*
*Thou sailest with Ra,*
*Thou surveyest mankind.*
*Thou art alone going round with Ra,*
*For thou art called Osiris.*
*I am the divine mummy.*
*What I say takes place.*
*I shall not be driven back from the gate;*
*its walls of burning coals show the way in Restau.*
*I have soothed the pain of Osiris,*
*When he supports him who balances his pedestal.*
*When he arrives from the great valley,*
*I have made my way to the light of Osiris."*

Both guards, a man with the head of a jaguar and a woman with the head of a dove, bowed and stepped aside. The companions passed between them, exchanging gestures of respect.

At the second gate, the Mad Hermit bowed and addressed its two guards, a smiling harpy and a small, furry sphinx.

*"The name of the doorkeeper is*
*He Who Shows His Face.*
*The name of its warder is*
*He With a Revolving Face.*
*The name of the herald is The Consumer,*
*Said the Searcher when he approaches the second gate.*
*He sitteth and acts in accordance*
*with the desire of his heart,*
*weighing the words as the second of Thoth.*

*The attributes of the Searcher are those of Thoth.*
*When faint the Maat gods,*
*The hidden ones who live on truth,*
*Whose years are those of Osiris,*
*Still I am mighty in offerings at the appointed time.*
*I have made my way out of the fire.*
*I march. I have made my way.*
*Grant that I may pass on freely,*
*that I may see Ra among those who give offerings."*

These guards also bowed and separated, allowing the companions to pass between them, their gestures of respect accompanied by friendly smiles.

At the third gate:

*"The name of the doorkeeper is*
*He Who Catches His Own Filth.*
*The name of its warder is The Watchful.*
*The name of the herald is The Great One.*
*I am He whose Stream is Secret,*
*who judgeth the Rebui.*
*I have come to remove all evil from Osiris.*
*I am the girdled at His appointed time,*
*coming forth with the double crown.*
*I secured firmly my suit in Abydos,*
*and I opened my path in Restau.*
*I have soothed the pain of Osiris*
*who balances his pedestal.*
*I have made my way*
*when he shines at Restau."*

At the fourth gate:

*"The name of the doorkeeper is*
*He Who Opposes Garrulity.*
*The name of its warder is*
*The Attentive One.*
*The name of the herald is*

*He Who Drives Back The Crocodile.*
*I am the bull, the son of the Kite of Osiris.*
*Behold, his father, The Fiery One, sat in judgment.*
*I poised the balance for him.*
*Life has been brought to me.*
*I stand unsullied. I have made my way.*
*I am the son of Osiris, and I live forever."*

At each of the gates, the respectful guards allowed them passage.

With glad steps, the companions stepped inside a vast garden surrounded by a golden wall, filled with bright flowers and trees heavily-laden with fruits. Pools filled the gaps between the tall greenery, lined with silver that shined through their shallow, lotus-filled waters. Across from them, their path led to an immense gate grander than any they'd yet seen.

As they stared, amazed at the scenic beauty before them, four women approached, each carrying a staff of polished wood, atop which was a flaming torch. One woman had the head of a lioness, another a leopard, the third a panther, and the fourth a tigress. In each of their other hands, they held out a wide golden tray covered with delicacies that looked delicious.

"Welcome, honored guests!" they said in unison, and the women offered them treats. "We honor you, in the name of Osiris, and bid you to rest and refresh yourselves. We are your humble greeters, your servants."

The Mad Hermit smiled, then glanced at his daughter, and gestured for her to respond. Alarika stepped forward and spoke to the cat-women.

*"In the name of Osiris, Ruler of All,*
*Rightful Master of Eternity,*
*We entreat your pleasure.*
*Ra the Sun brightens us,*

*And even to Nephthus we offer*
*Greetings with open arms.*
*Our hearts pure, we come to Thoth,*
*To seek the Judgement of Osiris,*
*for True and Rightful are His names."*

The cat-women and the Mad Hermit smiled, and everyone exchanged bows.

"We must bathe," the Mad Hermit said to the companions. "The clean offend not our gods."

The tall bushes allowed partial shielding, while not fully hiding any of them from view. The companions removed their armor and weapons, and unclad, stepped into pools of warm water, as fragrant and soothing as any pool could be, such that relaxation seemed to be a spell cast over them. The cat-women weren't alone; four men, with the heads of a loon, a seagull, a pelican, and an albatross, each of whom carried a torch-staff like the women bore, brought them soft towels and trays of honeycakes and small loaves bursting with jams of bright berries. The cat-women returned with small golden bowls of an elixir whose fermented smoothness no beer brewed by mortals could equal.

The companions welcomed these courtesies with much gratitude, and smiles beamed from every face. Henry felt especially delighted; *if he'd known of this place before they'd visited the Field of Wheat then this would've been his ideal.*

All too soon the bird-men returned with more fresh towels, and assisted the companions to stand and emerge from the water. They offered the companions fresh, new gowns of the sheerest flax, and thick robes, but Karl deferred.

"Forgive we who are strangers," Karl begged. "We gladly offer our thanks, but would the Gods of Egypt forgive us if we appear before them wearing the armor of Horus?"

"In arriving here, you have garbed yourselves in honor," the man with the head of the pelican said. "The Throne of Osiris welcomes you however you dress."

The Mad Hermit gladly changed his dull, red rags for a flax gown, and covered it with a voluminous robe of bright burgundy trimmed with wide edgings of white fur, which his snake-heads seemed to like, as they rubbed their faces against it and slid their long coils along its thick softness. The others dressed as they'd entered, in the armor of Horus, and girded their weapons.

"The Agate Circle of Osiris awaits you," the woman with the head of the lioness said, and she gestured to the ornate gate. "Are you prepared?"

"With all blessings and gratitude to you, yes, we stand eager to be honored," the Mad Hermit said, again bowing to the eight servants. Again, the servants and companions exchanged bows.

As the huge gate opened, a long chime resounded loudly over the city, like countless gongs being struck. Henry smiled, wondering what would come next.

The gate opened upon a loud celebration, the like of which they'd never seen.

A throng of thousands cheered as the gates swung wide, and the companions stepped through to find the shining City of the Gods filled with thousands of people, crowded as far as they could see, not half-creatures, but humans, Egyptians, all rising to their feet and crying out for pure joy. Every face smiled, all hands applauding or shaking fists in the air as if celebrating a tremendous victory.

"The Chosen," the Mad Hermit grinned. "These are the mortals whose faith and piety earned them eternal life in the City of the Gods."

"Each has passed the Test of Thoth," Alarika added. "Will we have to . . .?"

"Gladly I will, but for our companions, I can't say," the Mad Hermit said. "To my knowledge, none have ever entered this gate without enduring the unpleasantness of dying."

They stepped through the gate into a city of unequaled beauty and delight. Total strangers hugged them, warm greetings showered upon them, and countless hands reached out to touch them. Many spoke to them, but in Egyptian; only Alarika and the Mad Hermit understood and replied. Yet friendly smiles were universal. Henry shook many hands, and another small bowl, this time containing a fruity irep, was practically forced into his hands. He thanked them all, expressing gratitudes that he knew they couldn't understand.

The city was no less a paradise than the garden, filled with fountains, planters, tall trees, bonfires, shining lanterns, and endless splendor. Hundreds of stone dwellings stood, as elegant as the gleaming temples, and upon a tall pedestal stood a bronze statue of a sphinx, and even the metal woman's face seemed to be smiling. Yet the brilliance of one building, beaming the brightest light, came from a magnificent palace atop the tallest hill.

To no one's surprise, many residents of the City of the Gods gestured to the shining palace, and the companions obliged. Ten minutes they walked through the cheering crowd, and then they came to a wide, white marble stairs. Ascending, they left behind the celebrating inhabitants, whose joy never lessened, and approached the Palace of the Gods of Egypt.

Guards stood in layers of banded armor, with wide leather collars circling around their necks, with sewn-on metal plates, worn over bands of silver armor covering their chests. Under their short tunics, they wore tooled-leather greaves that matched their vambraces, and sandals upon their feet. Each guard carried a tall shield, a short spear, and tucked into their belts, a sharply-curved khopesh. A black headband tied back the white coif that draped down their necks, and theirs were the only faces in the city which weren't smiling.

Nine guards stood to each side of a blinding doorway, from which the brightest light was shining. As one, all eighteen guards tilted their heads toward the door, and every companion understood.

Taking deep breaths, they entered into the blinding radiance and proceeded through the door.

They emerged blinking into an impossible land. The doorway behind them moved aside as the last of them stepped through, and it seemed to elongate. As the door moved away, it spread out, allowing a moving view of the city below, its splendid mansions and temples, and the cheering crowd. Then the doorway grew small, too thin to pass through, and another thin gap suddenly widened, became a door, and stretched wide to encompass most of the palace. Through this doorway, the companions saw a vast, dark emptiness, but flowing, as if deep underwater. When it collapsed, a third gap widened, this one a vast, sun-bright desert, as they'd seen crossing the deadly Deshret. All around them the desert circled, and then suddenly a dark, shapely woman, that every companion recognized, emerged from the brilliant white light. She was tall, her midnight shoulders hovering above Roselyn's head, and beautiful beyond compare, black as coal, and real stars shined from her translucent skin, not jewels, but twinkling lights of the real night's sky.

"Nut!" the Mad Hermit exclaimed, and his snake-limbs lowered him almost to the floor.

Alarika knelt beside him, and the others paused, unsure.

The black eyes of the Goddess Nut shined menacingly, but her bright lips widened into a welcoming smile.

"Children of mine … and of distant lands," Nut said, her voice at once melodious and haunting. "Welcome to the Palace of the Sacred First Land. Where you stand, the first hill rose from the swirling Nu, and here came forth Atum, father of Shu and Tefnut. Here Thoth created himself, and Ra burst into existence. All are welcome. Enter, and be at peace."

Nut gestured them to follow her into the light, and suddenly the brilliant white light grew no less bright, but radiantly lustrous … and less blinding. A ring of many thrones surrounded a wide circular floor of polished agate, glistening of many colors. At the far end, between the largest thrones, a great earthen mound rose, grassy, but sandy on top. Upon that hill was lain the lid of a painted stone sarcophagus, covered with gold and gems, and behind it rose a throne taller and more magnificent than any other.

Many gods of Egypt stood before them, each before their throne, a blending of human and animal, each aglow with ultimate glory, shining with divine radiance.

Easily they recognized those whose cities they'd entered. Most prominent was Thoth, the ibis-headed god, with his long, narrow black beak, wearing a headdress of blue feathers and gold, with a long dagger upon his belt. Near him stood Ra, with whom they had dined, who nodded slightly to them, and his falcon-beak seemed to be smiling. Isis rose from her silver throne as they entered, beautiful beyond imagining, wreathed in sheerest lace, with a real, tiny sun shining from between the cow's horns on her crown, and she stood with a staff in one hand and an ankh in the other. Many others, over a dozen gods and goddesses, stood beside them, including one with the head of a hippopotamus, a thin, gray cat in human shape, and a woman with the face and fur of a lioness, who snarled threateningly as they approached.

Henry wished that he could remember all of their names, as Alarika did, fearing that he might accidentally offend one, but then, he never believed that they'd make it this far, and was certain that he'd make it no farther. Easily Henry recognized mighty Horus, the muscular, hawk-headed Champion of Egypt, whose statue he'd hidden behind when approaching the lightning-serpent, and who'd gifted them with the priceless armor that they all wore.

Yet most ominous of all stood Anubis, the jackal-headed God of Darkness. As with Mist the Valkyrie, a cloud seemed to permanently envelope Anubis, but where her vapors were white and misty, the cloud shrouding Anubis was black as pitch, and flowed across the floor like a dark, low fog to enshroud his legs and the feet of those gods and goddesses closest to him.

Before them all stood a small man, a human, but radiating an immense glow.

"*Athelwynne …!*" Roselyn shouted.

In the very center, perfectly still, stood a Saxon of England with iron black hair and eyes, wearing a long black robe, but shining with a brilliant sheen, lighting their afterlife with his glow: Athelwynne the Seer, the companion that they'd left Earth to find, for whom they'd passed through realms of foreign terror.

Roselyn and Eloise ran past sparkling Nut, onto the wide, polished agate circle, and seized the Seer in simultaneous tight hugs, but he never moved nor acknowledged either of them.

"Forgive us, great Gods of Egypt," Karl said loudly, and then he bowed deeply, drawing their attention. "We are strangers in your land, and wish only the knowledge of how we may properly honor you, Gods Who Preceded Our Own."

"We know why you have come!" barked a voice at once high-pitched and thunderous. "You seek to steal the last light of Egypt!"

The very darkness stepped forward, deadly and foreboding, seeming to drink in even the Seer's brilliance, and yet it remained ever in shadow. Jackal-headed Anubis stepped into the bright light of Athelwynne, illuminated, yet wreathed in gloom.

Karl bowed deeply to Anubis, and all the others mimicked his gesture of respect.

"We seek no ill to any, Great Anubis," Karl said. "Your light is our friend, and for friendship's sake we came to his aid."

"Your friend is mine!" Anubis said with ultimate finality.

"We offer …," Karl began.

"You offer lies!" Anubis snarled, and his glower deepened.

Eloise laid a hand on Karl's arm, and stepped forward and curtseyed.

"Lord of Darkness, we pose no threat … powerless mortals before gods," Eloise said. "You have an abundance of time. Can you not hear our petition?"

"Murderous mortals!" Anubis spoke, his words stabbing spikes. "You dare bring your curse into my lands …?"

"Curse …?" Eloise asked.

"Mortal lives are too short to see the doom you carry," Anubis said. "While Osiris sleeps, I maintain his realm … for as long as possible … and you seek to destroy it!"

"Destroy …?" Eloise asked. "How can mortals destroy …?"

"Hope," Anubis said. "Hope is the curse that you bring."

"Forgive our mortal ignorance, Great One," Eloise said. "How is hope a curse?"

"Hope fails," Anubis said. "Hope brightens a land on the edge of oblivion, and when hope fails, it leaves the land diminished, its spark dimmer."

"Our hope is real …," Eloise said.

"All hopes are real," Anubis said. "You've conjoined the wisdom of Yggdrasil and Elysia, but those faiths still burn; Winter hasn't extinguished them. Our realm burns no more. We are the dying flicker of a spent candle; soon we will be no more."

"Then let us help," Eloise said.

Anubis shook his jackal-head.

"For mortals, you are wise, but you see not your danger in our crisis," Anubis said. "What if your hopes fail? What if you attempt to unify us with your young gods … and their brightness only hastens our darkening? We have no sun, no moon, and most of our stars have died. However intended, if your attempt should fail, then our final day shall conclude. You ask gods to bet their immortality upon your assumptions, but your success isn't guaranteed. To us, you're infants. Would you, mortals, risk your brief existence upon the whims of a child?"

The companions stared at Anubis.

"He's right," Elaina said.

*"Mother . . . !"* Eloise snapped.

"No, let her speak," Karl said to Eloise, and he gestured for Elaina to continue.

Elaina curtsied to Anubis and all the gods.

"I stand willing to be corrected if I speak wrongly," Elaina said to all of the gods, but facing Anubis. "There is no guarantee … save what will happen in the end … if you try nothing new. Oblivion has swallowed other pantheons, if all that I've learned is true. Yet Winter can be survived; the Christian god has proved this, for His people survived their Winter as slaves to your people, and now His faith flourishes …"

"You asked for correction, mortal," Nut said, nodding to Elaina. "You grasp only the brief time in which you live, which is but a blink in the eyes of immortals. Time isn't the fixed ribbon mortals believe it to be. Time is as fluid as Nu, holds many beginnings, and suffers many endings. Time here passes not as any corollary to time in the mortal world. Think you that the stars in your sky will last forever? The Winter of Egypt brings our realm close to the final ending … where all stars fail."

"Can you not reproduce the renewal of Christ?" Elaina asked.

"We stand trapped in our doom," Nut said.

"We can't even argue amongst ourselves," Ra said, stepping forward, and his falcon-eyes met theirs with twinkles of familiarity. "Disunity weakens us, but I've met and feasted with these mortals, and I know their minds.

I'd take this risk, for without it, our pantheon passes into eternal darkness."

"This risk isn't mine to take," Anubis said. "Existence is my only goal. The light of Athelwynne the Seer enhances our existence. He must stay."

"Ask him," Roselyn said, stepping forward. "Athelwynne is wise, and carries the wisdom of two pantheons; if a chance exists, he'll know it better than we. Release his soul …!"

"Again, you words are unproven," Anubis said. "You would weaken our light for the possibility that the Seer possesses wisdom that your younger gods know … that we older gods know not, wisdom that you don't have."

"I can't leave without the Seer," Roselyn said.

"Then you shall never leave," Anubis said.

"Please, my sacred Lord, may I speak?" the Mad Hermit asked, bowing to all the gods.

"Speak, fallen disciple, before you return to your doom," Anubis said.

"My gods, my failure was momentary, yet I grovel before you," the Mad Hermit said, humility filling his voice. "I speak for the damned of the Duat; my failures in life darkened my spirit, my hope failed, and thus I succumbed to despair, so common in the lands where all once worshipped you …and are now removed from your intercession. All in the Duat are changed, in spirit as much as in mind and body, and would kneel before you in contrition, as I do, had they but the chance that these mortals have given me.

"The chance I speak of isn't the defeat of Aapep, which these mortals accomplished, but of …," the Mad Hermit slid one of his snake-arms around Sister Aspertine's shoulder, "… of faith itself, the faith of this one woman, whose staunchness wavered not before fear.

It is not their mortal strength or wisdom, but their friendship and devotion to each other which has brought them before you, where I thought that they'd never stand.

"I was wrong. Gods of Egypt, my gods, your will is mine, even if you would cast me back into the Cursed Tunnel, for never would I deny you anything. Yet I entreat you, my gods; give up not upon the advantages of faith."

"Gods are objects of faith, not its source," Anubis said.

"Combined, our faiths drove back your worst enemy, Aapep the Unslayable," Sister Aspertine said.

"As Ra drove back Aapep … with the faith of Osiris," Alarika added.

"Beware that your words carry no threat," Anubis said. "Think not that our wisdom failed with our power."

"If you would have faith …!" Sister Aspertine said.

"Enough!" Anubis shouted. "This discussion is ended. Only Osiris could accept the risk that you offer. I will hear you no more."

"Let me speak to Athelwynne," Eloise said. "Allow this, and we'll prove our claims … or make them no longer."

"You may speak, but he won't hear you," Anubis said.

"Please …?" Elaina asked.

"Without his soul, he knows you not," Anubis said. "His soul is mine … and I won't surrender it."

"You waste the power of Elysia," Roselyn said. "Just let us speak to him, and let him hear and answer; that's all we ask."

Anubis stood unmoved, but Thoth stepped forward.

"Wisdom says that such an entreaty can do no harm," Thoth spoke in a high-pitched twitter, the beak of his ibis-head moving only slightly, yet an eminence arose from him which wafted over their whole land, as if every word of Thoth carried the immeasurable strength of certainty.

Anubis turned to Thoth, staring as if amazed.

"Not in centuries have you shared your infinite wisdom," Anubis said to Thoth.

"Thoth shares only when truth may aid," Thoth said to Anubis. "For centuries, my truths would only weaken."

Anubis considered these words.

"Let all speak who will," Anubis said. "In this, I heed the voices of the gods."

"I will that they speak to their friend," Ra said.

"As do I," Nut said.

"I see no benefit, but I see no harm," Horus said. "I believe the hearts of these mortals are true, elsewise they wouldn't have risked their lives to rescue their friend. My curiosity arises, for I've seen them fight; I would learn how they hope to accomplish this victory."

"I care not," hissed Geb, one of the tallest gods, whose face looked both human and reptilian. A living serpent encircled his brow, like a crown, and a live bird stood upon his head. "My hope is lost, and I see none before me."

"Not all wisdom can be foreseen," Isis said, her voice like flowing warmth and comfort, and her beautiful face smiling. "I would give them this chance … in the hope that unforeseeable opportunities may present themselves."

"I see no hope, whether you deny them or not," Tefnut said, her head resembling a lioness. "However, as always, Thoth speaks truly; I see no harm."

The other gods said nothing, but Anubis met each of their eyes, as if their expressions needed no explaining.

"I weary of waiting," Atum said in a voice like the deepest roar of the stormy Nu. He seemed to be the most human in shape, and he also carried a staff and an ankh. "Let these mortals try; better death than endless despair."

Anubis stared at the other gods, several of whom shook their heads, refusing to speak, and then he stepped toward a black throne and held out his hand. From off a white stand floated a small, colorful chest.

From their previous revelations, Henry knew what it was: the memory box of Anubis, which held the trapped soul of the Seer.

The ornate box looked simple, as if created by a street artisan, made of thick, sand-colored clay, painted white but stained with faded pink, and decorated on all sides with patterns of colorful mosaics, swirling lines of blue dotted by polished turquoises, aquamarines, and amethysts. On its narrow front side opened two tiny holes, each barely the size of a finger, both surrounded by mosaics of eyes, making the holes look like dark pupils.

With a glare as potent as a clenched fist, Anubis stepped toward the Seer. Slowly, Anubis turned the eye-holes to face the Seer.

At once, the Seer's light lessened … and he blinked and breathed heavily.

"Athelwynne!" Eloise shouted.

The Seer startled, then looked at Eloise.

"You … you're … not a god," the Seer said.

"He may speak, but his memories reside in the box," Isis said.

"We're your friends," Roselyn said to Athelwynne. "Your memory is lost … we hope to restore it."

"My … memory …?" the Seer asked, his expression confused. "You're … strangers. I've never seen you …"

"You've slept with both of us," Roselyn said bluntly, and many eyebrows rose on both gods and companions. The Seer looked astounded.

"Athelwynne, we need your help …!" Eloise said.

"Servant, answer me," Anubis interrupted. "You have carried messages between Odin and the Lady of the Druids; know you of any way for gods to survive their Winter?"

The Seer looked at Anubis, then briefly glanced at the companions, but with no hint of recognition.

"No," the Seer said. "The other gods are … hopeful … but they've only begun to explore this mystery."

"Do you have any proof, or even evidence, that the Gods of Egypt can arise to a new Spring?" Anubis asked.

"I haven't … examined that …," the Seer said.

"Do you know if you'll still be able to relay messages from Yggdrasil to Elysia once they begin their Winters?" Anubis demanded.

"Yes, I will," the Seer answered.

Anubis startled, and Thoth nodded.

"He speaks the truth," Thoth said.

"I entered this land through a doorway from the Norse realm, through a crack called Mistyhel," the Seer said. "It is guarded, but that doorway to your realm is open … despite your Winter."

"I found another portal in Alfhiem, a living 'crack in the world' that only the fairies know of … that opens onto a whole other universe, one whose gods I've never heard of," Roselyn said. "We came through yet another portal, from the lands of Egypt, and that passage may still be traveled, and Bifrost is always open."

"That's four portals … and there may be more," Karl said. "Who knows what may be learned from the one that Roselyn found … to a realm beyond our knowledge …"

"A fairy realm, where everything is light and beauty," Roselyn said.

"Know you of such a realm, Gods of Egypt?" Karl asked.

"Enough!" Anubis said. "Your friend knows no proofs that he can help us …"

"Helping is what he's best at," Roselyn said. "I've seen his healing powers, so powerful that he can heal the dead legs of …"

Roselyn's eyes suddenly widened, and she grabbed and jerked the Seer's arm. "Athelwynne, if you don't remember us, then use your healing powers! Heal yourself!"

"I …," the Seer began.

"No!" Anubis said, and he turned his memory box away, so the eye-holes of the memory box no longer faced the Seer. Instantly the Seer staggered, as if he'd fall.

*"Athelwynne!"* Eloise cried, trying to hold him up.

*"Hel needs you!"* Roselyn shouted at the Seer, shaking him roughly. *"Hel loves you! Heal yourself!"*

The Seer met her eyes, but then he began to shine, as before, lighting the afterlife of the Egyptian gods.

*"Hel …?"* the Seer hesitantly asked.

Again the light of the Seer dimmed. The Seer lifted his right hand, as if reluctantly, yet confused, and he looked at his hand, and then he turned to face Anubis.

"Be silent, slave!" Anubis commanded. "Light my realm!"

The Seer's eyes went blank, but his hand reached out. All of the light he was shining with, from every inch of his being, suddenly coalesced on his right hand, and the Seer blasted out a beam of blinding intensity. His radiance struck the memory box in the hands of Anubis

… and shattered it into countless clay fragments, scattering jewels upon the agate floor.

A glowing smoke of many colors rose from the shattered fragments falling from the suddenly-empty hands of Anubis.

*"No!"* Anubis cried, and he waved his dark hands through the smoke of many colors, but it seeped through his fingers, rose into the air, and streamed into the Seer. Athelwynne staggered as the glowing smokes poured into him, the gold of the Ba, the silver of the Ka, the white of the Ib, the blue of the Ren, and the black of the Sheut. As each slipped inside him, he almost fell, but Eloise and Roselyn supported him.

*"You dare defy me …!"* Anubis shouted. *"Now you shall witness the power of Egypt … in your dooms!"*

*"Behold truth when you see real power!"* Karl shouted back.

"Real power …?" Nut asked.

*"You …!"* Anubis began.

"He must speak," Thoth said.

Karl frowned, then started to speak, his voice tinged with anger.

"You gods …!" Karl started.

"Most-honorable Gods of Egypt …!" Eloise interrupted him.

Karl hesitated, then began again.

"You … most-honorable Gods of Egypt," Karl began again, his voice softer. "You seek the power for your pantheon to endure. Yet you deny your own goal. You grasp at petty powers, and deny true power when you witness it."

"What power do you speak of?" Horus demanded.

"The only power here that can defy a god … any god," Karl said. "Hel is the Norse Goddess of Death. She and the Seer are …"

Karl hesitated.

"… Lovers," Roselyn finished.

The Gods of Egypt exchanged glances, and Nut laughed softly.

"You share your affections aplenty," Nut smiled at the Seer.

"Not anymore," the Seer said.

"Hel and Athelwynne are pledged," Roselyn said.

"You witnessed it," Karl said, "Devout as he is, as powerful as he is, the Seer's magic didn't protect him from the power of Anubis' memory box. Neither Yggdrasil nor Elysia saved him. Love saved him … his love for Hel."

"Even faith isn't as powerful as love," Elaina said. "You've seen this with your own eyes."

"Love suffers no Winter," Thoth said, his resonance emanating.

"Trust us," Karl said. "Maybe we'll fail, but you'll have Odin and the Lady's help, and they'll do all they can … far more than we can offer."

"You steal my lantern … and ask for trust …?" Anubis snarled.

"I'm not your …!" the Seer began.

*"Silence!"* Anubis shouted. *"You will obey!"*

"If you'd …," Karl began.

*"Enough!"* Anubis shouted, and thunder echoed across the sky. *"Mortals who defy Anubis pay with their lives!"*

*"No!"* Ra shouted. *"Anubis, fighting only weakens us!"*

"We didn't come to fight," Karl said.

"But we can fight," Sister Aspertine said. "We have faith …!"

"No mortals worshipped Aapep," Isis said. "Your young faiths can't harm objects of faith."

"Not all of us worship gods," Elaina said.

*"How dare you!"* Anubis cried. *"We are gods!"*

*"Then threaten us not!"* the Seer shouted. *"I know the secret of gods!"*

Godly gasps came from all around. The companions froze, and all, companions and gods, stared at the Seer.

"Gods aren't born divine," the Seer snarled, facing the entire Egyptian pantheon. "Even the first, the Self-Created, began small and frail. Their pantheons only formed eons after their births, after infinity forces insights which can't be denied. The gods aren't divine because they know powerful spells … or understand secrets that mortals can't grasp. The gods have ultimate power because they know the source of ultimate power: the gods know themselves!"

A dread silence fell over the City of the Gods, and not even a grain of sand shifted.

"Anyone can be a god," the Seer sneered. "It requires strength … the greatest of strengths: total honesty … and acceptance of all truths. It requires depth, the power to comprehend the darkest recesses of our own minds. It requires humility, our submission to reality, even when circumstances refute our desires. It requires courage, to face the deepest secrets that we hide from all, even from our firmest beliefs, but after eons, which mortals never live to experience, gods must finally acknowledge and accept. It requires wisdom, the understanding that all beings begin poorly, and that each of us, mortal and god, is but a step on a journey unfinished, evolving toward a perfection that can only be grasped when we attain it."

The Seer turned to face the companions.

"The strength of the gods is age," the Seer said. "They're vastly older, and wiser, with a consciousness unbroken by the cycles that wash away the thoughts of mortals. Time has taught them who they are. Yet, here stand their equals.

"Karl, you're fickle, but you know why: you want everyone to have what they want … and everyone wants different things. Your goal to make everyone happy can't succeed, but you can invent your own happiness, become a true font of happiness, and share your divine happiness with others. *Accept it!* You've shown the strength, the depth, the humility, the courage, and the wisdom of any god. You'll die before you reach their level, but you can continue in your afterlife … until you succeed.

"Roselyn, you're the strongest mortal ever. Even Hel thinks of you as an equal. You face external fears with excitement, determined to defeat everything. You have every quality of a god … even immortality. *Face your internal enemy!* You don't have to win … you just have to know … to grasp all that you are … and keep fighting.

"Eloise, you know the Lady, Her secrets, and Her wisdom … you already possess a dim reflection of Her powers. We're all part of the greater reality, and to understand ourselves, our place, wants, and motivations, is to see truly … and evoke powers greater than any spell. *Look into yourself, not Her!* The Lady sees Her subjects not as followers, but as infant brothers and sisters … that She hopes will someday grow. Don't wait to become a goddess. You're a seed of divinity, and need only to claim your birthright. *Be the goddess that lies within you!*"

*"You blaspheme …!"* Atum rumbled.

"He speaks the truth," Thoth said.

"Truth is always blasphemy to someone," the Seer said. "The power of the mind is infinite … if you have infinity to learn. The imagination is infinite. Strength of will can be infinite, if sufficiently determined. The end of mortals isn't death, it's despair. Those who surrender to opposition become trapped in their own minds, doomed to whatever fate they submit. But no one has to submit! We may be beaten. We may be slain. The worst of worsts may devourer us, but ultimate defeat comes not from without. While mortals stand resolute, mortals are gods!"

"Waste no more words on these liars," Anubis said. "These mortals die now!"

"If Thoth and the Seer speak truly, would you kill … other gods …?" Elaina asked.

Anubis snarled, and then waved his hand slowly in the air, toward the wide door circling around them, gesturing to the sandy hills now outside their palace. At once, a roar of shifting sands echoed, and thousands of mounds erupted on the gentle hills, bursting upwards, and from each mound rose an Egyptian warrior, armed and armored. Within seconds, the bare, empty hills around them sprouted ten thousand Egyptian soldiers, all risen at the command of Anubis.

Henry gasped and stared at the vast, armored throng; *even all of the Valkyrie could never defeat this army!*

"Hear me, Gods of Egypt," the Seer said. "Let not pride lead you to folly. I carry the strengths of Yggdrasil and Elysia. Battle with me shall weaken you far more than my light could aid."

*"Threats from mortals shall not be the downfall of the realm of Egypt!"* Anubis said.

"We don't threaten," the Seer said. "Believe me, Anubis; we, Odin, and my Lady, will do all that we can to delay your oblivion."

"You can't fight gods … or our army," Anubis said. "All the powers of the desert are mine to command. You will swear to remain … or our battle begins … and you and your friends will die!"

The Seer frowned, and then glanced at Eloise, Roselyn, and Karl.

"What would Eric Bjornson do?" Karl asked.

Eloise, Roselyn, and the Seer grinned.

"Great Gods of Egypt, I beg you to end this now," the Seer said. "I know the path to your lands, and will gladly carry your messages to my liege … and Odin. However, know what you risk before you threaten me; your army is equally as dangerous to you as it is to me."

All the gods of Egypt exchanged worried glances.

Confidently the Seer stepped forward, raised both his hands high, and then slowly spun around, facing the Egyptian army. The Seer's closed hands snapped open, and his fingers splayed wide.

Ten thousand soldiers screamed, a horrible chorus, and most fell, writhing onto the sands. The few who remained standing twitched and thrashed, as if overwhelmed by torment. Agonized cries rose and deafened. Where any skin showed on the Egyptian soldiers, especially their bare legs behind their greaves, fur exploded, thick and hairy. Screaming mouths elongated … and burst vicious fangs. Weapons fell from shaking hands … where trembling fingers sprouted long, deadly claws.

Eloise screamed, horrified, and Henry understood; *none feared the curse of the Wolfqueen more than she.*

Slowly, ten thousand armored werewolves arose, growling and slavering. Weapons fell from hands bearing claws that no metal blades could equal. Wolfish lips drew back in snarls, revealing teeth able to rend any flesh. Ten thousand reflections of the Wolflord stood and stared at those in the palace, gods, mortal, Valkyrie, and half-demon, with red, glaring, hate-filled eyes.

The Seer turned to Anubis.

"Release us all, now, or they attack," the Seer warned. "Even gods must fear an army of lycanthropes."

Henry quaked, terrified; the gods of Egypt might be able to fight a swarm of wolf-monsters, but he and the other companions had no chance. The Seer had turned the army of Egypt into a threat to both mortals and gods. Even many of the deities recoiled in fright.

Only Anubis, Atum, Isis, and Thoth seemed unaffected. They exchanged a momentary glance, and then Anubis burst out laughing.

Anubis faced the vast army of werewolves. He raised one hand … and at once, ten thousand werewolves dropped to one knee before him … and reverently bowed their heads.

Every companion, and the Seer, gaped open-mouthed at the hideous horde of werewolves, tamed by a godly glance.

Anubis laughed darkly.

"Fool mortal, did you think that I'd disgrace my beloved token with the boon of unequaled savagery?" Anubis asked. "I created this curse, which I blessed with the semblance of my cousins: the Warrior-Wolves of Anubis."

Henry gulped; the Seer had turned the entire army facing them into werewolves … *and made their formidable executioners deadlier.*

"Forward, my legion!" Anubis ordered his army. "Destroy my enemies!"

At once, every werewolf arose and stepped forward.

Henry had heard of the curse of the Wolflord as a child, and knew all the stories of Eloise's transformations … the sheer fury and unstoppable strength of the Wolfqueen. An army of such beasts could threaten even a god … and they marched at the bidding of Anubis.

*"Seer, take back the curse!"* Elaina shouted.

The Seer nodded, then looked at the approaching werewolves, raised his arms, and with a downward slash, gestured the curse away.

Nothing happened.

Anubis laughed, and even Henry understood; *over the curse of werewolves, its creator held ultimate dominion.*

Roselyn raised the Sword of Hel. Karl and Alarika drew their swords, and Nate and Phil matched their gestures. The others didn't bother; *what use were weapons against ten thousand werewolves?*

A loud, familiar chime rang out across the city, like the beating of countless gongs. The Gods of Egypt paused, and with a raise of Anubis' hand, the advancing werewolves halted.

"Is that … the gate chime …?" Nate asked.

"A petitioner approaches," Horus said to Anubis. "Their execution must be delayed."

Anubis scowled, but he didn't repeat his summons to his army. *The continued existence of these gods depended upon petitioners.*

Distant cheers rose from the inhabitants of the city, and the gods resumed their original positions. Isis sat upon her throne. Minutes later, the wide doorway, opened upon the sandy, werewolf-covered dunes, encircled them again, began to thin, and all the doors circled around the edge of the agate ring that they stood upon. As they rotated faster, other doors widened and then narrowed, surrounding them with dense forests, then glacial peaks, and then a steamy swamp filled with monstrous lizards. Finally a door widened and remained opened, and they were surrounded by more stars than they'd ever seen, and each shined brightly, as if newly-born.

The center of the agate circle fell away, opening upon a deep pit, a wide, swampy dungeon beneath them, filled with hissing crocodiles.

A large, golden scale, beautiful in its simplicity and taller than any god, came silently sliding forward, and it stopped at the edge of the newly-exposed pit … beside Thoth.

*"The Scale of Thoth!"* Alarika and the Mad Hermit exclaimed.

Suddenly a bright light blinded them all. Thoth lifted his hand, and with a gleam of warmth and sweetness that suffused everyone and everything, a large, magical white feather appeared, standing upright upon his palm: the Feather of Truth.

Into the divine palace came an old woman, limping, leaning heavily upon a cane. Behind her came dozens of townsfolk, silently reverent.

"Now comes the Final Judgment," Isis announced. "Approach, and prove your worth."

One of the townspeople, a tall man, stepped forward from the throng and bowed deeply.

"Gods of gods, rightful masters, and lords of my people," the man spoke in a strong voice. "We are the forty-two divine judges, who come to plea for this petitioner. Through your challenges, her faith was never lost, and she has won the right to approach. We, your divine judges, beg that she be tested."

"We hear you, divine judges, and accept your plea," Isis said. "Let the petitioner come forth. Let the petitioner speak."

The old woman shuffled forward, bowing as best as her aged frame allowed. She looked frightened, but determined, proud to have arrived. She looked at the gods and finally spoke with a weak, wheezy voice.

*"I am pure! I am pure!*
*I am pure! I am pure!*
*My purity is as that of the Bennu bird,*
*the bright Phoenix.*
*I come without sin,*
*without guilt, and without evil.*
*I eat of truth.*
*I have given bread to the hungry,*
*water to the thirsty,*
*and clothing to the naked.*
*I have provided offerings to the gods*
*and offerings to the dead.*
*Preserve me from Aapep, the Eater of Souls!*
*I pray to you, Lord of the Atef-Crown,*
*Lord of Breath, oh, great god Osiris."*

"This is the moment which evil-doers fear … and the good Ka welcomes with joy," Isis said.

From a golden sheath hanging upon his throne, Anubis drew a bright, thick silver knife. He approached the old woman, and his hand closed on her shoulder with a firm grip. Swallowing hard, the old woman lifted her free arm to her white linen robe, and pulled to draw open its edges. Anubis nodded to her, and with a swift motion, Anubis plunged his silver knife into her chest.

The woman screamed, but didn't fall, as if frozen in horror. She gritted her teeth, straining, and then Anubis lifted the bloody dagger to his long nose and sniffed it, opened his mouth, and bit upon the bloody blade, holding it in his teeth. With his hand freed, he plunged it into the fresh rent in the woman's chest. He tugged hard several times, and when his hand withdrew, Anubis lifted up the warm, bleeding heart of the old woman.

Anubis handed the bloody heart to Horus, and then took the silver knife from his teeth.

Horus accepted the living heart into his hands, and Henry was surprised to see that the heart was still beating. Carrying the pulsing heart, Horus walked up to the tall, golden scale beside Thoth. As one, Horus placed the beating heart upon one pan of the golden scale, while upon the other pan, Thoth placed the sacred, glowing white Feather of Truth.

The scale tilted, first one way, then the other, and every mouth held its breath, every eye focused upon each sway. Slowly the rocking of the pans, up and down, evened out, and the Scale of Thoth balanced.

Isis stood and looked carefully at the scale, balancing the beating heart against the Feather of Truth.

"The judgement of Osiris, my husband," Isis said, "… is that this woman … stands worthy."

No cheers met this announcement, but all eyes turned to Anubis. The jackal-headed god stepped closer, leaned in, and examined the scale intensely. Finally he stepped back.

"I concur," Anubis said.

Cheers erupted from the forty-two judges, and another chime rang, and joyous shouts burst from all the inhabitants of the city around them. All of the gods seemed pleased, and inhaled deeply, as if absorbing strength from the ceremony.

As one, Thoth lifted the white Feather of Truth from the golden scale, and Horus lifted the beating heart. He carried it back to Anubis, who took the heart, and with a sudden gesture, he plunged it back into the chest of the woman.

A white glow burst from the woman, and no smile shined brighter than hers. The glow radiated from every part of her, especially from the rent in her chest, and her shine beamed to the sky and dimmed the stars. She shined across all lands, brightening everything, as radiant and pure as the light of creation.

The gods visibly strengthened, widening their arms and absorbing as much of her glow as possible. Indulging, the gods all smiled, basking in the light as if absorbing both life and strength from her radiance.

When the glow receded, the woman stood before them, old no more. Youth had returned to her, and she stood tall and beautiful. She lifted her smooth hand, looking strangely at it. The forty-two judges from the city cheered again.

Thoth overspoke all.

"True and accurate are the words this woman has spoken. She has not sinned; she has not done evil. Let not the Eater of Souls devour her. Grant her the eternal bread of Osiris, and make for her a place in the Halls of Peace with the followers of Horus."

"Welcome, honored worshipper," Isis said. "You are triumphant. Join now your fellows … and rejoice forever."

The townsfolk rushed forward, surrounded the youthful woman, and lifted her onto their shoulders as the starry door rotated around, and returned their view to the wide City of the Gods. With loud shouts of joy, the forty-two judges carried the youthful woman out of the palace, back through the doorway, and down the white steps to the city. In the distance, more cheers arose in a great roar.

Thoth lifted the still-glowing, white Feather of Truth, and as he held it high, in his hand, it shimmered and vanished. The tall, golden Scale of Thoth slid silently back toward his throne, and the pit in the floor, full of crocodiles, sealed itself, and returned to bright, swirling agate. Anubis cleaned his silver knife and returned it to the sheath hanging upon his throne.

The doors spun again and returned to the sandy dunes … and ten thousand armored werewolves.

"Back to the execution …?" Anubis asked.

"If you must …," Horus said, shaking his head.

"Wait …!" Elaina exclaimed. "That's what your petitioners pray …? That's the final prayer required to live with the gods?"

"Of course," Horus said. "Only that prayer allows petitioners to be judged worthy."

Elaina slowly stepped forward, her eyes filled with wonder, and then she sank to her knees.

"You wish to be judged?" Anubis asked her.

"No," Elaina said. "I wish to give unto you … before I die … the worship that you deserve."

To everyone's amazement, Elaina closed her eyes, raised her open palms to them, and bowed, lowering her face to the polished agate where she knelt.

"You … woman of strange gods … would worship us …?" Isis asked.

"I do, great goddess," Elaina said. "I was born a Christian, and ruled over both Christians and Druids, then was stolen to the lands of the Norse, who worship the gods of Yggdrasil. I've studied and practiced many faiths … and many gods. All of them make questionable demands upon their followers. All desire their followers to worship them alone, as if worship of another deity is blasphemy against them, and most punish those who scorn not other gods. Some gods list endless rules, and commandments, to which all of their followers must adhere, or be denied paradise. Odin needs warriors, so his handmaids choose only the best warriors to enter paradise, and all others suffer cold and darkness.

"But you, the Gods of Egypt, you test those who would enter paradise to see if they desire to be with you, but your foremost demand is that they are good to each other … in life … that they '*have given bread to the hungry, water to the thirsty, and clothing to the naked*'."

"We of Egypt stood strong thousands of years before your gods were born," Horus said. "Our goal was not to dominate, but to civilize all lands, and our demands to our subjects were that they assume our goal. No act is more civilized than to offer what you have to aid those who suffer."

"Combined, we are Maat, Order and Civilization, the Heart of the Cosmos," Thoth said.

"And for this, I honor you," Elaina said. "A year ago I knew nothing about you … and now … now I wish to know all about you."

"You would worship us?" Anubis said. "After all that I have done to your company … and what I am about to do …?"

"Forgiveness is a requirement of all faiths … well … most of them," Elaina said. "I understand why you opposed us, and why you want to keep all sources of light to protect and strengthen your land. I can't say I know all about you, but of what I've learned, I see a greater reason to honor and respect the gods of Egypt than many other gods … about whom I know all."

Again Elaina raised her palms to the gods of Egypt, and then she bowed low before them.

"I, too, honor this final prayer, and the gods that require it," Sister Aspertine said, and she bowed deeply. "I worship my God, Jesus, and the Holy Spirit, but I can't deny your prayer … of the very deeds I deem the most-Christian. I can't worship pagan gods, but I honor you all … deeply."

"And I," Nate said, bowing. "I would show you equal respects."

"I'll kneel before you, if it pleases you," Roselyn said. "I serve Odin, chief god of my people, but his commands benefit himself first, his other gods next, and his people last. He doesn't command worship, like the Christian God, but rules by strength. He cares only for those mortals who die as warriors, who may in death add to his might. I envy your subjects, whose gods demand generosity and civility."

"I, too, bow before you," the Seer said. "My Lady would show you equal respect, I assure you, were She here to grace you with Her presence. Your concern for the neediest of mortals proves your civility."

"We all offer respects," Karl said. "Whatever you do to us, you are unquestionably deities worthy of worship."

With all reverence, Karl, and all the other companions, bowed, knelt, or curtsied. Alarika and the Mad Hermit prostrated themselves, and all the gods, even Anubis, looked surprised.

Suddenly a loud churning arose from the sands. The divine palace of the gods shook, and all the gods looked startled.

Illumination, brighter than the Seer or any petitioner could ever hope to shine, burst forward, so brightly that every star in the sky vanished, and the black sky became as blue as noontime over the desert. A radiance beamed up from the ground all around them, through the agate beneath their feet, from every stone and grain of sand. The shaking grew fierce, and a silvery brilliance blinded their eyes as the grinding increased.

"*Husband!*" Isis cried.

"*Father!*" Horus cried.

"*Osiris!*" cried all the other gods.

Drowning out even the shouts of the gods, the whole of the Egyptian Afterlife trembled and shuddered, and sands blasted from the tomb of Osiris, flinging the great silver light skyward. The vast golden throne rose higher, bursting sunrays beaming to every corner of their land. The gold throne rose to its full height upon a marble dais as white as snow, veined with green like the sea.

The sarcophagus of Set arose from the sands … and its shining lid opened. Wrapped in liniments and sacred bandages, the cerements of the grave, Osiris arose, and a new dawn came to their land.

Osiris was huge, thickly-bound in tight bands of white linen, a mummy, with only his face exposed. The face of Anubis shined with a glow of civility, a calmness that seemed unchangeable and eternal. His eyes beamed with divine radiance, and his forehead rose high and smooth to support his golden crown, from which extended a living cobra of solid gold. His strong chin moved, and a voice of pure music spoke.

"My brethren, my wife," Osiris said. "I awaken."

## Chapter 14

## The Ruler of All

# HENRY

The presence of Osiris beamed upon all like a warm, sunny day.

"Welcome, my beloved husband!" Isis said, tears flowing in her voice and eyes. "We rejoice at your return!"

He bowed to her, and then Osiris turned to Anubis, who also bowed deeply.

"My lord and father, I return rulership of your lands to the Master of All," Anubis said.

"I greet you, my son, gladly and with all thanks for your efforts in my absence," Osiris said. "You've overseen our lands through our darkest hours, longer than my light would have lasted, and protected all that we are."

Anubis bowed again.

"My brethren in eternity, we have all infinity to share thoughts," Osiris said. "Let me speak first to these mortals whose generous respects have awoken me. Always I knew that the fading faiths of our followers would fail us; this new, foreign worship has stirred my heart and resparked my hope."

Osiris turned to face the companions, and the glow of his attention warmed them. The companions repeated their gestures of respect … to Osiris.

"These mortals have good Kas, even the strangers to Egypt," Osiris said. "I see only small evils in them, such as hide in all mortals."

"Great Osiris, we worship you!" the Mad Hermit cried, and he flung himself prostrate, his daughter beside him.

"Arise, faithful servants," Osiris said to the Mad Hermit and Alarika. "Well am I pleased. Your faith empowers us."

"All blessings unto you, Master of All," the Seer said with a bow.

"Personally I greet you, Emissary of the Lady," Osiris said to the Seer. "While I respect my son's position, I have greater leniency in cultural communications. I grant you freedom to return to your lands, to carry my respects both to your Lady and to the young gods of Yggdrasil."

"I am delighted, and pray that I will be invited to return with their greetings and replies," the Seer said.

Osiris nodded.

"To you of younger faiths, I bid you welcome," Osiris said. "You've achieved your goal, and I grant you success. Your companion is restored and set free. We welcome your company, and I hope that you will be happy here."

*"Here …?"* Nate asked, but Karl waved him quiet.

"Great Osiris, Master of All, you honor us," Karl said. "We stand proudly in your presence, and offer all respects. However … we've no wish to stay."

Aghast, Alarika and the Mad Hermit turned their faces to Karl, but he gestured both silent before they objected.

"Here you may be judged … and celebrate forever," Osiris said. "Here all is good; you've no need to return to lands of evil."

"Our lands … do have evil," Karl said. "Well, I can't speak for Elysia, and I'm pretty sure Heaven is entirely good …"

"Yet Heaven has a counterpart, no less real than itself," Osiris said.

"Hell," Sister Aspertine said.

Osiris smiled at her.

"I watched the births of your young realms … and your gods," Osiris said. "I walked your lands when only savages lived there. I brought to them their first tokens of civilization. The faith of Jehovah has banished evil from half of its existence, but concentrated it in its other half. It has not vanquished evil. Likewise, Elysia hosts gardens of ultimate civility, yet forests of savagery equal to the curse of Anubis. Yggdrasil separates neither good nor evil, but embraces only the strengths of both, discarding their weaknesses."

"Odin is our Master of Battles, but also our God of Wisdom," Roselyn said.

"The young gods are fools," Osiris said. "Once I was like your Odin, determined to survive at any cost, to fight against evil. But what your Alfather does not understand is that … evil has no desire to win. Evil is evil even unto itself. Evil wants eternal destruction. If evil destroys good, then evil will turn on itself, and the cycle of destruction will be renewed. You can't win by fighting evil. This lesson I learned in the Lands of the Dead: *fight evil; delight evil.* Defeat evil, and evil always sprouts afresh, for the seeds of evil spawn anew in every beating heart.

"That's the price of free will; envy, jealousy, greed, and lust always torment the good … until someone succumbs, and then evil is born anew. That's why I surrendered my godly life during our dark centuries; to banish evil from my heart. I can't allow evil to devour my lands … or my people. I will not fight evil."

"Alarika and her father are your most-devout subjects; they'll willingly stay," Karl said.

"I'd advise against that," the Seer said, and Alarika and the Mad Hermit gasped. "I can return them both to Egypt. Their appearance could respark the faith of all your people. You've survived a thousand years of darkness. The renewed faith of your people could bring their light back to you."

"Your wisdom impresses me," Osiris said. "So let it be." He turned to Alarika and the Mad Hermit. "My children, return to our land of Egypt, and spread news of my greetings to my people. Tell them … Osiris cares for them."

"Your wish is our will," the Mad Hermit promised, and then he held up his snake-limbs. "Master, must I go like this?"

"Your current form will convince others more than words," Osiris said. "Will you suffer this … for me?"

"I gladly exist as Osiris wills," the Mad Hermit said. "The company of my daughter is all I need."

"I'll take you both, and drop you off with enough flashes and whirlwinds that your people will beg to hear your tales," the Seer said.

"We thank you," Alarika said.

"We could go with them," Karl said.

"No," Osiris said. "Your Kas are good, whatever fool gods you worship. Anubis was right; your presence here will help hold evil at bay."

"Contact with Elysia and Yggdrasil is assured, but their good will isn't," Eloise said. "Would you seek their friendship … and forcibly restrain their loyal followers?"

"Great Osiris, with all respects, I can't leave my friends …," the Seer said. "They came all this way …"

"Your duties are to bring to your goddess correspondences with other pantheons of deities," Osiris said. "You know your task, servant. Take my subjects and be gone."

"Is there no other way?" Karl asked.

"Only a mortal's sacrifice could empower us more," Osiris said.

"Sacrifice …?" Karl gasped. "We can't …!"

"Then you will remain," Osiris said. "You may live here forever … or the armies of Egypt will slay your Has … and your spirits will remain."

No one spoke. Henry looked out at the waiting army of werewolves, ten thousand strong, still waiting to attack them.

"Athelwynne …?" Karl asked. "Do we have any hope …?"

The Seer shook his head. The others looked helpless. Karl held up a hand, gesturing for patience, and seemed to be thinking hard.

"If … if one of us … would sacrifice themself for the others … then … would you let the rest go?" Karl asked.

"If one of you will sacrifice yourself … here, before my throne … right now, then I'll allow the Seer to take the rest when he departs," Osiris said.

"Karl, we can't …!" Eloise began.

"I'm open to suggestions," Karl said to her.

Eloise looked at him, but uttered no words.

Karl looked at each of the companions in turn, but none spoke. He sighed deeply, and finally bowed his head.

"Henry …," Karl said.

Henry froze; *he'd been expecting this.* He wasn't a baron, or a Valkyrie, or a sorceress, or a seeress, or a squire, or a nun. He was the most expendable man, a common sailor … the only one left of the four sailors … *to be sacrificed.*

After all his struggles, after all that he'd done, he was the one whom Karl called upon when someone had to die.

"I … understand …," Henry sighed heavily. "Rishard was stabbed, Thorkel and Dennel died in Italy, and Samuel took an arrow as we sailed on the Nile. I'm the least important … I knew that my time would come …"

Karl stared at him, incredulous.

"Henry, you dishonor me," Karl said. "No life is unimportant. I wouldn't trade the life of an infant to save a king … or anyone else. Henry, I called upon you first …. to say good-bye."

*"No …!"* Eloise screamed.

*"Master …!"* Nate and Phil shouted simultaneously.

"One of us dies … or we all die," Karl said.

"I'll die …!" Eloise argued.

"You must return to raise our children … and rule du Harmonn," Karl said. "My death was decided eight years ago … and my time has come."

*"No …!"* Eloise began to cry.

Karl took her in his arms and held her tightly.

"I wouldn't trade my last eight years for anything," Karl said. "I love you, my dearest wife. I love our children, and I can't deprive them of their mother. They need you. Our barony needs you; you were always better at politics. I've had eight blessed years … but the spare time that I was granted is over. It's time that I joined my brother, Eric."

*"Please … don't do this!"* Eloise whined.

"Who should sacrifice themself?" Karl asked.

*"I will …!"* Eloise sobbed, but Karl ignored her.

"Master …!" Phil said, but Karl cut him off.

"Squire, no arguments," Karl said. "You and Nate are too young, your lives unfulfilled. You've work to do and chores to perform. I leave to you the guardianship of Eloise, my children, Rafe, and Seren, … all our companions, and everyone in du Harmonn. Protect them; I leave you to be … my hands of justice."

Both squires stared, aghast and uncertain.

"Elaina, it's been an honor, and my greatest pleasure, to become your friend," Karl said.

"Then honor me," Elaina said. "I'm the eldest … let me save all."

"You spent years denied of your own daughter," Karl said. "You deserve those years undone, and she'll need you. Even if I make it back to England, my time there is short. I gave an oath to Odin … before the Gates of Valhalla … and it's time I fulfilled that oath."

Eloise whimpered but said nothing, and Karl held her tighter.

"Alarika, Mad Hermit, I wish you both the best," Karl said.

"You honor us," the Mad Hermit said.

"Someday I'll erect a monument to you … in the Hall of Horus," Alarika promised.

Karl smiled and nodded to both of them.

"Sister Aspertine, I leave to you the care of every soul in du Harmonn," Karl said. "I know that they'll be safe with you."

Sister Aspertine, her mouth hanging open but unable to speak, nodded her reply. Then he lifted up Eloise's chin and stared into her eyes.

"My darling, my love, mother of my children …," Karl began.

*"You can't … !"* Eloise cried, tears streaming down her reddened cheeks.

"I won't be gone forever … will I?" Karl raised his eyes to the Seer.

"I'll escort your spirit to Asgard," the Seer promised.

"Then I'll be Reginleif again, and carry you to Valhalla," Roselyn promised Karl.

Karl glanced at Roselyn.

"Is there any chance … that you could bring my children … sometime … for a visit …?" Karl asked Roselyn.

"It won't be the first time I've broken Odin's law," Roselyn smirked.

Karl turned back to Eloise.

"My dearest, we always knew that this day was coming," Karl said.

Karl pulled Eloise in tightly … and kissed her. Desperately Eloise kissed him back, clinging to him as if she could hold back fate. Finally, slowly, Karl released her, and Elaina stepped up and hugged her from behind.

"I love you," Karl whispered to Eloise. "Good-bye, my wife."

With a slow motion, Karl drew his sword, and then he turned to face Roselyn. He took a deep, steadying breath, and then his muscles tightened.

*"I call upon the Valkyrie!"* Karl shouted. *"For Osiris … and my friend's lives … I face death unafraid!"*

Roselyn nodded, and then, with a sudden burst of movement that surprised even the watching gods,

Roselyn whipped up Hel's sword, and in one quick motion, she rammed Hel's sword through Karl's golden breastplate. Blood splashed both before and behind him. Karl choked and shuttered, and his last gaze swept across his companions, and a pained smile grew upon his face. He hovered on his feet, as if immune to the steel plunged through his chest. A trickle of blood dripped from his lips … and then his eyes dulled and grew sightless.

Roselyn yanked out her red-drenched sword.

Karl's dead body collapsed onto the bright agate circle.

Eloise screamed … and fainted.

# Epilogue

## Egypt

## ALARIKA

Thunder pounded Giza from a cloudless sky, followed by trumpets blasting from nowhere. Despite the noontime sun, the sky suddenly blackened, and a brilliant, blinding light burst above the huge stone sphinx. From between the arms of the great sphinx, tall flames exploded, making those nearby scream in terror.

"By command of Osiris, heed these messengers!" boomed a deep, threatening voice, rumbling as if the sphinx had come alive again. "Obey them, and deny them nothing!"

A roar more terrible than the guardian's followed, echoing across the city and desert. Then a dread silence fell, the flames extinguished, and the thick smoke began to dissipate amongst the startled inhabitants of Giza.

As the smoke cleared, Alarika looked out at the many merchants and townsfolk of Giza, all watching her with horrified expressions. A snake's head slid across her armored shoulder, and its serpentine coil wrapped around her.

"I return!" Alarika shouted at all their stunned faces. "I, Queen Alarika, who awakened the great sphinx. I, who passed through the lost portal in the Temple of Osiris. I, who braved the lands of the gods of Egypt, and faced their challenges. I, who helped drive back Aapep, and entered the City of the Gods. I, who stood before Osiris, Anubis, Horus, Thoth, Ra, Nut, Sehkmet, and Isis, and all of the gods of our people. I return, she whom Osiris himself has sent back to you, to remind you of his rightful rulership of Egypt, and the duties that you owe to him … and to each other.

"I come to you, Alarika, Queen of the Valley of Thieves, daughter of the Mad Hermit, who has returned with me, an emissary of our ancient gods."

The crowd gasped … and many fell to their knees.

The Mad Hermit raised his snake-limbs, which hissed at the crowd, and many screamed.

"Fear me not!" the Mad Hermit shouted. "I am sent by Osiris … as proof of his power … and warning to all who have lost faith! I am the Mad Hermit of the Valley of Thieves, buried in the sands, and by the will of Osiris, I have returned from the dead!"

The eyes of the locals seemed horrified, fixated on her father's snake limbs, and they seemed to see nothing else. Alarika frowned; *this wasn't starting well.*

However, one old man finally shouted:

*"Praise to Osiris!"*

Within days, all of Alarika's dreams came true. She and her father were given a temple, treated like royalty, and they guested the wealthiest and most-powerful pharaohs and merchants, all of whom gifted her with generous tributes. Scribes documented the story of her fabulous adventure, and everything else that she said, and her tale became legend. Thousands flocked to hear her, and to witness her father's inhuman form … for a small, but respectable, fee.

Quickly the renewed faith of Egypt spread far and wide, and Alarika richly profited from the reverence of a hundred thousand new believers. She and her father never knew unhappiness again. After her father succumbed to extreme old age, Alarika founded many charities, and spent her twilight years looking forward to returning to the City of the Gods, to regain her youth, strength, and beauty … and to become the first warrior-maid of Horus.

## Epilogue

### Italy

# ATHELWYNNE THE SEER

The Seer set them down in a dark, narrow alley, only loud twangs of musical strings reaching them from the street. As they stepped out between two shabby buildings, the musicians begging for coins abruptly stopped playing, every conversation ceased in mid-sentence, and all eyes turned toward them.

The Seer wasn't surprised; his rescuers might be accustomed to gem-studded gold and silver armor, worn by both men and women, more ornate than the wealthiest knights could afford, but for a crowd of noble-armored strangers to emerge from a filthy alley behind a whorehouse left every peasant stunned and speechless.

The Seer smiled and stepped up to the musicians. Suddenly a bright silver coin appeared in his hand, and he dropped it into the basket before them.

"I … think it's this way," Henry said, and at once the whole richly accoutremented party began walking down the street.

The farther that they walked, the more attention they gained, and soon a crowd followed. Many crossed themselves and whispered prayers in Italian. Roselyn was recognized, and strangers began speaking to them, but the Seer was exhausted and recalled only a few words through their heavy accents; he let Eloise and Roselyn deal with the locals. No one stopped them, and finally Henry led them into sight of a white two-story charity hospital.

*"Samuel!"* Nate shouted, seeing three men talking outside the hospital.

Although startled, Samuel looked up and cheered, and Thorkel and Dennel stared in disbelief.

*"Henry!"* Samuel shouted, smiling. *"Still alive …?"*

"Looking better than you!" Henry laughed, and the four men hugged and greeted each other, and then shook hands with the other companions.

"Where's Rishard?" Eloise asked.

"Healing, but he still can't stand," Samuel said.

"Glad that you didn't come sooner … we just found him yesterday," Dennel said.

"What?" Henry said. "It's been weeks …!"

"We appeared at the docks, and Samuel couldn't remember which hospital," Dennel said. "This city is huge!"

"You … aren't you the man that we came to get?" Thorkel asked, offering the Seer his hand. "I saw you ride into Demril once, when I was young, before you, and the baron and baroness, stole that dragonship."

"Athelwynne," the Seer introduced himself, and each of the sailors gladly shook hands with him.

"Our full story will have to wait," Eloise said.

"We found a good boat for sale," Dennel said. "You can tell us on the voyage home."

The companions laughed.

"We don't need boats," Eloise chuckled.

"Could … could we rest a while, before we travel again?" the Seer asked. "To be honest, I'm pretty tired."

"There's a fine inn not far away," Samuel said. "Rishard's asleep; we can come back tomorrow."

They spent the night in comfortable beds. Samuel, Thorkel, and Dennel paid with the coins that Henry had given them in the Field of Wheat, where he'd brought them back from the dead. The next morning, they enjoyed sleeping in late, and then ate and drank their fill.

As they breakfasted, the Seer tried to calm their fears.

"If you'd died in their Afterlife, then yes, parts of your soul would have stayed there forever," the Seer told Samuel, Thorkel, and Dennel. "However, Henry summoned your souls from this world … where those parts of your souls never left … and then he returned you here. I don't think that you need worry; each part of your souls yearns to be reunited, even if you're unaware of it. Your souls feel complete to me."

The Seer was still tired, yet they had far to go, so when they returned to the white hospital, only he, Eloise, Sister Aspertine, and Samuel went inside. Rishard was awake, but convalescing, still unable to stand, yet far more healed than when they'd last seen him. They waited until the Italian nuns left them alone, and then Eloise finished his healing. As soon as she was done, and their path was clear, Rishard arose from his bed for the first time since he'd been stabbed, and they snuck out and joined the others.

However, walking out of a deserted alley in sparkling armor, with every eye in the city following them, was far easier than finding a secluded place from which to vanish.

"Who cares if they see …?" Rishard asked.

"We've been seen here before," Eloise said. "Our names are known, and I'd rather that we vanish quietly."

"That may not be easy," the Seer said, looking around at the large, staring crowd.

"Follow me," Roselyn said, and she marched toward the nearest building, a small candlemaker's shop. At the door, she gestured for them to wait, and then she entered. Seconds later, an old man, in a wax-splattered apron, burst out, with Roselyn waving the Sword of Hel at him.

*"She's crazy!"* he shouted, but the companions only laughed.

His tiny shop was cramped, but it had no windows and only the one door. The companions squeezed inside and shut the door behind them. Then the Seer cast his spell, trying not to laugh, imagining how surprised the confused candlemaker would be when he finally worked up the courage to open his door … and found his shop unoccupied.

## Epilogue

## London

# ELOISE

The King of England startled as, without warning, the largest stained-glass window in his castle shattered. Eloise clenched her jaw, preparing for the quarrel, as the Seer floated all of their company inside through the broken colored glass, into his royal hall. Servants and courtiers screamed, and guards came running … only to be blown backwards, off their feet, by a terrible wind. The companions floated across the hall, and then slowly descended until their feet struck the polished wooden floor … right before the Throne of England.

"Your Majesty!" Eloise cried loud enough for the whole castle to hear. "Your humble servant brings greetings!"

*"What …?"* the king gasped. *"Baroness Eloise du Harmonn …?"*

"That depends on you," Eloise said, stepping forward. "If I hear what I like, then I'll return home … and stay there. If I don't hear what I like, then I'll have you fed to a dragon … a real, fire-breathing dragon … and take your place as ruler of England!"

*"Ahh …, but … ummm …, perhaps … how …?"* the king asked.

"Meet Athelwynne, the former Seer of Madrone," Eloise said. "Don't bother calling for more guards, or attempting to attack us; your last army fell to thirteen women, Valkyries, including Roselyn, the daughter of Eorl Sir Guldwin, whose father lies dead."

Eloise smiled, and then gestured at Elaina.

"I believe you may also remember my mother, the former Baroness Elaina, whom you forced to marry Sir Vandeslidge du Harmonn …?" Eloise asked. "She's now a Norse Seeress, one of the most powerful women ever. Between us, we have power beyond your imagining, and we've just returned from yet another land beyond death, from a council of foreign gods, and if we can't find an agreeable tongue in your mouth, then you may well find yourself without a tongue …!"

The King of England quavered before them, and Eloise was amused to see Nate, Phil, and even Sister Aspertine attempting to look threatening.

The Seer lifted his hand, and the king screamed as he rose off his throne, floating into the air, helpless before them.

*"Please … let me down …!"* the king cried.

"You will never again send troops into du Harmonn," the Seer ordered. "You will never challenge Baroness Eloise's right to rule her lands, and you will never again ask her or her people for taxes … or anything else. You will take oaths now to all of these conditions. If you fail, in any of these, you'll find yourself the guest of the Norse Goddess of Death, trapped in her land of corpses, to be chased and devoured by her legendary pets. Do you agree to these terms?"

*"Anything …!"* the king cried. *"Please … spare me …!"*

"Make your vow!" the Seer commanded. "Let all your people hear it!"

"I … wish I could, but … there's an army headed there now!" the king cried. "Not mine; it's Sir Aledard … Eorl Sir Guldwin's son … Roselyn's brother! His army marches …!"

The companions exchanged worried glances.

"Is my brother leading them?" Roselyn asked.

*"No!"* the king shouted. *"He's in his castle … in Madrone!"*

"We'd better go," Elaina said.

The Seer dropped the king; he bounced hard upon his dais, and his crown fell off and rolled across the floor.

"If I ever hear Eloise complain about you, I'll crush this castle like an eggshell, and dispose of you … painfully," the Seer warned the king.

*"You won't …! I swear …!"* cried the king. *"Upon my crown …!"*

"Oh, and I never liked the name 'du Harmonn'," Eloise said. "Restore my barony's original name … or …!"

*"Consider it done!"* the king cried.

## Epilogue

### Castle Bristlen

# ELAINA

With a deep belly-laugh, Rafe came storming out of Castle Bristlen as the many guards on the wall cheered. Another army had stood outside their gate, but as the Seer descended from the sky, a huge wall of fire burst up around the castle, and every soldier outside the gate turned and fled, screaming insanely. The Seer gently lowered them all onto the grounds of the courtyard, and Rafe practically fell upon Eloise and Roselyn, hugging one in each arm. Within moments, Seren slowly emerged, walking with a cane, and her bright smile beamed. With her came Edith, little Eric, and little Roselyn, and behind her came a wetnurse carrying little Athelwynne, who was crying loudly.

Little Eric and Roselyn ran ahead of Seren, squealing with joy, and hugged and danced around their mother, simultaneously demanding her attention. Hugs were shared all around. Athelwynne was delighted by his namesake, and blessed all three of their kids. Yet he couldn't linger; he promised Seren that he'd visit them again soon … and regularly, but insisted that he had to take Karl's spirit to Asgard before it faded. He and Roselyn quickly hugged Rafe, Seren, the kids, and their companions, and then they rose into the sky.

"Farewell!" Elaina cried as she watched them rise into the sky. She wondered if she'd ever see them again … and knew that she'd miss them.

The flames around Castle Bristlen quickly died, but only dropped packs, discarded weapons, and a few fallen shields remained of the fleeing army. Rafe sent their soldiers to gather the plunder, and a few volunteers to scout for the enemy's position, and all returned with reports that they'd fled down the main road through Wolven Forest, westward toward Grusshire, and many were still running.

News of Karl's death burst tears from Seren's eyes, most of the castle women, and even many of the men. Rafe promised to host a requiem mass for Karl … despite his assurance of Valhalla. Seren cried all through dinner, which was sparse, as Sir Aledard's army had marched in secret, and they'd only had a day's notice that their army was approaching. They'd had no chance to gather supplies, and maintaining their quickly-gathered army, mostly farmers and fishermen, had drained their supplies.

Eloise delighted them with her description of their visit to the king, and once again Nate was requested to tell the whole story of their adventures since leaving Castle Bristlen.

While Nate talked and gestured dramatically, and entranced listeners sat mesmerized, Elaina tapped Phil on the shoulder and nodded toward a back door. She quietly exited through it, and while Nate held everyone spellbound with his enthusiastic storytelling, Phil followed Elaina out of the hall.

"Phil, we need to speak," Elaina said, lowering her voice to a whisper.

"How may I serve you, mi'lady?" Phil asked.

Elaina smiled.

"After all that we've been through …?" Elaina smiled.

"We're back in this world," Phil said. "You're a baroness … and a seeress. I'm a squire … born of a farmer …"

"You're the hand of justice of Baron Sir Karl, and his last command to you was to maintain order," Elaina said.

"I take Karl's command seriously," Phil said.

"My dances can help you maintain Karl's justice," Elaina said.

"I'm at your service, mi'lady," Phil said, and he bowed slightly. "Together, we can insure peace in these lands …"

"I hope we can do more than that," Elaina said. "Karl was just a farmer, too, before he married a baroness."

Phil looked confused.

"Am I too old for you?" Elaina asked suddenly, and Phil startled. She smiled widely. "I admire you, Phil, and I think you're a good man. I know that you like watching me dance. I just … thought you might like to know … I like moonlit walks, too."

Over the years, Elaina and Phil kept peace in all the lands around Castle Bristlen, and shared many moonlit walks. Yet Elaina always slept beside her daughter, who often cried herself to sleep. Elaina comforted Eloise as best she could, deeply regretting that the curse of Skafti had finally come true: Eloise had seen her mother's face, and Eloise would never again truly know happiness.

# Epilogue

## Madrone

### ROSELYN

*"Aledard . . . !"* Roselyn screamed up at the castle guards from the drawbridge.

The Seer cast her a nasty glare.

"We arrived quietly to keep from attracting attention . . . !" the Seer chastised her.

"I've been fighting with my brother all my life," Roselyn said. "The last time I saw him, I warned him to never again attack our friends."

"Families can be frustrating," the Seer said. "Just remember Grusshire; my father and brothers died because of me."

"Eric led us into Grusshire . . .," Roselyn said.

"If I'd kept a closer eye on them . . .," the Seer said.

"Not even Heimdal can see all places at once," Roselyn said.

"Still, even though we never got along, I'll miss them forever," the Seer said.

Finally an older, heavily-bearded soldier appeared atop the wall among the younger guards, and he looked down at them scornfully.

"Who calls forth the Lord of Northumbria?" the old guard shouted down at them.

"I, Reginleif, Valkyrie, once called Countess Roselyn, sister to Sir Aledard," Roselyn shouted up at him.

The guard's eyes widened, and they exchanged worried glances.

"Where are your sisters?" the older guard asked, his voice hesitant.

"Above the clouds," Roselyn answered.

"Are they expected?" the old guard asked.

"If I needed them, they'd be here," Roselyn snarled. "Bring my brother out here … now … or suffer his doom!"

The old guard paused, then nodded. "I'll inform the Eorl of your request."

As he departed, Roselyn glanced at the Seer, who nodded at something behind them. Roselyn glanced around, unsurprised to see every visible townsperson standing frozen, watching her with mouths agape. Roselyn wasn't surprised; seldom did women in golden, red-trimmed armor appear on the busy streets of the crowded city of Madrone, let alone stand before a fully-manned castle and command the city's ruler to appear.

The old guard soon appeared in the courtyard, on the far side of the drawbridge, walking toward them. He stopped just inside the castle gate and bowed.

"Sir Aledard, Lord of Northumbria, welcomes his sister, and bids her enter and join him at table," the old guard said.

"Inform my brother that he will come out here, now, or I'll crush his castle to rubble … with him inside!" Roselyn rebuked.

The old guard didn't laugh, and without expression he turned and walked back toward the keep.

"You're sure that this whole castle is supported by four pillars?" the Seer asked in a whisper.

"I grew up here," Roselyn said. "I know every inch of its dungeons."

Long moments passed, and Roselyn began breathing short, angry breaths.

"Patience," the Seer warned.

A clatterer of marching armored men arose, and six knights in gleaming armor stomped out toward them, one man protected in their middle. The scarred face of Sir Aledard radiated fury. All approached Roselyn and the Seer, but the knights stopped just under the portcullis. Only Sir Aledard stepped out onto the drawbridge. Diagonally, across his entire face, ran the long, nasty scar that she'd inflicted upon him.

"You look lovely," Roselyn said.

Sir Aledard glared.

"I warned you to send no more forces against du Harmonn," Roselyn said.

*"I don't answer to you!"* Sir Aledard snarled.

Roselyn and the Seer exchanged another glance.

"Your army was routed yesterday," Roselyn said. "Why weren't you leading them?"

"My duties …," Sir Aledard began.

*"Because you're a coward!"* Roselyn shouted, and the knights behind him trembled, and gasps came from the watching crowd. "Tell me why I shouldn't kill you now!"

Sir Aledard hesitated, his scarred face reddening.

*"You're no sister of mine!"* Sir Aledard shouted, surprisingly loudly, as if signaling a command.

Roselyn started forward, but the Seer grabbed her arm and held her back. Several *'sssshhhtttttssss!'* filled the air, and suddenly five arrows appeared, pointed at her and the Seer, frozen in mid-air, as if caught in mid-flight from the castle toward their targets.

The Seer raised his free hand, snapped his fingers, and the five frozen arrows dropped harmlessly to the ground.

Roselyn looked at the fallen arrows and snarled.

*"Assassin ...!"* Roselyn shouted at Sir Aledard, and she slowly drew the Sword of Hel.

Sir Aledard paled, and Roselyn started forward.

"Reginleif ...!" the Seer shouted. "Remember, you're immortal now. Whatever you do to your brother today will haunt you for all eternity ...!"

Roselyn paused, then glanced back at the Seer ... and nodded. The Seer met her gaze, and nodded in silent reply.

Wary seconds passed, and then the first rumble began. The tallest tower seemed to tremble, and then to tilt ... and its bricks began to fall. The tower's round, pointed, wooden roof slid off its crumbling bricks, fell, and crashed upon the courtyard's dirt. The whole tower suddenly broke apart into loose stones and toppled. Whole walls of castle keep shook, and the ground beneath their feet began to vibrate. One section of the castle's slanted roof crumpled, sank in, and broke away, and a crenelated corner of the top of the keep fell apart, and showered down a torrent of heavy bricks. A hanging balcony broke off and plummeted to crash onto the main steps before its shaking doors.

Countless screams filled the air, overwhelmed by the '*crack!'s* of shattering mortar, splitting timbers, and the '*crash!*' of falling stones. A deafening roar and cloud of dust blasted them simultaneously, and suddenly the central keep's roof entirely collapsed, and its tall walls crumpled and fell inwards.

A violent wind rose, and the expanding cloud of dust engulfing Roselyn, Athelwynne, and Aledard suddenly cleared, and ascended high into the air, forming a great black pillar hanging in the sky over a newly-decimated castle. Fallen to ruins, the last small bricks of the keep rained down, tumbling and shifting in the silence of the shocked aftermath.

The knights beneath the portcullis ran out of the castle, past Roselyn and the Seer, even as the heavy wooden gate fell and crashed shut, inches from Sir Aledard, who stood dumbstruck, aghast at his downfall.

A dread silence fell … a quietude of shock and horror … broken only by a few cries of agony from beneath the rubble.

*"Imagine what I'll do next time …!"* Roselyn shouted at her brother.

His scarred face ashen-pale, Sir Aledard stared at the remains of his once-mighty castle. Amid his horrified expression hung a slack mouth unable to speak.

"Time to go," the Seer said.

**Epilogue**

**Demril**

## SISTER ASPERTINE

Sister Aspertine dismounted, helped down by Nate, and looked at the unfamiliar tavern with quiet trepidation. She'd feared this moment …

*"Phil! Nate!"* shouted a rustic old man in farmer's clothes as Phil opened the door and the lantern light spilled out upon them.

*"Henry!"* shouted a stout woman of mature years before they were all inside. She ran forward and threw her arms around Henry.

Another woman, a barmaid, ran up and practically fell upon Thorkel as he stepped inside, hugging and kissing him.

The joyous crowd at the Bent Hook cheered loudly. Just inside the door, Sister Aspertine stepped to the side, fearful of being knocked over by their exuberant reunions.

Weeping, an older woman in an apron hurried close, and she seized both Nate and Phil in smothering hugs.

Others tried to push forward, but all were halted by the barkeeper.

"Let them come in!" he chastised his patrons. "Clear a table! Olaf, Megan, beers for everyone … starting with our guests!"

Rishard, Dennel, and Samuel stepped forward, and shook many hands amid glad greetings. His arm around his smiling wife's shoulder, Henry stepped forward, and he was equally greeted by lifelong friends. Still trapped in their mother's hug, an arm around each, and looking embarrassed, Nate and Phil came forward to greet the rustic farmer, who looked immensely proud.

"Welcome home, my sons," the farmer said to Nate and Phil, and unable to pry them from their mother's arms, he shook their hands heartily. "I can't wait to hear of your journey."

"Our tale puts Yggdrasil to shame," Phil said to his father, "but that will have to wait …" These words were followed by loud *'aaawww's* of complaint. "Nate will tell you everything, tonight, but first … we have a few … announcements."

The crowd hushed, and all eyes fell upon Phil. Phil and Nate both pulled free of their mother's grip and turned; Sister Aspertine saw them look back at her, and they gestured her forward. Sister Aspertine blushed slightly, stepped toward them, and several stepped back out of respect for her new habit, which felt strange after wearing the gift of Horus for so long.

"Nate will explain everything, but first, Mother and Father, we need you to meet our most-honored companion, Sister Aspertine."

The old farmer swept off his hat and nodded politely.

"Michael Tiller, at your service," he said to Sister Aspertine.

"Sarah Tiller," their mother said, extending a hand to greet the nun. "I know you …! Aren't you … one of the sisters of the Abbey of St. Dunstay …?"

"Not anymore," Sister Aspertine said. "But … it is an honor to meet you. Your sons have been … I can't say how proud of them I am."

Farmer Tiller and his wife started to beam with pride, but then confusion softened their expressions. Sister Aspertine blushed again.

"We've faced evils equal to those Baron Sir Karl met on his first journey, where he challenged the Norse gods," Phil said. "In our journey, we've met the living gods, and dead gods, of ancient Egypt, who are far older and more deceptive than those of Asgard. Many times we fell victim to their entrancements, so powerful that no mortal's willpower could endure. Their manipulations twisted our minds, our bodies, and time itself, making us perform acts we'd never willingly consider. The consequences of those acts walk with us … and deeply affect our family."

Nate looked uncomfortably nervous, and Sister Aspertine tried to restrain her trembles; *not before the great demon Aapep had she felt this afraid!*

"Sister Aspertine will live in Castle Bristlen, care for its chapel, and help Sir Rafe pray for the souls of those of us who've met and been influenced by pagan deities," Phil continued. "She can't return to the Abbey of St. Dunstay … because she … is pregnant … with Nate's child."

Incredulous eyes met hers amid intense silence, and Sister Aspertine bowed her head and tried to turn away, but Nate's hand reached out and firmly took hers. She accepted his grasp, and felt warmed and protected by his touch.

"Father, mother, we didn't intend this," Nate said, "We were ensorcelled by a land of pagan magics … and tricked into doing its bidding. I'll explain everything, but …"

"It was as much my fault as his …!" Sister Aspertine blurted out.

"It's no one's fault," Phil said firmly. "Nate and I already consider every member of our company to be part of our family … especially Sister Aspertine."

"W-when it comes," Nate stammered, and he looked up into his mother's eyes. "We, Sister Aspertine and I, have agreed … son or daughter, we'd like you to raise it."

Sarah Tiller's stunned expression slowly transformed into a bright smile.

"We'd be honored to raise our first grandchild," Farmer Tiller said.

Sarah Tiller, unable to find words, stepped forward and embraced Sister Aspertine tightly.

Nervously the crowded tavern applauded.

"We'll visit often," Nate promised.

Sister Aspertine smiled, truly grateful. She glanced around the aged tavern; every face was staring at her, aware of the blasphemy that she represented, but understanding that magic and strangeness followed all the folk of Castle Bristlen. No one had cheered the announcement of her pregnancy, but not one eye looked disappointed or disapproving.

*Perhaps this birth wouldn't be as shameful as she'd expected …*

Sarah Tiller took both of her hands in hers.

"You'll be my new daughter," Sarah Tiller whispered.

Thorkel stepped forward, he and the barmaid, with their arms tight around each other, and Dennel nudged him with his elbow.

"Where's my beer?" Samuel called, obviously attempting to break the uncomfortable silence.

"Thank you, Olaf," Henry said as he reached out and took a foaming wooden mug, passed to him by several hands, and Olaf continued filling mugs beneath his tap.

"Nate tells our story best," Phil said. "Let's all get comfortable; this tale may take all night."

Sarah Tiller pulled Sister Aspertine to a bench at the foremost table and made her sit beside her, and several men stood to give them room.  Nate remained standing, eager to retell their story, and Rishard sat down on Sister Aspertine's other side.

Soon The Bent Hook rang with gasps and cheers as Nate again orated their tale, with many theatrical pauses and flourishes, and Sister Aspertine smiled; *she was very proud of the father of her child.*

## Epilogue

## Asgard

# ROSELYN

From his golden throne, Odin's one eye locked upon Roselyn and the Seer. Both stood shoulders-pressed, sheilding Karl's wavering spirit from the fury of Odin's glare. Despite that no mortal, and few gods, could see Karl, and he couldn't speak or touch anything, both knew that Odin and his ravens were aware of Karl's presence.

Around them, the Norse gods and all the Valkyrie stood watching.

"Most-noble Alfather!" Roselyn shouted and saluted. "Behold Athelwynne the Seer, whom I return to your service! Greater than expected has my mission been. Once Athelwynne was charged only to carry messages between yourself and the Lady of the Druids; now he comes to offer conversation with the chief deity of an elder pantheon, Osiris, Ruler of the Gods of Egypt!"

Other Norse gods gasped, and whispered conversations began, but Odin stared unmoved, his frown fixed.

"Thus does wisdom prove fallible," Odin scowled. "I suspected that you'd find the doorway you needed; I'd expect no less of a former Valkyrie. I never thought that you'd escape the Duat."

"Former …?" Roselyn demanded. "You said that you'd restore me …!"

*"You defied me!"* Odin shouted. *"You placed your judgement above mine!"*

*"My judgement proved right!"* Roselyn shouted back.

Odin sneered and shifted on his throne, making the ravens on his shoulders caw in complaint. He glanced at the other gods, then returned his gaze to Roselyn.

"Correct judgement requires complete understanding," Odin snarled. "I ordered you to not seek the Seer. I didn't explain why. *I shouldn't have to explain why!"*

*"Without the Seer, how will you exchange messages with the Lady of the Druids?"* Roselyn demanded.

"I converse with the Lady is to prevent Ragnarrock!" Odin shouted. *"I die in Ragnarrock …!"*

*"You already died!"* Roselyn shouted. "You killed yourself to steal the Nine Secrets of the Dead, and you came back to life!"

"That was in our Spring," Odin said. "I was stronger. Now we're on the verge of Winter …!"

"Gods die all the time," Roselyn said. "You, Jesus, Osiris; all have died and come back."

"How does helping the Gods of Egypt escape their Winter help us?" Odin demanded.

"No pantheon has ever delayed their Winter forever," Roselyn scowled. "If we can bring the Gods of Egypt out of theirs, then we can do the same for ours … and you."

"How many pantheons do you think mortals can worship?" Odin asked.

"I never could've defeated Aapep," Roselyn said. "I couldn't figure out how to escape the City of Thoth, or alone defeat the Serpent of Horus. But I had friends, smart, powerful friends, and where my fighting skills failed, theirs didn't. Friends of other pantheons, especially elder gods who were ancient when Yggdrasil was a seed, could help you in ways that no others could."

*"You don't know that!"* Odin shouted.

"Anubis and I just had this same argument," Roselyn said. "Anubis was willing to face oblivion, at the end of time, rather than embrace a risk. Not even the Norns know the future. You don't know if Ragnarrok can be delayed … or won. You don't know if our Winter can be prevented. I'm doing all I can to save you …!"

Odin frowned, then snarled.

"The last thing that I need is a presumptuous Valkyrie," Odin said.

Roselyn grinned. She held her tongue, and stared at Odin while he glared back at her.

"Go back to Valhalla, Reginleif," Odin growled.

All of the Valkyrie cheered, and Reginleif lifted the Sword of Hel and saluted her master.

*Never had she smiled so brightly!*

Odin scowled again.

## Epilogue

## Valhalla

# KARL

Familiar roling hills, many trees, a blue sky, a wide, swift stream, and a bridge over the stream paved with crushed bones; the white road led to a gate of golden spears, whose fence surrounded Odin's battlefield, a vast land full of countless einherjar, but none could be seen. Inside Valhalla, on a distant hill, stood Elvidner, the Hall of Odin, where the Valkyrie feasted each night, yet not one figure stood in sight. Karl couldn't even see himself.

Only two stood before him; Roselyn and the Seer.

Never had Karl felt so empty. He didn't even feel numb; Karl felt nothing, no sensation, neither desire nor joy. He moved his arms, but no muscles flexed. He looked at Roselyn and felt no longing. The weight of his soul had vanished, as if he were floating in a river without feeling wet … no sensation at all.

He'd watched it all, but as a helpless spectator, unseen and unheard; their rescue of Rishard, Samuel, Thorkel, and Dennel, their intimidation of the king, their reunion with Rafe and Seren, the destruction of Sir Aledard's castle, and Roselyn's restoration as a Valkyrie.

"His soul won't survive much longer," the Seer said. "Open the gates."

*The Gates of Valhalla;* Karl's heart crushed. The last time that Karl had stood here, they'd been tortured by Hel, fought Loki, and Karl had watched Roselyn die. Eric had entered Valhalla and become an einherjar on this very ground. Odin had witnessed all, and transformed the woman that he loved, Roselyn, into Reginleif, the Valkyrie that Karl barely knew. Yet now Odin was back in his hall, the other Valkyrie had departed, and no crowd of einherjars were watching.

The wide, golden-spear gates of Valhalla slowly opened of their own accord, leaving no barrier to admittance. The Seer waved his hands, and Karl floated intangibly down, onto the white road of crushed bones … which his feet couldn't feel.

Roselyn, now Reginleif, held out the tip of Hel's sword and pointed it at Karl.

"Arise, warrior," Reginleif commanded Karl. "I summon you, in the name of Odin."

A tingling passed through Karl, the first feeling that he'd known since Roselyn had plunged the Sword of Hel through his chest before the Throne of Osiris. He knew what was expected of him; haunted by countless trepidations, Karl walked up the white road and stepped through the Gates of Valhalla.

Sensations washed over Karl, like a sudden deluge upon a sleeper. It overwhelmed his senses, soaking deep through every inch of him. He held up his transparent hand … and slowly color returned to his flesh, his clothes, and his armor. Karl was alive again … as he'd expected … but the joy that he'd hoped for didn't coalesce.

Karl looked up at the tall hill, past the long, grassy slope, at Elvidner, then he turned around and saw Reginleif, her face smiling, and behind her, the Seer.

"Thank you, Athelwynne," Reginleif said.

"Before I return to Elysia, I'm going to visit Hel," the Seer said. "I'll give her your respects, from both of you, and I'll be back to visit soon. Oh, and give my regards to Glororil and Silvana."

"I will," Reginleif promised.

The Seer nodded in silence to Karl, who nodded back; *they needed words no longer.* Instantly the Seer began to glow bright white, blinding, and when his brilliance faded, he was gone.

Only Karl and Reginleif remained.

"Well, here we are," Reginleif said, and never had a more uncomfortable silence followed.

"Alone …?" Karl asked, nodding toward Elvidner.

"I asked my sisters … for privacy," she replied.

Karl frowned, unsure what to say.

"Roselyn … Reginleif …," Karl began.

"Call me anything you like," Reginleif said. "I'm both, and I know that now. I need to be Reginleif … because that's who I am. I need to be Roselyn … to be worthy of you."

"Well, you have me now … for all eternity," Karl said.

"Eight years have passed since you made that vow … eight years with Eloise," Reginleif said.

"Neither of us are the same …," Karl said.

"No, we're better," Reginleif said. "You're Baron Sir Karl, einherjar, and I'm Queen Reginleif, Valkyrie … and I need you … to keep Roselyn alive."

Reginleif stepped forward, one step, two, and crossed the bridge. As she entered Valhalla, she held out her arms. Karl hesitated, and then tried to smile. Neither of them were the love-struck children who'd fled from Hel and Loki.

"I … want the love … that we used to have," Karl whispered.

"We will," Reginleif smiled. "We can have both … for we are both."

Reginleif stepped closer. She wrapped her arms around him. She closed her eyes … and kissed him, long and slowly. Karl kissed her back, deeply.

"I loved you … the instant that I saw you," Karl whispered. "Wrapped in that blanket … while Baron du Harmonn slept. But … it wasn't love. It was a little boy's infatuation … with the most beautiful girl that he'd ever seen. Now we're … older … and wiser. Our love … must be wiser … an adult love."

"That's the only love … that lasts forever," Reginleif smiled.

Karl smiled back. They kissed again, and Karl was suddenly very glad that they were alone.

# The End

# Books by Jay Palmer

## The Grotesquerie Games

Martin's dream of being a sports hero is crushed when his mother declares that school athletics are "too dangerous". Then a misfired spell from another realm drops Martin into the playoffs … of the Olympics … in the Monster world … and all of Martin's dreams come true. Martin becomes the star of the monstrous Grotesquerie Games … destined for greatness … if he can survive.

## The Magic of Play

Audrey doesn't want to play with dolls anymore, but Great Aunt Virginia's magic tea set carries her and Audrey to the enchanted land of Arcadia, where the baby dolls have been kidnapped, the tin soldiers attacked, and the marionettes, hand-puppets, and paper dolls are helpless. All their magic is done with jump rope chants, but Great Aunt Virginia can't jump rope anymore. Only Audrey can save the dolls, but she must first master the mysterious, unlimited powers of the magic jump rope.

## Jeremy Wrecker

Shanghaied by cutthroats, and their treasure map stolen, young Jeremy is forced to scrub the pirate's ship. Captain Beckett had Jeremy's uncle and older brother, wounded and bound, imprisoned deep in the hold, and Jeremy's only prayer of rescuing them lies with a mad pirate who lives in the rigging. But even freed: how can three unarmed captives scupper a crew of bloodthirsty buccaneers? Can he survive without revealing the dread secret of what Wreckers really are?

## The Seneschal

Torn from his well-ordered castle, young Galloway is commanded to be the Royal Seneschal, to provide the King's army with food, water, horses, and supplies … at a distant mountain pass surrounded only by desert. Even before their enemy arrives, Galloway's inadequate resouces earn him hatred from the starving troops and squabbling commanders. Yet, as the fierce fighting begins, Galloway discovers that victory in war depends on his non-martial skills as surely as on any soldier!

## The VIKINGS! Trilogy

### DeathQuest
### The Mourning Trail
### Quest for Valhalla

Unwilling to let old age sap his fighting prowess, Eric Bjornson seeks to impress the Valkyrie by earning the most glorious death any Norse warrior has ever enjoyed. Strangely, his horrified Catholic companions are reluctant to sacrifice their lives so that Eric can enjoy his death.

After forcing a war that Eric arranged, the others find themselves hunted outlaws in England. Attempting to flee, and led by a Druid Seer, Eric's doom haunts them.

Their only hope: to find a mystical portal to enter the lands of the Norse Gods. Finding themselves trapped on the roots of Yggdrasil, the companions wander lost, until they stumble into Niflhiem and are captured by beautiful Hel, the Norse Goddess of Death, whom they must escape, and then are angrily pursued by immortal fiends through Nidavellir, Jotunhiem, Alfhiem, Svartalfhiem, Asgard; every realm of Norse mythology.

## Dracula - Deathless Desire

Dracula hates his cursed existence. He never asked to become a vampire, and learned of his bloodlust when he murdered his beloved father and fiancé. Horrified by his unexpected transformation, Dracula fled into the blackness of his own despair. Four centuries later, recognizing that his dreadful beginning took him upon a wrong track, Dracula desires to begin his existence anew, to find a beautiful, worthy bride ... and with her arise to the highest status that his vampiric powers can acheive. Abandoning his homeland and his three treacherous brides, Dracula embarks for England ... but can the King of Vampires escape the very darkness that he embodies ... and embrace enlightenment among the living?

## Viking Daughter

Teenage Hávi, an 8th century goat-rancher, is forced to marry a strange visitor, three times her age. Hávi tried to refuse ... only to find that women had no legal right to refuse a marriage. Then she discovers that her aged husband rules the largest clan in Sweden. Forced from her only home, and imprisoned in the first castle that she's ever seen, Hávi is swept up in deadly politics which threaten her new-found position and her life.

To spare other women from the rape and ignominy that she suffered, Hávi determines to take clandestine lessons in the den Skaanske Lov, the law-code of Scandinavia, which is forbidden to women, in the vain hope of giving women the legal right that she was refused ... but the only jarl willing to teach her is her husband's most-hated enemy, and revelation of their meetings could plunge all of Sweden into civil war.

## Viking Son

Thron, Garad, and the other village boys dream of going viking, of sailing south, of slaying countless enemies, and plundering golden treasures. Their fathers come home every Harvest with wonderful, exciting stories of adventure, bravery, glory, and riches.

The village boy's can't wait to join them!

However, the fathers only tell their sons the stories that they want their wives to hear. The reality of going viking was risking deadly invasions into hostile lands and seas, against fortified castles and cities manned by vengeful soldiers … and after centuries of vikings, their enemies know that they are coming.

Hard lessons must be learned; the pleasant dreams of going viking clash against grim reality … but will either boy survive the discovery of the truth that haunts all Norse warriors …?

**For more details, see my website:**
**JayPalmerBooks.com**

# ABOUT THE AUTHOR

Born in Tripler Army Medical Center, Honolulu, Hawaii, Jay Palmer works as a technical writer in the software industry in Seattle, Washington. Jay enjoys parties, reading everything in sight, woodworking, obscure board games, and riding his Kawasaki Vulcan. Jay is a knight in the SCA, frequently attends writer conferences, SciFi Conventions, and he and Karen are both avid ballroom dancers. But most of all, Jay enjoys writing.

JayPalmerBooks.com

Made in the USA
Monee, IL
06 February 2024